by

Craig Gallant

Zmok Books

Zmok Books is an imprint of Winged Hussar Publishing, LLC
1525 Hulse Road Unit 1
Point Pleasant, NJ 08742

www.WingedHussarPublishing.com
Twitter: WingHusPubLLC

www.Wildwestexodus.com

Cover by Michael Nigro

Wild West Exodus, the characters, inventions and settings were created by Romeo Filip, who own all rights, registers and trademarks. This book is published by Winged Hussar Publishing, LLC under agreement with Wild West Exodus.

ISBN: 978-0-990-3649-5-5
LCN: 2015947854

This is a work of fiction. All the characters and events portrayed in this book, though based in some case on historical figures are fictional and any resemblance to real people or incidents is purely coincidental.

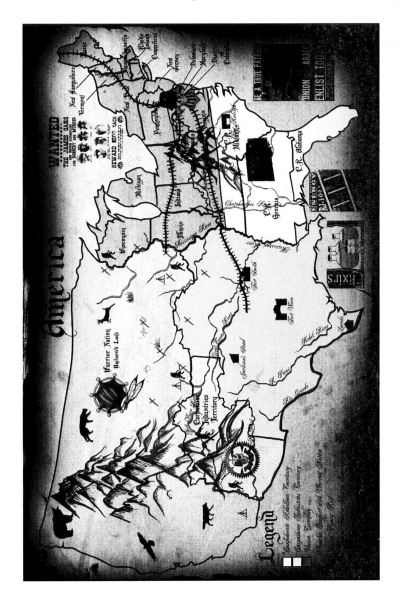

Prologue

The old man settled in behind a gnarled old oak tree, grunting with the pressures of age as he rested his shoulder against the rough bark. Gears in his metal legs whined, a less-than-gentle reminder that they would need serious maintenance after this recent expedition. His mouth bent in a sour grimace. He had had years to acclimate himself to the artificial components forced upon him by fate, but a small part of his mind resented them, what they represented, and his lost humanity.

He grasped a heavy, box-like contraption in one hand, lifting its red-tinged viewing screen to narrowing eyes. The far side of the valley snapped into focus.

The images within the monocular were shaded with crimson highlights, but clearly showed the forces forming rigid, disciplined lines out in the hot sun. Waves of heat from the yellowing plains further distorted the view, but the uniforms were unmistakable. The technology they prepared beneath the hot sun as they arrayed themselves for battle was familiar as well, brazenly stolen from him years before.

"He's not here." A gruff, heavily-accented voice muttered behind him. He waved an impatient hand, silencing his majordomo.

"He was never going to be here, Vladimir. We are not here for him." Thin lips twisted into a sneer beneath the stark white whiskers of his sweeping mustachios. "Although, this is closer than we have been in many years."

Vladimir Caym, his brother-in-law and chief lieutenant, grunted. The old soldier's own monocular hung loosely from one gauntleted hand. Sweat poured from beneath his bowl-like helmet, and he scowled before turning sharply away. His heavy boots crunched in the thick underbrush as he moved farther into the deep shadows, walking with a pronounced limp.

Through the monocular, the Union battle line had finished its preparations. Soldiers in dull armor stood shoulder to shoulder as heavily-armored vehicles sent their red-tinged smoke belching up into the clear sky overhead. The garish red, white, and blue banners snapped in the fitful breeze, and brass glinted as trumpets were raised. The sound of the horns was thin with distance, but it sent a chill down his old spine nonetheless.

There had been no brave trumpets that night so many years ago. Limelight, hissing in the light rain, and the strobing blades of rifle-fire had been the harbingers of the Union presence that night. But the heartless, brutal efficiency had been the same; as had the thoughtless violence, the night they had killed Veronica Carpathian, Vlad's sister and his beloved wife.

Burson Carpathian lowered the monocular and eased himself down against the tree trunk. He seldom thought about Veronica these days. His revenge against General Grant, the man who had led the attack that night, had been a long time in coming. Guilt had been his constant companion for years. His inability to exact his wife's blood price from the masked monster, no matter how great his own army of animated dead became, was a harsh reminder of his continued failure.

The doctor raised the monocular again and focused on the dun-colored mob below the Union lines. A large Warrior Nation war party was gathered there, the tanned skin and cured hides of their clothing blending uncannily into the yellowed grass. Although they outnumbered the Union forces on the ridge by about half again, the disparity in technology seemed insurmountable. However, he knew that the Warrior Nation throng concealed men and women capable of calling upon the strange powers of their 'Great Spirit' to perform all sorts of wondrous tricks and feats of strength. This mystical power would make them a deadly match even for the soldiers wielding the latest in weapons and technology above them.

Carpathian pushed himself away from the tree with another grunt and rose to his feet. The powerful metal legs pushed him forward with a speed that even his natural legs, lost now these many years, could not have matched. He followed Ursul back to their clearing.

The Warrior Nation was his true problem now. Who would have thought that the unwashed savages would be able to hold the greater share of Grant's power in the east for so long? Carpathian knew that Grant was as eager as he to meet in open conflict, their hatred brutally mutual. The technologies the vile Union general had stolen from him on that beach so long ago formed the basis for all the Union advancements since the end of their Civil War. In fact, without those advances, who knew how that war would have ended? But the hatred remained. Years of clandestine work and fortunes spent tracking down every rumor and innuendo had revealed the true source of Grant's animosity.

Carpathian's discovery of the potent, mysterious power source he called RJ-1027, now colloquially known as 'RJ' or 'Devil's Blood', had been the culmination of a lifetime of arduous work. That early work had benefited greatly from a series of mysterious patrons, and had slowly transitioned from the healing efforts of his youth to the weapons and machines of destruction that had dominated his more recent years. Despite setbacks and difficulties in his home nation of Romania, he had believed himself to be the sole master of this new and daunting power.

But before he had even arrived on the shores of America, someone had used that power to assassinate General Grant's entire family. The attack had left the general alive, although terribly disfigured in body and soul. Somehow, Grant had decided that Carpathian was to blame, and had ordered the doctor's murder, along with his wife, their servants, and the entire crew of the steamship Lady B, on that cold, wet beach. Carpathian had survived against the odds. His beautiful Veronica, however, had not.

More mysterious patrons had spirited the doctor away from the site of the massacre and brought him deep into the American west, to the thriving town of Green Valley, now transformed into his own personal fiefdom, Payson, buried deep within the Tonto Forest. Hidden away within the maze of pines, valleys, and majestic buttes, he had constructed an empire that would one day change the world. Mines sunk deep into the ruins of the once-lush valley produced all the power he needed, and the Boot Hills and bone orchards of the Wild West had provided him with the raw materials for his animation armies.

Carpathian stumped into the clearing. The dull metal hide of his Doomsday wagon, flanks dappled by the fluttering shadows of the leafy canopy overhead, was silent and menacing in the shifting darkness. Around the vehicle stood a squad of his animations, all completely still as only corpses could be, awaiting his word to lurch into obedient action.

There was still some debate within his inner circle as to the practicality of using animations over more durable, artificial automatons. The Union Lawmen made excellent use of their own automata; the UR-30 Enforcers, K9s, and others. But using the readily available raw material of the dead, plentiful at any time in history but even more so in the rough and tumble world of the American west, meant that his ranks could be replenished again and again, without the complex industrial support structure creating squads of automata would require. That left his manufacturing capacity free for other projects, such as the weapons and equipment needed to ensure his freedom and extend his power, as well as the goods and services he provided to towns and villages that were smart enough to bow to his will without a more expensive show of force.

Which did not mean you ever got used to the smell.

Vlad Caym rested with his back against one massive iron wheel, his enormous sniper rifle, Old Pusca, cradled in his right arm. Nearby stood the twins, Schultz and Dieter Kaufmann, their long gray coats hanging loosely from tall, muscular frames. The Kaufmanns had been a regular fixture around Payson for over a decade; two of his most gifted agents, especially when it came to clandestine work or helping to lead animations in the field. They lacked the refinement and finesse of some of his more gifted followers, and enjoyed the work perhaps a little too much, but he would stake his life on their loyalty, and there were no better men available to him when violence was in the offing.

"You believe us now?" Schultz stood straighter, his face a petulant mask. The guttural tones of Germany could be heard rumbling just beneath his voice.

Dieter's expression mirrored his brother's. "We told you there was no getting to them."

"Those damned savages are a better defense for the blue-bellies than anything Grant could come up with!"

Carpathian grunted, tossing his monocular into a cargo box on the Doomsday wagon and reaching down to snatch his atomic blunderbuss from the ground by the wheel.

"They continue to present a most irritating obstacle, I'll grant you." He turned to look in the direction of the battle as if his glowing red eye could pierce the intervening forest. In the distance, the dull roar of fighting could be heard. "What of your other task?"

Dieter shook his head. "There's been no sign of him on this side of the river."

"I'd be very surprised if he pushed this far east." Schultz added. "He's a creature of the desert, now."

Carpathian grunted. "We must follow up on every rumor. It is imperative that we find him as soon as possible."

Schultz looked at his brother and then at the doctor. "Billy the Kid would know where to look. They're not friends, but the Kid always seems to know where to find him."

Carpathian rolled his eyes. "I would rather not have to deal with William Bonney unless absolutely necessary. I've managed to keep the loathsome toad out of Payson for months, I'd like to maintain that blessed state for as long as possible."

"Ze ozer vun vill be returning to Payson again before too long as vell." Vlad's scowl deepened, and he rubbed at one thigh. "Zere vill be hell to pay, if Vayvard and James meet, and talk."

The doctor waved the concerns away. "There's plenty of time to deal with that dilemma before it gets out of hand." He quirked an eyebrow down at Vlad's leg. "Would you rather me not have struck that little bargain?"

The stout man snorted. "He dropped me down ze lift shaft. Vhat more vas he going to do?"

Carpathian shook his head and turned back toward the sounds of distant conflict.

"There must be a way." The statement was low, almost as if the old doctor were addressing himself rather than the men around him. "They're primitive savages. How they lasted this long will redound to my eternal bafflement."

"You've been fighting zem, and every ozer wretch able to spit in your direction, for so long now I've lost track." Vladimir's sour tone matched his heavy-browed expression. "Ve have greater zings to vorry about zan ze savages or ze foolish Americans."

Carpathian shook his head, shooting his brother-in-law a surly look of his own. "You, more than anyone, Vladimir, should know that nothing is more important than making Grant pay for his crimes. The man's offences are infinite. But even ignoring that, unless he is removed from the world stage, our wider plans will forever be plagued by his violent opposition."

"Ve cannot reach him. You said it yourself." He pushed his massive weapon toward the sounds of violence and death. "Ve cannot fight two foes at ze same time. And meanwhile, ze smoke still hangs over Payson. Ve need to take care of our own, before ve launch some ill-conceived attack zat vould make Napoleon cringe."

The doctor shot Vlad a vicious glare, then settled back against the studded ram of the Doomsday. "Mister Wayward and his merry band have been taken care of, Vladimir, and those other mercenary fools will meet their doom in time." He looked up through the branches overhead, watching the thin clouds stream off to the east as the sounds of battle rose to a violent crescendo. "Payson will endure, and the time has come to turn our thoughts back to first causes." Carpathian's head dropped, his eyes flat. "Grant will pay, and with his fall, the Union will be ripe for the kind of change that will bring our ultimate plans to fruition."

"Zere are ozer sings ve must focus on as vell." Vlad's stubborn tone was hard, his chin lifting in defiance. "Ze Confederacy is still in disarray. Zere defeat at ze new Union fort has knocked zem all back on zere heels. Ze world is not bending to your vill, Herr Doctor, and it von't vhile you spend your time and effort focusing on Grant."

The Kaufmann twins looked uncomfortable, their eyes flicking between the two older men behind their silver-tinted lenses. Schultz nudged his brother with an elbow, and jerked his chin toward the defensive copula of the Doomsday. "Maybe we should look to the Hellions?"

Dieter's eyes were fixed upon Caym's taught face. He nodded absently, moving toward the tall metal ladder that stretched up the flank of the wagon. He did not take his eyes from the older man's tight expression until he turned to follow his brother up onto the warm metal roof.

"Zere is anozer matter I vish resolved." Vladimir broke his brother-in-law's gaze and turned back to look out at the woods around them. His eyes skimmed over the still, silent forms of the animations standing watch; he had grown accustomed to them over the years, if not comfortable.

Carpathian shook his head with a mixture of worry and distaste. "Nothing has changed since the last time you broached this subject, Vladimir. Our situation is more precarious now that it has ever been. It is too dangerous for the boy and his mother to –"
"	He is no longer a boy, Burson. He is a man, and has been for years. He celebrates his twentieth year zis month. And I have been away from them both too long." He bowed his head. "I mourn my sister, Burson, but I miss my wife and child. Zey are still alive." He turned his head to speak over his shoulder. "He needs his father. I have heard stories—"

A look of distaste flashed across the doctor's face before he could banish it completely. "I have heard the tales as well, my friend. Mere idle gossip, I am sure. There is no way such a sweet boy could be guilty of such terrible crimes." He turned his eyes away, knowing they would betray the lie he told.

"His mozer is constantly vorrying; the boy is so wrapped up in his studies. Dreams of joining us in America have driven his every action for years." His tone was concerned, not that of a man entirely convinced of his own son's innocence. "She hardly sees him, zese days."

"It is merely the energy of youth, Vladimir, nothing more." He hardened his tone, stiffening it against his brother-in-law's paternal concerns. "But we can hardly take the time and effort to shepherd such a spirited young man through the vagaries of maturity with our current difficulties, no?"

The shorter man's next words were firm with sudden resolve. "If I cannot send for them soon, I will leave you eventually. They need me."

"Where will you go, Vladimir? To Paris?" Carpathian's voice was sharp and cruel. "I don't see you deriving much satisfaction from the salons and cafes of the City of Lights, my friend. And Romania will no longer have you, as you know." He pushed himself away from the wagon and reached out to pat the other man's shoulder with a metal-braced hand. "Vlad, the time will come. The lad and his mother will be with you before you realize it. Do not forget our most recent reverses. Do you not suppose the havoc caused by Wayward could happen again? Would you want your boy caught in the middle of a conflagration like that?"

Caym tensed as the heavy hand landed on his embossed pauldron, then made an effort to relax. He nodded, not turning around. "As you say."

Carpathian nodded in turn, moving towards the rear hatch of the Doomsday. "And as I say, they will be with us before you know it." He turned to speak over his shoulder in an off-hand tone. "I look forward to meeting the lad, as you know."

Vlad followed, Old Pusca clanging against his armored shoulder, his tone growing light. "You vill love him, Burson. A mind like a machine, he has. Far more ze man of science, like his uncle, than a man of action, like his father."

"I cannot believe any child of yours is entirely lacking in a tendency toward action, old friend." Carpathian slung his weapon and reached up for one of the handholds bracketing the rear stairway. "Such direct impulses could not have been entirely bred away."

The other man looked vaguely uncomfortable. "Well, he vas always a feisty boy—"

Vlad's response was cut short as a blazing trail of sharp blue light struck the armored flank behind him, sending a swirling cloud of cerulean sparks dancing off in all directions. The detonation echoed across the clearing while the big man dropped, his heavy rifle falling across one forearm as he searched the wood line for targets.

"Savages!" One of the Kaufmann brothers shouted down from the fighting platform above them. A blast of super-heated plasma flashed out to ignite one of the ancient oaks nearby.

"Defend!" The doctor's brusque voice snapped as he hopped down from the ladder, his blunderbuss swinging up to point threateningly into the mottled shadows.

At the sound of their master's voice, the animations in the clearing lurched into motion. The decaying synapses of their dead brains came to a sluggish resemblance of life, as RJ-1027 flowed through their desiccated veins. Pre-programmed responses sent them turning toward the source of the original blast.

Indistinct forms moved through the shadows of the deep forest. They appeared human in shape and size, and the doctor breathed a sigh of thanks. He had no doubt he would be able to handle one of the shape-changing chieftains of the Warrior Nation, but it would be more of a challenge than he currently savored.

Several more bright-blue bolts snapped out of the shadows, flashing against the armor of the wagon and sending him skittering back behind the tall rear wheel. One of the bolts hit an animation as it turned to face the threat, its blaster rising to fire. The sapphire missile struck, blasting the thing backward and igniting the rotten tatters of clothing that clung to its gaunt form. Pale, cloudy eyes stared sightlessly into the branches overhead as smoke curled up from the charred crater in its chest.

"Guard ze doctor!" Vladimir yelled up to the twins as he rolled awkwardly away from a string of bolts that slapped into the moist loam of the forest floor. He clanged like an ironwork as he moved, streaks of crimson fire lashing wildly from the muzzle of his gun as he tried to suppress the attacking warriors long enough to reach cover.

Another blast of searing plasma flashed from the top of the wagon, and then the chuffing sound of Dieter's gas launcher sent a spinning canister of hissing poison into the trees. High-pitched screams and violent thrashing followed, as several savage warriors succumbed to the vile fumes. Vlad settled his back against the bark of a tall tree, his heavy rifle clutched to his chest. He rolled to his right, collapsing into a prone firing position, and brought the targeting reticule of his personalized sniper scope down on the first figure emerging from the shadows and toxic fog. The man was tall and well-muscled, like most of the Warrior Nation. His dark eyes glowed a deep blue, as did the ancient weapons he clutched in tight fists. Droplets of azure fire hissed into the moist loam.

Glaring eyes scanned the clearing, a cold sneer pulling at one cheek as he saw the animations lumbering toward him. The warrior gave a shriek filled with terrible anticipation, two stone axes rising over his dark hair, when the blue fire went dark without warning, a look of confusion stuttering across his proud face. He looked down, uncomprehending, at the massive hole that had appeared in his chest. The flesh around the wound was charred and smoking, while blood and viscera began to seep through the blackened meat.

Vlad nodded as he watched the warrior's corpse tumble bonelessly to the dirt. Behind the still form, noxious fog drifted through shafts of afternoon sunlight. Several figures still staggered within the cloud, clutching at their throats; their bodies wracked with wet, hacking coughs. Too many had made it into the clearing, however, and Vlad could tell it was going to be a close thing.

The animations had staggered into a defensive line, hacking methodically at warriors who whirled and skipped around them, punishing them with weapons of flame-wreathed energy. Atop the wagon, the Kaufmann brothers were trying to keep the savages away from the doctor. Carpathian was not cowering down, but rather stood indignantly by the tall metal wheel, clearly put out by the unforeseen intrusion.

The doctor brought his blunderbuss up across his chest, an eyebrow cocked in annoyance, and moved away from the wheel. One particularly energetic warrior spun over the line of animations, whirling in mid-air, to land before him, a long stone knife in either hand, a vicious grin twisting his dark face.

The grin disappeared as the blunderbuss barked a sharp blast into his midriff. The man flew backward, taking a stumbling animation down with him. The savage's stomach was a smoking, red mess as burns and purple rot swept out from the initial wound. The man staggered to his hands and knees, trying to push himself back up to his feet, but his arms were shaking with the strain. Eyes wide with disbelief, he slowly fell to the earth and lay still.

"Dieter, launch the Hellions! Let us get some use from this lot of ruffians, shall we?" Carpathian moved back to the cover of the Doomsday wagon while he slid another atomic shell into the mouth of his weapon. With his other hand he fidgeted with a series of knobs and dials on a small box at his belt. One of the downed animations, not damaged enough to knock its RJ-1027 connection out of the doctor's link, staggered back to its feet despite a massive slash in its side.

High above, behind the iron parapet, the Kaufmanns exchanged a look and then turned to the spindly forms huddled in one corner of the fighting platform. Thin strips of rotting skin stretched across gangly frameworks of bone and metal, twitching with each sound of the battle below. Dieter shrugged, reached down, and flicked first one small switch, then two more. Each was hidden behind a desiccated ear, set into the soft, decaying flesh of a nearly hairless-head.

With a high-pitched shriek, the first Hellion launched itself into the sky, erupting from the top of the Doomsday in a flash. The loose bundle of bone, flesh, and metal swept over the battle, its face a mass of flapping skin and metal plates, a single ruby eye flashing down from its iron forehead.

The savage warriors tensed, looking up in confusion as the creature circled once amidst the branches overhead, its screaming cries a mix of tormented scream and predatory raptor call. The tattered wings folded and it fell from the sky, striking one tall fighter so hard in the chest that the feathers of his headdress exploded into the air, drifting down in slow, gentle patterns. The Hellion dug into the warrior with the gleaming metal hooks that had replaced its hands. It chewed at the man's throat with metal teeth, and the spirit energy flickered and died as his concentration was lost in the churn of pain and terror.

Kicking off the twitching body with its metal talon-feet, the Hellion launched itself back into the sky with a victorious cry. All around them the remaining warriors wavered in their resolve. When two more Hellions leapt from the Doomsday, they broke and ran, more willing to brave the poison gas lingering among the trees than face the terror from the sky. Dieter and Schultz continued to fire into the fleeing savages. One man was dashed into the rough bole of a thick tree as one of the massive shells from Vlad's rifle slapped into his broad back.

Carpathian smiled as he watched the warriors run. He looked up, his eyes flashing with vindicated pride, just as the Hellion, barely visible through the leaves overhead, seemed to jerk spasmodically in its flight. The thing stiffened, its arms, legs, and wings arcing with tension, and then it tumbled back toward the earth, lifeless.

The other two Hellions, sweeping up past their falling brother, cleared the trees just as a muscled form, half warrior and half enormous bird of prey, flashed by overhead, a bow gleaming sapphire in its outstretched hands. The two Hellions stopped in their flight, looking with empty red eyes at the fierce creature soaring toward them. Before they could bring their weapons to bear, the altered warrior pulled up, his pristine white wings flaring, and gestured as if to draw the string of his bow. A fiercely burning arrow shaft shimmered into being, and the warrior loosed the phantom missile, repeating the motion in a blur. Each arrow of light and flame struck a Hellion in the chest, blasting them both off-balance and tumbling them toward the ground.

The doctor was cursing in harsh Romanian as he watched his latest creations fall through the branches. Two trailed blue-tinged smoke and fell lifelessly toward their imminent destruction. But with another series of convulsive shudders, the first Hellion sprang back to awareness before it struck, rolling over to glare down at the earth once again, its wings splaying. The head scanned the field, and without hesitation, it fell upon one of its earth-bound cousins, taking the other animation in the back and ripping its head off with one wrenching pull of its bladed hands.

"Oh, pentru numele lui Dumnezeu!" Carpathian lapsed into Romanian again in exasperation. Always considering himself a man of the world, he almost never used his native language outside of moments of sheer frustration and anger.

The Hellion lept off the still form of its latest victim and surged back up for the clouds. Carpathian raised his clumsy-looking weapon and struck his creation out of the sky with a contemptuous snarl. The atomic bolt struck the flying creature in the head, incinerating the putrescent brain and the artificial command runs, leaving nothing but a black and purple stump trailing thick, icorous fluid as its limp form fell heavily to the dirt.

From the firing platform, Schultz cursed. "Verdammten wilde!" He sent the flying eagle warrior screeching away with two sun-bright bolts of searing plasma that lit small fires amidst the leaves and branches overhead. "What in the name of damnation was that?"

His brother called out. "Not Sky Spirit. Too small."

The clearing was silent for a moment, surviving animations staring sightlessly into the forest around them while Carpathian and his brother-in-law stood, glaring at the twisted wrecks lying amidst the steaming mud and loam. Fingers of black smoke rose lazily toward the branches overhead. The doctor looked up at the fighting platform atop his wagon. The Kaufmann brothers peered over the parapet, eyes wide behind their silvered goggles.

"Come down and gather these useless pieces of rahat so we may return them to the lab." He looked as if he wanted to spit.

"I swear, one more miscarriage of this magnitude, and I'll scrap the entire project."

As the Kaufmanns climbed down from their perch, Vlad stumped over from his shooting blind, Old Pusca over one shoulder. "Vell, that vas invigorating, eh?"

The sour look on Carpathian's face twisted even tighter. "You have strange taste in pastimes, brother. You always have had." He gestured at the wreckage all around them, from the torn and bleeding bodies of the native warriors to the stinking wreckage of dismantled animations, to the shattered wreck of the Hellions. Each time a Kaufmann brother pulled on a limb or wing to straighten it, the appendage pulled free with a sickening sucking sound.

"And this is the land you would subject your wife and son to." He shook his head. "Leave them where they are, my friend. We need to secure our position here before we can trust our new home with such precious cargo. They will be much safer where they are, for now."

Vladimir looked at Carpathian in silence, and then turned away, his head bowed.

Chapter 1

The predator stayed to the shadows as he crossed the Pont d'Iena, careful lest his prey should see him in the dim illumination of those few functioning gas lamps. The prey walked with a jaunty spring in his step, walking stick tapping a sprightly beat on the stones of the bridge as the dark waters of the Seine slid beneath them. The predator's teeth gleamed in a sudden, vicious grin. The bald old tromper in the salon had been right: this was going to be an easy take.

Ahead of the prey, the trees of the Champ de Mars loomed out of the late-night fog, domes of indistinct gaslight doing more to confuse the scene than illuminate it. They did provide a fine backlight to the swaggering target, however.

As the tall man in the fancy clothing stepped off the bridge, the stone Saracen and Greek Hoplite guarding the Right Bank loomed out of the fog, looking down with sad, regretful faces. The predator watched with a widening sneer as the man tapped the brim of his tall hat with his cane, first to the Mohammedan, then to the Greek, and then continued on his way toward the Quai Branly, and the park beyond.

The night was cool, which probably explained the fog. Summers were fickle in the City of Lights, but a night this cold was rare, and often coaxed a thick mist from the black waters of the river. The predator did not care. The fog would make approaching his mark laughably simple, and any brief noises from the struggle would echo confusedly through the fog, giving him plenty of time to escape, should the gardes decide, against years of habit, to take an interest.

The predator's eyes flicked to either side, acknowledging the statues of the warriors with a knowing smile. Those ancient killers would have nothing on him. He had ended more lives in Paris than any other three tueurs added together. And the gardes had not once come close to catching him. The city was very much his playground, and its citizens were toys that he used and discarded as he pleased. He usually chose his targets himself, without requiring or accepting assistance, but the old bald man had been so adamant, and there had been something in his eyes that could not be denied…

The prey entered the Champs de Mars, the barren, dirt lot of the northern end of the park offering him nowhere to hide. Rumor in the city claimed that this was to be the spot of some exciting new structure for the Exposition Universelle, but like most things in Paris, and in Europe at large over the last few years, grand plans had been scrapped, leaving the beautiful park scarred and empty. Not that the hunter cared a whit for monuments, expositions, or parks. He would stalk his human quarry through forests, alleys, or deserts with equal ease.

Ahead of him, the prey kept to the center of the muddy swath, away from the shadowing trees and piles of grass-sprayed dirt. It was almost as if he were seeking to make it easy. As the tapping of the walking stick subsided with the man's diversion off the stone street, the predator picked up the pace. A small killing knife appeared in his left hand. The man ahead seemed tall and fit, and would most likely provide a welcome challenge before watering the grass with his blood.

"Hey!" The predator's voice was pitched low, and echoed in the fog, confusing its direction. He began to jog toward the quarry, anticipation gleaming in his eyes. Ahead of him, the man stopped, looking off to either side as if trying to locate the source of the call. A moment's disappointment caused the predator's smile to falter. This might not be the challenge he had hoped for after all.

The man ahead turned quickly as the predator closed the remaining distance, his knife swinging in from the side. The blow would not be lethal, disabling the prey's right arm at worst. But it would be painful, and there would be a great deal of blood. The predator's smile widened once again. Even if the mark was not going to provide a challenge, at least he would offer a modicum of entertainment while he lived.

The knife slashed through the fog, through the air, and then passed beneath the target's rising arm. The man spun faster than the predator would have expected, and shocked him with a wide-eyed, voracious grin of his own that he recognized all too well.

The prey's formal coat flared around him as he spun, one hand striking the attacker's knife-arm down and away. The predator staggered as his follow-through failed to meet any resistance at all, and was in fact helped along with a sharp push on his left shoulder. His feet rushed forward, trying to get back beneath his center of balance, but the last push was too much. He hit the hard packed dirt on his left shoulder, grunting with the impact.

The attacker rolled across his shoulder blades and came up into a crouch, smile replaced with an angry scowl. The knife reflected gaslight dully, and he tossed it from one hand to the other and back again, forcing his opponent to guard both sides at once. Through narrow eyes he waited for the hesitation that would indicate his opening had arrived.

Except that, again, his prey did not oblige. The man's devilishly fast arm darted out as the knife arched from one hand to the other, and caught it in mid-flight. With a childish snort of amusement, the would-be prey stepped in, reversed the knife, and punched the small metal pummel into the predator's gut. With a surprised grunt, he fell back, one arm clutching his sore stomach, the other reaching back to catch himself as he fell.

"You're not as quick as I had hoped, Jacques." The prey stood tall, one gloved hand idly flipping the small knife along agile, rippling fingers. "Hugo promised me a challenge, and there you lie, wallowing in the mud like a pig." The voice had a strange, hard accent.

Jacques du Eventreur was not a smart man, but he was cunning. One did not rise through the brutal aristocracy of crime on the streets of Paris without a sufficient supply of artifice and smarts. But there, in the mud of the defunct construction site at the north end of the Champ de Mars, the comfortable roles of predator and prey reversed, he was at a total loss.

"Nothing more to say, Jacques? The great stalker of the night, the most lethal man in the City of Lights has no words for his challenger?" The man's cheeks were smooth, lending him an air of youthful innocence that was entirely belayed by the cold emptiness in his eyes. Thin lips pulled back in an open smile that sent a wash of cold dread through his gut when paired with the dark, frigid eyes.

"How... how do you know me?" Jacques cursed the fear he heard in his own voice. He moved slowly away, crabbing backward, his stomach tight and bruised.

The man standing over him shrugged. "A little digging, a little listening here and there. A man of your reputation is not that hard to find, if one is willing to spread a little gold in the right quarters."

"Who... are you?" Again the fear caused him to stutter, and Jacques' scowl deepened as the warmth of anger began to leech into the cold of his panic.

The man paced casually to his left, then pivoted on one gleaming shoe to pace off to the right, all the while twirling the little knife without apparent thought or effort. "Well, you see, you have to earn that knowledge." The man stopped and smiled down at the most successful killer in Paris. "Do you think you can earn that knowledge, Jacques?"

Jacques' eyes narrowed as pieces of the evening began to fit together. "The old man in the salon."

The mysterious stranger he had meant to kill nodded, an almost apologetic furrow appearing above his eyes before smoothing over once again. "Hugo Digne: teacher, companion, and confidante." Once again he began to pace. "This was all his idea, you see. Take out my more ... ... aggressive ... ... impulses on the criminal element. It was meant to both avoid undue notice from the admittedly lackadaisical authorities, as well as provide more of a challenge than randomly selecting victims from the casual run of pedestrians wandering the streets at night."

A shadow crossed the man's face. "Not that the latter portion of the scheme seems to be proving overly efficacious."

Jacques' anger had achieved a suitable temperature to launch him back to his feet. Who was this man to speak to him

so here, in his own city? The man's French was barely under-
standable with that terrible, guttural accent. With a growl, the killer pulled a long, broad-bladed knife from a sheath along his left
thigh. The metal hissed against the leather, and the razor's edge
gleamed in the dim light.

"I'll give you a name, secousse. I call you viande morte!"
The long blade flashed forward. His wrist twisted, bringing the
sharpened edge up as he snapped the knife at the man's gut without warning.

The prey's long coat flared again as he stepped back,
one gloved hand slapping the blade aside with a ringing, metallic
sound that brought a flash of confusion to Jacques' eyes. Was the
man wearing armored gloves? He did not let the errant thought
distract him, however, and twisted his wrist again to bring the long
blade back around in a hacking attack at the arrogant man's eyes.

Arching his back, his arms thrown to either side to maintain balance, the blade swept through the air where his head had
been only a moment before. The very tip of the blade nicked the
flesh of the quarry's temple before sailing past, causing no further harm. Before Jacques could recover and bring the blade back
again for another swing, the man was standing upright, his right
arm flashing out, and Jacques' own small blade was lodged in his
left shoulder.

Pain and anger warred within him as terrible, violating agony surged through his body. His arm curled against his chest in
an instinctual, protective posture that threw off his balance, cost-
ing him the return swing of the massive blade. He took several
staggering steps back, trying to clear some distance between himself and the figure with the cold smile.

The man stood before him now, that awful grin still firmly
in place, not a mark or scuff marring his appearance. He settled
gloved hands on narrow hips, almost as if waiting for Jacques
to recover enough to rejoin the battle. The stance infuriated him
even more than the man's words. Despite the burning cold of his
dead left arm, he tightened his grip on the long dagger, preparing

himself for another rush. One way or another, this man would die here in this forsaken park.

The man in the formalwear crouched down, ready for the criminal's charge, but then stood up again, a look of mild curiosity on his features. He held up a hand to forestall Jacques' rush. The gesture was so strange, so against all convention, that the street tough paused, cocking his head to the side, shoulders heaving with exertion and pain.

"What's your number, Jacques?" The tone was calm, the cold eyes suddenly warming just a touch.

But Jacques could make no sense of the words. "My number?"

The man nodded. "Your number. How many? How many people have you killed?"

For a moment Jacques stared at the strange foreigner in numb disbelief. The words seemed to carry no meaning while at the same time, they drove into his mind, infusing his every heart-beat with wrath. When he suddenly rushed at the twisted mad-man, he was rewarded with the first look of surprise he had been able to illicit. The man danced aside, batting at the wildly swinging blade with the flat of one hand, again causing a sharp ring to echo off into the fog. Jacques' vision was hazy and tinged with red. Anger and blood loss conspired against him.

As the enraged killer rushed past, the strange, cold-eyed young man planted one hard palm on the center of his back and gave what appeared to be a negligent push. However, the force of the blow was out of all proportion with what a man that size should have been capable of providing. Bones snapped, waves of shock rolled through his body, and deep within, he could feel his organs shifting and rupturing. Jacques lost all control of his momentum, flying several yards before he tumbled into the dirt, fetching up against a dense hillock, sparse grass dusting it with green.

Jacques' vision continued to blur. His entire body ached. The cold from his numb arm was now spreading into his chest, and he could feel his thoughts wandering. Hot flickers of anger flashed within his mind, but they were weak, distant images in the soft confusion that reigned there. He could hear footsteps nearby, but his head would not turn no matter how hard he tried. He thought his teeth were gritted, he thought his hands were clenched. But as all sensation leached away, he could not be sure.

"So, Jacques." The words came from somewhere above him, and he felt, like pangs of dull pain, pressure and pulling as he was gently rolled onto his back. A pale object floated before his vision, and he focused all of his dwindling energy to bring it into focus. The face of the man he had planned to kill. The eyes were still cold, emotionless. The smile was gone, the thin lips straight. The curiosity, however, still rode the man's brow as the eyes searched his face as if looking at some mildly interesting puzzle. "What's your number?"

Blood bubbled up onto Jacques' lips. His breath was harsh and shallow. Each wet gasp brought a fresh stab of dull agony. The question seemed to worm into his mind, writhing through the boil of fear and anger and pain. He coughed, and thick blood splattered his face. He tried to smile, as vestiges of pride pushed the words past his lips.

"Twelve." It was barely a gasp, and his red-stained teeth gleamed wetly as he smiled.

The man who had killed him stood up, brows rising in disbelief. Then he leaned down, his sharp teeth shining in a smile of his own. "Well damn, son. You're my twentieth. You lose."

* * * * *

F.R. Caym rested his wrists on his thighs as he squatted beside his latest kill. The light left Jacques du Eventreur's eyes as he watched, and the moment carried with it the electrical thrill he had come to expect from such events, although the fear of a helpless victim had been lacking, and the fight old Jacques had been able to offer had not really compensated for the deficiency.

He was going to have to discuss this further with Hugo. He was not sure preying upon the criminal element of Paris was going to be the panacea his old mentor had promised after all.

"F.R., if you're quite done?" The voice from the fog was muted, with a barely-contained note of distaste. "I believe your mother is expecting us?"

F.R. stood, still looking down at the cold, dead form. He brushed a single drop of blood, tracing a line down his cheek, away from the shallow wound at his temple. It was not often that his prey was able to mark him. Jacques had not been quite the slouch he had thought him after all. He had contemplated taking trophies from some of his past victims. He knew that many of the great killers of history had done that. But nothing had ever called out to him. After a moment, he crouched down again to pull the small blade from the meat of Jacques' shoulder. The knife, caught in the dense muscle, resisted a moment before it slid out. He cleaned the blade on the street killer's shirt, and then slid it into his coat pocket as he stood again.

"Yes, Ern, I'm coming." He moved toward one of the main paths heading west through the Champ de Mars.

"I'll never understand your need to indulge these baser instincts, my friend. A mind such as yours, to be a slave to such hungers..." A tall, well-built man loomed up out of the fog as F.R. walked, his recovered stick tapping once again on the stones.

F.R. grimaced, not wishing to have the same conversation again. Ernest Rutherford was the closest friend he had. Next to his own mother and old Hugo, Ern meant more to him than almost anyone else in the world. Certainly more than his absent father, lost to distant America. But the young genius from New Zealand he had met all those years ago back in the storage locker beneath the Gibb's Building, King's College, Cambridge, completely lacked the thirst for extreme sensation that drove F.R. to these more risky outings. Ernest seldom wanted to discuss the issue, but when he got his dander up, he could be quite tiresome.

F.R. raised a hand to forestall further comments. "Ern, I'm tired. Can we do without the lecture and hurry home? As you say, mother will be worried if we're much longer."

The other man smoothed his full mustache, still shaking his head. "Was it a great challenge? Taking down a street tough?"

He pushed off the inoperative gaslight post he had been resting against, falling into step beside his friend. "One would think not, what with your ... ... advantages, and all." He flicked one finger against F.R.'s sleeve, the nail pinging off something metallic beneath.

F.R. shrugged his arm away from his friend. They crossed the Avenue de Suffren, its stones moist with fog. The distant clopping of a horse's hooves could be heard echoing off somewhere to their right, toward the river, but they could see no one as they moved up toward the Rue Desaiax.

"My advantages, as you say, do nothing but enhance the abilities I was born with, and continue to enhance through every means necessary. And if I do not test myself, and my enhancements, how will we know they are effective?" He grinned at his friend. "I would think, as a scientist, you would understand the process."

Ernest shook his head. "In the furtherance of science, I understand. But I do believe you have begun to take a more than seemly enjoyment in the entire process."

The elegant old townhouses of the Rue de la Federation rose up around them. Here, many of the most rich and powerful of Paris' foreign inhabitants made their homes, not far from the embassies and consulates of the 7th Arrondissement. When his family first fled Romania, they had travelled around Europe, eventually settling in Paris against his father's wishes. Using a large portion of the family's remaining wealth, they had purchased, outright, the elaborate townhouse at 52 Rue de la Federation, where they had lived ever since.

The townhouse was a brownstone, with elaborate marble carvings gracing the tall, thin front. It had been home for as long as he could remember, and even after his father had followed his uncle to the New World, it had been a place of safety and comfort for him. His own rooms and laboratory, taking up the entire basement level of the structure, provided him with a safe haven for the experiments and studies that had dominated his life for years now.

F.R. took the steep steps up to the front door with a jaunty air, tapping on the heavy paneling with the topper of his silver cane. A maid opened the door quickly, smiling at the young master of the house and moving demurely to the side. He gave her a warm smile of his own, but Ernest merely pushed past, more gruff than usual.

In the receiving room on the main floor, his mother sat in a tall, wing-backed chair, a book in one hand. She looked over her reading spectacles at the two young men as they entered, a smile creasing the wrinkled skin of her forehead.

"You boys are late." She stood, setting the book on a reading table beside the chair. "Dinner is in the warming pan beneath the oven, if you're still hungry."

The tall, stately woman approached her son, grasping him gently by the shoulders and placing two gentle kisses upon him, one on either cheek. As she drew back, she saw the cut just to the side of his eye, and frowned in disapproval.

"You've been fighting again." The iron in her voice was unmistakable, and F.R. bowed his head to break their eye contact.

"Just a minor disagreement, mother. Nothing major." He muttered. His mother would not understand his need to test himself and his advances in the streets. She had married a soldier, that was true. And a fierce one, if the stories were to be believed. But she had no concept of the scientific method, and the need to constantly test ones hypotheses in the laboratory of the real world.

"Just a street tough, mum." Ern's lilting, foreign accent never failed to charm Mrs. Caym from her occasional parental disappointments, and she smiled at him with returning warmth, taking him by the shoulders in turn and giving him a quick peck on either cheek as well.

"You must try harder to keep him out of trouble, Ernest. You know he can't be trusted on his own."

F.R.'s friend smiled for the first time that evening, his full mustache curling with the expression. "You have no idea, mum."

"Enough, the two of you. I'm not a child, to be spoken of as if I'm not present." F.R. grabbed his friend by the sleeve and pulled him back toward the door. "We'll bring the food down with us, mother. We'll be in the lab late, tonight, I'm afraid."

His mother shook her head, resuming her seat and picking up her book. "When are you not? Try to get some sleep. It's not seemly, for you boys to sleep through the mornings like you do."

"Yes, mother." He rolled his eyes at his friend as he steered Ern out the door and into the hall. "I swear, she thinks I'm still ten years old. As if the neighbors care a whit for my sleeping habits. We're barely tolerated in polite society as it is, barbarians that we are."

Ernest shrugged F.R.'s grasp away and moved into the vast, echoing kitchen with its gleaming black and white tiles. The servants were all gone for the night, left for their own homes or retiring to the servant's quarters in the upper portions of the house. The heavy door to the warming pan clanged as he pulled it open, drawing two plates, each covered with a napkin, into the light. He stood, kicking the door closed with another resounding crash, and placing the plates on the pristine surface of the kitchen's island countertop.

Pulling the napkin from one plate, Ern sniffed in dismissal. "Duck again." He grabbed the small hunk of meat in one hand and tore a chunk out, chewing around a big grin.

"And they consider my family the barbarians." F.R. opened a drawer and removed two forks and a pair of knives, sliding one set pointedly at his friend. "Tell me, Ern, does anyone use tableware in New Zealand, or is it all hands and sticks, like the natives?"

His friend laughed around the food in his mouth. "Oh, please, F.R. The Maori are far more civilized than us colonials. If we want forks and knives, we borrow from them!"

F.R. shook his head and picked his plate up. "Come. There are some adjustments I would like to make, and we have yet to resolve the volatility issues with the latest admixture."

"If it's all the same to you, old son, I'd rather not eat around the materials down there." He gave a theatrical shudder.

"Perhaps we could finish our repast here in the upper world, and then delve down into the secrets of the universe below?"

F.R. stood still for a moment, then shrugged. "As you say."

The meals were polished off quickly, F.R. hungry from his exertions in the Champ de Mars, and Ernest eating, as always, with the appetite of a young man who grew up within limited means. As F.R. watched his friend finish his vegetables, he rested his elbows and back against the counter and looked casually up at the ceiling.

"Has there been any word from your father or your uncle?" The words were so aggressively nonchalant, F.R. had to smile as he looked back down.

"Not since the last regretful denial, no." He drew the napkin across his narrow lips and placed it over the empty plate. "I'm starting to doubt father's sincerity, to be honest."

"The stalwart war hero, dissembling to his own progeny? Say it isn't so." Ernest's face had taken on a sour look.

F.R. nodded. "Do you have any idea how long it has been since I have seen my father?" His voice was bitter as he stared down at the wrinkled napkin. "He left to follow my uncle when I was barely into trousers. He's been gone for more years than I care to remember, and hasn't been home once in all that time."

"Well, they did kill his sister, your aunt." Ern looked as if he were having second thoughts bringing the topic up. "Given his soldierly bent, I'm sure he felt responsibility toward vengeance. And your uncle, by everything you say, is far more a scientist than a warrior."

"And so he rushed off to America, abandoning us here to rot in this horrific, gilded hellhole, while the two of them write their names in blood across an entire continent." Anger was seeping into F.R.'s voice. It was an anger he was familiar with, that he usually denied himself in favor of the discipline of an educated, scientific mind. But this time, he embraced the fury rising within him.

"My aunt's death has been nothing but a pretext for years now. Uncle Burson pushes back the walls of conventional wisdom and knowledge, bringing ever-greater advancements and inventions into the light of history, establishing himself as a dominant force on an entire continent, and I am left here, with no goal or objective to set my mind to, told only to wait, interminably, for some ephemeral future time when I might be able to join them in their established glory."

Ernest looked skeptically at his friend. "I know you revere your uncle, F.R., but do you not think you're putting too much upon him? Writing his name across a continent? The scientific journals of Europe don't even mention your uncle at all, never mind speaking of great advancements and world-shaking theories. I mean, if—"

With a dismissive wave, F.R. turned to his friend. "Jealousy. How often is RJ-1027 mentioned in those self-same journals? And yet you and I both know it exists, we both know small quantities have been arriving in Europe for years now, used by secretive cabals of pseudo-scientists who would rather throw themselves into the Channel than admit that they have followed in Burson Carpathian's footsteps. Hell and damnation, Ern, we have several canisters of the infernal stuff in the basement right now!"

"But if so much is happening over there, while science is slowing to a crawl here, why won't anyone say anything? It makes no sense."

"Science? Say, rather, society as a whole. Europe is dying. Cut off from the most important advances of the new age, in complete denial of the new potential while denied the proof and inclusion by the iron fist of the American Union across the ocean... is it any wonder that things here have gotten so bad?"

Ernest shook his head. "There is no denying that Cambridge was not the Mecca of learning I had hoped, when I accepted my scholarship. But if things are so bad here, why would your father and uncle want you trapped here, when you clearly have so much to offer?"

F.R. barked a sharp, bitter laugh. "And how would they know what I have to offer? All they have are my letters. The scribblings of a creature they both believe to be nothing more than a child. No matter how many collaborative projects I enter into here, with the greatest minds this benighted continent has to offer, I'm merely playing at being an adult, as far as they are concerned."

"But, surely they know Hugo, and what an influence he has been upon your learning?" The strange old man was an object of awe and devotion to the young New Zealander, opening entire worlds of possibility and wonder for the two young men to pursue.

"Hugo Digne is only a name to them both. He became my tutor years after father left. The man is a genius, but he has always worked in secret, and so there is no published proof of his accomplishments. His endorsement means nothing to Uncle Burson or to my father."

"The man is more of a father to you than Vladimir Caym ever was, F.R., you've told me that yourself. Surely there is something—"

F.R. put up a hand to silence his friend, shaking his head with a rueful smile, his anger subsiding. "There's no use gnawing at this old bone now, Ern. My uncle and my father have denied my latest request, and we must come to heel, like good little boys, and wait, and trust that our time will come."

"Well, it better come soon." Ernest was slower to let his bitterness go. "I'm due to return to Spring Grove soon, and I'd rather not board the slow boat south if I have other options available."

Grasping his friend on the shoulder, F.R. led the way through a small door in the back of the kitchen and down into the bowels of the townhouse. "You won't go back any sooner than you want to, my friend. The work we have ahead of us is far too important. We will go to America one day, and it will be one day soon. I would rather go with their blessing, is all. And barring that, I cannot leave my mother alone here among these bohemian sybarites."

The air in the stairwell was warm and close. Darkness closed in around them, until they were in near-total blackness, standing before a heavy door made of reinforced metal and clearly of new construction, with a small, glowing red vial sitting in a bracket on the wall. A small dial set into the door where a knob might be expected was turned in a quick series of flips, first one way and then the other. Something within the door gave a heavy click, and the slab of iron swung silently open.

F.R. moved into the room, a proud grin sweeping across his face. The chamber was vast, taking up almost the entire footprint of the townhouse. It was broken down into different work areas, each obviously outfitted for a variety of different tasks. The floor was illuminated with tubes of glowing material fixed to the ceiling, the light a strange orange-red that cast odd shadows across the lustrous white surfaces of the tables below.

The two young men moved past a long structure that supported a series of packs and bundles attached to heavy armored vests. Several of the bundles, toward one end of the line, had bulky shapes attached to them, comprised of hoses, nozzles, and tanks. One pack, the last in the line, had a small collection of such materials down its center with a sweeping wing-like vane rising up off of each side.

F.R. moved through the chamber, looking fondly at one area after another. He reached out to trace his fingers across one particularly vicious-looking weapon that looked like a cross between a hookah pipe and an elephant gun. Eventually, he stood at the back wall, looking up at an array of tubes, pipes, tanks, and gauges. Ernest stopped several steps behind him, arms folded defensively across his chest.

"Will you come up here? You told me yourself that the substance was harmless." A smile was clear in F.R.'s voice.

"I said most likely harmless." Ernest's voice was hard. "This is an entirely new discipline. No one has ever broken apart the constituent components of reality as we have. These materials shed the very atomies that constitute their existence, and those microscopic pieces of creation must go somewhere. What effect they might have as they pass through other matter is something we need to study in far more detail before I become entirely comfortable with the process."

F.R. grinned over his shoulder. "Well, we've been doing this for over a year now. If it's dangerous, I'm afraid the damage has already been done." He gestured with one hand at two tanks dominating the right-hand side of the wall. One tank glowed a pulsing, sullen crimson, the color of old, drying blood. The other tank glowed with a bright orange-yellow. The fluid within each tank moved sluggishly behind the thick glass. Each tank was connected to a third, smaller tank, situated below and between them and connected by heavy iron pipes with wheel valves at each juncture.

This third tank glowed with the same vermillion, orange-red light of the over-head tubes, but with far more intensity. The substance within the tank surged violently within the confines of the thick glass walls and around a heavy rod of some golden substance suspended in the middle.

F.R. bent to peer into the tank, his smile reflecting the bright, pulsing light.   "It looks like the control rod you devised is minimizing the violent interaction." He turned to look at Ernest, who had not moved from his original position. "With a little more work on the mixture, and maybe some refinements to the rod material, we should have a power source that we can start to incorporate into our other designs." He gestured at the rest of the room with a sweep of his still-gloved hand.

Despite himself, Ernest nodded. "Perhaps more lead in the alloy would further deaden the impact. And I was thinking, with a little more monoatomic gold added to the RJ-1027, the deterioration effect that powers the reaction might be further mitigated..."

Smiling at his friend's tone, F.R. settled back against a workbench with a nod.

Ernest, with Digne's help, had been breaking down the mysteries of particularly volatile substances whose dissolution could provide vast amounts of power. If coupled with his uncle's RJ-1027, which was clearly unstable and less-than-reliable, F.R.

had no doubt that he would have the key to unlocking a whole new world of technology and power. Once he had his mother situated, and he was ready to unveil this new discovery to his uncle, he would be ready to begin writing his own name across not just a single continent, but the entire world.

Chapter 2

The sun was setting over the distant, pine-skirted mountains; a flaring red corona all that remained of the blazing heat of the day. Through the strangely clear windows of the tower office, Vladimir Caym watched the golden beams of the dying sun spearing out over the landscape. Far below, in a valley whose once-verdant beauty had given the town of Payson its original name, the bustling figures of animations stripped the depths of the earth for the ingredients of RJ-1027, the power source that had made it possible for these immigrants from distant Romania to challenge the lords of America for domination of their continent.

Vlad's eyes flicked to the right, where the city of Payson sprawled out beneath him. Much of the damage they had suffered at the hands of that band of shiftless mercenaries had not yet been repaired. Burnt-out buildings and tumbled vehicles stood in mute testimony to the vulnerability of the doctor's stronghold. Vlad had spent more than a month leading the repair crews in the worst sections of the town, as well as organizing the installation of a new series of defenses within the surrounding forests. It had been weeks since he last enjoyed the comforts of the palace.

"Would you not agree, Vladimir?" Doctor Carpathian was sitting in his wing-backed chair; a brandy dangling in one relaxed hand, while he peered through his bushy white eyebrows, clearly expecting a response. The doctor had returned from their foray in the east with his renewed determination to make the Hellion project work, to the exclusion of many of the things that seemed far more important to Vlad. The man went on and on about altitude, autonomy, and aerodynamics; all subjects sure to cause the old soldier's eyes to glaze over with boredom and frustration.

"I'm sorry, vhat vere you saying?" Vlad stumped away from the window and dropped himself into a comfortable chair across from his brother-in-law. His own snifter sat, untouched, on the small marble table beside him.

Carpathian smiled and shook his head in a manner that never failed to irk the old soldier. "You can't pine over the sunset each evening, Vladimir. There are great things in the offing, and we need to discuss what comes next before we can put things into motion."

Vlad grunted. "Vhat comes next should be clear." He swept one thick arm at the eastward-facing bank of windows. "Ze town is in total disarray. If anozer attack vere to be launched right now, zere vould be no vay for us to defend ourselves. Ve must make good on our losses to ze tampit, Vayvard."

Carpathian's smile widened. "Ah, the eloquent language of a soldier. Vladimir, I cherish the way you keep me grounded, my friend." He then dismissed the meat of Vlad's statement with an indifferent wave of his snifter. "Marcus Wayward is of no concern, trust me. He has been dealt with. And there will be no further attacks for the foreseeable future. We must discuss the Union Forces just over the Mississippi, and the savages that stand between us."

An expensive, hand-drawn map sat in an ornate cherry-wood frame on the wall behind the doctor. Silver pins embossed with elaborate symbols and heraldry showed the dispositions of the various military units currently vying for control of the continent. A large mass of pins faced each other over the northern stretch of the Mississippi, several hundred miles northeast of Kansas City. More pins were scattered across the map, including a glittering array across the Great Plains to the north and into the Rocky Mountains, dense concentrations along the east coast and the border with the nearly-defunct Confederate Rebellion, and a surprising collection floating around Rebellion territory.

Vlad knew those pins represented a rather large force, scattered since their defeat at Fort Knox. Despite their defeat, that shabby group of insurgents were relatively well-supplied and well-led, thanks to a small coterie of officers and sergeants who had continued to pursue the war long after the vast majority of southerners had given up all hope. Vlad was not privy to the details, but he knew that the largest group of militia, centered around the port city of New Orleans, were beholden in some way to the doctor; that his influence stretched even into the fetid swamps of old Louisiana.

"I don't understand," Vlad kept his tone level. Burson was a man of science, and was often cold and calculated in his dealings with the world. But occasionally, he had a temper that would do justice to one of the great bears of the mountains of their homeland. "Our enemies are right zere, gathered togezer, ripe for a killing blow. Ve have done great sings here, Burson. A veritable empire for ze ages, growing up in ze forests around us, zat ze Romans or ze Greeks vould barely believe! Ve need only unleash your veapons on ze vorld, and all of zem vill fall! Grant vill fall! The savages vill fall! Zere is no vay zey vill be able to stand against us!"

Carpathian shook his head, taking a slow sip of brandy. "You are a direct soul, Vladimir. And God knows, your military knowledge has saved us on more than one occasion. But even were I to utilize every body within a thousand miles of Payson, it would not be enough. And I do not have the RJ-1027, nor the weapons and equipment, to arm even that many."

Vlad snorted and jerked his head in violent negation. Storming up out of his seat, he charged across the room and slapped his blunt-fingered hand against the map, square in the center of Confederate Rebellion land. "Here is everyzing you say you need!" His hand crashed against the wall again. "Men." Again, "weapons." Again, "equipment." He turned, unable to contain his anger. "You have ze world hanging before you, ripe for ze picking, and yet you balk!"

Carpathian sat as still as an ancient statue, staring at his brother-in-law with cold eyes. "You think, if this were all true, I would not seize the moment, and revel in the glory we have pursued for so many years?"

Vlad's breath game in sharp, angry huffs. "You sent zat pacali, Jesse James, down zere to gazer zem up and srow zem at ze Union. You can do ze same again, but at ze real threat! Find James, and send him to lead zem against Grant, if ve cannot lead zem ourselves! Crush ze masked madman once and for all, and let us rise up to take our rightful places at ze forefront of zis entire continent!"

Carpathian's eyes were hooded as he made a sour face. "Lest you forget, first we would need to find James. Since his ... ... abrupt, departure soon after I replaced his ruined arm, we have not had a great deal of luck in that regard. The man is like a ghost, wandering through the territories without a trace, leaving only whispers behind him."

Vlad snorted. "Then use ze ozer vun! If you must have Marcus Vayvard on a string, srow him at ze Union!" He paused, and then pointed one blunt finger at the doctor. "Or is it zat you lack ze courage of your convictions, after so many years of preparation and planning?"

There was a moment of cold silence in the tower room, and Vlad thought for a moment that he had pushed the other man too far. He had seen what Carpathian was capable of when his anger had been aroused, but he could not bring himself to care. They had both sacrificed too much, and suffered their exile too long, to bear it any further. If he needed to slap his brother-in-law in the face to make him see reason, he would do that. He tensed, waiting to see which way Carpathian would jump.

The laughter caught him completely off-guard.

The doctor began with a slight, lilting chuckle, but soon he was convulsing with deep, hooting mirth. By the time he had wrestled himself back under control, his face was red and he was wiping tears away with the back of one braced hand. "God bless you, Vladimir. You are like a breath of fresh air."

The tight concern, the anticipation of violence, evaporated, and Vlad's body stiffened as a cold anger rose up to take their place. "I fail to see ze joke, Burson." His hands tightened into fists, knuckles popping with the power of his growing fury. "I am not accustomed to being an object of humor."

Carpathian shook his head back and forth, waving away Vlad's concern with a single, airy hand. "No, no, of course not. No offense was intended, I assure you." He wiped his eyes one last time and shook his head quickly, as if to clear his mind. "In fact,

I'm heartened by your faith in me. That you honestly believe we could face both the Union and the noble savages of the plains, and prevail, is quite a show of confidence."

Vlad would not let his confusion temper his anger, and kept his fists tight, his eyes narrow. "I do not understand."

Carpathian waved him back to his chair, and after a moment, the gruff old soldier moved stiffly back to sit down, his spine ramrod straight. When both men were sitting across from each other again, Carpathian, schooling his face to seriousness, looked Vlad in the eye.

"We will never rule America."

Vlad surged upward again, fists rising, lungs filling to bellow his frustration and annoyance, but Carpathian's calming hands rose quickly, and there was such sincerity in his eyes that it gave Vlad pause.

"I'm not saying we couldn't rule America, Vladimir." The doctor shook his head. "But why would we want to?" The tone was laden with such iron-willed self-confidence that Vlad had nothing to say.

"We could rule America, but to what end?" Carpathian sat back in his chair, picking his snifter up from the table where he had placed it. "Nothing but heartache, back-breaking work, and all the million petty details that have plagued rulers throughout history."

He raised a finger to forestall Vlad's questioning glance. "Now, think for a moment, Vladimir. Who knows the lion's share of peace, happiness, and satisfaction: the man who sits upon the throne, hearing every petty complaint of the lowest of his subjects, or the man who provides not only everything the king needs to rule, but every modicum of comfort and security his people know, as well?"

Vlad sat back in his chair. He felt this way whenever Carpathian's plots and schemes became too convoluted for him to follow. He knew the man was a genius, and he was dedicated to him and his vision. Or so he chose to believe. But he also knew that he, himself, had not been built for such intrigues. The headaches they caused were a good indication whenever he was in too deep. His natural environment was on the battlefield, leading men into conflict for clear, tactical goals. His brother-in-law's world of a thousand shades of gray did not suit him well.

"I do not understand." It had taken him years to be able to say those words without the taste of defeat flooding his mouth. He trusted Burson, believed in him completely. Such trust was not easily earned, but together they had brought a continent to its knees, and every step of that march of conquest had been orchestrated by Carpathian.

"Vladimir, which of the dusty little hamlets and villages that surround the Tonto and Coconino forests are the most loyal to Payson?" The reasonable, lecturing tone was one Vlad recognized, and it created for him a role he knew, and was comfortable with. "Which of them thinks of us most fondly, and with the least resentment? The towns that came to us willingly, because we provided them with power, warmth, and security when their own government could do none of those things? Or the towns that we needed to bend to our will through force?"

A glimmer of understanding began to burn within Vlad's mind, and he found himself nodding.

Carpathian nodded in turn. "Exactly. We were more than capable of pounding any township we needed into the dirt until they succumbed. We easily had that strength. But those towns that came over to us willingly? Those that were eager for the things we provided for them, and willing to help us in turn? Our investments in those towns were far more profitably rewarded, and for far less exertion. If we had enough time, I am confident, if those bunglers in Washington continued to oblige, that we could win the entire continent over to our cause without firing another shot."

Vlad could feel his face betraying his dismay at the thought of suspending conflict with the Union, and the doctor raised a hand to reassure him. "But we do not have that time, my friend. And so we will be forced to use brute strength, where the powers of the mind would be so much more effective, were the option available to us. And because we are required to resort to violence, we are afforded the opportunity, when the moment arrives, to achieve our more personal goals of vengeance."

The doctor leaned forward and rested a hand on Vlad's shoulder. "Veronica's ghost will be stilled, Vladimir. Grant will die, and he will know why he dies before the light fades from that lone, hate-filled eye."

Vlad was still for a moment as his understanding of their goals shifted slightly within his mind. "Ve vill confront ze Union..."

"We cannot take our rightful place, providing the peace, security, and advancement this continent is so hungry for, while the decrepit institutions of the Union hold the nation down with their benighted, antiquated beliefs." Carpathian looked almost sad. "Many will die before we are able to secure peace for the rest." He looked up at Vlad again. "Only the sure knowledge that Grant will be among the dead allows me to sleep easy knowing that."

Vlad felt a slight smile tug at the corner of his mouth. "Zere is nossing I vish more." He stood, slowly this time, and moved to the east-facing windows. The lights of Payson were coming alive. The darkened stain that pointed like an arrow at the palace, marking the burnt-out buildings of the stronghold's recent difficulties. Both Wayward's assault and The Wraith's escape had left scars that were harsh reminders of the danger that remained.

"Ve have done so much here, Burson." The dark shadows of the Tonto stretched out beyond the city limits, reminding him, just a little, of the deep forests of their own Romania. Despite the desert that crouched just beyond those trees, waiting to envelop everything it could reach in dust and death, here in the Tonto Forest, Vlad felt more at home than anywhere since they had been forced to flee their homeland, superstitious peasants hard on their heels, and a great deal of their families' wealth lost behind them.

Vlad felt Carpathian approach, standing by his shoulder and sharing the view. "We have, Vladimir. And we will accomplish a great deal more before we finally rest."

Vlad nodded, looking not out the window, now, but at

his brother-in-law's reflection in the smooth glass. With a quick breath, he changed the subject to something more sensitive, and yet more important to him, than any other.

"Burson, I vish to bring my vife and son here, to share vis zem vhat ve have accomplished, and to show zem vhat has come from all ze sacrifices and loss."

Carpathian stiffened, caught off-guard. Vlad knew the man had assumed their quarrels were done for the evening, and that he would resent this newest sortie. But he kept his tone firm, and his eyes were like stone as he turned to face the doctor.

"Zis land vill provide great opportunities for us, Burson. F.R. should be able to take full advantage of zem. You owe it to me, and you owe it to my son. But most importantly, you owe it to Veronica, to see zat ze boy achieves his full potential here in zis new world to which you convinced her to come, and vich killed her at its first opportunity. He is her blood-kin, Burson, and ze debt zis nation owes us is every bit his to collect as ours."

There was tempered steel in his voice, and he stared into the other man's emotionless face. Carpathian was forced to break away first. Something in his eyes troubled Vlad more than it should have, for reasons he could not have said. But he was not surprised when Carpathian's response, lower than his earlier harangues, reached him.

"Now is not the time to bring new blood into the organization, Vladimir. Not even our own." He moved to his massive desk and sat down, rearranging the papers and files upon it in a manner that did nothing to bring order to the chaos. "It is a delicate time for us. We need to be placing all of our focus and energy in preparing our next moves, and in consolidating our support. Edison and Eiffel alone—"

Vlad snorted before he realized it. His contempt for both of Carpathian's chief scientific underlings had grown in the face of the rising threats to Carpathian's power in the west. "Neizer of zose men warrant any consideration, Burson. Zey care for nossing beyond zere own fame and fortune."

Carpathian nodded distractedly, still not looking up. "True, to a certain extent. Still, there is a definite strength in such consistency. Men like these are easy to control and understand, and thus make perfect tools in the delicate work we are about. And yet, lately they have become more and more unruly. Edison whines like a child whenever we dispatch a formation for possible combat. After his sorry showing against Wayward, he is eager for any chance to redeem himself." Vlad's snort at this was even more pronounced, but Carpathian ignored him. "And Eiffel, who has added more to our arsenal than any man other than myself, refuses to refine his designs, or see them properly tested in the field, but instead barricades himself in the labs downstairs, immersing himself in new, untested theories and projects, and refuses to emerge for any incentive less dire than a blaster to the back of the head." He shook his head. "Only J.P. Smith comes even close to following my wishes lately, and even he—"

Vlad sniffed dismissively at mention of the demented clock maker.

Carpathian's eyes snapped up to Vlad's, and the soldier's smile faltered. "And then there's you, trying to push me into open war with every man, woman, and child in the nation. Is it any wonder that I lack the energy and impulse to put playing nursemaid to a psychotic child prodigy on my docket as well?"

At the word 'psychotic', Vlad's temperature surged. His hands landed on the desk, scattering the papers, and he leaned down to put his eyes on a level with the doctor's. Before he could speak, however, Carpathian sat back, genuine regret in his warm, human eye, and raised both hands in a gesture of surrender. "I am sorry, Vladimir. I did not mean it. I am certain the boy is no more guilty of the crimes rumor places before him as you or I were in our youths."

This statement gave Vlad pause, but did not provide the comfort that perhaps it was intended to.

"It is too much, my friend; too much." The doctor seemed to cave in upon himself, resting his elbows on his desk and his head in his hands. "Some days, I feel that I have no friends, and all the world is against me."

Vlad looked down at this man, a giant in the scientific community, who had pioneered so many new areas of discovery and enlightenment. If there was any justice in the world, his name would one day appear beside the greatest thinkers in history. And yet, he was only a man; subject to the stresses, frustrations, and confusion of any mortal.

"I accept your apology, Burson." Vlad forced his voice into rigid formality, and tamped his paternal anger down in the face of his brother-in-law's obvious distress. "It is not time yet. I vill accept that, for now. I shall let ze boy know. Can I give him some hope, at least, zat his time is not too far off?"

Carpathian nodded without looking up. "Of course, Vladimir." When he did look up, there was more energy in his eyes than his recent moment of seeming-weakness might suggest, and a niggling doubt whispered in the back of Vlad's mind. As usual, he ignored that voice, believing it to be a vestige of the simple soldier's mindset that had dominated his thinking for most of his life.

"We need only push the Warrior Nation back long enough to allow Grant and his monsters to surge west. Then we will crush him between the deserts, our full power, and the returning might of the savages. I have a plan that will see this all resolved in mere months, my friend. I have summoned everyone of any import to a meeting here, in one week's time. We will put into motion a grand design, and then F.R. and his mother will be welcomed here with a splendid parade down High Street, I promise you."

Vlad paused again. Very seldom was there any sort of meeting he was unaware of, and never the sort of meeting that Carpathian would describe as calling 'anyone of any import'. In fact, such councils were few and far between, given the scattered nature of the doctor's holdings and his most trusted advisors and agents. If such a meeting was only days away, and he was only hearing of it now, then something truly momentous must be in the offing.

"Vy vas I not—"

The doctor smiled away the doubt. "Things move so quickly, Vladimir! It is nothing! You have been overseeing the reconstruction and the work on our defenses in the forest. I did not want to trouble you." He leaned over the desk. "It is the Hellion project. I believe we will be able to seize control of the skies over any battlefield. As soon as I've proven the latest designs, we will need to move rapidly."

Vlad stared at the doctor for a moment, uncertain how to respond. A sharp knock at the ornate door, however, cut his thoughts off before they could fully form.

"Enter." Carpathian sat up straighter in his chair and pulled at the front of his vest. It was of a shiny black material, with very fine silver pin stripping that must have cost a small fortune. Vlad had not noticed earlier, too distracted remembering his work in the city and the confrontation with his brother-in-law. But now that he noticed the vest, and looked a little closer, he saw that Carpathian's entire outfit was new, and of markedly finer make than he was accustomed to wearing. The man had never been a fashion-conscious clotheshorse before, and the change struck a strange note with the old soldier.

The door swung open and a tall, lithe figure strode into the room. The woman's honey brown hair fell in an artful cascade that swept her shoulders and down her back. She was dressed in tight-fitting clothing obviously designed for combat, with a sleek RJ blaster on one narrow hip, a long thin blade sheathed on the other. The lines of her body spoke of a physical strength and grace that marked her as a dancer or athlete, but did nothing to diminish the feminine aura of her presence. As his eyes moved, of their own accord, up and down her taught figure, they rested once again upon her face, and he recoiled slightly as what he saw there finally registered.

The woman wore a beautifully-painted golden mask. It covered her forehead, swooping down around her left eye to the line of her jaw. The design painted upon the mask was elaborate, incorporating a dizzying array of swirls and flourishes in a subtly-shifting pattern of warm colors that complimented her hair and sparkling green eyes. Despite the mask, she was a stunning woman, but with that added embellishment, there was not a single room in the world she would not have dominated upon entering. Vlad was struck speechless, sitting mutely, his mouth open in mid-word.

"Ah, my dear!" Carpathian rose quickly, meeting the woman in the middle of the room and reaching out with one hand, taking her own and bending to kiss it lightly. "Welcome home! I trust your journey was uneventful?"

The woman nodded with a slight smile, tilting her head in silent greeting to Vlad, then returning her gaze upon the doctor. When she spoke, it was with a refined sensibility that seemed forced, as if every word and phrase needed to be planned ahead of time so as to avoid the pitfalls of a lifetime of less-polished speech.

"Nothing we couldn't handle, sir." Her voice was smooth despite the almost imperceptible hesitation beneath it. And as she spoke, a vague, undefined chill swept up Vlad's back. Somehow, this woman sounded very familiar.

Carpathian gestured for the woman to take his own seat, and then moved to fetch another from the conversation group closer to the door, pushing the chair so that it was closer to the woman's than to Vlad's.

"You must tell me all about it. But first, I'm not sure if you have met Vladimir Caym, known to many as Ursul? My brother-in-law, majordomo, seneschal, and all around guardian." He turned in his chair to look at Vlad with a raised eyebrow. "Vladimir, you've met Miss Mimms?"

Several things snapped into place at once. Misty Mimms. The mysterious woman who had appeared in Payson at around the same time Doctor Carpathian had begun to turn Jesse James onto his present path with the gift of one of several vehicles Carpathian had convinced the outlaw was the only one of its kind. There had been whispers among the doctor's associates for some time that the woman had been associated with James, and that they had parted on less than amicable terms; some even said the woman held an undying, bitter hatred for the outlaw. If that were the case, her presence here, given how important Jesse James was to the doctor's over-all plans, was confusing.

"Ve have." Vlad rose from his chair and gave a perfunctory bow to the woman with the mysterious smile. "You are looking lovely as ever, Miss Mimms. I believe I heard that you are a friend of Jesse James—"

"No." The single word shot out across the room like the report of a pistol shot. Her elegant face had frozen, the soft, warm lines of the visible side hardening to match the stiff visage of the mask. "No, I am not." She looked at Carpathian with cold eyes. "In fact, that is why I wished to see you. You said that if I obeyed your instructions, I would have my opportunity to repay the twisted monster for what he and his metal hand did to me." One graceful hand rose, as if without conscious thought, toward the left side of her face, before falling back to her lap. "I have done everything you said. I have trained, I have learned, I have travelled, all as you directed. I have spent almost a year in that miserable, sweating pit on the gulf, and I refined my skills and abilities with the assistance of Madame Laveau. I am ready."

Carpathian nodded, his smile fixed and a touch pale. "Yes, yes, of course. And in due time, you will have your chance." He changed the subject with a hasty lack of grace. "But tell me, how is Madame Laveau? Is she with you?"

The young lady jerked her elegant neck in one rapid nod. "She is. Getting away might have posed some interesting puzzles, but she managed. We arrived just this afternoon. She has brought several specimens with her that she thinks you will appreciate." She shrugged, as if admitting something against her will. "Her work with that snake of hers, Nzambi, is quite spectacular, if you like that sort of thing."

The chill creeping up Vlad's back continued to work its way into his spine. The woman's proud, confident bearing was affecting him, reminding him of something, or someone; but he could not isolate the thought or memory, and it was beginning to concern him.

"Excellent." Carpathian's smile was more genuine again, but Vlad noticed that his eyes were pinned to the woman's face with an almost feverish intensity. He did not know if she was aware of that concentration, but it began to feed his misdoubts, and the chill burrowed deeper.   "And so Madame Laveau and her people are situated comfortably?"

Misty Mimms looked vaguely insulted by the question. "No, I left them in the stables to fend for themselves and went to take a bath." She shook her head, sending a soft wave rippling down the long fall of her hair. "Of course they're comfortable. They're in the east wing, and her animations and Creations have been provided space in the barracks hall across the parade ground."

Carpathian's smile had slipped a bit at her sarcasm, but he rallied admirably. "Very well. And the rest of our guests? Will they be available for our little gathering?"

The woman looked down at her lap and took a deep breath as if martialing her patience. "Well, Doctor, those invitations were not my responsibility, but from what I heard down below, it appears that attendance at your little soiree is going to be nearly one hundred percent."

The doctor's smile returned full force at this. "Excellent!" He rubbed his hands together, seeming more his old self than he had since the girl had arrived. "Then all the pieces are falling into place." He stood, bowing slightly to the strange, lethal-seeming woman. "And it is wonderful to have you back at last. If there is nothing else, however, sadly, I must beg your indulgence. Vladimir and I were just finishing up here."

She rose in one smooth motion, unfolding from the chair with a grace that would make a royal ballerina proud. "There is something else, actually." Her head was tilted up at an aggressively imperious angle. "I spoke to Dieter and Schultz downstairs. They told me about the foray north." Her head ratcheted up another degree. "I want to go."

Carpathian seemed nonplussed for a moment, and Vlad looked between the old doctor and the young woman, the chill deeper than ever.

"I don't think that's a very good idea, Miss Mimms." The doctor's tone was awkward. "This is a very delicate operation—"

"And I can't be trusted?" A smoldering fire flickered in those deep green eyes, and the chill within Vlad's chest snapped into a clear, crystalline focus.

"Of course you can! But you have yet to lead our forces in battle, Miss Mimms. Your training and your talents lie in a different direction, as you well know." It appeared as if a sheen of fine sweat was breaking out across the doctor's brow.

"And how can I learn if you do not let me into the field?" Her hands rested on her narrow hips, not far from her elegant but deadly weapons.

The old iron finally settled back into Carpathian's voice, and Vlad found himself relaxing from a tension he had not realized had gripped him. "Young lady, do not think I am a feckless old man, unaware of the heated passions of youth. I know why you want to venture north with the Kaufmann twins."

She opened her full lips to protest, but he raised a single peremptory hand and her mouth snapped shut. "Jesse James is not in the north, Miss Mimms. Your time will come, but it is not now. Now, I need you to continue your training, and your invaluable assistance to me. The Kaufmanns will lead this latest assault, you will remain here, close at hand to assist me with our guests as they arrive, and the future will unfold as I have promised." His eyes grew harder. "It is the future, Miss Mimms. It will come, but not today."

She sneered, her body stiff. She nodded sharply, but there was no retreat or surrender in her pose. "As you say." She spun on one heel and moved away, then casually tossed a parting comment over her shoulder as she swayed through the door. "Thomas will not be pleased you are sending the twins either, Doctor."

The door closed with a heavy sound, and Carpathian breathed a sigh of relief that pushed his grand mustachios upright. He shook his head, gave Vlad a rueful smile, and returned to his chair.

"Were we ever so young, Vladimir?" The casual tone struck a false note with Vlad, who sat back into his own chair, staring at the doctor.

Rubbing one blunt-fingered hand over the fine fabric of the chair's arm, Vlad casually muttered. "She seems a spirited girl." He looked up from beneath his heavy brows. "She reminds me of someone." He waited a moment for a response, and then continued. "Does she not remind you of someone, Burson?" He was surprised he had not noticed it before, himself.

Carpathian shook his head in genuine confusion. "No, I can't say that she does."

Vlad's smile was sad. "Perhaps, after all these years, our memory blurs." He shrugged. "Probably it is nothing."

Leaning forward in his chair, Carpathian placed his elbows on the metal-bracings of his knees. "Who does she remind you of, Vladimir?"

The old soldier shook his head. "It's probably nussing, Burson. But zere is a certain cast to her, I felt, zat reminded me, somehow ... ... of my sister."

Carpathian reared back in his chair with a snort of denial. "Misty Mimms? Reminded you of Veronica?" Again, he snorted. "No, I don't believe so. Miss Mimms is far less ... ... refined ... ... ? Aside from the manifold other differences, of course. No, I can't say I agree with you, old friend. Just heartsick nostalgia, I would have to assume." The words were fast and hard, without an ounce of spring to them.

Vlad nodded slowly, looking away. "Perhaps I vas mistaken." There was no conviction in his tone, however. He tapped on the arm of the chair, and then continued. "She seems terribly eager to come to terms with James. Do you sink it is entirely vise, though, to have zat woman about? Jesse James is fairly integral to your plans vis ze Rebellion. If Miss Mimms vere to achieve her goal..."

The doctor shook his head. "I am not yet sure what our best course of action toward Jesse James will be, Vladimir. For now I want him found, not killed. I fear Miss Mimms might do one part of that job well, while finding the second part far more difficult."

"As you say." Vlad pushed himself up out of his chair, shaking his head as he moved toward the door. "You are a vise man, Burson. And you have my complete trust." He turned, his face stern and his strong arms folded over his chest. "But you cannot juggle zese knives forever. Ve must make a move soon, or zey vill begin to tumble down around us, and ve vill all be cut."

The doctor nodded, still sitting, staring into the middle space, nearly oblivious to his brother-in-law's words. "Yes, Vladimir, I know." His eyes became sharp again, and he turned to look at the retreating soldier. "Let us see how our Hellions do in their latest iteration, and we may just be able to see these knives you speak of alighting where they will do the most good."

Vlad looked at the old man wordlessly for a moment, then nodded. He moved toward the door, but stopped when Carpathian's voice snapped out into the silence.

"Do you ever wonder about them, Vladimir? Those strange, crimson-eyed patrons that were so instrumental in our rise?"

Vlad paused. The Doctor generally kept him quite isolated from the mysterious benefactors he credited with so much of his good fortune. He had, however, wondered about them. He had never met one, to the best of his recollection, and that alone was strange.

"To be honest, I give zem little sought at all." Another lie, but again, harmless, he thought.

Carpathian had risen and was staring through the wide windows at the night outside. "I wonder about them often. It would be a glorious thing, to be free of them, don't you think?"

He could not remember the last time the doctor had spoken in such soft, whimsical tones. An icy wind seemed to blow over the old soldier's neck, and he shivered without really knowing why.

Before he could respond, Carpathian shrugged. "All things in due time, I imagine." He sighed. "All things in due time."

Vlad stared at the still form of his friend for a long moment, and then turned away muttering some mindless agreement that even he himself could not have articulated. He closed the heavy door quietly behind him.

Chapter 3

The Doomsday wagons had been in place for more than a day. Their iron bulk lay hidden by tree branches snapped from the trunks of ancient pines through the brute force of the heavily-muscled Creations bolstering the large force of animations and monocav. The heavy wagons, their massive Gatling cannons pointed down the length of the valley, would provide a final line of defense should the enemy break through the main force of the Enlightened army.

Schultz and Dieter Kaufman stood atop the central Doomsday, monoculars pressed to their eyes as they scanned the distant mouth of the canyon. They had sent two groups of monocav scouts out into the hills to find a suitable target, and the warband that approached, entirely unaware of the death that awaited them, seemed like the perfect mark.

The Warrior Nation, although still concentrating much of their force in the east to hold the Union army out of their ancestral territory, was also scattered across the northern territories of the United States, all the way out to the west coast. The nomadic bands calling these more remote areas home would send columns of reinforcements from time to time to bolster the line that held against the Union and to hone their warrior's skills against the eastern invaders.

Although Doctor Carpathian had never been able to ascertain exactly why the Warrior Nation held such a violent, negative opinion of him and his works, it had been clear from the beginning that no alliance against the Union would be possible. Every attempt to come to a meeting of the minds had met with total disaster. Not even a token effort had been made in years, and whenever the growing might of what the doctor had come to call Carpathian Industries came into contact with any element of the Warrior Nation, only violence and bloodshed had resulted.

And that suited the Kaufmann boys just fine. They had not followed the rumors of a mad Romanian genius to the ends of the Earth for nothing. They had come seeking fame and fortune, leaving a land that had lost its sense of wonder and adventure many centuries ago. As was true of many of Carpathian's underlings, the twins were eager for any chance to prove their value to the old man and his organization. This was the largest assault the forces of Payson had mounted in years, and the fact that they were leading it carried weight that had not been lost on either of them.

Although the vast bulk of their force was made up of the animated dead and reconstructed monstrous Creations of the doctor and his scientist allies, there were several living, breathing fighters with them, eager to seize their own chance to shine and gain a little of the doctor's favor. J.P. Smith held the far right flank, his monstrous Creation 5 standing in the shadow of the tall, gangly man's Doomsday, its rail gun nosing forward, eager for targets. The battering rams at the end of 5's arms were larger and heavier than either twin remembered. They had been repaired and enhanced after the damage dealt to them by the Union's mercenary attack. The twins had been away on a mission for the doctor when the attack had landed, which was one of the many reasons they were so eager to put a little more polish to their reputations with this day's work. Both Kaufmanns hoped that they would be returning to Payson with a rousing success under their belts, leaving many dead savages in the canyon behind them to feed the vultures.

There was no movement at the mouth of the valley, and both brothers lowered their monoculars in unison. A slight breeze stirred the ponytail that hung down Schultz's back, ruffling Dieter's shorter hair like a proud parent. From the back of the Doomsday, they could just make out the array of animations standing with the deathly stillness of the dead. The creatures were armed with an assortment of weapons, from blasters integrated into the putrid flesh of their arms, to rusted, ill-kept metal implements that had surgically replaced their hands.

Most of the animations stood upon the rotting legs that had carried them in life, albeit with crude iron braces bolted through their tattered clothing and into the bones within to provide stability. Some, however, had been so far rotted by the time the scientists beneath the palace had prepared them for the conflict, that even with artificial enhancements, their legs would never have supported the heavy, lifeless weight of their bodies. These animations were far less-human looking, their legs replaced with spider-like constructs that scuttled over the uneven landscape, or smaller versions of the single-wheeled monocav design, pushing them along on single, fat wheels at an alarming speed.

The wheeled animations would be of limited value, given the broken, rocky surface of the canyon floor, but the spider-legged creatures would be priceless, climbing up the sides of the canyon and across the shattered stones scattered about with equal facility.

The muscle of their strike force, the Creations that often encompassed the flesh and matter of several dead bodies recombined into one monstrous whole, were scattered among their statue-like brethren, their nightmare faces oriented in the direction the Warrior Nation column must come. Aside from the Gatling cannons mounted on their vehicles, these creatures carried the heaviest weapons that would be available to the brothers. One gigantic brute cradled the barrel of an enormous cannon in four muscled arms, the sinews and threads of the creature's stitching straining with the great weight.

But the true reason they were all gathered in the dusty valley that day were held atop the remaining Doomsday wagons. Each of the vehicles carried a dull metal box strapped to their roofs, rather than a fighting platform like the command wagon. These boxes could be opened to the sky at a single order from either brother. Each box contained five of the newly-engineered Hellions that Carpathian hoped would prove far more effective in battle against the Warrior Nation than their predecessors had.

Schultz smiled at his brother, sharing the satisfaction, without words, of what the day could mean to them. Too many of the doctor's other men and women saw the twins as nothing more than dumb muscle, sent out to scare local villages into complying, or waylay Union supply convoys when the need arose. But today, leading the largest force to leave Payson in years, and testing the doctor's dearest new machines in the field, would change all that.

"They should have been here by now." Dieter's eyes were worried behind the silvered glass of his goggles. "You don't think they took another route, maybe?"

Schultz smiled at his brother. "They're savages, Dieter. What do they know of schedules?" He patted his brother on the back. "They will come. And we will crush them from before and above, and we will be back in Payson in plenty of time for the champagne toasts."

Dieter returned the smile, looking back out over the tumbled floor of the canyon to sweep the monocular over their forces one more time. He had a perfect view, therefore, when disaster struck.

The first hint that something had gone wrong was the sudden appearance of several bolts of eye-searing blue streaking down from the clear sky and into the still forms of their lead animations. Each spear struck straight down into the balding head of an undead soldier, blasting the corrupted structures from the top down with steam and shock that tore the dead bodies into shreds of rotten meat and spinning metal components. A small, crimson detonation within each cerulean fireball denoted the RJ power cells cooking off under the intense heat.

Both twins looked up in horror to see shapes falling from the sky, their feathered wings wide behind them, gleaming bows unleashing a second barrage of spirit arrows before their first victims could collapse to the ground.

"The Hellions! Release the Hellions!" Both brothers were shouting, looking off to either side where the other Doomsdays lay hidden. Animations standing stationary by each of the armored boxes lurched into movement, pulling levers and lifting switches.

Six boxes opened within moments of each other, and thirty spindly shapes hurtled aloft, clawing at the air with their tattered, skeletal wings. Each creature's head was horribly swollen to accommodate the additional control runs and the armored RJ-1027 casement that Carpathian's scientists had decided would solve the issues that had rendered earlier generations of Hellions worse than useless in large-scale action. Each globular head, sparse hair waving wildly in the breeze, feverishly hunted the skies above with three large lenses that flashed red in the warm sun.

A scattering of ruby beams rose into the air, but failed to hit any of the eagle warriors. Off to their right, the zipping sound of a rail gun sang out, but the ghostly trail of its shot went far wide, as Creation 5 proved unequal to the task of targeting such agile foes.

Lurid cries echoed off the walls of the canyon as the squadron of flying nightmares rose into the air to confront the twisted forms of the savage eagle warriors. The Hellions each bore a massive blaster in place of a right forearm and hand, and gleaming bladed weapons where their left hands should be. They reached out with their gun-arms, and thunderclaps roared down the canyon as clouds of red-tinged smoke billowed out. Each Hellion soared through its own cloud, the motion of their wings causing the ruddy exhausts to swirl out behind them in graceful eddies that provided a stark contrast to their own lurching flight.

Blasts of coherent ruby light slashed through the descending formation of Warrior Nation fighters. The graceful fliers spun and wove through the flurry, altering their own aiming points and sending a sheet of gleaming azure arrows streaking across the sky. One savage was not quick enough in his maneuvers, and a bolt struck him in an outstretched wing. As he staggered, several more bolts slapped into this body, tearing him to bloody pieces that dropped down to land among the animations shuffling around on the ground, trying to come to grips with the surprise attack from above.

Dieter's shout of celebration was cut off in mid-breath, however, as first one, then two more, then another of the Hellions were blasted backward by spirit arrows sleeting in upon them as they rose. The wreckage of the destroyed constructs fell down upon the rocky soil where it steamed in the sun, RJ-fueled components gleaming a dull red.

The Hellions, lacking the sense of self-preservation or doubt that might have halted the charge of living creatures, continued to rise toward their tormentors, blasting away with their fearsome weapons. The nine remaining eagle warriors dove for the earth, their wings flaring as they slowed, while the Hellions, now nearly level with the lip of the canyon on either side, had trouble redirecting their fire. Their heads pivoted woodenly on stiff, leathern necks, trying to track the swift, graceful movements of their targets.

A heavy boom roared out from the top of the canyon, rolling down upon the waiting animations and their masters, and a Hellion ceased to exist as a massive sapphire beam struck the thing in its chest. Wings and bits of flesh and fabric fluttered through the air as the remaining Hellions, slow to react to this new threat, paused in confusion, hovering on rotten wings as the real trap closed.

The Hellions were unable to adjust their positioning and target priorities as a line of warriors rose up on either side, spirit arrows flaming against their bows, and unleashed a double salvo at the fluttering corpses hovering between their lines. Over a dozen of the creatures, unable to avoid the incoming fire and incapable of coming to grips with the rapidly evolving situation, were struck multiple times, falling limply out of the air and hitting the hard ground with dull, muted slaps.

Dieter and Schultz looked up in dismay as the Warrior Nation lines, appearing at the lip of the canyon, fired again, sending even more of their charges tumbling down to destruction. They were so concerned with what was happening above them, and what it might mean for their mission and for their reputations, that they were caught, again, completely by surprise when a growing rumble of thunder and dust produced a wave of enraged warriors crouched upon the flanks of enormous, shrieking energy beasts charging down on them from the front.

The horribly-altered horse creatures screamed in torment as their riders, bouncing smoothly with their mounts' furious gait, launched their own storm of blue energy into the animations. The arrows flew true despite the great, pitching speed of the warriors, striking a score of targets. Each automaton that took a gleaming arrow staggered backward a step or two and then tumbled limply forward, wisps of blue-tinged smoke curling up from their scorched wounds.

Suddenly, the twins found themselves directing the battle before them, desperately managing their own defense, and forgot all about the conflict in the sky overhead.

"Fire the sonic Gatling cannons!" Schultz barked out, stomping on the metal floor of the fighting platform. The savage warriors were far out of range for the brothers' own weapons, but if the animations manning their vehicle would respond, maybe they could do some damage. Again, the rail gun sang out to their right, blasting right through one energy beast and striking the rider of another off its mount behind.

The massive rotary cannons hanging to either side of their wagon's control house creaked to life, spinning slowly at first, but then whirring with a lethal, high-pitched whine. Both brothers, familiar with the weapon, fell down and forward, pressing their shoulders against the bulkhead of the firing platform just as the cannons tore out their first volley of crimson fire. The shells streaked through the intervening air, shrieking like lost souls. The initial burst was low, blasting a furrow into the dusty earth and throwing dirt and rock into the air. The energy beasts and their howling riders tore through the drifting cloud, heartened by this pathetic show. The animations within were correcting their fire, however, and one trailing beast was caught by the last, errant shell from the fusillade.

When the sonic Gatling cannon shells struck a target, they burst with a mind-numbing blast of force and sound as a small RJ-1027 cylinder within ruptured, its energy channeled through a series of baffles to form a spear of power that stabbed through the impact point and into the target. Although the weapon was most effective against the hard, stationary armor of large vehicles, it made a bloody ruin of the energy beast's chest. The warrior riding upon the stricken animal was thrown into the air, a look of near-comic surprise on his face.

Both brothers, peering over the edge of the parapet, shouted in excitement to see the beast go down. The rider was able to turn himself in midair, however, tumbling down onto the stony earth, rolling with a graceful flip, and bounce up in a fighting crouch. His bow had been lost in the tumble, but he grasped a heavy stone hammer in either hand. They exploded into blue-tinged flames to match the fire in his eyes as he looked for an opponent, his fellow warriors pounding past him, crashing into the shuffling mob of animations.

The battle was joined in earnest as the automatons finally surged into dull motion, their weapons raised over their heads to meet the riders in combat. Here or there, the crudely-stitched hulking shoulders of a Creation rose up out of the sea of dead flesh. Massive dead hands flexed, blades and drill bits whirled and hissed, and the screaming of the energy beasts rose an octave or more, this time in pain rather than fury.

The riders had been halted, and the battle raged all across what should have been the line of their ambush. The Doomsday wagons continued to tear the air with short bursts from their Gatling cannons, striking here or there when a target presented itself. The towering Creation with the cannon, showing more initiative than most of its kind, had turned the enormous weapon in its arms upward, and was pummeling the canyon edge high overhead with blasts of ruby force. Following suit, the rail gun was turned on the canyon wall as well, keeping the warriors there pinned down.

As the Warrior Nation attack stalled, the twins were able to spare a moment to look up to their primary charges once again, and were alarmed to see that things had continued to go poorly for the doctor's newest chosen constructs. Only a handful of Hellions were left, flapping around in desperate spirals as they attempted to defend themselves from the eagle warriors, most of whom now brandished pairs of burning long-knives. It was clear, even from the quick glance they could spare, that the Hellions were hopelessly outmatched. More of the carrion creatures fell from the sky.

"We need to get out of here!" Schultz gripped his brother's shoulder, pointing up. A savage warrior, larger than all the others, was swooping down upon the last remaining Hellions, two grasping, misshapen raptor claws where its feet should be. "Sky Spirit!"

Dieter looked from his brother, down to the furious battle swirling around before them, then to the Doomsday wagons stretched out to either side. Other than the gigantic Creation with the cannon, the big vehicles were their only heavy weaponry, and the sonic Gatling cannons were fixed in forward mounts incapable of being brought to bear against the bird-men above them. He shook his head.

"If we return with nothing, it will go poorly for us." He gestured to the battle raging throughout the length of the canyon. "We press on here, and maybe at least rack up an impressive enough body count that we won't be laughed out of Payson!"

A terrible scream from overhead dragged their eyes back upward. Something was happening to the remaining Hellions. The survivors, seeking to escape the flaming blades of the eagle warriors and Sky Spirit's burning tomahawk, had soared up into the clear sky, well beyond the edge of the canyon. They were twitching and spasming in their erratic flight, much as the creatures who had flown too high had done in their last encounter. Even as the brothers watched, the survivors fell upon each other, not even bothering to flap their tattered wings as they blasted at point blank range, tearing hunks of cold, quivering flesh from their brothers as they fell.

The last of the Hellions fell screaming from the sky like grotesque, crimson shooting stars. One pair, in a particularly spectacular display of bad luck, struck the giant construct with the cannon from behind with such force that the thing's stitching ruptured, sending its component parts off in various directions and allowing the heavy weapon to crash to the earth, silent.

Both of the twins stared at the jumble of limbs and machinery without a word. Small, cherry-red flames burned unnaturally bright here and there among the pieces, as the excess RJ was consumed.

The battle in the canyon was not a total loss. Any time a warrior leapt into the air, or rose for a dramatic strike, several of the Doomsdays would open fire with the tearing sound of their Gatling guns, shredding the savage with explosive bolts. Toward the mouth of the canyon, the bloody remains of an enormous creature was splashed against the rock walls, its massive antlers canted up into the sky at a morbid angle.

The desire to escape with their lives and the knowledge that retreat could forever tarnish their work with the doctor contorted both twins' faces. The fighting on the field before them seemed to be going more their way. If they could clean up the savages down here, and pull their forces out of the canyon and away before the warriors up on the cliffs could make their way down, they might just salvage something from the day. After all, the Hellions were no work of theirs. They had no responsibility for their effectiveness in battle. That would fall to Carpathian, Edison, Smith, and the other scientists. They were only to unleash them, and the scientists' alterations and adjustments should have done the rest.

Both men's eyes had hardened with resolve just as a massive shadow passed over the sun. Schultz ducked as if an eagle warrior had appeared over his head, but Dieter, diving to the side, looked up again, dreading what he would see.

The creature was massive, larger even than the Great Elk that lay crumpled at the mouth of the blasted valley. Its wingspan was easily half again the length of a Doomsday wagon when at full extension, and its proud eyes scanned the battlefield with a disdain that could be felt despite the creature's animal, alien presence.

"What the—" For once Dieter's quick wit was caught flat-footed, and words failed him. The bird was enormous, and as it soared down into the canyon, the brothers knew they had nothing at their disposal that could face it.

The thing folded its wings and fell into a graceful, harrowing dive, headed for a concentration of blaster-armed animations that were driving a line of warriors back across the bloody ground of the canyon floor. Dieter fully expected the monster to grab two of his automatons and scatter the rest with the hurricane winds of its passage. It would break up the only offensive his forces had managed, and could spell the final disaster for him and his brother on a day that had already turned quite sour enough.

"Shoot the bird!" He shouted, again stomping upon the iron grating beneath his feet, and then cupping one hand around his mouth to call out to the rest of the Doomsdays. Their combined fire sent burning ropes of flame streaking out across the canyon, blasting massive holes in the stones downrange, but never once coming close to the swift, agile creature making its final approach on the unsuspecting constructs.

"Duck!" Schultz shouted, knowing even as he drew breath for another try that it was futile. The animations did not respond to such generic orders without careful arrangement ahead of time. There was nothing they could do but watch as the shadow swept across the dry, stony ground.

But the enormous bird did not make any sort of conventional attack against the formation. Rather than fly on through, raking them with its talons or beak, its wings spread wide, and the giant eagle's head came up and then stabbed its raptor beak toward the man-shapes still more than ten feet away. Dieter could see that the things eyes were glowing a fierce blue, just before the flames billowed from its screeching, open beak.

The flames were the same luminous, half-insubstantial cerulean of Warrior Nation spirit energy, more than sufficient to burn the entire contingent of animations to the ground. These constructs were not living targets. They did not scream and thrash about as live men would have. They continued their advance, some of them turning their weapons upon this new threat, oblivious to their sudden danger.

The flames consumed each construct, and as their sinews burned away, and the metal struts that supported them warped and melted, each stumbled forward into a smoking, still pile of meat, metal, and fabric.

The eagle soared past, moving upward and away, weaving effortlessly through the ruby streams of light that lashed toward it from the ponderous wagons. In a flash, it was up past the lip of the canyon, beyond the reach of anything the twins could bring to bear, and circling once again, looking for another concentration of foes to burn.

"What the hell is that!" Dieter repeated, even as his brother began to shout the order to retreat to the surviving animations and constructs that littered the field. The automatons began a slow, steady withdrawal over the ground they had been defending with their borrowed lives only moments before without a hesitation or a thought.

The twins' Doomsday wagon shook as the rugged RJ engine deep within its armored hide roared to life. To either side, the other wagons were starting as well. J.P. Smith had already loaded Creation 5 onto his vehicle, and it was in the lead as they all backed out of the canyon. They had walked the bulk of their troops into the valley only a day ago. There were so few left now, they would all be able to ride out with the wagons by the time they were able to disengage.

Schultz met his brother's eyes. There was more than fear for their own reputation there now, and he saw the same through Dieter's goggles. "I don't know what it was, brother. But Carpathian was right. If all we can throw up to answer that monster and its ilk are Hellions, then Heaven have mercy on us all."

Dieter shook his head, his lips pursed. "Heaven has little mercy for the likes of us."

All around them, the shuffling remnants of their force moved away from the line of contact, keeping the native warriors at bay with a scattering of ruby bolts.

Their first foray out of Payson at the head of an army would not be one anyone remembered fondly. Least of all, themselves.

Chapter 4

The sickening, squelching noises from his sodden shoes echoed off the close brick walls of the alley. He had wanted to make directly for the Rue de la Federation and home, but Ernest had suggested they stick to the darker byways and narrow backstreets, avoiding the wider avenues. It was late enough, they could expect to get home without running into any inconvenient witnesses, but F.R. could see his friend's point. In his current state, there would really be no way to conceal that something horribly untoward had occurred to them on the streets of Paris that night.

"I told you the mixture was still unstable." Ernest had been grumbling ceaselessly since the test. F.R. had conceded that Ernest had several good points, but he was growing less tolerant with each messy step he took. The fluids that drenched him were congealing quickly, drops and gobbets falling with sickening little plopping sounds to the cobbles. All he wanted was a bath and a long sleep. He did not want to listen to another lecture from his overly-cautious friend.

"I mean, the packs have been working well, but I told you, the weapons would not be ready for weeks yet." The tones grated upon F.R.'s last, fraying nerve.

"In the lab, we saw exactly the same violent reactions with living tissues. The new atomic material has such an explosive reaction with flesh. I warned you—"

"Ernest, enough." F.R. grimaced as some of the offal slipped from his upper lip into his mouth; yet another highlight to the day. He had known, from the moment the footpad had experienced his unfortunate reaction, that discussing the trial with Ernest would be a bad idea. He had allowed his frustration and annoyance to drive that resolution from his mind.

"I just want you to remember, it was you who pushed for this test." The petulance, even in the dark alley, was so palpable, F.R. wanted to push Ern into one of the rough walls.

"I had no idea this would happen." F.R. reached out, gesturing to the side with both gore-covered hands. "You made no mention of catastrophic detonation." He shook his hands, dark matter shedding off into the alley's native garbage like a soft, sickening rain. "When you wanted to call it a Death Ray, I thought you had something somewhat more ... ... elegant ... ... in mind."

Ahead of them, the dim light of gas lamps illuminated the empty main street. Ernest stopped at the mouth of the alley, looking furtively in either direction. They were the only souls abroad, and he gestured, without looking back, for F.R. to follow.

"Do I sicken you so much you cannot bear to look at me?" His frustration gave way to grim humor as he realized there may have been more than one reason Ernest had insisted upon such a dark path home.   "Do I serve as a grim reminder of the finite nature of mortality?"

Ernest glanced back, shuddered, and hunched his shoulders against the chill of the night, hurrying his gait. F.R.'s smile widened as he imagined what his gleaming teeth must look like, grinning from the blood-slick mask of his covered face.

The mischievous young scientist lengthened his own stride, the clatter of his boots finally shedding the muffling coating of gruesome mud. "Come, Ernest, embrace your brother before all the world."

"You are a child, F.R., and I will not play your disgusting games, shrouded as you are in the mortal remains of a fellow human being." Ernest tossed the disgusted comment over one hunched shoulder as hopped over the gutter and onto the sidewalk.

"A fellow human being that preyed on other fellow human beings who were, on the whole, far more worthy of your esteem." F.R.'s mood turned sour once again, and his pace slowed in response. "Seriously, Ernest, choosing these ill-favored children of the night over other targets was a decision made in no small part to appease your cursed guilty conscience. If it won't have that moderately-salutary effect, perhaps I will have to rethink the entire scheme. These vermin smell horrible, as I'm sure you know.

Wearing their innards as an overcoat does nothing to improve the aroma."

At the foot of the tall, steep stairs leading up to the Caym townhouse, Ernest Rutherford finally turned around to confront F.R. "I feel no special delicacy toward the villains we exterminate in our tests, as I think you well know. But your blithe disregard for the solemnity that any ended human life should engender gets under my skin at times." He stood straighter, forcing himself to meet the ghastly mask face to face. "This, I am afraid, is one of those times."

F.R. could not stop the grin from resurfacing. He felt the blood and viscera drying on his face cracking and flaking away. "Well, we certainly got under this chap's skin, anyway."

There was a moment of terrible stillness on the Rue de la Federation. Ernest's eyes did not flicker, there was not a moment's acknowledgement in his face that he had heard the statement at all.

F.R.'s smile widened even further, completely unaffected by his friend's stolid demeanor. He waggled his eyebrows like a dance-hall comedian, sending a further cascade of dried matter fluttering to the street.

With a snort, Ernest shook his head and turned away. He was halfway up the stairs, F.R. still standing at the bottom, when the large, ornate door slammed open.

A man staggered onto the upper landing, fresh blood sprayed across his arms, chest, and face, glistening in the gaslight. His eyes were wild, darting this way and that in nervous confusion, not settling on any sight for more than a moment before flicking away, as if entirely unsure of anything he was seeing.

Grasped in one shaking hand was a long kitchen knife, dripping blood.

"F.R., your mother!" The call came from within the townhouse, and carried with it a weight of horror and fury that nearly twisted it into incomprehensibility.

The man on the stairs looked lost and confused. He was dressed in a fine jacket and trousers, an embroidered vest flashing silkily beneath the lapels of the coat. He certainly did not look like a common criminal, to be bursting out of the house drenched in blood; F.R.'s tutor's high-pitched, horrified voice screaming horrible accusations into the night behind him.

The bloody man took two staggering steps down toward Ernest, his eyes slowly shifting from a confused, glassy impenetrability to a pleading, desperate hope. "Please, sir, I don't ... ... I didn't ... ..."

Ernest recoiled, both from the blood and from the accusation hanging unspoken in the air.

"It wasn't me, sir." His accent was upper-class, his French that of a native speaker. But there was still an edge of hysterical confusion in his eyes and in his voice. He held up shaking hands to the young scientist, F.R. hidden in the shadows behind. The man's head jerked as he seemed to see the knife in his own hand for the first time. He stared at it, as if only now realizing he was holding some terrible, poisonous serpent, and let it drop with a sharp snap. The metal clattered down the stairs to land at F.R.'s feet.

Above, the doorway was again filled, this time with the tall, gaunt form of Hugo Digne, the sleeves of his own white shirt slick with blood. The tutor's normally-placid face was twisted with rage, and an eerily-familiar crimson flare seemed to flash within the depths of his dark eyes.

"He killed your mother, boy! Don't let him get away!" The words were snarled out, the voice barely recognizable as the instrument of a thousand thousand lectures down through the years. It was a voice that had earned his affection, his admiration, and his trust for all the years he had lived in this strange, foreign city, all-but abandoned by his own father.

A terrible coldness rose up within F.R. unlike anything he had ever felt before. At the same time, a burning fire seemed to ignite behind his eyes as Hugo's words finally registered. He looked down at the bloody knife at his feet, and then felt the heavy shape of Ernest's Death Ray weighing down his own coat's wet pocket. He was not sure there would be a sufficient charge left in the weapon, given the spectacular display it had facilitated earlier in the Jardin des Tuileries. A darker shadow within the rising cold discarded the thought as irrelevant. It would not be satisfied by some calculated, distant kill.

The specter at the bottom of the stairs bent down with a swift, smooth motion and rose with the long knife in a tight red fist. His white eyes, luminous in the gory mask, fixed upon the stranger, and he took one, heavy step onto the stone.

The blood-spattered man gripped the wrought-iron railing, his face, pale beneath the burgundy stippling, shook back and forth in hopeless fits. The eyes rolled like a mad horse's, looking back up at Hugo's terrible form, then to Ernest, then the nightmare phantom stalking up the stairs toward him, blade flashing in the street light.

"Please…" The man's voice was low, he sank down upon the stairs, shaking his head, the last vestiges of hope draining from his face. "Please, I did nothing. I don't know... I don't even know where I am!" Tears coursed down his cheeks, drawing pale lines through the tracery of blood. "I couldn't have..."

"F.R., wait." Ernest reached out to him as he stalked up the stairs, but even now, with this terrible and bizarre turn of the evening, the younger man could not bring himself to touch his friend's bloody clothing. "F.R., we need to let the Sûreté—"

"F.R., your mother lies dead! She gasped out her last breaths in my arms, while that man laughed! Will you be trusting some foolish policemen with the justice of her killer?" Hugo pointed down at the stranger, his long finger as implacable as the Grim Reaper selecting a worthy victim. The tutor's face was demonic, twisted beyond all recognition. There was nothing of the old instructor there; only the cold face of divine judgment, weighing an errant soul and judging it horribly wanting.

Long, smooth strides carried F.R. past his friend as the knife rose high into the cold night air.

"No, please!" The man collapsed against the railing, one hand outstretched to ward off his attacker, the other wrapped hopelessly over his head. He still shook slowly from side to side, but his voice was low and despondent, muffled as he ducked his face into his shoulder. "Please, please, no."

The words were nothing but meaningless sound to F.R. as he fell upon the man, knife flashing. There was no challenge, no sport, no thought. The knife rose and fell, rose and fell, tracing graceful ruby arcs up into the air before slamming down once again. It plunged into the cowering man's shoulder, his arms, his neck. The coat became heavy with blood, and the body sank lower with each blow, but the despairing pleas for mercy would not end, although they grew weaker and weaker as the attack raged on.

F.R.'s world shrank to the back of the man who had murdered his mother, the flesh nothing but a target for rage and pain and guilt that had not even seeped into his conscious mind yet. Each time the man moved, or moaned, or cried out, the flames of his cold anger were fanned all over again. The stairs, the townhouse, the street, and even his friend and tutor faded away. There was no reality but this man and his crime, and there was no punishment or judgment but that which F.R. would mete out himself.

"Get off of him! He's dead!" Hands grabbed F.R. from behind, pulling him backward and down the stairs.

There was no understanding or thought in F.R.'s reaction. He knew only that he must continue to beat the lifeless flesh before him. He had no memory of why he must do this, only that he knew he must. He must strike the cowering form over and over again with his fists... wait... had he not started with a knife? Where had it gone?

But the pulling was insistent. The arms locked around his chest were strong, and he found himself dragged from his prey despite the weak protestations that rose to his lips.

Only a single coherent thought swirled around the darkness in his mind. A string of sounds, or words, whose meaning was too terrible for him to focus on more than a moment at a time. "Your... mother... lies... dead..." The words were not his. They were in a voice familiar and yet strange. Their meaning was like smoke or fog, refusing to settle into his mind. And yet they carried with them a terrible weight that even in his addled state, he shied from.

"Your mother lies dead."
What could that possibly mean?

* * * * *

Ernest stared at his friend slumped at the servant's table in the gleaming kitchen. He was wrapped in a thick woolen blanket, his skin and hair cleaned at one of the massive slop sinks as well as Ernest could manage.

At Hugo's insistence, he had dragged the body of the man F.R. had mutilated back into the house, and then doused the stairs with several enormous soup-cauldrons full of warm water. It would not hide the blood from a determined study, but at least the worst of the stains had been diluted enough to pass casual observation.

The one-time tutor, as Ernest continued to stare in concern at his friend's empty face, had been very helpful, in fact. The usually-quiet man had taken charge, snapping orders and setting priorities while Ernest could only stare in horrified fascination at the bloody scene before him. The man's tone had been cold and formal, almost as if he were addressing a servant rather than a long-time guest of the family.

Hugo had disappeared while Ernest was sluicing the blood from F.R.'s face and hands. With the killer laid out in one of the cooling rooms, he assumed the man was taking care of Mrs. Caym, elsewhere in the house. In truth, Ernest was not terribly concerned with the man's whereabouts. F.R. had not emerged from his catatonic state since the last moments of that terrible assault, and Ernest was starting to fear that he would not be able to pull his friend back from the brink.

"F.R., you need to come around, old son." Ernest gripped his friend's shoulder, giving it a gentle shake. "There's still much that needs doing, and I'm not entirely sure old Digne will be up to the task. I need you, F.R., you need to come back now."

The other man's head shook slightly as his shoulder was

moved, but there was no acknowledgement in his eyes, his face slack and without animation. The eyes were hollow and dark, staring off into the middle distance and refusing to focus on anything before him.

"Really, son, you're going to have to come around." There was a dead body in the other room, the cause of death terribly obvious. A trail of blood, hastily mopped up, was still detectable from the foyer and into the kitchen. And elsewhere in the house was F.R.'s mother, herself murdered with the same knife that lay upon the table beside her son even now.

"F.R., we aren't going to be able to stay here. We need to be gone before the Sûreté notices the front steps. There will be questions, and I don't think we can answer them right now."

He was having trouble articulating his concern, even to himself. Someone had broken into the Caym townhouse and murdered the lady of the house. Her son had returned home (from where, now that he was cleaned up, would be unimportant), discovered the killer, and in a fit of rage, had exacted his revenge. It was not a particularly outlandish tale, and not something the local police would take undue interest in.

But that ignored the rumors and dark whispers that had swirled around F.R. for years now. Even though the local Sûreté had never taken action against him, a situation like this would push even their well-greased complacency. And the whispers that had followed F.R. back from his time in London had never quite gone away either. Should the wrong witness appear, or an unfortunate piece of evidence emerge, their grand plans to join Doctor Carpathian and Vladimir Caym in America and take their places upon the world stage would end before they ever truly began.

There were great things to be done, great discoveries waiting to be made. And they would not be the ones to tread that golden path if the local Parisian gendarmeries were allowed to interfere now. He hated the appearance of impropriety, but Ernest could not see any other way out of their current predicament.

"Why."

The word was rough, the voice harsh. There was no emotion or force behind it, and yet it seemed to carry a great deal of weight for such a short, innocuous sound.

Ernest looked quickly back to F.R.'s face, and almost smiled to see the sense flickering back into those dark eyes. Almost, he smiled, until their current situation leapt back to his mind. But before he could marshal his thoughts, F.R. spoke again.

"Why."

The voice was smoother, but still jagged and rusty, as if from a throat that had not spoken in long, strange years.

"Why what, old son?" He leaned closer to his friend, squeezing the shoulder reassuringly before the hard metal beneath the blanket reminded him that there was no avenue of comfort to be given there.

"Why is my mother dead?" F.R.'s eyes flickered from the lost horizon to meet Ernest's own gaze with a sudden, shocking firmness. "Why is my mother dead?" The words, repeated, carried even more weight as F.R. came back to life.

The question bothered Ernest; it was the very thought that had haunted his mind the entire time he was trying to clean up the evidence of the fight as best he could. He shook his head.

"I don't know, F.R." He forced himself to refrain from the sarcastic response that rose into his mind. If F.R. had not slaughtered the man on the stairs so ruthlessly, they might have learned something from him. As it was, there was nothing to be gleaned at all.

"I need to know." F.R. was whispering, but the intensity was still building beneath the words. "Where is Hugo?"

Ernest leaned back, casting his eyes around the kitchen and out the main door into the rest of the house. He looked back with a shrug. "I don't know, to be honest. He disappeared a little while ago."

"I want to see my mother." Ernest stood and came around to stand beside his friend in case he needed help to stand after his shock. But F.R. rose smoothly, without apparent trouble, and wrapped the blanket more tightly around his shoulders as a king pulling together his robes of state. "Where is she?"

Ernest shook his head, embarrassed. Now, it seemed like something he should have seen to almost as once, but there had been so many other things that needed doing, Digne had snapped so many orders at him, that he had not settled down to thoughts of the murdered woman until right now.

"I don't know, F.R. Upstairs, maybe?" He followed his friend to the big doors, pushing out into the receiving lounge that connected to the formal dining room. "I would assume Hugo might be with her."

That was another thing about the evening that was bothering Ernest. What had Hugo been doing here, apparently alone with Mrs. Caym? The lady had never particularly cared for the man who had supplanted her husband's affections in her son's mind. They had never been alone together, to the best of Ernest's recollection.

F.R. moved through the lounge, peering into the dining room, and then moving down the dimly-lit hall to the receiving room at the back of the house. As he pushed the dark wood of the door open, he stopped, blocking Ernest's view for a moment. But by the stiffening of his shoulders, Ernest knew what his friend must be seeing.

The room was lit by several dim oil lamps, their wicks each turned down low to provide only a soft, glowing illumination. The paneled walls reflected the golden light, as did the small glass and metal knickknacks that F.R.'s mother had liked to keep around the room, reminders of their native Romania and her husband, kept from her across the vast, impenetrable ocean.

On a low table at the far side of the room, the shrouded form of Mrs. Caym laid, a soft, elegant sheet draped over her still body. Her face was hollow, her once-serene features caught in an expression somewhere between confusion and fear. There was no sense of serenity or comfort there, no modicum of peace-in-death that her son would be able to solace himself with in the days and years ahead.

Sitting beside the table with its sorrowful burden, Hugo Digne looked over his steepled fingers at F.R. with sympathy. Despite the warmth in his eyes, however, there was iron there that Ernest, looking over his friend's shoulder, did not miss.

"My son, words cannot tell you how sorry I am." The tall man stood and approached, his arms wide. "It all happened so fast."

F.R. stepped back, nearly bumping into Ernest, who quickly stepped aside, and raised his own hands within the blanket. "Why is my mother dead?"

Ernest moved around F.R. and into the room, to stand by the dead woman's head, looking down into her face while the confrontation unfolded by the door. The welcoming soul of the woman who had granted him a home thousands upon thousands of miles from his own was gone. There was nothing of her warmth or her thoughtfulness left in the husk laid out on the table before him.

"F.R., the man came to the door, he said he was from your father. His clothing, his words, everything indicated that he was a man of education and distinction." Digne's words took on a calming pattern, and Ernest winced. His friend did not deal well with being handled.

"Why is my mother dead?" F.R.'s response was nothing but the cold repetition. Looking up, Ernest could see that his friend's eyes were fixed on the tall bald man, not so much as flickering in his mother's direction.

Digne shook his head, his shoulders slumping. "I don't know, son."

"And we will never know, now." The room seemed to grow chill with the tone of the words. "You told me to kill him. You drove me to that. And now we will never know why."

Digne's hands fluttered before himself. "I'm sorry, son. I was not thinking clearly. It all happened so fast. There was nothing I could do! And the guilt!"

F.R. shook his head, and then pushed past, to stand with Ernest to look down at his mother. It was clear to his friend that he derived no more comfort or peace looking down at the body than he had. F.R. looked back at Hugo.

"Now what?"

The tutor nodded, his hands folded together before him, and gestured back toward the door. "I think we should perhaps speak somewhere else." His eyes flickered down to the dead woman. "I don't think we will be able to best apply our minds to the problems we now face in the company of your mother's sad remains."

F.R. stood quiet for a moment, and then silently gestured to the door. He nodded for Ernest to follow the tutor, and then came after them both. He turned to close the door gently on the now-empty receiving room with all of his mother's books and curios.

In the kitchen, the men sat around the servant's table, and for the first time, Ernest thought to wonder where, exactly, those servants were.

"F.R., you're going to have to leave France, and you need to do it soon." Hugo was sitting on the edge of his chair, leaning forward with a strange intensity in his eyes. "There have been too many whispers already, and now, between your mother's death, and the attack on the stairs… there will be no way to avoid official notice."

The young scientist nodded, but without strength or conviction.

"How would you suggest we flee, Monsieur Digne?" Ernest felt he needed to jump in to defend his friend from this sudden decision. "We hardly have the financial wherewithal for that kind of move."

Hugo smiled at the New Zealander, but it was a cold, reptilian expression without any reassurance in it. "Of course, Monsieur Rutherford, there are practical considerations to be taken into account as well." He looked back to F.R. "Many of your compatriots and research partners over the last several years have recently expressed renewed interested in a variety of your newer discoveries. I have kept them at bay, believing you would have no interest in selling your best work, even to such men." He shrugged. "But now, in extremis, if you will, it may be the best way to gain the financial independence you're going to need to get to America—"

"America?" The word escaped Ernest's lips before he experienced the thought. "Are we going to America, then?"

F.R. stared down at the tabletop before him, the blanket still wrapped tightly around his shoulders. "Where else would we go?" His eyes rose to meet his friend's. "We were going there eventually." His eyes dropped. "There's nothing holding us here, any longer."

"You cannot access your family accounts without arousing suspicion, sadly." Hugo looked from one young man to the other. "Of course, I will not be able to sell these technologies at a moment's notice, but I should be able to secure you the funds you will need for your crossing by the time you arrive in England. You should have enough currency with you now to get that far, I should think?"

F.R. nodded, and Ernest shrugged. As a scholarship student at Cambridge, he did not have a great deal of wealth to call upon, himself.

"Excellent. I think you should both dress for travel then. You will want to repair to your laboratories, collect all of your research, your notes, and such. Break down what material you can bring with you." He stood, looking down upon the two boys with a smile that contained more warmth than he had shown since the front door had first slammed open. "I will contact a transportation company to assist you in getting to England. Your best chance to get to America will be to leave from Liverpool or Southampton. I can have your funds available through the Bank of England in either port."

F.R. nodded again, not looking up. "We have sufficient crates and such, we should be able to bring most of the packs. We will also bring the Death Ray, and the other weapons."

Hugo held up one long finger. "You'll need to leave enough behind that their sale will pave your way to America, don't forget."

Ernest stood as well. "We should try to bring as much of the materials with us as possible as well."

"The RJ-1027 will fetch the most hard cash, gentlemen." Hugo smiled again. "After all, you should not have trouble gaining more, once you reach the New World."

F.R. hesitated a moment, then pushed himself away from the table. "We will keep all of the atomic material, and a sufficiency of the RJ-1027 that we will be able to continue our work, when time allows, as we travel." He held up a calming hand toward Hugo. "That should still leave plenty to sell to your mysterious contacts, Hugo. Don't worry."

"Of course." The tall man tilted his head, his scalp gleaming in the lamplight. "I will go and make the arrangements for your travel to Calais, then. Once you are in Dover, you can find your best paths to a port of departure." He nodded one last time and then turned to push out past the main doors.

"America." F.R. said the word as if it were a wonder. Ernest could see that his friend's eyes were still dull with shock, and so merely smiled and nodded.

"We have been so eager to leave, and now, knowing the cost..." He shook his head. "Is it wrong, that I feel even the slightest thrill of expectation?"

Ernest reached out once again for his friend's shoulder, this time being sure to grasp higher up, toward the neck, and squeeze the living flesh he found there with a reassuring pressure. "You have looked forward to this journey for most of your adult life. And you are going to your father in a moment of terrible loss. There is no shame in feeling some expectation, I don't think."

It was odd, though, to realize that after so many months of anticipation, of refusals from F.R.'s father and uncle, that they were going to be leaving for America.

Ernest had gotten so used to his friend receiving those rejections, he had almost reconciled himself with the idea that they would never see the New World. And now, in the course of one tragic evening of blood and death, their path was clear, means were at hand, and they were leaving, without hesitation or celebration, for this next phase in their lives.

Chapter 5

Sweat dripped from Vlad's nose as he paused to draw one gloved-hand across his brow. It was often easy to forget that Payson was in the middle of the dreaded western territories, with the tall, stately pines swaying in soft breezes and formidable roseate escarpments providing shelter from the harsh heat and arid winds of the surrounding deserts. But after spending the better part of a day in the blazing sun, directing a party of animations in the demolition and clearing of a building ruined during the invasion of Marcus Wayward and his sălbaticmercenaries, the taste of the arid wastelands was in every breath he took.

Vlad harbored no illusions as to his place in his brother-in-law's organization. Burson was a genius of the first order. His mind was a marvel, and would secure them all a venerated place in the history books. But he was a scientist. He lived in a world of clean laboratories and calculated experiments. Vlad was a soldier, a man of war that lived in the harsh and dirty world of reality, where only skill and confidence stood between a man and utter disaster.

There was no doubt in Vlad's mind that Carpathian's nature, always looking for the main chance, always looking to try to bend people to his will, opened him up to this kind of betrayal. Wayward and his crew had devastated Payson, blowing a broad swath through the town and reaching into the very palace itself. He pulled at his chin with one hand, remembering with bitterness the beating Wayward had given him in the cargo lift. He still walked with a limp, the leg he had broken as the lift hurtled back down the shaft having healed poorlydespite the doctor's best efforts. Whatever had happened in that dingy tower room after his fall was still not entirely clear to him. There were many aspects of that day that he found confusing, elements of Burson's deal with Wayward that he had not been made privy to.

Vlad held the doctor in highest esteem, but he was a man of action, and he grew tired of the waiting and the scheming and the planning. They had assets all over the continent, and if the time was not ripe for them to rise up and claim their place among the great men of the age, he knew it had to be close, or they would lose their chance forever.

All of the work they had put into positioning Jesse James with the Confederate Rebellion, with an entire army at his disposal, and it had been thrown away for nothing! As far as Vlad had been able to ascertain, there had been no gain at all from the entire Fort Knox endeavor. There was still a well-armed and well-prepared army down in the swamps, only waiting for James, or someone like him, to return and lead them. The decrepit leaders of the Confederate Rebellion would fall in a matter of days, with more than enough support among the people to raise Jesse James to the position of president of the whole fetid mess. Many, many men and women had died to put all of those pawns into position. Once they ruled the south through a malleablepuppet, they would be able to crush Grant and the Union Army. Between the forces sweeping up from the vanquished states and the army of animations and Creations Carpathian had stockpiled in Payson and other towns loyal to his cause throughout the western territories, they had power to spare.

But instead, everything had started to fall apart. Jesse James had fled into the night, his injuries only half-healed, his motivations and intentions unknown. He had disappeared into the wind, leaving no trace. The doctor had been forced to send his minions far and wide, fruitlessly chasing rumors and ghost stories that never quite panned out. Wayward's aborted assassination attempt had killed hundreds of their best workers, devastated a large portion of the city, and rocked the very foundations of Payson beneath them. To say nothing of their latest trouble with miserable mercenaries. It was a wonder Carpathian did not close to the city completely. And still,the good doctor had them holding the line to the east, wrestling with the filthy, flea-bitten savages to the north, watching their best chance at victory slip through their fingers. Every day the armies around New Orleans were forced to wait, sitting in their own filth in the nightmare swamps, more and more of the guerillas melted away, returning to their farms and shops and families. With no grand vision to hold them together, many saw no reason to suffer those terrible conditions any longer.

Vlad's opinion of Jesse James was not high, but he did think, with the doctor behind him, that the outlaw would at least be able to fulfill the role of figurehead to the lost and feckless ghosts of the former Confederacy.

Vlad hoisted his massive sledge high over his head and brought it down on the brick wall in front of him. He would much rather be leading the charge against the powers of corruption and privilege that had killed his sister and enslaved the entire continent. Instead, he was sweating through his clothes, swinging a giant hammer, knocking down walls they had spent years putting up.

With a grunt, he blasted through the wall and toppled it, sending a cloud of pink dust billowing down the uneven slope, engulfing the putrid animations working around the base of the pile, shoveling debris into waiting wagons. Some of the creatures were his front line soldiers, their weapons set aside as they worked with less-destructive implements. Others had been borrowed from the mines behind Payson, their hands permanently replaced with hammers, chisels, and other tools. They all bent to their work with mindless vigor, tearing down walls and pushing piles of debris toward the wagons. Neither group made very good company.

"Excuse me, sir." The high-pitched voice was soft and diffident. Vlad looked around wildly for a moment, thinking that perhaps his mind ws fooling him, starved for the sound of a human voice. He had been the only living man in the entire, devastated neighborhood for hours.

A small boy stood at the foot of the slope of wreckage, his clothing ragged and dusty, his face streaked with dirt. The child's dark eyes were huge in his thin face. Dark hair flopped over his forehead, waving in front of those big eyes. He said nothing more, merely standing, looking up to where Vlad stood, hammer now resting on one broad shoulder.

"Yes? Vhatiz it, boy?" If this was some messenger from the doctor, sent to remind him that it was below his station to get his hands dirty, then he was going to have another conversation with his officious brother-in-law.

"Are you trying to dig up my mommy and daddy?" The high voice was dull, as if the words carried no meaning. "We lived at the other end."

Vlad's head jerked slightly as if he had been slapped. His head tilted to the side. "Vhat?"

"We lived at the other end. My mommy and daddy are probably down at that end." He looked at the animations, none of whom had stopped their work at the boy's appearance. Fear almost broke through the child's apathy, but then he shrugged, returning his big gaze to Vlad.

"Son, vere your parents in zis building ven it fell?" Vlad put the hammer down and made his slow, careful way down the ruined slope. Payson was a strange town. The undead animations made up much of the population, but there were many living, breathing people as well. Not many families, that was true, but there were some. He had thought this particular block had been mainly storehouses and manufactories, but maybe he had been wrong. He admitted, other than the few saloons he frequented, he did not spend much time outside of the palace in Payson.

"Yeah." The boy shied away as the big man jogged down the last few feet to stand nearby. "My dad wanted to come out to fight the bad people, but mommy wouldn't let him. We lived at the other end, though. So, if you're trying to dig them up, you gotta dig over there." He pointed to the far end of the block of wreckage, then brought his thin arm back in to wrap around his narrow chest.

Vlad sighed, looking around the ruin of the neighborhood. If there had been anyone here when it camedown, there was no way they would have survived. He sank to one knee, grunting at the stab of pain. "Son, if your parents vere in zis building when ze bad people attacked, I'm afraid zey are gone."

The boy stared at him, uncomprehending. "Gone?"
Vlad nodded. "Zey are gone. Dead." Something about the little boy reminded him of someone, and he leaned in a little closer. "I'm sorry. Vhatiz your name, son?"

The boy sniffled, drawing one bare arm beneath his nose. "Benny. What do you mean, they're dead?"

He bowed his head. He wanted to be leading armies, crushing foes, and making the way for the future...Instead, he was clearing wreckage and caring for orphans whose parents should never have been in danger.

"Zey are not vis us anymore, child. Zey are gone." He wanted to reach out and bring the boy in for an embrace, to comfort him in any way he could. But the poor waif looked like he would run if Vlad approached any closer. "I'm so sorry, Benny."

The little boy shook his head. "No. My daddy would never leave me. He wouldn't leave me alone." Huge tears hung just within those luminous eyes, and Vlad would have done anything to stop them from falling. But there was nothing he could do.

When the realization struck, it hit him like his own sledge-hammer, striking the back of his head. This little boy, with his dark hair and dark eyes, was like a ghost stepping from the past. His son, F.R., had not been much older than this when Vlad had been forced to leave him, kissing him goodbye on the landing of their Paris townhouse all those years ago.

"He wouldn't leave me." The little boy repeated.

The words were like a knife sliding into his heart.

Vlad stood slowly. He needed to help this child, whatever else he did. He reached out, but a harsh voice called out from down the rubble-strewn street, echoing off the slumping, shattered walls.

"Ursul! You have perhaps forgotten the meeting?" Vlad looked up and cursed. A broad-shouldered form stood at the end of the street, hands on hips and big smile stretching between wild muttonchops: Thomas Henry Huxley, one of Burson's newest protégées.

"Vhat?" He remembered Burson's damned meeting as soon as he had heard the Englishman's voice, but he needed a moment to think.

"The big meeting, you old bear!" Huxley was one of the few scientists Vlad genuinely liked. The Englishman was almost as much a man of action as he was a man of science, and he had a rough and ready sense of humor that was at odds with the majority of the stodgy folkBurson surrounded himself with. "It's shaping up to be something you really don't want to miss! He wants you up at the palace early!"

Vlad cursed, and then looked down to the little boy, trying to decide if he could trust Huxley with the child.

But little Benny was gone. The newcomer must have scared him off. Vlad cursed even louder. He could not very well tell the animations to find the boy; that would terrify even a grown man. And Huxley was a good sort, but probably not the ideal type to go digging through rubble looking for a poor, starving orphan boy who believed his father had abandoned him.

With a shrug, Vlad tossed his hammer onto the slope of brick and clapped his hands together, sending a cloud of dust skirling down onto the shattered ruins. He would have to come back after Burson's foolish meeting and find the boy later.

As Vlad joined Huxley at the entrance to the street and moved away, a small shape stepped out of a ruined doorway to watch them go with a blank, expressionless face. Deep within its brown eyes, a deep, crimson flash twinkled in the shadows.

*****

Vlad refused to clean up before being ushered into his brother-in-law's tower-top office. He rapped once on the ornate doors, leaving a layer of pink dust to settle down across the ornate 'C's raised from the wood.

"Enter." The voice was muffled, but easily recognizable. After all these years, not only could Vlad recognize Carpathian's voice, he could also tell, from a vague combination of tone and cadence, that the doctor was not alone.

The room was much as it had been during their last meeting; much as it had been for many, many years. Doctor Carpathian was not a man who concerned himself overmuch with decoration. The doctor was sitting in one of the large chairs, his back stiff and proper. A cup sat on the table beside him, steam rising up in gentle curls, carrying the subtle fragrances of the far east into the room. In another of the chairs sat an elegant-looking woman in a thin, lacey white gown whose cut and style was far more reminiscent of the Old Country than of current fashion in the western territories.

Vlad could not see the woman's face, as she was turned away from the big doors. But even if she had been standing in the center of the room, caught in mid-pirouette, he would have had very little attention to spare her. His eyes were immediately caught by a shape shifting in the shadows of a far corner. He caught vague hints of coiled muscle, flashes of dull metal, and the gleam of two saucer-sized, pale, milky eyes staring at him.

Vlad's killing blade, Vendetta, was out before he even realized it. The thing in the corner shifted, its entire mass seeming to move in too many directions at once, while the whole merely shuffled forward against the dictates of common sense. A dusty, rasping sound accompanied the movement, like air wheezing through an ancient vent, and a foul gust flowed over him with a stench as familiar to a denizen of Payson as anything.

The scent of death.

"Is it not grand, Vladimir?" Carpathian surged from his chair, a wide smile stretching over his bright, white teeth, his cheeks flushed with excitement beneath the grand muttonchops. "MademoiselleLaveau has truly outdone herself this time, has she not?"

Vlad's eyes snapped from the thing in the corner to the woman, who now turned with stiff dignity and grace, to bring her bright smile fully to bear upon him. He shivered in response.

There was no denying the woman's beauty, despite the frosty chill in her gold-flecked eyes. But it was a distant beauty, like that of an ancient queen assessing the potential value of a new servant. She nodded in greeting, but the slight smile pulling at the corner of one full lip gave the gesture a more condescending flavor than he would have liked.

Her café au lait skin was a shade darker than might have been fashionable in the more traditional quarters of the bigger cities back east, appearing even darker against the soft white of the gown. Although he was no expert at the ethnic breakdowns of the United States, he would have put a small sum down on the woman having mixed racial heritage somewhere in her past: Marie Laveau, Voodoo Queen of New Orleans, and on-again-off-again ally of Doctor Carpathian. Her apparent connection with the criminals responsible for thelatest destruction visited upon Payson still rankled. He did not know why the doctor had been so quick to accept her back into his good graces.

Vlad forced himself to nod in return, consciously keeping his gesture short to match her own. He looked back at the corner, where the enormous, coiled mass shifted restlessly.

"Vhat is it?" He slid his knife back into its sheath, but he kept his distance, sideling around the edges of the room to rest in what he hoped was a casual pose against a heavy sideboard laden with glittering crystal decanters.

Carpathian's smile widened. "This, Vladimir, is a genius solution to our most perpetual difficulty: raw materials."

"Please do not allow Doctor Carpathian to belittle my favored creation, MsyeCaym." The woman's smile grew perceptibly warmer, but did not touch the core of Vlad's unease. She glided across the floor toward her creation. For some reason, her movements reminded him of Misty Mimms, and his unease ticked up a notch. Sheglided to a halt beside the thing in the crimson-tinged shadows. She rested one thin hand upon something that rose up out of the mass, the two eyes still staring unblinkingly at him.

The thing's head was massive, but clearly rotten. Tight stitches joined neat sections of scaled hide together over the sharp shape of bones beneath. A pair of gleaming metal mandibles had been bolted to bones through the scales and flesh, and an elaborate metal exoskeleton emerged from the creature's spine, with ribs of iron embracing the rotten whole at regular intervals, providing the putrescent corpse with stability and strength.

"This is Nzambi." She stroked the hard scales at the top of the wide, flat head.

She giggled girlishly, covering her mouth with one raised

hand. The sound and gesture seemed terribly out of place in the tower room, especially with the enormous, awful serpent coiled beside her. "Well, this is really the fifth Nzambi. I only ever have one at a time. I use the ancient name for each in turn. Simply the silly habit of a foolish girl, I'm sure."

If half the stories he had heard from the doctor's agents were to be believed, this woman was neither foolish, nor a girl. None of the tales agreed, but they all seemed to indicate that Marie Laveau was much older than her beauty would indicate.

"Can you imagine, Vladimir?" Carpathian had moved no closer to the serpentine creation, but his excitement was undeniable. "No longer beholden to the cemeteries of this barbarous territory! To be able to unleash Nature's own wrath upon our foes!"

Vlad continued to eye the giant snake warily. "Zere are not so many creatureszis fierce in ze territories, Burson."

"However, the swamps and bayous around my city are very well-supplied with nature's bounty in this regard, Msye-Caym." Her accent was refined, and yet it had a burr within it that reminded him of France. It reminded him of hisfamily, relegating the manipulative woman and her writhing creation to a position of far less importance and fascination.

"Very vell." Vlad turned stiffly back to look at the doctor, drawing himself up to his full height. "I must speak vith you, Burson."

The light of excitement and engagement faded slightly from the doctor's eyes. The dimming was not lost on Vlad, whose mood cooled further at the sight.

"Of course, Vladimir." The doctor took the woman's hand and brushed the back with his lips, bringing the smile back to her face. "Madamoiselle, if you would excuse us? I look forward to continuing this conversation later in the evening, perhaps after our little conclave?"

She inclined her head, again reminiscent of a great queen. "Of course, Doctor. I look forward to it." She pivoted on one heel toward the door, drawing a finger across the rigid surface of the snake's head, and gave the two men a smile with a mocking edge. "Come, Nzambi. I require rest before this grandas-sembly."

Vlad stepped aside as the woman brushed past, his eyes riveted on the thick shape of the serpent as it writhed by. The met-al framework clicked a rapid tattoo across the floor. The beast's body was nearly as thick as a rain barrel, and he saw with a fur-ther lurch of distaste that its tail had been bifurcated, each half neatly sewn and then embellished with a massive, flashing axe-blade.

When the doors closed behind the woman and her pet, Vlad turned back to the doctor, his back stiff, his face firm. He braced himself for what he knew was going to be an unpleasant encounter. It had been weeks since the last time he had broached the subject, but the soft words of the boy in the ruins had decided him. There would be no denying him now, or he would be going back to Paris presently.

"This is about young F.R. and his mother, yes?" The words caught Vlad off-balance, and his carefully-framed argument stum-bled to a halt. He nodded.

"You feel very strongly about this, then?" Carpathian moved to his chair and settled back, taking the tea cup in one hand. He sipped from the fine china, but his lips curled as he swallowed. "Cold." He muttered under his breath.

"I cannot vait any longer, Burson. If my wife and son can-not be brought to Payson, zen I vill be forced to take my leave of you and return to Europe myself. I vill not spend anozer day separated from zem, vith no light of reunion in sight."

Carpathian sat back in his chair, his metal legs hissing softly as they were relieved of his weight. His face was calm, even considerate, and he nodded. Vlad was caught completely off-guard.

"I understand, Vladimir. I know the pain of separation, and I know that all human patience is finite." He shook his head, looking up at the tin panels of the ceiling. "I have no right to keep you from your family." His eyes came back down, settling upon Vlad's face with an intensity that made the old soldier want to squirm. "And I need you too much to let you wander away now."

Vlad shook his head, moving to sit in another chair. "I do now vish to leave, Burson! Ve are doing great sings here, and vis much greater sings to come! Humanity vill see us as champions of freedom and liberty venve are done here. But—"

"But you see no real reason to do this without your family by your side." Carpathian sighed. "I know, Vladimir. I know."

"Not just to have zem by my side, Burson, but to sharezis greatness viszem!" Vlad leaned forward, his fingers squeezing the arms of his chair to the point of cracking. "F.R. vill be a great asset to you! And zeyvill see, venzey arrive and see vhatve have accomplished, zat our separation has not been in vain!"

Carpathian nodded again, one hand raised. "I know, Vladimir. I have no doubt." And with his mind clouded by this un-foreseen appearance of a thaw, Vlad believed him.

The doctor gave another great gust of a sigh, and then nodded firmly in one decisive gesture. "I relent, Vladimir. F.R. and his mother shall join us here, and take their rightful places beside us as we move into the future."

Vlad's surge of joy was so strong that he almost missed the doctor's single raised finger, and threatened to flash into cold fury when he did so. "I just have one request, Vladimir, if you would indulge me?"

Vlad's eyes were cold, his joy checked, as he muttered, "Vhat?"

"We are scheduled to have a very important meeting in..." He pulled on the chain emerging from his vest pocket and a golden watch slid out, dangling in his long fingers. "The meeting is in less than an hour. It will change everything, I promise you, and I need you there beside me. Do you think you can give me this day? And perhaps, depending upon what happens at this meeting, a last brief respite, should immediate action be required based upon what we learn today?"

Thick, dark brows fell over his cold eyes, and Vlad felt the hope twisting in his gut. "Zevoman called it a 'grand assembly'... Vhat did she mean by zat?"

Some of the excitement rekindled in the doctor's eyes and he leaned forward over his creaking legs. "It's very exciting, Vladimir! I have brought so many people together today, to secure our future and to move our agenda forward. You will not believe it, my friend! And you will be beside me through the entire ordeal, won't you?"

Vlad settled back in his own chair. His eyes closing in surrender even as he imagined he could see his son, a little boy with dark hair and eyes, falling away from him. Would F.R. ever forgive him?

Almost against his will, he nodded. There would come a day when the doctor would lose him. But he had spent so many years now trying to build something his wife and son would be proud of, something that they could partake of, and know that all those barren years were worth something, that the world would see that he had not abandoned his family for no great purpose.

All the same, there was something in the doctor's answering smile that struck a dangerous note in Vlad's mind.

Chapter 6

Doctor Carpathian's grand conclave occurred in one of the most majestic rooms of the doctor's palace. It was a long, narrow room filled with an enormous table of dark, heavy wood gleaming in the ruby glow of elaborate wall sconces containing swirling orbs of RJ-1027. Long sideboards stood against one wall, with ornate serving sets displayed on each.

Overhead, a series of crimson chandeliers hung from the high ceiling, providing even more light that reflected off the silver cutlery and the porcelain service. The walls were ornately paneled wood, and the floor was covered in thick carpets whose rich reds, greens, and blues could only have come from the Far East.

Everything about the room screamed elegance and refinement.

The men and women gathered there, however, did not.

Along one side of the table were the collected scientists of Doctor Burson Carpathian's Enlightened Movement. All of the rising stars were there, each accompanied by a small coterie of assistants and technicians. They were huddled together as if for protection against the others, although it was clear from the way they eyed each other that there was no love lost amongst themselves, either.

First among equals, Thomas Edison sat at the center of the table. Edison had been the first scientist to make the pilgrimage to Payson, and thus had been serving the doctor longer than anyone else at the table. His early work with ion weaponry had been the cornerstone for several technologies used to control and limit the powers of RJ-1027. This was becoming more and more important, as the substance saw widespread use across the continent. Edison still had a boyish cast to his features, his skin a more healthy color than the pallor evinced by most of the others around the table. Although a proven scientific mind, his conceit of being a field commander as well had met with total failure at the hands of Marcus Wayward in the recent unpleasantness. He had been eager to redeem himself ever since.

Sitting to the left of Edison was the famous Frenchman, Gustav Eiffel. Two assistants sat between the men, both as a show of how important they were and as a buffer to keep them from having to speak directly to each other. Eiffel was the doctor's master of mechanisms, his work essential to the movement's vehicles and the more advanced automatons Carpathian Industries had recently turned their attention toward. Eiffel's flesh was as pale as parchment. He seldom left his laboratories unless absolutely necessary, and was clearly put out at having been forced to abandon his work for this particular, mysterious meeting.

The others were all much more recent arrivals, and thus lower on the ladder of power and prestige within the enclave. The big-shouldered English geneticist, Thomas Henry Huxley, sat back in his dark, carven chair with a more relaxed air than the rest of them. His smile was genuine, and he spoke to the men around him with confidence and humor. A fierce believer in what he saw as Carpathian's ultimate goals, Huxley was often referred to as Carpathian's Bulldog, equally able to argue the scientific and moral merits of the discoveries and their place in the world, as to beat any foe senseless in the casual violence of a saloon brawl.

Beside Huxley, hunched in his chair and leaning slightly toward the Englishman, was the newcomer, Heinrich Friese. Friese was a German biologist who specialized in insects. As yet he had not provided a great deal of insight or advancement to the projects of the Enlightened Movement, adding to his air of vulnerability. The man was terribly eager to prove himself, but he had not yet been granted the chance to do so.

Other scientists and technicians gathered around these luminaries. At the far end of the table sat the dark and gloomy man known as J.P. Smith. The renegade clockmaker's face was bitter, having been an integral participant in the latest defeat of Carpathian's forces at the hands of the unwashed savages. An RJ-1027-powered staff, his pride and joy, rested against the wall behind him. Despite his close work with the doctor on the enormous Creation 5, the man's mysterious arrival in Payson and his

reluctance to speak of his previous life had made the others hesitant to accept him into their brotherhood.

Beside the thin man sat the massive shape of Kyle the
Black, Carpathian's personal surgeon, and the man who knew
more about the doctor's own augmentations and enhancements
than any other. The alien shapes of his Corpse Grinder claws
swayed gently behind his peaked head. The two men made for
a strange dichotomy, the gloomy, thin J.P. beside the maniacal-
ly-grinning, hefty surgeon.

On the other side of the table both of the Kaufmann brothers sat in brooding silence. Never truly welcomed into the brotherhood of scientists at the core of the movement, Dieter and Schultz
were always uncomfortable when called to full meetings like this.
Their defeat at the hands of Sky Spirit did nothing to make them
feel more at ease.

Vlad entered the room through the massive double doors,
and all conversation stopped as the men and women watched
him enter. The scientists knew Vlad only as the majordomo of
the master; the man who often cracked the whip over their heads
without fully understanding the demands he made. The men of
action among them had more regard for him, he knew. Everyone,
however, knew that he helped Carpathian fashion the strategy
and tactics that would see them all elevated to the positions of
authority and power to which they believed themselves entitled.
This explained the wide range of smiles that greeted him.

His gaze paused for a moment as he saw J.P. Smith.
The man's furtive eyes skittered away from his own, once again
reinforcing his distrust of the man. Vlad had told Carpathian on
more than one occasion that he should have sent the wease-
lylittle clockmaker on his way, but the doctor swore the man was
a genius and deserved a place among the other great minds of
Payson. Carpathian had repeatedly refused to listen to the merest
criticism about the man.

Vlad never enjoyed meetings such as these, and as he
cast his gaze around the room, he saw that there were a few
empty chairs on the scientists' side of the table, and far more free

space opposite them. But rather than join the contentious rabble, he moved quickly to the end of the table and the elaborate, throne-like chair that crouched there on polished wooden lion's claws. He stood behind it in silence, pretending that he knew what to expect next. There was at least one more outsider due to arrive, and he could not wait to see what throwing Marie Laveau into this mix was going to do to the status-obsessed idioti that lined the far table edge.

The doors were pushed silently open moments later, and the graceful lady herself glided into the room. She made her usu-al, regal entrance, and surveyed the chamber without seeming concern for what she saw there. She nodded once to Vlad, that damned smile on her full lips, and then moved to an empty seat on the far side of the table from the rest of the scientists. He allowed himself a moment's relief when the enormous undead snake did not slither in after her.

She arrayed herself in a chair, her arms out to either side, allowing the fall of her gown to drape across the rich wood. Thus settled, folding her hands before her, she regarded the men and their retinues across from her as if they had come to beg some boon of their indulgent queen.

After a few moments of uncomfortable silence, the scien-tists looked to each other, befuddled. Edison looked completely taken aback, while Eiffel muttered something under his breath to the assistant sitting beside him. Several of the women among the technicians standing along the wall watched the new arrival with open hostility, and Vlad wondered how much of that might be the result of the innate antagonism womenfolk the world over always seemed to exhibit for a strange, beautiful newcomer.

It was clear, though, that Marie Laveau felt no driving need to speak with any of them, and so, perceptibly comfortable and confident, she merely sat draped in her regal silence, smiling disdainfully at the lot of them.

The Voodoo Queen's relationship with Payson was al-ways nebulous, given her tendency to go her own way and con-sort with forces and powers of which Carpathian did not approve.

Rumors of her latest exploits, running with men indelibly tied to Grant's Union, were even more confusing than normal. He found himself intrigued by what affect her current disposition might have on this latest venture.

The door opened again, and another beautiful woman strode in. Although she was familiar to them, they were no more comfortable with her entrance. Everyone in Payson was aware that Misty Mimms held a special relationship with the doctor, although no one knew precisely what that relationship might be. She had only been back in town for a short while, and although she was clearly working in the capacity of a bodyguard, especially when the Kaufmanns were away, she seemed to spend more time with the doctor than any of his previous protectors. Vlad believed that only he might understand, even in part, Carpathian's attachment to his newest vassal, and he refused to think upon it too closely.Misty swept into the room, looked at each person at the table, and then came to join Vlad behind the massive chair with a crisp nod. He knew she spent almost all of her time away from the doctor in an intensive training regimen that would have done any soldier or athlete proud. He had no doubt that she could hold her own against any opponent even near to her own size, and that appreciation had mitigated his opinion of her. In turn, she seemed to have thawed toward him as well. It was only when Vlad saw Misty and the doctor together that his original misgivings would resurface.

Behind Misty, Carpathian stumped in, his eagerness to beginclear. He allowed his eyes to skim across the room, taking note of each person's presence and location. He smiled when he saw Marie Laveau sitting near the Kaufmanns, opposite the rest of the scientific community. She nodded majestically to him, and he returned the gesture with a slow tilt of his head.

"Well, we might as well begin. Our other guests will arrive soon, but I believe some introductions among those here present may be in order." The doctor settled into his chair, his ironwork legs whirring. "Ladies and gentlemen, please allow me to introduce to you MadamoiselleLaveau, a woman of scientific accomplishments nearly the equal to her physical beauty."

The local scientists nodded and murmured vague welcomes, although none of them seemed inclined to look her in the eyes. All of them had heard the rampant rumors about the monster serpent she had brought up from the deep south, and there were whispers that spoke of other, even more terrifying creatures in her retinue. None of them would have denied her intelligence or her beauty, but her commitment to the doctor's cause was always suspect.

"Excellent." The doctor settled back in his chair, smiling as if completely unaware of the undercurrent of tension in the room; unaware, or indifferent.

"I know you are all wondering why I brought you together today. It is no secret that our ultimate plan, to bring the Union to its knees, has not been faring well of late. You are all aware of the surprising efficacy of the Warrior Nation's confrontation with those forces, and our own difficulty in bringing Grant's forces to action with the savages in the way." The man's voice was firm and unemotional, merely putting out the realities before moving on to possible solutions.

"Most of you are also aware of the new arena that has come to dominate combat out on the plains. Our own efforts, with the Hellions, have been no secret to you. Neither has been there abysmal failure." Here he made no attempt to avoid the Kaufmann's eyes, and the twins looked away quickly, knowing that they had not yet been forgiven. "The savages have come to dominate the skies over the battlefields of this new world. Sky Spirit now leads a force of eagle warriors whose guiding spirits are similar to his own, if not as powerful. These brutes have made it nearly impossible for us to maneuver against them."

The doctor took a breath, and then tilted his head marginally toward the Kaufmanns again. "Thanks to Dieter and Schultz, we now know that these warriors are the least of our worries. The savages have unveiled the next weapon in their Great Spirit's arsenal; an enormous, twisted bird of prey capable of destroying many soldiers at a time, both with its natural weapons and a most unnatural evolution... These creatures can, apparently, breathe spirit flames, not unlike the mythical dragons of my native land."

Vlad grimaced. He had heard the reports, of course. But he still had a hard time giving credence to the idea of a giant creature belching flames across the battlefields of the modern world. Still, far more outlandish things fought men's wars these days. There were far more bizarre things in Payson alone, in fact, if he was to be honest.

"You can rest assured, having fought the Warrior Nation even longer than we have, that Grant and the other foes ofEnlightenment are wracking their own brains to counteract these self-same difficulties. They will, undoubtedly, come to their own conclusions. With men like Tesla and Tumblety serving him, those conclusions will vie for the skies just as ably as the eagle warriors and their fire eagles."

The scientists looked at each other, several muttering in distaste. Edison, in particular, looked perturbed. It was clear the man would have spit, if it had not been for the priceless rugs spread beneath them.

"Ladies and gentlemen, we need to create our own response to these threats from above. We must either solve our problems with the Hellion program, or we need to develop a new theory that will better serve us against these current and future threats."

"I believe I might be able to assist with something." Marie Laveau's smile was condescending as she looked across the table. "There are several animals that I believe might be altered to serve your purposes."

Eiffel and Kyle, who had taken the lead on the Hellion program with Carpathian, sneered in automatic rejection. Kyle moved forward, his mass surging in his chair, but Carpathian slapped one hand on the table and everyone stopped moving, looking up at him with a wide array of emotions playing across their faces.

"I do not care to discuss our possible responses now." His voice was cold. "There will be plenty of time in the days ahead. I believe there is much to salvage in the Hellion program, but we will be looking at alternatives as well. I merely want all of you to understand how important securing the air will be. We will craft a response, and you will all work together to make it happen.

"Now." Carpathian put both hands flat on the table before him and took a deep breath, a smile settling over his face that even Vlad could sense, standing behind him. "The primary purpose of today's meeting is to discuss the overall strategic goals of our organization, and how best to achieve them."

Again, the men and women exchanged glances. There was more concern in most of the faces than curiosity, however. Carpathian's grand schemes often encompassed more audacious ambitions than even the megalomaniacs who inhabited Payson found comfortable.

"You are all aware that we intend to end Union domination of the continent." Careful nods from most, as each realized that the doctor was going to start slowly. Marie Laveau did not nod, but rather smiled her unfathomable smile, her eyes not moving from the doctor's.

"The ultimate goal of our Enlightened Movement is not now, nor has it ever been, to take over the country, or to rule in any overt way." There was some muttering at this, as there was still a great deal of opposition to the idea that they would never be able to take the reins of power in the bright light of day. Who better to lead the world than the most gifted minds of the age?

"We will shatter the power of the Union, deny them the ability to dictate to the masses and control the common run of man, and then we will step aside to allow others to rise up and rule in their stead." He raised a hand to forestall the growing rumble of unease. "These new leaders will be carefully selected, and will benefit from our great store of experience and knowledge. Together, we will guide the people of this continent to a great and shining future!"

Polite applause replaced the grumbling, and a few genuine smiles. As long as they were not relinquishing their power and privilege, the vision was not nearly so onerous. Vlad watched the various faces for deeper response, and was alarmed at what he saw. It was clear that Eiffel cared nothing for ruling, only wanting to return to his labs as swiftly as possible. Edison, however, was surely scheming as to how he could secure the largest portion of power for himself. He had cast a wary eye toward J.P. Smith, the man he felt most likely to usurp his favored position with the doctor. The others balanced their ambitions against each other, casting covetous eyes to either side. If such infighting was allowed to flourish, it might undermine everything Carpathian was trying to create. And it was Vlad's responsibility to see that that did not happen.

The word 'Rebellion' was muttered more than once, and Carpathian nodded. "The Confederate Rebellion has always featured prominently in our plans, and continues to do so. When we have crushed the Union, the power vacuum will need to be filled. By preparing a suitable government in the south, we will be able to provide the needed leadership, almost seamlessly, when the time comes."

Kyle the Black coughed, one beefy hand tapping on the table before him. "If we're talking about the Confederacy, what about James? That's supposed to be his part in all this, isn't it?"

Carpathian smiled and nodded, but there was an edge to the smile that made many of the people around the table nervous. Only Marie Laveau and J.P. Smith, in fact, did not look at least mildly ill at the expression.

"Until now, Jesse James was, in fact, central to our plans to secure the Confederacy for our purposes. Sadly, the young man seems to have had a change of heart." The doctor waggled his hand back and forth over the table, and then pointed to each of his scientists in turn with a gnarled finger. "You are all well aware that he is no longer an honored guest in Payson. Nature seldom provides a stable platform for any endeavor, and often chaos and violence breeds more advancement than a hundred years of peace, as you know. We need an agent of violence and chaos more than anything, and it just may be that Jesse James is not the only option available to us."

Many of the men and women around the table had been central in one aspect or another to Payson's long association with Jesse James. The fact that the charismatic outlaw was the heir apparent, as far as Carpathian was concerned, to the throne of the south, and eventually the entire nation, was as established in their minds as the most fundamental scientific laws.

"Tangential to the issue of James, I would like to discuss more mundane difficulties." He looked first at the Kaufmanns, then at the rest of his scientists. Again, his glance slid right over Marie Laveau, and again her position as favored outsider was driven home. "How many of you have been having difficulties with the lawmen in your various areas of responsibility when beyond Payson's walls?"

The twins both nodded, as did Kyle, J.P., and Huxley. All of them were required, in the pursuit of their duties for Carpathian, to venture into the wider territories on a fairly regular basis. Each of them had suffered setbacks at the hands of Over-marshal Wyatt Earp and his lawmen. Often, when a town was ripe for the doctor's influence, a deputy, UR-30 Enforcer, or one of Earp's infernal assistants would descend upon the burg and wreak havoc with the Enlightened's plans. Even Edison and Eiffel had suffered setbacks in their forays beyond the Tonto Forest.

Carpathian nodded in sympathy to their looks of frustrated agreement. "I know, my friends. We had not anticipated, back when we first began our hallowed struggle, that such a force for order would arise amidst the benighted Union horde." His smile returned, and his hands spread out before him, as if presenting some great offering. "However, I believe, much like our situation with the Confederacy has grown and changed, our relationship with the lawmen might well evolve in turn, solving more than one of our issues with a single blow."

The doctor pulled his watch from his vest pocket and consulted the red-glowing face. "In fact," he muttered around his smile. "I believe someone who could shed further light on that very subject is due to arrive at any moment now." He twisted around, nodding to Vlad before addressing the woman beside him. "Miss

Mimms, if you would be so kind?"

Without a word, Misty moved from her station by the wall and went to the door, opening it silently.

On the other side, revealed as the heavy slab of dark wood slid open, stood the dusty and battered figure of Virgil Earp.

*****

Virgil's skin crawled as the door swung silently open before him. He had almost managed to convince himself this inevitable moment would never come. But from the moment he had fled Tombstone and turned his back on his brother to beg Carpathian to repair his devastated arm, something in the shadows of his heart knew that he would return to Payson one day, as just another creature of the damned European.

He could only hope the price he would be called upon to pay would not undo all the good Wyatt and the rest of the lawmen had accomplished.

As he stepped into the room, Virgil kept his back straight and his gaze steady. A throng was gathered at the far side of the room, arrayed down the length of a large banquet table. He recognized many antagonists from down through the grim years, and it became easier to maintain the slight sneer he decided was the most fitting expression for this darkest moment of his life. He had to maintain as much dignity as he could.

Carpathian's pet four-flushers and shysters all stared at him with open hostility. Edison, in particular, looked like someone had pissed into his beer. Eiffel looked distracted, as always. And the bloated form of Kyle, called 'The Black', was almost comically wedged behind the table with those grotesque mechanical claws waving over his head. A newcomer, a thin man with curly, elaborate facial hair and a bowler hat with far too much ironmongery riveted to it, stared at him with a look that a lifetime of lawman's instincts told him meant nothing good. Two other men he was unfamiliar with looked confused and startled, although the large brute with the muttonchops had an aggressive set to his broad shoulders that sent warning bells off in the old lawdog's mind. Behind the brain-trust stood their army of blowhards and sycophants, a wide range of expressions passing across their faces.

Sitting on the nearside of the table, Virgil saw the twins, violent, German scum who had caused untold havoc as they rampaged across the territories. He knew they were each wanted for more murders than you could count on both hands...

As the thought came through his mind, Virgil looked down at his right hand. The crude iron arm Carpathian had given him had served him well, despite the tension it had created between him and his brother. But it was not his, and a day never passed without a keen reminder of what he had lost, and what he had given up to replace it.

Virgil shook his head and continued to glance up the table. Nearest him, facing away and only turned to reveal a quarter-profile, was a stately woman in an ornate white gown that looked out of place amidst the frontier fashions, long white coats, and men's finery in the rest of the room. The woman's profile was stunning, and his brain froze for a moment at the twinkle he saw in the corner of her brown eye.

"Marshal Earp, thank you for joining us." The words snapped Virgil back to the dark present, and he looked to the head of the table, his gut twisting behind his gun belt.

Carpathian was sitting in a chair that could easily have been confused for a throne. Given how grand the rest of the room was appointed, it was obviously the effect he was striking for. The Great Man was sitting back casually, master of all he surveyed, chin propped on one metal-braced hand, elbow on the carven arm of the chair. His smile was almost enough for Virgil to draw his UR-30 Blaster and end the charade right there. If they hadn't taken his grenade launcher at the front door, the massive weapon that Wyatt had laughingly named The Gift, he might have turned his back on this Faustian bargain then and there, and blasted them all back to Hell.

But more than his own pride was at stake. His family name, and the legacy Wyatt, Morg, and the rest had worked so hard to build, was on the line. Virgil could not afford to indulge himself in a suicidal purge, no matter how good it would have felt.

Behind Carpathian crouched the big, hairy brute of a soldier that never wandered too far from the doctor's side. The man most of the hardened folks of the territories knew as Ursul stared at him with dark, piercing eyes. Somehow, Virgil knew that the man had seen the thoughts ticking through his mind, and realized that he would never have been able to skin his blaster from its holster, even with the added speed of his mechanical arm, before the old soldier burned him down where he stood. It was a sobering thought, and one he knew he needed to keep in mind.

Virgil finally looked at the last person in the room, and his breath caught in his throat. The woman was beautiful, despite the mask that hid the right side of her face. In her tight-fitting trail gear, she looked more like some dancehall character than a fitting addition to this nest of vipers. But the woman's eyes were hard and cold as she met his gaze, and he reassessed his original impression. She might seem soft and lithesome, but she was as much a killer as the rest. Although there was still something about the girl that caught in his brain... and was there a nervous twitch, there, at the corner of her steady eye?

He could not shake the feeling that he had seen her somewhere before...

"Marshal Earp, if you would care to take a seat?" Carpathian once again dragged Virgil's mind back to the dark moment at hand, and he reluctantly dropped down between the mysterious woman in white and Carpathian at the head of the table. The lawman took his hat off as he sat, resting it on the gleaming wood of the table before him.

"I came, Doctor. Say yer piece." Virgil knew he had no room to negotiate or maneuver, but that did not mean that he would meekly bow down before the black destiny of the moment.

Carpathian seemed amused by Virgil's response, and a chill settled down his old back as he realized just how vulnerable he was, here.

"Marshal, please." The smile warmed, but Virgil was not

fooled. Carpathian could afford to appear magnanimous in the center of his power. It carried no reassurance. If it came time to shoot or drop iron, Virgil knew he was done for.

"I have asked you here so that I could thank you for your most recent services." Virgil looked away. He had been passing along harmless-seeming information on Union movements and the attitudes of townsfolk ever since the doctor had replaced his arm. The Union had denied him the medical help he needed despite all the work his family had done for them. He felt no guilt, passing along that information. But at some level, Virgil knew the information about the townsfolk, about their attitude toward the Union and Carpathian's Enlightened, and their own plights here at the back end of nowhere, was more of a betrayal of his family's legacy than all the rest combined.

"I would like to take this opportunity to reaffirm that you have been asked to do nothing that worked against your family's best interests?" The doctor's hand waved before him, as if granting some boon upon a peasant. Virgil's jaw tightened, but he nodded. There was nothing else he could do. Carpathian's smile widened.

"Excellent." The man nodded to the rest of the table, and the assembly nodded mechanically in turn.

Carpathian looked back to Virgil, leaning forward, his face realigning itself into a more reassuring configuration, his eyes softening. "Marshal, it is important that you believe what I am about to tell you. The future of the entire continent depends upon it."

Virgil's stomach gave another sickening heave. He swallowed the sour bile down, and jerked his head in a single, violent nod. Out of the corner of his eye he could see that the monsters around the table were staring at the doctor, clearly eager to hear what the man had to say. Whatever was happening, Carpathian was being true to form, indulging in high drama, and his posse of twisted flannel mouths were learning about this scheme at the same time as Virgil himself.

"You must understand our ultimate goal, Marshal, to understand why we do what we do." The man's face was severe, his hands splayed on the table before him. "We are concerned with the freedom and wellbeing of the common people of the land, first and foremost."

Virgil snorted before he could stop himself. Carpathian and his clan had killed just as many innocents as any of the other outfits tearing the territories apart between them. And none of the rest of the factions bothered to raise the poor pie-eaters up from the dead after they were murdered.

Carpathian raised a placating hand, nodding in rueful agreement. "I know, I know. Our work has often redounded to the detriment of the common people." The man seemed genuinely sorry, and Virgil had to force himself to remember all the crimes that were laid at the doctor's feet. There seemed to be less than universal agreement with the sentiment around the table. Some, like the strange, dark-skinned woman in white, smiled in genuine amusement.

"Often, in our pursuit of the most enlightened path for humanity, we lose sight of the cost upon the common man." Carpathian shrugged. "It is a fault not uncommon within the scientific community throughout history, I'm afraid. And yet, I assure you, our ultimate goal should not be doubted."

Virgil managed to repress his reaction this time, but he made no attempt to hide his skepticism.

"Marshal, let me approach this from another angle, perhaps." Carpathian looked up at the ceiling, his fingers drumming on the fine wood of the table. "Has the Union been a good steward to the men and women of the territories?"

The churning in his gut hardened to an icy anger. Even though he knew he was being manipulated, Virgil refused to deny his own convictions regarding the leadership in Washington. "You know it ain't."

Carpathian nodded. "And do you truly believe that the men of the Union, specifically men like Ulysses S. Grant and President-in-perpetuity Johnson, have the best interests of the common people in their hearts?"

Virgil had never met Grant or the president, but he had seen the results of their policies within the territories. They pursued their vicious, selfish agendas throughout the west, and spent no effort to help those wronged in that pursuit. Hell, it was like pulling hen's teeth to get them to cough up a red cent for the Marshal's Service.

"You know I don't." Virgil's anger with the Union government, raw and bloody in the aftermath of his maiming, had made him vulnerable to Carpathian's manipulation during their negotiations for his replacement limb.

"Do you believe that another party, perhaps outside of the traditional leadership of the Union, might better serve the common folk?"

Virgil started to nod, and then stopped, caught by surprise by the laugh that rose up in his throat. "You mean ya'll?" He gestured to the mismatched crew around the long table, each face a mixture of confusion and irritation. "Ya'll are gonna be the new lords of creation? Rulin' the rest of us poor sods from your mansion here in the Tonto?"

Carpathian was quick to shake his head, a look of annoyance flashing beneath the calm, kindly facade. "No. It is important for you to know that we do not seek to rule. We seek a stable environment from which to assist the growth and wellbeing of the people." Virgil did not miss the looks of misgiving and rejection that flashed across several of the faces around the table. Not everyone, it seemed, was completely convinced that they did not want to lead in this brave world the doctor was conjuring up.

"We seek only to usher in an age where our work can best benefit the innocents most adversely affected by Washington's careless disregard and draconian, imperialist policies." The doctor's face was so sincere, Virgil forced himself to stifle the laughter again rising in his throat.

"And you do this by diggin' up the bodies of folks' loved ones, slappin' guns 'n knives on 'em, an' drivin' 'em into fights to get shot up and burned down by anyone who don't agree with you?"

Carpathian's eyes hardened. "Nothing we do is illegal, I assure you, Marshal. And would you rather the forces of chaos that run rampant through the territories, from the savage, to the road agents, to the minions of Washington, be allowed to do so with only the Marshal's Service to stand between them and the innocents that call these dry, inhospitable lands their home?"

Virgil stared at the doctor in silence, and then turned his eyes upon each of the scientists sitting across from him. Each of them looked as if they had swallowed something bitter. He sensed where this was going, and he thought they must as well. Their expressions, more than any words of Carpathians, made him think there might be some truth to what the madman was spouting.

"You saying you want to work with the Marshal's Service?" The words were heavy with scorn and disbelief, but he was brought up short when Carpathian shook his head in sharp, immediate denial.

"No, Marshal. We will not work directly with your brother's forces, any more than I believe Wyatt Earp would be willing to stand shoulder to shoulder with me." He tilted his head down as he continued. "But I suggest something of an alliance of convenience. You will assure your brothers that we mean no harm to the lawful status quo within the territories, that we work toward a stable nation where laws, the laws your brother is so enamored of, will truly be upheld and affirmed; not the laws of Washington, but the laws civilized men have agreed to abide by for thousands of years. We will work in our way, and you shall work in yours."

Carpathian's heavy gaze fell upon Virgil with the force of a sledgehammer. "You will convince Wyatt Earp that we are not his enemy; that our agents moving through the western territories work with the same overall goals as the marshals themselves. You will convince your brother to stay out of our way."

Something within Virgil's chest snapped, and a flood of ice melt rushed through his veins. There was no negotiation or compromise in those dark eyes. Virgil Earp had arrived, at long last, at the final destination of his ill-fated choice to accept the doctor's assistance in that dark moment long ago.

"He won't listen." The words sounded dead in his own ears. "He'll disown me if I push it too hard. I can't."

"You have no choice, Marshal Earp." The iron in the tone was clear. The faces across the table had settled into surprised, delighted excitement as the doctor's intention became clear. "You will see to it that your brother and his deputies stay well clear of my forces from now on. I assure you, I have been nothing but honest with you today. But whether you believe my intentions to be pure or not, you have no choice. You will do everything in your power to further those intentions." A cold, stony smile formed on the doctor's face. "Unless you would like to relinquish your arm, and languish in my mines for the rest of your short, miserable life?"

Virgil looked down at the clenched metal fingers of his right hand. The fine mechanisms of the joints squeaked slightly at the tension. A sudden, stabbing pain flashed through his numb mind, and the arm twitched as he watched.

"And should thoughts of betrayal cross your mind, Marshal, remember, please, that by accepting that shiny limb, you accepted my intrusion into your body and mind." The dark eyes were burning over the cruel smile. "Any act of betrayal will be met with the most terrible pain you have ever imagined."

Virgil's eyes lost their focus, the arm and table blurring before him. The pain had subsided, but he would never forget its cold invasion, nor the man who had caused it. Deep within the frozen chill settling into his heart, a burning anger began to smolder. He was Carpathian's creature now, as surely as Wyatt had told him he would be. But nothing lasted forever...

"In addition, Marshal, I would greatly appreciate your further assistance in another endeavor." The doctor's voice was casual, but a certain roughness caught his attention, and Virgil cocked one bushy eyebrow at the madman. "A certain well-known person of interest is currently at large within the territories. A well-known outlaw of no small reputation...?" The old man shrugged. "Perhaps, if you could see that the Marshal's Service made more than a casual effort in finding and apprehending Jesse James..."

Virgil barked a quick, bitter laugh. "You lost your tame killer, doc?" He enjoyed the flash of annoyance that crossed the old face. "You want we should do your dirty work for you?"

Carpathian's flat eyes turned cold. "Keep your eyes open, Marshal Earp. If you should find the man, bring him to me." There was no soft negotiation or cajolery in the voice now.

Almost as if a switch had been flipped, Carpathian was all casual smiles in a moment. "Marshal, if you would do us the honor, I would appreciate you perhaps taking the place beside Vladimir, for the next portion of the meeting?" The cool, condescending tone hurt almost as much as the sliver of ice that had slid into his mind earlier.

Virgil rose slowly, not meeting the gloating eyes of the creatures arrayed across the table, and moved around Carpathian's enormous chair. As he slid past the woman in the fighting leathers, he felt again that sense of familiarity, but in his own misery, he could not care to dig. He turned as he came up beside the man he knew as Ursul, and was surprised to see a brief flash of pity in the man's eyes before he looked away.

"Ladies and gentlemen." Carpathian addressed the room again, as if the display of his power, and Virgil's humiliation, had not occurred. "Many of you have wondered about the absence of Jesse James from our assembly. You further asked how we were to move forward without him." The smile widened as he sat back, gesturing widely to the room at large. "You felt perhaps we had wasted our time and effort, I know." He turned to look at the man standing beside Virgil. "I know, Vladimir, that you felt our assets in the south were going to waste."

Carpathian rapped on the table once with his knuckles, the sound echoing through the wood-paneled room. "There is one more guest lacking from our little assembly, my friends. And I think his appearance will answer all these questions and more."

The door swung open once again, revealing a man standing there, a dark, dusty overcoat of indiscriminate color draped over gleaming steel. An ornate suit of articulated armor chased in a bright metal that might actually be gold sat over a brown shirt, and more plates of armor were fastened over tan trousers. A massive RJ-powered pistol sat in a custom holster on his right hip, while an ornate scabbard held a cavalry saber whose hilt featured several glowing indicators and vents. Unruly dark hair swept down over mischievous, flashing eyes.

Behind the man stood another figure, much taller and broader, with a gnarled, craggy face held in a permanent sneer. The man's dark clothing was obscured by bits and pieces of salvaged armor and a rig of belts and buckles that held an array of weapons, including a brace of heavy blasters, several knives, and at least two grenades. A goatee encircled the contemptuous mouth, while his own dark hair was held in place by the goggles that rode high on his forehead. The man carried an enormous rifle casually in one hand.

Virgil did not recognize the men, but the sudden tension in the room was unmistakable. Many of the members of the brain trust surged to their feet, hands reaching for weapons. Beside him, Virgil felt Ursul move, and saw a glittering knife appear in the man's clenched fist. Kyle the Black pushed at the table, freeing himself even as the claws over his head flailed eagerly. Other knives, blades of various lengths, and pistol barrels stabbed across the table at the pair in the door. Down the table, the Kaufmann brothers jumped up, steel flashing in their fists.

The big man with the goggles crouched down, the rifle coming up to pan across the room. His eyes were hard as his nostrils flared. Virgil saw the desire for bloodshed plain in the man's face. His own pistol remained holstered against his screaming lawman's instincts, for reasons he did not wish to investigate at that moment. He saw, as he scanned the room, that the woman in white had not drawn a weapon either, her slight smile unwavering. Because she knew this was going to happen, or because she truly did not fear the violence that hung in the air? Who was she, anyway?

Aside from Virgil and the woman, only Carpathian and the man in the long coat had not reached for their weapons. The man in the door folded his arms over his gleaming armor, muttering something over his shoulder with a mocking grin. The bigger man spat a low response that Virgil could not make out, but then lowered his enormous gun as the armored man nodded.

"Ladies and gentlemen, if you would be so kind as to lower your weapons," Carpathian's face wore the expression of a man whose highest expectations for the moment had been met. "I do believe it will be easier to conclude the business of this assembly without all the cutlery and firepower in evidence?"

Beside Virgil, Ursul tightened. "You expect us to velcomezis beast into our midst?!" The man's accent was thick, but did nothing to obscure the anger or hatred that coursed beneath the words.

Carpathian turned, putting one hand out in a calming gesture. "Vladimir, I know. We have had our differences with Captain Wayward in the past—"

Ursul's face paled at the words. "Differences?Ze man burned down half ze town! He—"

"Hardly half, there, Ursul." The man Carpathian had called Wayward, his grin still wide, rose up on his toes and sank back down again. "I'd say, what, about a quarter, Jake?"

The man behind Wayward nodded once. "Woulda been more, if we hadn'ta been interrupted."

The tension rose again, and again Carpathian raised his hands, shooting Wayward a look. "Captain, please?"

The man in the coat put one hand out, palm down. "Sorry, Doc. Habit." Over his shoulder he tossed another comment, "Jake, enough."

"You got it, Cap." The man settled back on his heels, cradling his gun in a way that made it obvious he could bring it up again at a moment's notice.

The newcomer sauntered forward and dropped into an empty seat, his grin firmly in place. Virgil knew the type. He'd arrested countless such braggarts in his day. This man, Wayward, was full of himself, and only meeting a bigger, badder curly wolf was going to cure him of it. He watched the man scan the room and stop at the leather-clad woman behind the doctor, his eyes drifting up and down appreciatively, ignoring the heat of her re-turning glare.

Something told Virgil that the mercenary was going to re-gret taking that liberty some day.

"What is the meaning of this ludicrous display, Doctor?" Somewhere, Edison had found his voice, and the strength to con-front his mentor.

Carpathian stared for a moment at Wayward, then forced a mild laugh, leaning forward and resting one forearm on the ta-ble. "Straight to the point then, eh Thomas?" He nodded. "Fair enough."

The doctor rose to his feet, one arm swinging out in a dra-matic gesture towards the grinning mercenary. "My friends, please allow me to introduce you to the next president of the Confederate Rebellion."

The room erupted in chaos and anger.

Chapter 7

The wet cobbles of the alleyway were slick underfoot, and F.R. was forced to spend more than his usual amount of attention to where he put his feet as they walked from the Bank of London offices toward the Alexandra Docks on the far side of the Derby Road thoroughfare. Behind him, lost in his own thoughts, Ernest walked along, his own footsteps echoing off the brick buildings to either side.

"I still don't understand." The New Zealander's voice was muffled as he spoke at his shuffling feet. "How could it have burned down? What about Hugo?"

The numbness F.R. had felt since his last night in Paris had not faded in the slightest with the passage of time and distance. It was almost as if, with the death of his mother, something inside himself had perished as well. More and more, his mind was fixated upon crossing the Atlantic and finding his father and uncle, as if those two men could make sense of what had happened. The news, communicated to them by the concerned clerk at the bank, that 52 Rue de la Federation had burned down, leaving two bodies, assumed by authorities to be the lady of the house and her son, had hardly made an impact.

"The money was there, so he managed to do that, anyway." F.R.'s voice was cold. He felt a small twinge of shame, knowing that the loss of his childhood home, and the disappearance of the man who had all but raised him, was having a more profound impact on his friend than on himself. But he could not force himself to care where his heart felt nothing, and so he shrugged, continuing along his chosen path.

"But, I don't understand." Ernest repeated as he hurried to catch up, pulling his short coat more tightly around himself against the Liverpool chill. "The bodies were still inside... that means it happened right after we left! And the Sûretéthinks it's you and your mother in there? How would that happen?"

F.R. stopped and turned toward Ernest. His friend recoiled from the chill in his eyes, and again the small shiver of sadness passed over him, that he could not bring himself to care. "Ernest, what does it matter? My mother is dead, the man who killed her is dead, and now the Sûretébelieve me dead as well, and so will not pursue us. Hugo Digne is a grown man, quite capable of taking care of himself, and so I feel no particular need to expend further energy in worrying for him. There was no further report of other bodies to be found. He's probably fine."

"But why has there been no further word?" Ernest would not let it go, and F.R. felt his anger rising. "If Hugo is fine, why not a word, after he put the money into the account in Paris?"

F.R. spun around, lunging forward, his hard fingers closing over Ernest's lapel, seizing him, and turning to shove him hard against the dirty wall of the alley. His friend's breath gusted from his chest as he winced with the pain of impact. He leaned in, feeling the snarl sweep over his features, and not caring at all.

"I am leaving this cold, wet, miserably little country, Ernest. I am going to America, where I will find my father and my uncle, and take my place by their side." His grip tightened, gathering the fabric in tight, groaning knots. "You are free to accompany me if you wish, but if you burden me with your maunderings, I will leave you behind in the blink of an eye."

F.R. lowered Ernest back to the cobbles, his hands loosening from the coat with a series of clicks and whirs. He brushed out the bunched wrinkles gently, and patted the other man on the shoulder. "I am sorry, Ernest, but that is the reality of our situation. Nothing behind us matters to me now. All that matters is finding our new place in America. I truly want you with me, I do. But nothing can come between me and what is left of my family. Do you understand?"

Ernest nodded, his head bobbing with a nervous jerk. But there was a resentful tightening around his eyes, and he brushed at the front of his coat before stepping away from the wall and continuing down the alley toward the wide roadway ahead. "You have been under a great deal of pressure, F.R. And so I will not hold this moment against you." He looked over his shoulder as he walked. "However, do not presume that you can manhandle me that way again. I have friends all over the world, sir, and I can get by quite well with or without you, also."

They walked in silence, coming out onto Derby Road, where they had to wait for several large horse-drawn wagons to pass before they could cross the street toward the large bank of warehouses on the far side. F.R. noticed that a wagon coming toward them, carrying a heavy load of crates and boxes, was not pulled by horses at all. Instead, a smaller wagon was attached to the first, grunting and growling as it rumbled along, crimson glowing from vents and indicator lights along its stubby length.

"Ernest, is that an RJ-1027 powered wagon?" He pointed toward the vehicle, and the other man turned to look.

"Why, I believe it is, F.R." His friend spoke in cool, aggressively neutral tones. "We knew there was some RJ in use here in Europe. It's been a long time since you've traveled this far west, after all. That might be the largest such engine I have seen, however." He looked back at F.R., working to put the past unpleasantness behind him. "Have you seen anything like it?"

F.R. shook his head. "I've seen sketches from my father of even larger machines, of course, and heard stories. But all of my work with colleagues on this side of the Atlantic has been with much smaller quantities and less-impressive machines."

"Well, it looks like the future will eventually reach even these benighted shores after all." Ernest tried to marshal a smile for the cause.

The wagon grunted on past them, dragging the pallet of crates toward the warehouses of Albert Dock in Liverpool-proper, off in the distance. Soon, the street was quiet again, the clopping of horses' hooves and the sharp crack of drovers' whips replacing the harsh, guttural growl of the RJ engine.

"Come, Ernest, we need to secure our materials and arrange for them to be transported to the Celtic before the offices close for the day." F.R. crossed the street with a quick step, tipping his hat to a wagoner that pulled his team up to let them pass.

"How do we know the Celtic's destination is where we want to go?" Ernest followed after, jumping back up on the raised walk along the block of buildings. "Do we know where we want to go? I thought your uncle's retreat was in some dark and secret location, known to no one?"

F.R. chuckled as he came to yet another dark alleyway. He looked up and down the broad, well-lit Derby Road, and then moved into the darkness of the close backstreet."It's secret, yes. But I've been in contact with all sorts of folks in America, preparing for this day. One particular clockmaker, very eager to work with RJ, was especially helpful. Just a few months ago he provided me with some very detailed information on how to find Uncle Burson and my father."

Ernest looked up and down the street, then into the mouth of the alley, before shaking his head and following. "And you trust him?"

"I have since had the information verified through other sources. I have no doubt we will be able to find this fabled Payson without much difficulty. We will land in New York, and then se-cure passage westward on one of those monstrous Heavy Rail trains my father spoke so much about." He jerked a thumb over his shoulder. "Those put that little mule wagon to shame, I promise you."

The warehouses on either side of the alley stretched up into the gloom overhead, blocking out the sun and plunging the dank length of cobblestone into a darkness much more profound than the alley on the other side of Derby Road. The gloom of twi-light was barely enough to provide relief at the far end, where the sounds of the bustling docks beckoned them on, echoing and distorted by the high walls.

"And are you so sure they will be happy to see us?" F.R. turned with an exasperated snarl, but Ernest raised his hands to stave off another confrontation. "All I am saying is, we have more than enough money now, and you have contacts all over Europe. The Continent isn't so bad, is it? We could continue our work any-where. We don't have to go to America." He shrugged. "They have been telling you that you aren't wanted, after all."

F.R. looked at him for a moment, and then turned to continue on his way. "They will have no choice, Ernest. The ties of blood will be too strong for them to send me away once I am standing before them." He smiled over his shoulder. "And besides, is there anywhere else in the whole wide world that such work is being done? No." He shook his head. "We are heading to the Wild West, my friend. We will turn our top hats and bowlers in for Stetsons, and wrestle a new life from the dusty landscape like the frontiersmen before us."

"Well, 'ello, 'ello, 'ello." The gruff voice echoed out from a side alcove completely shrouded in shadow. In the dim light F.R. stopped and turned toward the sound, an anticipatory smile sweeping over his face. He had been sticking to the dark alleys all afternoon, weaving his way through the darker Liverpool neighborhood of Bootle, waiting for just such a greeting.

"You lot off to the colonies, then?" There was a hint of movement within the shadows, but nothing definitive that F.R. or Ernest could have acted upon. A low shuffling seemed to indicate that there was more than one person emerging into their alley, but they could not be sure in the gloom.

A different, high-pitched voice, broke in. "Oit'ink we should give 'em a send orf, Sydney, wot?" At least two of them, then.

There was no doubt in either young scientist's mind that they had fallen under the scrutiny of the more unsavory elements of the port city. But where Ernest, despite his athlete's body and years spent on the rugby paddocks of his youth, did not cherish the kind of confrontation he now knew was in the offing, F.R. had been actively seeking out just such a distraction for most of the day.

"We'll at least take their hats for 'em, I t'ink." The first voice, deeper than the other, was definitely moving toward them. Judging from the menacing chuckles coming through the archway, there were more than two.

Ernest turned to the dim shape of his friend and muttered to him. "No Death Ray."

The flash of teeth marked F.R.'s grin as he responded, "Of course not, old son. It's been packed away. And even if it hadn't, our spare clothing has. I'm not going to board the S.S. Celtic tomorrow morning wearing these fellows' guts as an overcoat."

"You ain't bordin' nuthin' tomorrow, old son." The man emerged from the deepest shadows, ducking down to fit beneath the keystone of the old archway. In the dim light it was hard to tell details, but he looked like he had the battered face of a habitual pugilist, the kind of man Hugo used to force F.R. to face on a regular basis in his youth, when he decided it was important for the boy to toughen up. The man was dressed in tattered dark rags, but thin chains were wrapped around his fingers, bulking out his fists and providing a real danger, should any of his blows land.

Behind the leader came three other men, none of them nearly so big nor so frightening in appearance. They spread out along the blank wall, and Ernest looked down the alley toward the fading light and the glittering of the wide River Mercey beyond. F.R. knew that his friend did not relish this kind of rough entertainment, but that he would not run, regardless. If he fled, the four ruffians would fall upon F.R., then alone, and Ernest would not be confident enough in his friend's ability to deal with such uneven odds to leave him to such a fate.

There was a great deal to be said for loyalty, at moments like this.

"I must confess to being in a bit of a quandary." F.R.'s grin had not slipped, and his flippant tone had to have struck an odd note for the men confronting him. The leader, in particular, looked nonplussed by the statement, his head tilting to one side as his nose wrinkled in a sneering smirk.

"Honestly, friend." His tone was so unconcerned, that the attacker hesitated again. "Should I use my pistol, and risk getting blood all over my friend and me, or should I refrain, and risk missing my appointment, should subduing you with my bare hands prove more onerous than I anticipate?" He drew a large pistol, making a comic show of trying to spin it around his trigger finger.

A nervous giggle escaped Ernest's lips at the words 'bare hands', and he quickly stifled the embarrassing reaction.

F.R. smiled broadly at his friend, and then shrugged, clumsily returning his weapon to its holster inside his coat and settling down slightly in a boxer's crouch, his arms rising, moving his gloved fists in tight, controlled loops. "Hands it is, then, I guess."

The brute leading the dingy crew shook his head, deciding he did not need to understand the mutterings of this foreign madman, and put his own fists up, scuttling forward with just a little more caution than he was used to.

Ernest took several steps backward, putting more space between him and the other three men in case they took it into their heads to attack, but it appeared they had no concern for him, and instead were watching their leader approach F.R. It was a situation for which the country boy from Spring Grove would be truly appreciative.

The big brute came in with his back straight, his hands weaving before his face and chest to distract F.R. and provide some defense should the stranger attack early. But F.R. had fought more bouts of this type than he could count. Hugo had trained him well, and he immediately recognized the error of the other man's form. He was standing tall, trying to intimidate with his height and bulk, which meant that his center of gravity was a touch too high.

A sharp jab to the point of the man's jaw drove him back with a pained cry, his nose and chin a bloody ruin. F.R. knew that it must have felt like getting hit in the face with a lump of iron, and he smiled at the thought. Even as the man stumbled backward, F.R. spun on one heel, his other sailing in to crash against the man's ribs, tossing him back against the greasy wall. He came down hard, his head striking against the bricks with a hollow sound that made his companions wince.

"I certainly hope that's not all." F.R. moved backward, giving the man room to rise if he was able. Either the catastrophic blow to the face or the impact of his head against the wall could have ended the fight too soon. The Romanian cursed under his breath. Was he going to have to go easy on these clouts, for even half a chance to work his frustrations out?

But the man was tough, growing up on the streets of a sprawling port city, fighting for every scrap of respect and opportunity he had been able to wrest from an uncaring life. He came lumbering up onto his feet in a rush, grunting with the effort and the pain, and charged with an inarticulate roar that echoed off the wet walls. The man's eyes were wide with insane fury, bright in the mask of blood and torn flesh. Big arms, chains clinking, swung back and forth in wild, haymaker blows. If even one of those strikes landed, F.R. was not going to be worrying about America any longer.

Ducking and weaving among the flailing blows, F.R. guided first one swing past him, then another. Stepping forward, he was soon inside the sweep of his opponent's arms, and the man was forced to bring his forearms in to protect his injured face as he stumbled backward, trying to escape.

But this time, F.R.'s target was not the man's face. First one piston blow and then another drove into the man's soft gut. Foul breath gusted out into his face as the man lost his wind, his backward stagger collapsing into an uncontrolled fall that almost fetched his head up against the wall again. The man's arms, already high to guard his face, flew back to brace against the wall, arresting his fall just as his leg twisted beneath him. With a delighted skip-step, F.R. moved forward and drove one iron-hard fist into the side of the man's head with a wet crack.

The thug settled into a loose heap of stinking fabric and disjointed limbs, no hint of life or movement visible.

The three remaining toughs moved forward in the gloom after a brief hesitation. The three men spread out to threaten F.R. from different angles, but the young man's smile only widened. He bounced on the balls of his feet, his hands loose as he shook them out before him, snapping them from the wrist.

"Excellent, gentlemen! Congratulations on finding the courage of your convictions!" There was no animosity in F.R.'s smile, his eyes were clear and friendly despite the shadows. But the three men saw this lack of hostility as an insulting challenge, and all hesitation evaporated in the face of their injured pride. With their leader still and silent behind them, all three charged at the same time.

The assailant on F.R.'s right was slightly slower than the other two, and so in less time than it would have taken to blink, he pivoted to the left, grin widening as first the center attacker, and then the man on the far left, reached him.

F.R.'s right arm lashed out to strike through the center man's upraised block and slap him, open-handed, in the forehead. The hit stung, but was not enough to stop the man's rush. The left that sailed in after it, however, balled into a tight, smooth fist, was another matter. The man was still flinching from the slap, and so did not see the strike hooking in until it was too late. The fist met his jaw with enough force to shatter the bone. The man's eyes glazed over as the side of his head deformed beneath the impact. His bloody teeth began a brief voyage across the alley, and by the time they were skittering along the cobbles, the man was lifeless, following his dentition limply to the stones.

Knowing the target was out of the fight, F.R. brought his left foot back to stabilize his stance, reeling his left arm in like the crank arm of a locomotive. Without pause, he drove his elbow into the left cheek of his next attacker. The man's advance ended abruptly, pulling up short against the terrific force of F.R.'s arm. There was a sharp crack as the man's head twisted on his neck. Without a sound, the man folded up, his knees buckling as he dropped to the ground.

The right-most assailant, seeing his two companions put down in a flash, tried to pull up and thus slid into the combat in complete disarray. His old boots skittered on the slippery stones of the alley floor, and he fell onto his back with a nervous cry. As F.R. approached him, the man scooted backward on his palms and heels, coming up against the wall beside the body of his boss.

F.R. followed swiftly behind the retreating man, standing over him as his back slapped against the bricks, his breath coming in ragged, desperate gasps. The young Romanian leaned down to give the man a clinical, scientific inspection, and then placed his boot on the soft flesh of his neck. With inexorable pressure, he stood, pushing the man down into the slimy cobbles, grinding his heel into the cartilage of his victim's throat. The man's eyes widened even further, his hands coming up to scrabble against F.R.'s ankle, fruitlessly scratching for a handhold.

F.R.'s eyes were cold as he watched the man's final struggles with a tilted, mildly curious angle to his head. With a last, horrible, choking gasp, the man relaxed, his eyes drooping to half-mast and his tongue sliding out between his stained teeth as his body slumped to the ground.

F.R. released the pressure on the man's neck and watched for a moment longer, then leaned down, one hand reaching out to rifle through the vagrant's pockets. Behind him, Ernest began to protest, but F.R. cut him off with a sharp word. "Enough." He shot his friend a look over his shoulder. "To the victors! Am I right, old son?"

Scuttling to the side in a low crouch, F.R. went through the pockets of the dead boss, as well, grunting in sour annoyance at the dearth of hard coins he found there.

Standing up with a sigh, F.R. arched his back, looking back to where Ernest still stood, knees bent slightly, by the far wall. "If you don't mind, Ernest, I'd rather not do all the work myself?" He tilted his head toward the last two shapes lying prone on the alley cobbles.

Ernest hesitated for a moment, torn between indignation and distaste. "Do you think such … ostentatious displays are wises, F.R.? We are in Detective Inspector Reid's bailiwick, after all." The London policeman had nearly caught the Romanian genius at the very beginning of his criminal career, several years ago when F.R. had discovered and then taken the place of a very prominent killer stalking the back alleys of Whitechapel. Fear of the redoubtable Reid had loomed large in Ernest's mind, he knew, from the moment Hugo had mentioned that their path must lead back to England. F.R. cocked a single eyebrow at his friend, however, and he dropped down quickly with a nod.

There was only a little copper in each man's pocket, but he collected it and stood, holding it out to his friend. F.R.'s grin was almost maniacal as he looked down at his handiwork lying sprawled across the alley floor.

F.R. looked at the offered coins, and then shook his head, his grin fading into a less-terrifying expression of amusement. "You can keep them, Ernest. I just didn't want them to go to waste. And I don't think this lot will have much call for their coinage any-more."

Slipping the money into his pocket with a slight grimace, Ernest nodded, stepping back away from the bodies. In the last glimmers of fading light, his face looked pale. This was the first time his friend had seen him face such overwhelming odds, and it had probably been almost as shocking as witnessing some of the more gruesome side effects of the impressive array of weapons they had created together.

"Well, Ernest, have I earned my Stetson now? Will I have to embarrass a squadron of American wastrels when we make landfall, do you think, or will this prove sufficient?" F.R. took his top hat off and spun it on one upraised finger while looking at it with a quizzical expression.

"I... I think you have more than proved your worthiness of a Stetson, F.R." He shook his head ruefully, unable to take his eyes from the men scattered across the alley. "In fact, you have probably earned yourself the right to wear one of those legendary ten gallon hats now, if you really want one."

F.R.'s laugh echoed off the walls that had only recently been host to the cries and groans of the defeated. "I think I'll stick with the common size, if it's all the same to you. Ten gallons is an awful lot of hat to fill." He drew his pistol from within his vest, and again spun it clumsily around his trigger finger, not quite able to bring the weapon through a smooth spin.

He looked at his friend with steady eyes, his smile, for the moment, faded into the background. "In all honesty, Ernest, I hope you have taken a useful lesson from this, as well as the obvious entertainment value. The world is a rough place, where the strong take from the weak. If we do not establish our position amongst the former, we will suffer the most melancholy fate of the latter." The smile disappeared completely.   "I   will not suffer that fate. I will do whatever it takes, no matter what is required, to avoid it."

With a last look down at his vanquished foes, F.R. shrugged and moved toward the sounds of the river and the last light of day. A more tame variation of his manic grin returned. "Come, Ernest, we still have business to attend to. The Celtic will not load herself, after all. And we will be of very limited value to my uncle and my father without our materials."

As the two young men abandoned their field of victory, the tall body leaning against the wall opened its eyes, the terribly agony of the raw gore-and-bone ruin of the face seemingly for-gotten, and watched them leave with a strange tightness around the eyes that hinted at grim amusement. The last glimmer of the setting sun cast a single, ruby beam from the figure's eyes before true darkness engulfed the alley.

Chapter 8

Vlad hesitated at the ornate doors, his fist hovering over the elaborate letter 'C', really not wanting to knock. Carpathian had been in a foul mood for days now, despite his wildly successful assembly a week ago. Since, however, his minions were not coming into line. None of them were happy to have the mercenaries who had devastated so much of Payson only a few months ago now welcomed with open arms into the doctor's plans. The constant bickering and in-fighting among the scientists had only grown worse as the woman from New Orleans and her mechanical menagerie had come to dominate so much of Carpathian's focus and praise.

The woman had finally taken her leave, a caravan of supplies, power canisters, and her strange collection of twisted animals in tow. The lot of them, with her enormous animations in their dancehall stage makeup manning the wagons in grim silence, had looked more like a circus than the vanguard of a new age. But before things could be allowed to calm down, this newest aggravation had once again reared its ugly head.

There was no way Carpathian was going to want to deal with this little dunderhead and his ham-fisted sidekick, but Vlad had been fobbing the lot of these haiduci off with vague promises and veiled threats for too long now, and if the doctor would not see this particular little tâmpit this time around, he had no doubt that there were going to be difficulties out in the plains soon.

Steeling himself for the reaction, Vlad rapped sharply on the door. Carpathian was alone, he knew, so he pushed the door open without waiting for a reply. It was something he never would have done had there been anyone else present, and even then, he probably would not have done it at all just a few months ago.

"What is it now, Vladimir?" The doctor was standing at the broad windows behind his desk, hands clasped behind his back as he stared down into the bustling valley far below. There was no anger or resentment in his voice, but rather the exhaustion of a man who was tired of the world failing to conform to his own ideals. If his brother-in-law was coming in unannounced in the middle of the day like this, the news was hardly going to make him feel any better.

Vlad stopped before the desk, his body snapping to a stiff, military pose that he retreated into when the guilt of passing along an uncomfortable decision was forced upon him by the chain of command. "It's VilliamBonney, Burson. He vill not be put off any longer." He knew that if he did not impose upon the doctor the urgency of the outlaw's request, there would be worse to be had down the road.

"I have been putting him off for months, and he no longer believes me. He demands to see you." Vlad shrugged. If the doctor denied him permission to kill the vermin, the doctor had to live with the consequences.

Carpathian's head fell to his chest and he shook it with a weariness that made Vlad wince. "These particular pestsare proving to be less and less useful, and more and more of a burden, with each passing day."

"Perhaps if you tell him somesing of your new intentions toward Jesse James?Zere has never been any love lost zere…"

"And risk him blathering that to James before we can contain him?" The doctor turned, a look of condescending disbelief twisting his face and erasing much of the guilt Vlad had carried into the room. "William Bonney cares next to nothing for Jesse James, aside from coveting the advantages I have already bestowed upon his rival. He wants the strength and speed of James' augmentations, nothing more."

"And you have no intention of giving him anysing of ze sort, zen?" Vlad thought as much, but wanted to make sure. Having one out-of-control outlaw roving the territories with unnatural strength and speed was bad enough. At least Virgil Earp, with one such arm, was being kept more in line these days. And of course, the doctor had established that he could turn off any of these RJ-powered augmetics at will, which went far to limit the advantages when someone like Jesse James might go against the will of his true master. But James had been a handful for years now, and Vlad had no desire to have to deal with another such creature now that they were about to put one mad dog down for good.

"Of course not! I'm not going to trade one untamed beast for another." Carpathian collapsed loosely into the heavy chair behind his desk, gesturing with a vague wave that Vlad should take a seat of his own. "Marcus Wayward is a far more manageable tool, all things considered, with his military discipline and the native strength of his convictions. We will work with him, place him in a position of authority to which he never could have aspired without us, and he will know by whom his bread is buttered. None of these more-common rabble would have ever agreed to such a civilized settlement."

Vlad grunted, but kept his thoughts on that subject to himself. Wayward had come close to bringing all of Payson to its knees. He scowled as he remembered the beating he himself had suffered. In fact, he found it hard to reconcile his brother-in-law's trust in the man, given that Wayward had beaten him, as well, and turned one of their missing ion pistols against the doctor, rendering him helpless at the hands of the grasping mercenary. Trusting such a man would never come naturally to Vlad. He still harbored strong doubts as to how Carpathian and Wayward had reached their secret agreement in the first place.

"Well, as distasteful as this will undoubtedly prove to be, I suppose you better send him up, Vladimir." Carpathian sighed. "Maybe, if I can convince him he's important enough, he'll leave us alone for long enough that we will be able to render even the illusion of his assistance moot."

Vlad nodded and stood. "He has zatdezgustător fat man with him, as vell. Should I send zem both up?"

Carpathian nodded despite the look of distaste that crossed his features. "Williamson. Of course he does. He seeks to intimidate me with the beast, no doubt. Show them both up, please, Vladimir, and we will see if I cannot tame both animals at once."

Vlad was nearly to the door when the doctor tapped the top of his desk with his knuckles. The soldier turned around, one bushy eyebrow cocked questioningly. "Please escort them, and share the displeasure of their company, if you will? And see to it that their damned hand cannons are left downstairs."

Vlad nodded, and closed the doors quietly behind him.

*****

"Doc, you have any idea how long this damned uppity little coot has been keepin' us downstairs, coolin' our heels?" The man that stormed into Doctor Carpathian's office looked to be just exploring the early years of his third decade, although the infamously invigorating effects of RJ-1027 exposure meant that he could be years or even decades beyond that. Those that spent every day in the presence of the wondrous material tended to live longer and look younger than people who did not.

Doctor Carpathian looked up from the papers he was vaguely holding in one braced hand. He nodded to Vladimir as his brother-in-law moved around the posturing outlaw, taking a seat in a darkened corner off to one side. Behind the boy known far and wide as Billy the Kid stood an obese bald man with a prodigious handlebar mustache drooping down on either side of his thick-lipped, rubbery grin.

"William, would you care to have a cup of tea? Or coffee, perhaps?" Carpathian did everything in his power to remain calm. Whenever these unwashed beasts came storming into his inner sanctum it was all he could do not to have his animations drag them to the basement laboratories to make an object lesson of them. He had been aiding and abetting the outlaw community of the western territories for decades, using them as his cat's paw against the Union, the Lawmen, the Warrior Nation, and anyone else that threatened to get in the way of his grand design. He had never, however, developed a taste for their company.

Now, however, the changing paths of the world seemed to be altering at a staggering pace, with the situation warping day by day. With Virgil Earp riding herd on the lawmen, and the Warrior Nation and the Union tearing at each other up in the north, and with his secret deal with Marcus Wayward providing for a more stable alternative to the volatile, still-missing Jesse James, he was realizing that depending upon the criminal element of the territories may well have been premature. Now, however, he needed to find a way to get rid of them that would not see the weapons and materials he had been provided for so many years turned against his designs just as everything was coming together.

"You know I don't drink that piss-water, Doc." Carpathian would not allow the grimace that struggled to twist his lip with its disdain to show. Billy knew that he disliked being called 'Doc', and had watched Jesse James discomfit him more than once in the past with just that tactic. It would not do to let him follow the same path now. "You got any whiskey?"

The smile that rose to his lips at that was far more genuine, and he let it show forth. "I believe I can accommodate your thirst, William. Would a local single malt do, or were you hoping for another taste of my Glenlivet reserve?" It would be much easier to handle Bonney if he could get him swinging drunk, first.

The wily grin was almost enough to convince Carpathian to have Vladimir kill the fat one and drag the little om de nimic to his just fate. Just how smart did the little gutter rat think he was?

"Oh, I'll take the good stuff, Doc." The smile never wavered as he dropped indecorously into one of the expensive wing-backed chairs.

Carpathian nodded to his brother-in-law, and Vladimir rose and moved wordlessly to the sideboard where he poured a generous three fingers of fine amber liquid into a gleaming tumbler.

"Don't you forget ol' Smiley, now!" The grin never wavered as Bonney twisted in the fancy seat, throwing one knee up over the sculpted armrest to toss a glance back at Vladimir.

Vladimir paused for a moment, his back to the room, and then, still in silence, reached out for another tumbler. Carpathian watched his majordomo with admiration. Vladimir had less use for the outlaws than he did, and it took a great deal of self-control for him to maintain his composure in the face of the determined antagonism.

Bonney nodded in ironic thanks as he accepted the glass. Jake Williamson only rumbled as his fat fingers closed around the crystal. He tossed the expensive whiskey down in a single gulp, and thengrunted as he gestured for Vladimir to take the glass away. The old soldier did so, his face a stony mask.

"William, if that takes care of the preliminaries, perhaps you could tell me why you have decided to once again grace Payson with your presence? There is a great deal in the works right now, and I am afraid I am particularly busy." He thought he did an admirable job of keeping his voice light and even. If he was going to require Vladimir to be a paragon of self-control, he should endeavor to do the same.

Bonney tossed a slug of the whiskey down, licking his lips as if had just tossed down a mouthful of common rotgut. "Well, Doc, I reckon you know why we've swung on by." He gestured with the glass at the doctor, squinting with one eye as if taking aim with a pistol. "You ain't exactly been straight up with me an' mine, you know. I do believe you might just owe me a bit o' compensation, and I been thinkin', I think I'd like to collect sooner rather than later."

Carpathian nodded, folding his hands together on his desktop and nodding for the outlaw chief to continue. "Well, Doc, it ain't been that long since you had me drive clear 'cross the country to pull Jesse's ashes out o' the fire down on the border with Reb territory. You were terrible sweet-tongued, tryin' to get me to jump down there an' lend a hand."

"And you have received a great deal of weaponry and equipment since then, have you not?" Carpathian could not remember exactly what his people had sent the little rat's outlaw band, and he knew it would not have been of the best stock, but it had to have been something substantial. "Is there something specific you would like to request?"

Bonney slouched further down in the chair, tapping the

empty glass on the wooden arm. "You know what I'm lookin' fer, Doc. It ain't right, we gotta compete with Jesse James and those devil-arms of his." He shrugged. "I'd like to have a taste of bein' the fastest draw in the west, you wanna know."

Behind Bonney, the fat bruiser grunted again, his wide smile unwavering. Billy nodded as if his friend had made a valid point. "It's time Jesse had some competition, Doc, and with everything you promised me, it ought to be me."

It was everything Carpathian could do not to flick his eyes toward Vladimir. Should he tell this little imbecile about James' bleak future? But no... he needed to keep all of these vermin at arm's length until he could dispose of them when it came time to consolidate his influence over the territories.

He was certain Virgil Earp would appreciate the chance to turn the Marshal's Service to the purpose, when the time was right.

"William, I understand your desire... but you yourself have seen firsthand the many difficulties that James has had with his augmented arms." He tried to sound reasonable, waving one hand in a calming gesture. "Do you really wish to open yourself up to that sort of grief? Perhaps one of the three wheeled vehicles you were so fond of—"

"No." Bonney's empty hand slapped hard wood. "You mean another one of those Blackjacks, as Jesse calls 'em, now? You told 'im he got the first one, hell, you even let him name the damned things, when you knowed damn well I had one first!"

Carpathian's smile grew strained, and he caught his brother-in-law's head drop, shaking, at the accusation. "Of course I did, William. Jesse has a fragile ego, as I'm sure you've noticed." Birds of a feather, after all. "I told him what he wanted to hear. You know you were riding one long before he received one. It was just as well, for me, that your paths had not crossed while yours was still functioning." The outlaws were notoriously hard on equipment, and the elegant three-wheeled vehicle he had given William Bonney had not lasted more than a few months, he knew.

But Bonney was not going to be pawned off so easily. "You might wanna give me another one o' them, Doc. Sure, that'd be sweet. But I want arms to rival that chiseler's, and I want 'em now."

Carpathian sat up straighter at the tone, noticing Williamson standing taller, his grin wider. Vladimir slowly eased a pistol from within his long coat. He was just about to indulge himself, when an unscheduled knock from the door caused Bonney to jump, and everyone turned quickly, tension rising again.

"Enter." Carpathian rose from his chair, his hands out in a placating gesture meant more for Vladimir than for the two outlaws.

The door opened smoothly, and Misty Mimms stepped into the room. Her mask gleamed in the warm sun streaming through the windows.

Carpathian did not know what it was about the woman, whether it was merely her beauty, scars notwithstanding, or the fact that she had once held Jesse James' heart and now hated him with equal measure, but he found her fascinating.

Bonney rose slowly, his eyes transfixed, and Carpathian felt a creeping chill across his shoulder blades at the look that swept over the outlaw's face.

"Doc, you been holdin' out on me?" Billy's smile was admiring as he moved toward the girl, his hand reaching out to grasp hers.

Misty's face behind her elaborate mask had settled into hard lines of dislike, and only grew stonier as the outlaw took her hand and raised it to his lips. Carpathian's own eyes tightened, and he thought he caught Vladimir watching the entire interplay carefully from his corner. Damn the man and his suspicions. The girl looked nothing like his dead wife.

The doctor's heart was warmed when Misty pulled her hand away from Bonney's grasp in mid-kiss. She sidestepped the nonplussed outlaw and approached the doctor as if no one else was in the room, her face composed to professional barrenness.

"Doctor, Smith has returned. The Nation is moving south." She indicated the outlaws with a tilt of her head. "And there's more."

More. More bad news, she meant, and the last thing he wanted was for William Bonney to know what sorts of difficulties were plaguing him at the moment. He nodded with a bland smile even as he cursed violently in the silence of his skull.

"Excellent, Misty, thank you." He gestured for her to have a seat while moving around the desk to take Bonney by the shoulder. "I am sorry, William, but urgent business calls."

The outlaw spluttered a bit as he was ushered toward the door. Williamson looked uncertain, one hand hovering over the massive cleaver in his belt. Carpathian maintained a steady stream of words to keep them both off balance; as eager to get Bonney away from Misty as he was to hear the news the girl had not yet revealed.

"If you are certain you are willing to undergo the difficulties and risks, William?" The outlaw nodded, still not certain what was happening. "Well, then, who am I to second guess a man of such courage?"

Vlad appeared behind Williamson, moving the enormous man toward the door with the sheer power of his presence. "Head west, William. Go to the old trading post at Tolchico. You have the sacred word of Doctor Burson Carpathian that I will send someone for you, and you will be brought back here for the full and total reward of which you are so richly deserving."

Bonney looked like he was trying to decide whether to smile or scowl as he was almost pushed out the door, Jake Williamson on his heels. Before the door closed, though, Carpathian nodded at them, and then turned to his majordomo. "Vladimir, could you please see our guests from the palace? And see that William receives one of the new production run of the tri-wheel vehicles, as well?"

As the door was shutting, all three men on the other side looking less than pleased, he could not deny himself a parting shot. "The new production run is perfection, William, and you will drive the first one beyond our city limits!"

The door clicked shut, and Carpathian bowed his old head, taking several deep breaths before turning, a casual smile firmly in place, and stumped to one of the chairs near Misty.

The girl's eyes were still hard. "I thought you were done with that kind of scum, sir." There was no room for confusion as to where her heart was set, where outlaws were concerned.

"Just a loose end, I promise you. The days when we need to entertain men such as William Bonney are severely numbered." He settled into the nearby chair, trying to minimize the impact of his braces on the movement of his limbs. "Now, my dear, you have more to tell me?" He sat down, trying not to notice her from-fitting leathers, or the curve of her full lips.

Damn Vladimir, anyway.

*****

Smoke from the large fire in the center of the longhouse rose in a solid-seeming column up to the vent hole in the leather roof. The atmosphere within the structure was heavy, many of the most important leaders and elders of the Warrior Nation crowded around the fire, their dark eyes gleaming in its clean light as they contemplated the future of their world.

In the center of the group, standing before the fire, was a tall man whose skin had a pallid cast layered beneath the dark complexion of the free people. His doeskin trousers and vest were humble and unassuming, and the few decorations and icons he wore featured long, flowing eagle feathers and the burnished claws of giant birds of prey.

"The Fire Eagles have once again proven their superiority over anything the wielders of the red fire can bring to battle." The man was tall, even among the imposing legends of the Nation, but his body was bowed, as if on the verge of collapsing. "But the cost is always great. They are few in number, and as you know, each that gives itself freely to the power of the Great Spirit must end by joining Him in the sky, and may fly no longer among the clouds of our world."

The man looked down, and it was clear that each such death caused him great pain. His sadness and fatigue were obvious as he continued. "My eagle warriors, fighting beside the Eagles, have prevailed in each battle, but they are beyond exhausted. The attacks are coming more and more frequently, leaving us without sufficient opportunity to recover from the great change between battles."

Arrayed before the tall warrior were a semi-circle of the most important men and women on the continent, including the most revered war leaders fighting against the hated easterners. Sitting Bull, first among equals and the man who had welded the disparate tribes together into the relatively unified force that it had become, nodded slowly, as if he had anticipated his friend's words.

"You must rest, Sky Spirit. Your efforts against the spawn of the European will be for nothing if you are too tired to rise when you are needed most. We will deal with these new flying constructs from the ground for now. From all I have heard, they do not yet pose a real threat."

Sky Spirit nodded. "They are slow and clumsy. But when they remain close to the ground, they can be effective. And they bear the same weapons as the spirit-less creations that fill the European's ranks."

"They are few, and ineffectual." A big burly man with thick black hair and broad shoulders grunted. The man's face was clouded with frustration, and he shook his head as if to stave off arguments that had not yet arisen. "We have been too long fighting in the east. All of our power is concentrated against the invaders, while we allow the European and his minions to pollute entire swaths of the Earth with their poison."

Sitting Bull sighed, looking down at broad hands that rested loosely on his knees. He did not look up as he spoke. "You speak the truth, as always, Goyahkla." The war leader the white men knew as Geronimo paused, his eyes tightening at the use of his tribal name. "But we cannot ignore the easterners now. The true danger to the Great Spirit is in the south, as you say. But until we can destroy the Union, those who pose the most direct threat to our people, we cannot ignore them to confront Carpathian and his minions."

"Despite the fact that they are the source of the poison?"Another war leader, whose elaborate headdress featured a sweeping pair of buffalo horns soaring up on either side of an arch of shimmering turquoise, slapped his own knee for emphasis. "This Enlightened Movement of the European's spreads the poison further with each day. We can well struggle against the Union for another score of seasons and prevail, only to find nothing behind us but the burnt and twisted landscape of our darkest visions."

Sitting Bull looked through a fall of dark hair without raising his head. "White Buffalo also speaks the truth." White Buffalo was a new type of war leader: one of a group of men rising in prominence within the Nation, who eschewed the metamorphosis offered by the Great Spirit in battle. Instead, they wielded the raw power of the Spirit itself, lashing out with the energies of the Earth in all manner of manifestations. White Buffalo and the quiet youth beside him, Grey Hawk, were the most prominent of this new breed, both having earned battle honors sufficient to gain them access to this chief's council, and their words were weighed carefully by the elders.

"There is often more than a single truth." Sitting Bull raised his proud head at last, casting his dark gaze around the circle before nodding to Sky Spirit to return to his place in the second ring. "The truth of the Enlightened cannot force us to ignore the truth of the Union. Most of our war parties are locked in conflict all across the eastern plains. We have very little strength to send south and west, and were we to throw those few we can spare into the desert without proper support, we would accomplish nothing against the Great Enemy but the deaths of our people."

A voice from the shadows spoke up, as a lean form pushed itself off a far wall. At the sound of the first words, Sitting

Bull's eyes slid shut like a man hard-pressed to keep his composure.

"My father dances around the concepts of truth and reality as has ever been his way, with the nimble grace of the medicine man he is, beseeching the Great Spirit for life-giving rain." The figure moved gracefully through the crowded press of warriors, leaders, and elders without a pause or hesitation in her smooth gait. When she stood before them all, her beautiful face masked by a strip of soft gray cloth, she placed her hands upon her hips and moved her head as if she were glaring at them all through the fabric of her blindfold.

Walks Looking was the daughter of Sitting Bull, and as such, would have been granted respect by the men and women around the fire no matter her own accomplishments. But from a very young age, it had been clear that despite her blindness, the girl could somehow see as well as any young warrior. This miracle of the Great Spirit had given her even more power within the Nation, and her near-constant opposition to her father, the great chief, war leader, and medicine man, had been a hardship he had lived with for many years now. The inevitable opposition to his work within the constantly shifting loyalties of the once-disparate tribes often coalesced around Walks Looking. Whether this was simply a natural offshoot of her own opinions, or by her own careful design, he had never been able to ascertain.

"We are beset in the east, pinned in place by the war machine of the Union. We are sorely tested to the south, as the European poisons the Earth with near-impunity. And here we sit, speaking in circles around the council fire, listening in rapt attention while my dear father dances."

The warriors around the fire looked uncomfortable in the face of such disrespectful speech. Even those leaders who still harbored allegiances to their ancient tribes, and resented Sitting Bull's prominence in the councils of the united Warrior Nation, saw the man as a figure to be respected and revered for what he had accomplished against the easterners and the other enemies of the free people. None of them would dream of addressing the great man in such a way before the entire ruling council.

But Sitting Bull was accustomed to his daughter's cutting tongue, and with a small, tight breath he maintained his composure and inclined his head up at the woman standing before him.

"Thank you for sharing your thoughts, daughter." Dark whispers had arisen around Walks Looking in recent years, of alliances with strange, western bands, and opinions regarding the evil red fire that went against everything the Great Spirit had revealed to the Warrior Nation since its great reawakening in Sitting Bull's youth. But the man had never shied from a challenge, or a difficult reality, and so steeled himself for the worst, and continued. "Do you have any suggestions, as to how we might be able to better use our numbers as they now stand?"

The full lips twisted in mockery, and the girl gave a shallow bow to her father as she laughed a soft, insolent chuckle. "We all know how you fear the red fire, father, so I will not broach that subject today." Did that mean the rumors were true? Was Walks Looking advocating, among certain, like-minded warriors, that the Nation stoop down to pick up the weapons of their cursed enemy? Sitting Bull shuddered at the thought. If the Warrior Nation could be corrupted as thoroughly as the Europeans, then the Great Spirit could well one day find Itself without any champions at all. But Walks Looking had continued her speech, and he forced himself to concentrate, fearing what she might have to say next.

"There are free peoples in the far west that have not yet joined your cause, father." She put one hand on her hip, standing with an insolent ease that touched a nerve in her father's chest. He forced the reaction down, schooling his features to a steady, placid mask. "Could we not solicit the aid of these distant cousins against the European?"

Sitting Bull's eyes tightened at the suggestion. For several councils, now, the Warrior Nation leaders had debated that very course of action. The free peoples of the far west, beyond the deserts and the tall mountains, had been slower to embrace the unification of the tribes, but with the growing power and consciousness of the Great Spirit, most had seen the wisdom of such a union. Among those who were moved to join their cousins in the great struggle were several chiefs who seemed on the verge of moving eastward, but as yet, none had opted to begin the journey.

"There are many great eagles in the mountains, Sitting Bull." Sky Spirit muttered. "Such a journey could be made to serve more than a single purpose."

The chiefs and elders around the fires nodded, murmuring agreement. They were facing an age old dilemma of too many fires on the plain and not enough water carriers. Beseeching the peoples of the west might bring them enough warriors to save the south, and the Warrior Nation as a whole.

"Such a journey will not be easy." White Buffalo said, his chin rising in a challenge. "The spirit people of the mountains have not stirred in many turnings of the seasons, but if they still walk their ancient paths, they may not take kindly to outsiders sharing those trails; even less so to an entire war party coming back in the other direction."

"The spirit people dwell within their mountain still." The growling rumble of another turquoise-bearing chieftain, with wide, feline eyes and a snub nose, brought the quiet susurration of whispered conversation to silence, White Buffalo yielding the council's attention with a tilt of his head.

The fire flickered deep within the almond-shaped eyes. The big war leader, Iron Tooth, came out of the great Rocky Mountains to the west. His people were the most familiar with the spirit people who lived there, and thus in any matters concerning those strange denizens of the high places, his word was always carefully considered.

"The spirit people come and go from their mountain fastness as they ever have. Our ancient pacts and agreements still stand, and so long as travelers upon the trails and passes abide by those, there should be no trouble."

The spirit people were an ancient mystery, even to the ancestors of the Warrior Nation. They lived in a massive fortress carved into the living stone of the mountains, and seemed to hold the Great Spirit in as much reverence as the free peoples. Venerable agreements between the free peoples and these mysterious spirit people had existed for many, many generations. The Warrior Nation held the spirit people of the mountain in reverential awe, and did not lightly trespass upon their territory in the high mountains.

"The difficulties of the passage this time of year will be in contending with the Earth, not with any of the people upon her." Iron Tooth looked to Sitting Bull. "The spirit people will not hinder our work."

Sitting Bull looked to his daughter, then back to Iron Tooth. "Can you offer any guidance in the west? Are there any war leaders, in particular, who might join us?"

Iron Tooth looked from Sky Spirit, to the still-standing Walks Looking, and back to Sitting Bull. "There are two war leaders of the western coasts who have sent emissaries across the mountains of late. In the cool northern coastal waters, Qwoli, chief Thunder Wolf, and Bayaq, the Raven Warrior, have sent word they wish to join us." He looked back to Sky Spirit. "Bayaq is a skin-changer such as yourself, flying into battle when the Great Spirit calls upon him. Qwoli is a great warrior, one who single-handedly destroyed an entire war party of easterners that had invaded their lands." Iron Tooth shrugged. "Together, they might command the strength of some thousand warriors."

Sitting Bull rocked back on his heels, his lips pursed thoughtfully. "A thousand warriors led by two such leaders could well turn the tide in the south, when combined with the power we could free from our struggle with the Union."

Walks Looking smiled a small, sharp-toothed smile, and Sitting Bull felt a chill run down his spine despite the fire's heat. "I will make this journey for you, father. I have always wanted to see the great mountains, and walk the paths of our cousins in the sunset lands."

The thought of his daughter being an emissary to these new warriors was an uncomfortable one, and her eagerness did not sit well with him. Still, there was no easy way for him to deny her the right, now that she had made her offer in open council.

"I, too, will go." Sky Spirit, hands on knees, would not look at the woman standing in the middle of the circle, but kept his eyes steadily on those of Sitting Bull. "I will have a greater chance of enlisting the aid of the great eagles along the way." He inclined his head toward Walks Looking without moving his eyes in her direction. "Together we should be able to bolster our forces such that we can challenge the European for dominance of the desert territories to the south."

Something happened to the smile on Walks Looking's face, and the chill in Sitting Bull's chest deepened, although he could not have said why. After a moment, he nodded, rising in one fluid motion, and moved to stand beside his daughter.

"If no one protests, then, may we assume that Sky Spirit and Walks Looking will make this journey at the behest of the Great Council of the Warrior Nation?" None of the leaders around the fire spoke, although White Buffalo and Grey Hawk exchanged a cold look that seemed to carry weight he did not quite understand.

When no objections were raised, Sitting Bull nodded again and gestured for Sky Spirit to join him. The three figures, silhouetted against the council fire, cast long shadows against the far wall.

"We shall entrust this work to my daughter, Walks Looking, and my good friend and ally, Sky Spirit, then." He looked to each of them in turn. "The future of the free people travels with you. We know you will do your duty to the Nation. May you return with our cousins in our time of need."

"Of course." Sky Spirit stood tall despite his exhaustion, his chin high and his eyes steady.

"Of course, father." Walks Looking stood tall and proud as well, but a gleam in her eye made him uneasy, nonetheless.

Chapter 9

The streets of Kansas City baked in the hot sun, and ripples of heat rose from the surrounding rooftops. Ernest Rutherford had not felt such heat since he had left his native New Zealand. He knew people around this part of the world were fond of speaking of a 'dry heat' when describing the hellish fury of the western territories, but he was still more than ready to turn back east at the first opportunity.

F.R. and Ernest had arrived in Kansas City, on the edge of the Contested Territories, by way of the massive Union Heavy Rail. The RJ-powered monstrosity was a revelation, given how rare the substance was in Europe. To see something he and F.R. had had to beg, borrow, and steal to acquire, now used so prolifically, would have hurt his heart if it had not been so awe-inspiring.

The Heavy Rail had travelled through a landscape that had been permanently altered by the technology of Doctor Carpathian, even though the government-sanctioned news flow to the rest of the world had shrouded that fact in mystery. Factories had gushed red-tinged smoke into the clear blue sky, while the smallest wagons glowed with a crimson gleam from vents and lights. Massive construction automatons worked ceaselessly to expand cities and towns along the flowing tracks, and leather-draped metal statues patrolled the streets, keeping the peace as the sons and daughters of the dawning century were sent off to war in the west.

The towns had gotten smaller as the giant train rumbled westward, with brick and stone giving way to rough-and-ready frontier wood construction. The view out the wide, glossy windows had gone from vibrant greens to the drab, dry tones of the desert that dominated the area around this last great metropolis on the edge of the desolation.

Ernest smiled out the window at his use of the word metropolis as the heavily-armored passenger car hissed to a stop, the titanic halls of the Kansas City Terminal swallowed the train, leaving the dust and the heat behind. The frontier city might be large compared to the other townships within several hundred miles, but by the standards of Europe, or even the east coast of the United States, the ramshackle architecture would have elicited nothing but contempt from him even a month before.

"Ernest, if you're quite finished gawking at the local grandiosity?" F.R.'s smile was easy as he hoisted his valise from the overhead compartment, grunting with the weight. Each of them had taken to carrying several weapons in their baggage in case they were set upon by the outlaws from the tales that even the government control of information could not curtail. The Death Rays and blasters weighed a great deal more than their frontier fashions and unmentionables, however, and carrying their heavy cases was getting to be quite a chore.

Ernest grunted as he pulled his own case down from the compartment. "Grandiosity, indeed. Other than this edifice to misplaced civil budgeting, I don't think I saw another building that broke three stories all the way to the horizon."

That easy smile widened, and F.R. nodded with a grunt as he lifted his case. "Well, we only need to stay here until I can arrange for our passage to Payson." He made his way down the tight aisle between leather-covered benches. "The crates will be handled by the freight office in the terminal. We can claim them after the rest of our travel plans are finalized."

The two scientists left the cool darkness of the terminal, their cases pulling on their arms, and trudged out into the dusty street. The rough wooden buildings rising up on all sides were all from a similar design; giant boxes with windows and doors, with fancy facades lending the only sense of individuality and style. Large signs with intricate, swirling lettering picked out in glowing RJ-powered bars of light proclaimed the purpose of each building. F.R. passed several saloons and hotels, sparing none more than a moment's glance before continuing his stoop-shouldered trudge across the dust. A steady stream of loud wagons growled down either side of the street, forcing them up onto the raised wooden walkways, away from the traffic.

"F.R., are you looking for anyplace in particular? I've seen several establishments that looked quite promising, given how long it's been since my last drink..." Ernest put his suitcase down for a moment, dragging the arm of his coat across his forehead.

The dark-haired Romanian looked back, rolling his eyes at his friend's lack of endurance. "We're not on a sightseeing tour, Ern. We've got people to meet and places to go."

Ernest picked up his case and hurried after. "I know, I know." He caught up to F.R. and rolled his shoulder with the strain.

F.R. continued along the walkway, looking at the signs on each building they passed. He had, indeed, traded his bowler hat for the iconic Stetson of this wild territory. He wore a long coat made of a lightweight material that covered his arms to the wrists, and leather drover's gloves that hardly attracted any notice this close to the frontier. He wore broad-lensed goggles tinted with a vermillion coating that rendered his eyes nearly invisible, floating in the red-orange haze.

Ernest forced himself to remain silent as they made their way across Kansas City. He was about to give in to the very human temptation to grouse some more, when F.R. stopped before a rundown old building whose fading sign graced it with the grandiose-sounding title, 'Arcadia Saloon'. A set of batwing doors, one of them slightly askew, swayed as if from a breeze he certainly could not feel.

"Here we are." F.R. turned the smile upon him, nodding his hat-graced head toward the darkened doorway.

A lively combination of odors assailed Ernest's nose as he pushed the creaking door aside. There was stale beer, of course, and sweat. He thought he caught the sweet undertone of vomit, and the coppery scent of blood that he would not have recognized had it not been for F.R.'s late-night forays into the violent criminal worlds of Paris, Liverpool, New York City, and various smaller towns between the great east coast port and their current location.

He did not want to think too much about why there might be a trace of blood in the air.

Within, the saloon was much like similar establishments he had seen across the world. A selection of mismatched tables and chairs was scattered throughout, while a long, beaten bar stretched across the back wall. A ragged-looking man stood behind the counter, wiping glass tumblers with a dingy rag of questionable cleanliness. Several of the tables hosted small groups of men and women drinking from similar glasses, often with a bottle or two close to hand, speaking in low, tired voices.

F.R. stepped in out of the sunshine and looked around the room, scrutinizing the occupants of each table before moving on to the next. He made no attempt to hide his inspection, and before he had finished glancing through half the room, conversation had stilled as everyone stared at the intrusive newcomer with the piercing eyes.

"Um..." Ernest dropped his valise and tugged at his friend's long sleeve. "I don't think your Eastern European directness is going to be the order of the day here in the Wild West, F.R...."

But the other young man hardly seemed to care. He found what he was looking for in a far corner, near a set of rickety stairs that led to an upper landing with multiple doors, probably rooms for rent, by the night or by the hour, if Ernest was any judge of quality. Sitting at the corner table, wedged behind its scarred surface with his back against the rough boards of either wall, was a tall man with a scraggly goatee. A metal-plated bowler hat sat on the table beside him.

As Ernest saw the bowler, he smiled, and almost directed F.R.'s attention to the hat, but his friend was gone, bulling his way through the annoyed patrons as if they did not exist.

"J.P. Smith, I assume?" F.R.'s voice was warm with familiarity, and the man reciprocated with a smile nearly as bright as he stood, arm extended.

"Indeed, sir! And might I assume that you are Master Caym?" The man's voice grated on Ernest's nerves, and he could not help but notice that he had been paid no consideration at all.

F.R. and this man, Smith, shook hands and sat down, talking excitedly to each other as if long lost friends. Ernest glanced around the corner. The man had left a pack against one wall, and an elaborate staff leaning into the corner itself. The six foot length of iron was covered in tubes, pipes, and glowing crimson jewels. It whirred as he watched, and he saw that through several cutaway sections, minute gears and wheels were visible, churning away on some imperceptible task.

"And please allow me to introduce my dear friend, and a scientist of no small note in his own right, Ernest Rutherford, of Spring Grove, New Zealand." F.R. clapped Ernest on the arm, bringing him back to the moment.

"New Zealand!" The man's voice was no more pleasant for all that it spoke the near-magical name of his beloved homeland. "Such a journey, to come to our miserable little neck of the global wood!" Smith reached across the table with a wide smile, and Ernest was forced to take it or appear like a churl before a man who seemed just this side of polite society.

"Yes, well, I left New Zealand several years ago, so the lion's share of the journey is so far in the past as to have no bearing." The man's grip was aggressively firm, although there did not seem to be a great deal of muscle behind it. As a rugby man since his youth, Ernest knew he could crush the man's digits if he had felt a driving need. He was almost ashamed at the sense of satisfaction the thought gave him.

"Sit, sit! I'm afraid there's not much to be had here in the way of civilized drink, but there is a passable whiskey, if you're of an adventurous bent." With another wide grin, Smith gestured for the barman, who hurried over with a dusty bottle and two additional glasses. He began to put his hand out for payment, but when Smith only looked pointedly at him, one eyebrow rising in a wordless threat, the man paled, nodded without a word, and retreated behind his bar.

"The commoners here will come to grips with the new world order soon enough." The conceited sentiment seemed particularly galling, coming in the flat twanging accent of the American east coast, and Ernest decided he really did not like the man at all. He did, however, sample the whiskey that was pushed his way with an ingratiating smile, and it was quite good.

"I assume that neither my father nor my uncle know of my impending arrival?" F.R. rolled the amber liquid around in his glass, smiling as he watched it swirl in his hand.

"Of course not!" Smith seemed offended by the question. "If it hadn't been for you, F.R., I never would have gotten into Payson in the first place! It has not been an easy secret to keep, working as closely with your uncle as I have been, finalizing the new enhancements on our Creation 5." The light in the man's eyes took on a strange cast that put Ernest off even the fine whiskey, as Smith leaned forward into his words. "You will be the perfect heir to his genius, if you don't mind my saying so, sir. When the Enlightened Movement takes its rightful place in the course of human events, your name will shine at least as brightly as his own! Your work in Europe, such as you have seen fit to allow me to peruse, is truly world breaking! Doctor Carpathian, when you unveil it, will be very glad, indeed, that you have seen fit to grace our poor shores with your presence!"

The man's drivel seemed to have no end, and Ernest expected his friend to crush the sycophantic worm with the casual cruelty he had always shown such men in the past. But instead, to his growing dismay, he saw that F.R. was actually lapping the pabulum up like a dog licking at a mess in the street. He felt something in his gut give a sick little twist.

"Are we staying here for the night, Mr. Smith?" Ernest wanted to curtail the mutual admiration society's meeting any further, and spoke without thinking. But as soon as the words left his mouth, he found himself fervently hoping that a night's sojourn in the Arcadia was not on the agenda. He had made it this far through the American wilderness blessedly free of vermin…He would rather not contract a case of scabies or lice this close to their final destination.

Smith laughed as if Ernest had made the best joke he had ever heard, which further put him off the man. "No, of course! The Arcadia's good for a noonday meeting, or carousing with the lower-classes, but it's hardly a fit establishment for the likes of you gentlemen!" The men and women in the room, already annoyed by F.R.'s entrance, looked even more irritated by these words. Several were reaching under their tables, and he would not be surprised if they were forced to blast their way out of the saloon if F.R. or Smith were allowed to rattle on for much longer.

"Gentlemen, if we're not long for the Arcadia, perhaps we should take our leave?" Ernest tilted his head, his eyes wide, to indicate the surrounding locals and their hostile looks. "If we have a long journey ahead of us...?"

Smith paused for a moment, nonplussed, and then nodded, his smile returning. "Of course! We should be on the road soon, or we won't make our first stop before dark."

The man stood and twisted to reach for the long staff, stooping to pick up his pack. "I have secured us an Ironhide wagon for the afternoon. It should be more than sufficient to carry your gear and material out to where I have one of Doctor Carpathian's Doomsday wagons waiting for us."

The Ironhide was behind the Arcadia, and followed enough of the design concepts of standard, horse-drawn wagons. It was vaguely similar to the RJ-powered mule tractor they had seen in Liverpool, although much larger and with a completely enclosed passenger cabin perched up front. Behind the cabin was a long, flat bed with raised sides that looked like they would probably come up to a man's knees, were he to stand within.

"Your material is with the freight office in the terminal, I assume?" The access doors of the vehicle were perched high up on the cabin, accessed by an iron ladder nearly the height of a man, situated between two tall wheels. Smith lifted his foot onto the first rung, setting his staff against the wagon's iron flank. "You gentlemen can go around to the other side and enter through there. The steering mechanisms will make it rather difficult for you to scoot across from here."

Ernest allowed F.R. to climb up first, and after a moment, followed into the cramped confines of the armored cabin. The air in the interior was searing, catching in his throat as he tried to breathe. A single long seat stretched across the entire chamber, its leather covering burning to the touch. Smith was already seated behind what appeared to be a small ship's wheel and several levers and pedals, obviously designed to control the vehicle. What little light there was slanted through long, narrow vision slits along the front of the compartment and set high up on either door.

Smith was hoisting his staff through the small doorway, angling it back to sit on a rack behind the bench seat, and turned around to smile at his two passengers as they settled in, Ernest closing the heavy metal door behind him.

"You might have noticed the mounting points outside the cab?" Smith was fiddling with several of the controls as he spoke. Ernest had noticed three large holes just forward of the doors on either side, so nodded. F.R. seemed far more fascinated with the controls, and was watching the man's hands closely, paying no attention to the words. "The doctor designed these rigs to carry heavy weapons, in case things got hot out in the desert." His smile was wide as he reached down and did something complex looking with a small lever. The grin grew mischievous. "The locals get uncomfortable when we flaunt our weaponry, so we generally dismount the cannons when we're near what passes for civilization around these parts. This particular vehicle is on loan to several business owners in Kansas City, so it hasn't had weapons for some time."

With one last twist of the lever, the cabin around them gave a lurch as a hellish sound roared up at them from underneath. The vehicle was shaking violently, and Smith grinned, shouting to be heard over the noise. "They aren't taking very good care of her, it would seem! Even these crude beasts aren't usually this loud!"

*****

As the Ironhide rumbled its way out of Kansas City, a tarp securely tied down over the crates and bundles in the back, Ernest craned his neck up to look out of the viewport at the run-down buildings of the city's outskirts rolling by. The engine had settled down a bit once they had run it for a while, but it was still too loud to comfortably hold a conversation, and he was just as glad. Not having to listen to their guide's voice was doing wonders for his disposition, and he found himself once again eager to be on his way.

F.R. had been fascinated with Payson long before he had ever met Ernest, and he had transferred that excitement to his friend. The tales of the place, of its manufactories, towers, mines, and palaces had become their favorite topics of conversation when working late in the lab. He also knew that Carpathian and F.R.'s father did not take security lightly, and so was intrigued to see how Smith intended to get them into the city.

"Oh, damn it." Smith spat the words so loudly that they were clearly audible over the RJ engine. "Dash it all."

Ernest shifted on the leather bench to look out the front vision slit, and nearly gasped when he saw what was blocking their way. A metal man, its surfaces burnished to a coppery sheen, stood before them in the middle of the road. A single blazing red eye glared out from beneath an incongruous Stetson, and the thing held out a broad-palmed metal hand in an obvious gesture.

"Damn it, damn it, damn it!" Smith muttered. The motor below them had dropped down to a hollow rumble as he fiddled with the controls some more, bringing the wagon to a slow crawl, then a stop, then reached around to unlatch the door. A gust of dusty air washed through that felt like a winter breeze for a moment, before the air equalized, and the misery returned with full force.

Ernest leaned over to F.R. who was also looking out the narrow window. "Is that what I think it is?"

F.R. nodded. They had seen UR-30 Enforcers during their trip west, but never this close. The automaton was a work of art, moving with the smooth, natural gait of a living man, pistons and gears glittering in the hot sun. On each hip the lawbot carried a massive blaster, although it had not yet bothered to draw either.

"We're not doing anything illegal, you infernal machine!" Smith jumped down from the cabin to the dirt street, his long coat flaring and a cloud of dust rising up around his feet as he stormed around the tall wheel and confronted the iron figure. "We're just driving down the street!"

"This vehicle has been identified as being involved in a grand larceny on October 11 of the preceding year." The machine's voice had an irritating, buzzing quality that set Ernest's inner ear itching uncomfortably as he opened his own door to look out.

"That was over a year ago!" Smith stood before the tall robot, looking up into its crimson eye despite his own not-in-considerable height, his hands on his hips. "I've just borrowed it for the day! You can't stop me because someone else used the damned—"

"This vehicle is being seized by the Marshal's Service under statute 34970-A22B." The machine stalked past the man, its head tilted upward to cast its baleful gaze at Ernest, hanging from the hatch. "Please exit the vehicle." One skeletal hand hovered over the grip of a blaster, and the young man realized that things might be more serious than he had first thought.

Ernest put both of his hands in the air, and then realized he would not be able to descend the ladder in that posture. He glanced to either side, and then with a slight shrug slid off the bench and into a fall, dropping heavily to the packed dirt and getting a cloud of grit in the face for his efforts.

"Sorry," his apology was automatic, from a lifetime of polite behavior. "Thought I had that."

As he stood, Ernest saw a flash of movement from the corner of his right eye. Someone was in the bed of the Ironhide, moving through the boxes, head down as if looking for something. As Smith came around the big wheel on his side, he realized there was only one person it could be.

"What does he think he's doing?" The tall man whispered

to him as they watched the Enforcer, now ignoring them, following the movement along the bed of the wagon. The blaster was now clutched in the thing's metal hand, tracking the movement.

"I have no bloody idea." Ernest muttered, not able to tear his eyes away from the drama unfolding before them. There were all sorts of weapons packed into the wagon's bed, and any number of them might be able to deal with a UR-30.

"If he attacks that metal moron in the full light of day, here on the streets of Kansas City, we'll be trapped here for days disentangling ourselves from the legal ramifications." The man leaned in close to whisper in Ernest's ear. "There will be no concealing your arrival, then."

Ernest knew that F.R. was hoping for an epic, dramatic revelation when they arrived in Payson, but he was not sure there was anything he could do about the situation. He shrugged, on the verge of admitting that he thought it was a lost cause, when a booming voice echoed from beneath a shadowy overhang off to their left.

"Stand down!" An older man, big, bushy mustache and loose fall of hair beneath his hat peppered with gray, stepped off into the dust. A glittering silver star was pinned to the man's flowing leather overcoat. He walked with the ginger pace of a man feeling his age, but he held himself ramrod straight as he addressed the lawbot now turning toward him, fugitive forgotten behind it. The thing slipped its blaster into the worn leather holster, and something about its stance seemed to indicate that it was no longer ready to spring into action.

Ernest looked from the newcomer, then to Smith, then back again. Smith was standing still, his eyes dark as he watched the man approach. His shoulders were hunched, his arms bent, as if not sure if he should run or fight.

As the lawman came up to them, Ernest was shocked to see that the man's right arm had been completely replaced with a metal limb, much like the robot's. Before he could stop himself, he flicked a wondering look up at the back of the wagon. F.R. was there, peering over one of the largest wooden crates, his hands hidden by his sides.

Smith gave a nearly-imperceptible nod. "Marshal."

The man looked like he had just swallowed a mouthful of rotten fruit as he stopped nearby, his hands on either side of his belt buckle, flesh and metal fingers in stark contrast. He did not return the nod.

"You're the clockmaker?" He spat the words as if they were a deadly insult.

The tall man straightened, pulling at the lapels of his coat, and nodded again. "I am.Or… I was." He straightened even more. "I am."

The lawman nodded, moved his head back slightly to spit a wad of dark fluid into the street near the broad front wheel of the wagon, and then looked the vehicle over with the keen eyes of an experienced gendarme. "You about his business, I suppose?" The man's jaw worked furiously as he spoke. It looked almost as if he were chewing on nails.

"I am, Marshal." Smith maintained his careful pose of indifference, but a cruel gleam flashed deep in his eyes.

The old man nodded again, gave the vehicle one last glance over, shading his eyes with his mechanical hand to get a good look at F.R., who tipped his hat from the wagon bed, then shrugged.

"Let 'em go." The man muttered the words in the direction of the UR-30, and the robot balked for a moment, standing still, then pivoted on one booted heel and strode away as if the encounter had never occurred.

The man looked up and down the street casually, without a care in the world. "You'll tell him."

Smith nodded, the cruel gleam erupting into a full, wicked grin. "I'll tell him you are following the letter of your agreement, of course, Marshal Earp."

Ernest jumped as he heard the name. He stared at the man in open fascination, then to Smith who nodded with an unctuous inclination of his head, and then back at the lawman, who was patently ignoring him.

"Tell him there's been no sign of his missing boy, neither. Nothing but rumors, anyway. The man's a ghost, lost in the wind." Again Earp spit into the dust. "And you might want to get rid of the wagon. It's going to catch their attention every time they see it. There are no permanent Enforcer units hereabouts, I've just got some with me as I chase the rumors. But the next one you run into, I might not be there to stop 'em."

Smith frowned. "I believe the doctor intended for greater protection than you, alone, could provide, Marshal."

The man's jaw knotted again. Ernest thought he could see a snarl lurking just beneath the man's calm face. "I'm workin' on it."

"Very well, then, Marshal. Thank you." The tone was more in line with a master speaking to a servant rather than a polite expression of gratitude, and Ernest figured that Smith had just gotten the lawman back for his watchmaker comment.

The legendary lawman stood stock still for a moment, his eyes swiveling to capture Smith's in an ironclad net, and then he spat once more and stalked off without another word.

With a wide grin, Smith gestured for Ernest to remount the vehicle, and then called for F.R. to join them. As he turned back to the passenger-side ladder, Ernest stopped the tall man with a sharp call. "Was that Wyatt Earp?"

The grin grew broader. "Wyatt? Hell no! If that was Wyatt, we'd probably be dead by now. That was his older brother, Virgil."

F.R. dropped with a grunt from the wagon bed, dusting off his coat with gloved hands, a wide smile on his own face. "He didn't seem too pleased with you, J.P."

The man in the armored bowler rocked his head up and down, the smile firming. "No, but he'll get used to it. Like I told you boys, the commoners will come around soon enough."

He slapped Ernest on the arm and then turned back to go around the front of the Ironhide, turning to call out over his shoulder. "This is a great time for you gentlemen to have arrived. It's a good time to serve Payson, that's for sure."

*****

The hour they spent in the stifling heat of the Ironhide's cabin was the most grueling of their entire journey so far. At one point, Ernest asked Smith if he could ride in the back with the cargo. The tall stranger gave a tight-lipped little smile and his blessing. Less than five minutes into their resumed journey, however, the young man from New Zealand was banging on the armored roof of the passenger compartment, heavy grit and dust clinging to his sweaty skin and coating the walls of his dry mouth. He crawled around the access ladder to clamber back into the cabin, miserably hot and now coated in a layer of sand.

He remained silent until they reached their destination.

The dirt roadway, barely visible through the narrow slit, turned right in a sweeping curve that came around a tall butte and revealed another armored wagon. Taller even than the Ironhide, this wagon's rivet-covered shape included a protected rear compartment for cargo or passengers, as well as a fighting platform on top, with a steel parapet all around. Two enormous Gatling cannons hung to either side of the vision slits, in the same location as the mounting points on their current transport.

The Ironhide grumbled to a halt beside the other vehicle, and with a giddy smile, Smith leapt down, reaching up to pull his staff out after him. "Come, we really need to be going!" He yelled for the other two men to join him, and soon they were standing behind the two wagons. Ernest looked up at the heavy wooden crates, then over to the small access hatch in the back of the new wagon. Back at the terminal, the cargo had been lifted up onto the Ironhide by RJ-powered cranes. Ernest looked out to the desolation all around them, and then sighed. It was going to take them hours to transfer the boxes.

"I know what you're thinking." Smith's smile was like that of a child with a delicious secret, and again Ernest was reminded of how much he had come to dislike the man. He wanted to slap him, or at the least share some biting words with F.R. at the man's expense. But his friend had grown more and more quiet as they travelled. His eyes were distant as he walked around one wagon and then the other, closely examining each.

Ernest gave up, shrugged, and gave Smith a sour look. "What?"

"You're thinking that you don't want to have to lift all of that heavy material in this heat, covered in dirt, and dry as a bone." The grin was now frighteningly wide. "Am I right?"

Ernest grunted. As far as he was concerned, the sentiment went without saying.

Smith's head jerked in a spastic nod, and then he struck the ground twice with his staff. The metal gave out a vibrating ring that seemed to move Ernest's guts in a disturbing way.

"Five, get out here!" Smith called out toward the new wagon. For a moment nothing happened, then the locking panels slid apart and the hatch opened, swinging like a set of double doors, and a nightmare creature peered out.

Ernest had heard a great deal about the animations that Doctor Carpathian had perfected during his time in America. He had seen the plans and the journals much of the early work was based upon, kept in the townhouse in Paris for safe keeping. He had even taken part in experiments with F.R. that used various body parts acquired through several less-than-reputable means, bringing them to life with an infusion of RJ-1027 for brief periods of time. Once, at F.R.'s insistence, they had even brought a neighborhood dog, struck by the iron-rimmed wheel of a ragman's cart, back from the dead.

None of that work had prepared him for the creature who had answered to the call of 'Five'.

The skull was enormous, the skin stretched across it pallid and slack, with a roughly-stitched seam running diagonally between its sunken eye sockets. The thing's left eye was a pale, milky white, while the right had been replaced with a metal contraption, a red orb glowing ominously from its depths.

The smell that hit Ernest as he gaped at the nightmare creation defied description.

"I know, I know." Smith bobbed his head as he approached the rear of the wagon. "You get used to the smell, trust me." He smiled almost apologetically with a shrug. "I know you probably don't believe it now, but you will."

The tall man turned back to the wagon and struck the hard-packed dirt again with the butt of the staff. "Out, Five!"

The thing hunkered within the shadowy interior looked all around, then gave a snort, and began to push its bulk through the small door. With a convulsive heave, it leapt down to the dirt below, and Ernest was shocked again to see that it had no hands, but rather an enormous metal barrel shape, wrapped in tight leather, at the end of either arm. From the waist down it was entirely machine, with short, stubby legs that reminded him more of a gorilla than a man. All over the body, various gem-like lights twinkled with the intense crimson glow of RJ power, and some sort of metal trap on the thing's back might have been intended to carry a large weapon of some kind.

"Gentlemen, it gives me great pleasure to introduce you to my first creation, a collaboration between the great doctor and myself, Creation 5." With a flourish of his hat, Smith gestured toward the hulking behemoth. For its part, Creation 5 only stood, swaying slightly from side to side. Something beyond the obvious was bothering Ernest, and after a moment he realized what it was: the thing was not breathing.

"Fascinating!" F.R. came around from the side of the armored transport, his eyes wide with admiration as he walked a circuit around the animated corpse. "Are they all this big now?"

Smith chuckled. "No, of course not. Most of the animations are still made from the corpses of ordinary men. But Five, here, he's different. Aren't you, Five?" He tapped on the thing's broad forehead with the staff. It did not so much as flinch.

"We obtained Five from a traveling circus moving through the area. He was not entirely sane, the poor lad, and so we were able to perform even more augmetic surgery than we had anticipated." He tapped the squat metal legs with the staff. "He had been known as the Man with Hands of Stone, and would crush wood, stone, and metal with equal facility for the squealing mobs of the hoi palloi. His mind was not the only faulty element he was born with, you see."

Smith came around Five and patted one of the enormous metal rams with an affectionate hand. "Where the hands of a normal boy would have been, our Five had only massive gnarled lumps of calloused flesh and exposed bone. And the bone of his arms and vestigial hands were far denser than normal." He rapped on the metal. "We encased those ugly stumps in reinforced steel, creating one of the most terrifying weapons in the western territories!"

A sour looked crossed Smith's face. "He ran into some difficulty recently with a mercenary band, but he's been repaired, better and stronger than before! It's one of the many advantages of using animations over purely metal automatons: the ability to repair and enhance endlessly."

Five continued to sway slightly, not acknowledging the conversation going on around him. F.R. continued to walk his circuit around the construct. "And was he alive for those first augmentations?" There was no condemnation in his voice, only scientific curiosity.

"For some of it, of course, but only for purely clinical interest. The RJ-1027 programing and revivification really only works when the body and the mind are dead. So, when the surgery proved too much for his heart, we let him pass, and brought him back with this." He reached the staff up and tapped on a metal structure that protruded from the back of Five's domed skull. A cylinder glowing ruby red sat in the center of the contraption. "This will bring nearly anything back to life, as long as it still had a functioning brain when it died."

"Fascinating... truly fascinating." Ernest was glad to see that F.R. had come out of his brooding fugue, but he was much less sanguine with the methods that had been used to turn a poor half-wit circus performer into the monster he saw before him. Creation 5 lacked any sort of style or polish, and seemed a great waste of potential and effort.

"Without hands, will the brute be able to transfer the cargo?" Ernest made no attempt to keep the distaste from his voice. As far as he was concerned, there were avenues of research within the crates that would put Creation 5 to shame. If this was the latest and greatest of the doctor's mechanicals, then he and F.R. would have no problem securing a high station here.

But they had to get their equipment to Payson, first.

The smile slipped a few degrees on Smith's face, and F.R. shot Ernest a reproving look, but the moment was soon past, and as the two other men continued to talk amiably about 5 and other Creations they would meet when they reached Payson, Ernest oversaw the transfer of the heavy boxes from the Ironhide to their new vehicle, which was apparently called a Doomsday. The hulking Creation would simply place an enormous iron ram on either side of a crate, press them together, and lift without apparent effort.

Before he would have believed it possible, the Doomsday was loaded, and the three men were preparing to transfer their personal cargo to the new vehicle. Ernest was not eager to jump into the passenger compartment with the giant, rotting monster, and so was greatly relieved when an amused Smith assured him that they would be riding in the forward cabin again, and that the internal hatch would remain closed.

"Of course, we have a little unfinished business we must conclude before we begin the next leg of our journey." Smith looked critically over the rusting length of the Ironhide. "The marshal was not wrong when he said we should get rid of this wagon." He looked back at the Doomsday, then at the Ironhide, then back at the Doomsday. When he turned to the other two men, the wild look in his eye was frightening. "Do you lads like making things go boom?"

As the rear hatch slammed shut on Five's malignant, glowing eye, Ernest pulled F.R. aside, pretending to guide him to the passenger's side hatch, then lowered his voice. "What do we do when we reach Payson? Will we be following this organ grinder and his monkey all the way to your uncle's palace?"

F.R. seemed taken aback by the tone and Ernest's choice of words. "Organ grinder?Monkey? Are you alright, Ern? You usually reserve this depth of rancor for second-rate restaurants and overly officious sommeliers."

Shooting his friend a dirty look, he gestured for him to climb to the boarding ladder first, taking one last look at the desolate landscape, and breathing in the warm-but-clean air, in case the internal hatch was not quite up to snuff. "I'm just not sure we want to be tied too closely to this man, is all. We're already arriving unannounced."

F.R. moved up the ladder with his usual, easy grace, looking down at his friend with an open smile. "God, Ern, you are an elitist's elitist. You know that, right?"

Ernest grunted and looked down to put his foot upon the lowest rung. "He's not our sort—"

F.R. leaned down, his own voice now in a whisper. "He is exactly our sort, Ernest." The words were nearly spit into his ear, and Ernest reared back at their vehemence. "Without J.P. Smith it would take us months to find Payson, and then longer to get inside." He moved his head back slightly to stare into Ernest's eyes. "No one else was willing to help us in this, Ern. Not my father, not my uncle. No one. Without J.P., we would be left out in the cold."

F.R. stared for one more moment into his eyes, then turned and climbed the rest of the way up to the access hatch, opened it, and leapt inside. A muffled, jovial conversation began, and Ernest shook his head.

Smith brought the enormous RJ engine at the heart of the Doomsday to life. Somehow, although it was much quieter than the Ironhide's old power plant, its low growl seemed to convey a far greater sensation of menace. They still only had narrow vision slits to look through, but for some reason Ernest could not have explained, the Doomsday felt less-confined.

"I think you're both going to get a charge out of this." Smith giggled as he maneuvered the vehicle back and forth several times, bringing the front-oriented weapons to bear on their late, unlamented wagon. "I think you will find the Sonic Gatling Guns spectacularly effectiveagainst a lightly armored vehicles such as that heap of rubbish."

The man's grin was tight with anticipation as he hunched over the controls of the Doomsday. To either side of the cabin, the massive cannons spun up with a fierce whine, and then shook the entire vehicle as they began to send double streams of crimson bolts lashing out into the still form of the Ironhide. The missiles struck with a thunderous tattoo, shattering the side panels of the old wagon and then pushing it bodily over, continuing to chew at the smoking underside until a stunning detonation ripped the vehicle's body apart. The powerful shockwave even pushed the Doomsday back on its springs.

"That was the RJ going up!" Smith gave a resounding whoop, and for the first time, the eastern tinkerer resembled the Wild West ruffian of his own imagination. Out beyond the vision slits of the Doomsday, the swirling red-tinged explosion cleared, revealing only a twisted mess of metal and columns of thick black smoke rising into the sky.

"Damn, if that wasn't a hoot!" Smith smiled at them both, threw the wagon into gear, and they rumbled around the smoldering wreckage, their broad metal wheels clawing their way onto the packed dirt of the road and turning west.

Smith had told them that it would take several days, traveling at top speed, before they reached the edge of the Tonto Forest, and another day or more of wending their way through the dark pines and rocky canyons before they reached Payson itself.

Something told Ernest, between the giant undead thing in the back of the wagon and their strange guide, the days would not speed by.

He thought they would one day enjoy the fruits of this journey, despite the sad cost of its beginning. But he did not know if he would ever be able to reconcile how quickly their fortunes had turned.

Chapter 10

The mountains rose up in majestic splendor all around them; the Great Spirit's power made manifest through earth and stone and tree. The air was cold, with a bite to it that the warm plains and the arid deserts lacked at this time of year. There were even small piles of snow hunkered down in the sheltered shadows of broken stone. Walks Looking and Sky Spirit rode their horse companions in comfortable silence, each lost in their own thoughts. They moved through the valley forests toward the mountain pass that would see them clear of the Bitterroot Range, down toward the coastal regions beyond.

The two had achieved a wary camaraderie over the course of their travels despite their many differences. Sky Spirit, one of the first great warriors to revere Sitting Bull and support him in his efforts to unite the tribes, was fiercely loyal to her father, and would hear no words uttered against him. Walks Looking had learned early-on that she needed to watch her words, or she would earn herself a sharp, repetitive lecture about duty and honor and then hours of stony silence.

She smiled as she thought about the times she had goaded him into such a reaction for the sheer amusement of it. She grew bored easily without the excitement of combat or confrontation, and urging the grave, puritanical warrior into fits of pique had served well to pass the time in those dragging periods of tedium.

She could feel those darker urges shifting behind her eyes again, and contemplated how best to divert herself. She turned her head from side to side, seeking for Sky Spirit with her unnatural vision. As always, the echoes of stone and dirt around her appeared hazy and indistinct, while any living thing shone with an intense, vibrant light, the strength of its aura corresponding to its connection with the Great Spirit. The men and women of the Warrior Nation blazed like stars in a cold, winter sky. The pale Europeans glowed with the soft, muted light of a distant lantern. Every living thing around her glowed with intertwined, echoing ripples, affecting even the rock and sand nearby, tying everything together into the complex tapestry of the Great Spirit.

She realized with a soft sigh that she would rather not contend with Sky Spirit's fierce loyalty to her father this time, but perhaps they could have a more grounded, honest conversation. He would make a great ally in her constant efforts to defend the Nation from the dangers of hidebound inflexibility that often held them back from achieving the greatness that was their due.

"Sky Spirit, do you mind if I ask you a question?" She kept her tone light, so as to not alarm him. Whenever he sensed she was on the verge of teasing him, he would shut her out, urging his horse to greater speed, and pretend he could not hear. Once, he had undergone the painful transformation into his spirit warrior shape, sprouting wings and talons, his head contorting into a twisted version of an eagle's, and launched himself right from the horse's back without a word. He had later claimed it was to scout ahead, but she knew it had only been to escape her sharp tongue.

"Yes?" His answer was wary, but not overly so. It had been days since last they fought, and it was possible she had lulled him into a false sense of security.

"I would like to speak with you about my father." She allowed her mount to pick his way along the vaguely defined path, her face cast down in a humble pose.

She saw him, with the corner of her vision, glance suspiciously in her direction. "Not if you intend to speak disrespectfully, no."

She conjured what she knew was her most alluring smile and unleashed it upon him without mercy. She saw the echo of his aura shiver in subconscious reaction. Such manipulation was really too easy with her special gifts. Sometimes it even brought a slight twinge of guilt. Not this time, though.

"I have no intention of being disrespectful, I promise." She allowed her horse to ramble for several more paces, and then tilted her head back toward him. It always made people feel better talking with her when she faced them, despite the fact that it had no effect on her ability to sense them clearly.

"I would very much like to know why you think the Nation follows my father so readily." She needed to be careful, trying to lead him to the right thoughts while letting him think he had reached the destinations on his own.

"The Warrior Nation does not follow any one man, Walks Looking. You know this." He frowned down at the path. "We are a free people, and only follow when one leads where we wish to go. Your father is merely one chief among many on the Great Council." He tilted his head, as if considering his words. "Of course, he is also a great war leader and a medicine man of immense power. Very few, even on the Council, can make such claims. His communion with the Great Spirit is strong, and it is that, more than anything, that grants him such a voice among the people."

Walks Looking nodded. These were all arguments she had heard many times before. "But he is a man like any other, no?"

Sky Spirit shook his head. "No, he is not." He held up a hand to stop her immediate, violent reaction. "He is a man, but not like any other. The Great Spirit has granted to him the visions that have guided us since the unification of the tribes. There would be no way we could have stood against the easterners alone, constantly fighting among ourselves, never mind protected the Great Spirit from the European and his foul poison."

And now it was time to strike. "But are we?"

He stopped his horse and turned to look at her, his face a combination of confusion and distrust. "Are we what?"

She shrugged, urging her mount around his and continuing on up the trail. "Are we protecting the Great Spirit from Carpathian? So much of our strength is entangled with the Union. Could we not do so much more, if we were only to pick up the weapons that have been left at our feet?"

He hurried to catch up, genuine confusion on his proud, noble face. "What weapons?"

She stopped, turning to him, and schooled her face to a mask of utter innocence. "Could we not turn the poison of the European back upon him?"

The horror in Sky Spirit's eyes was clear, even through her spirit vision, and the strength of his aura echoed with his reaction to her words. "You would suggest we use the red poison? We should pick up the weapons of our enemies, knowing full well that each activation scars the Earth forever?"

She held up a placating hand, nodding slightly beneath her blindfold. The thought was there now. It would germinate and flower or it would not. To push the issue further would only harden his instinctive resolve against it. She pursed her lips in what she knew men found to be a fetching expression, rewarded with another flutter of his aura. "You're right, I know." She reached out to touch his arm with a smile, hiding the satisfaction as another shiver rippled through the golden glow that surrounded him. "Please, forget that I even mentioned it."

Without waiting for a response, she urged her mount forward as if embarrassed. In truth, it was to hide the smile she felt creeping across her face, knowing that she could contain it no longer.

*****

Sky Spirit's mount found his own path as his mind wandered dark trails of its own. Ahead of him, Walks Looking sat her horse with a carefree, sinuous grace that he found somehow disturbing. His eyes were constantly drawn to the shimmering fall of her long hair down her back, and he had to grit his teeth and force himself to look away. She was the daughter of his sworn chief! They were nearly of an age, but still... Walks Looking was almost as much an icon within the Warrior Nation as Sitting Bull, and Sky Spirit had no right to the thoughts that continued to sidle into his mind.

Her words of a few days ago troubled him far more than her physical presence, and he found himself wishing, repeatedly, that he had not volunteered for the journey. Had she really suggested the Warrior Nation take up the weapons of the European? The thought was repugnant. Each time one of those terrible weapons was fired, it cut at the Great Spirit's power a little deeper. It was almost as if the strange crimson material somehow leached the very spirit from the world.

To use such weapons, even in a cause as righteous as ending their use for all time, was unconscionable.

And yet, Walks Looking, one of the most influential warriors among the free people, had clearly been thinking along those lines. Sky Spirit was not naïve enough to take her mask of innocent simplicity at face value. But still, for her to be contemplating the use of such power, and to suggest it to him openly... Did she expect that he might join her in such thoughts?

The notion was more than enough to distract him from thoseimpulses that had surfaced to plague him from time to time since they left the plains behind. There was nothing attractive about the harnessing of such evil. He shook his head, kept his eyes on the ground, and whickered to his horse, urging it onward, trying to empty his mind through force of will.

They had been moving up into the high places for several days when they saw their first glimpse of Iron Tooth's spirit people, watching them from a distant bluff. Sky Spirit noticed them first, his keen eyesight touched by the spirit of the eagle even when he wore the form of a man. At first, he thought he was seeing a group of Iron Tooth's people who had stayed behind in the mountains when the Nation had marched off to war. But as he concentrated on them, details came into clear focus; their clothing and gear resembled far more that of the easterners than any tribe of the free people.

"We are being watched." Sky Spirit pointedly looked away from the bluff, but he flicked one hand in that direction, indicating where Walks Looking should direct her vision.

"Free people?" Walks Looking kept her voice even, looking off in the other direction with a casual flip of her head that sent her thick braid swaying down her back.

Sky Spirit shook his head. "Not by their dress; perhaps the spirit people. They wear the heavy clothing of the easterners, and their weapons look like Carpathian's work, although there is no ruby aura of poison about them."

As he mentioned the weapons, Walks Looking dropped her pretense of nonchalance, turning to look at the distant overhang. She gasped at what she saw. "They glow!" she whispered the words, her lips parted in awe.

Sky Spirit had no idea what she meant, but something about the watchers had affected her deeply. "Are they the spirit people?"

A transformative smile swept across her face, and she nodded vigorously. "They must be! They appear to be as connected to the Great Spirit as any within the Nation."

Sky Spirit looked up again, and saw that one of the people on the cliff had raised a slim, gleaming object to his face, appearing to look through it down at them. The figure lowered the cylinder, spoke briefly to its companions, and then turned back. Slowly, with the formal weight of ritual, the figure raised one empty hand, palm toward them, into the air.

Walks Looking turned her shrouded face to Sky Spirit's in that direct way that always unnerved him. How much did she see, through that opaque shroud? He shrugged, and then looked back up to the cliff. The entire party there was now standing with one hand raised high. With one last glance down to his companion, he raised his own hand to return their salute. After a moment, Walks Looking turned and did the same.

A long moment passed, both groups locked in stillness. Then, as if with some silent signal, the party on the bluff lowered their hands, and Sky Spirit thought he could see the figure who had first noticed them nod once. The group turned and disappeared behind a lip of stone. In a moment, it was as if they had never been there at all, and he almost wondered if he might have imagined it.

But when he turned back to Walks Looking, she was still staring at the distant point, her face inscrutable.

"Well, that was intriguing." He said it with a smile, uncomfortable with the blank wall she now presented to him. "Iron Tooth was right; the spirit people do still wander the high places."

She continued looking up for a moment longer, and then turned to him. "But whoare they? To possess such a strong connection with the Great Spirit and to bear weapons so much like Carpathian's?"

That had bothered Sky Spirit as well, although not as much as the tone with which Walks Looking voiced his own question. "Very little is known about the spirit people of the mountains. For many, many generations, Iron Tooth's people have lived here in the mountains, coexisting with them in peace." He smiled slightly. "Say what you will of Iron Tooth, but he is not one to turn a blind eye toward evil that might endanger his people."

Walks Looking's expressionless face gazed blindly at him for a moment more, then she nodded and urged her horse back to the path as if the event had never occurred, forcing him to hurry after her.

The next day, as they reached the peak of the Lolo Pass, Sky Spirit began to ride with his eyes on the sky, distracting himself from the many uncomfortable paths his mind had wandered since their journey began. The great eagles often made their homes in these high places. If he were going to recruit more flying warriors onto the dark warpath into the east, this would be his best chance of finding them.

Their travels had been nearly silent since seeing the spirit people the day before. His companion seemed lost in her thoughts, and he knew he had more than enough to occupy his own mind as they approached their destination. At least she seemed to have lost her taste for goading him into verbal wrestling matches over the past few days, for which he was more than duly grateful.

The more the warrior thought about the sacrifices of the great eagles, and their growing importance to the efforts of the Nation, the more he thought about the growing threat of the unclean dead flyers Carpathian's forces had been throwing into the air to contend with them. The abominations were not terribly effective in battle, often flying into berserk rages as dangerous to their nightmare kin as to the forces opposing them. But each time they were encountered, the carrion constructs improved.

At almost the same time that these horrors had first made their appearance, a greater number of warriors had followed him into the path of the sky. On more than one occasion, Sky Spirit had wondered if the Great Spirit had caused this change, knowing that the skies would be the next great battlefield in their war against the polluting evil. Without the emerging eagle warriors and the Fire Eagles coming to their aid, the Warrior Nation would have no way to respond... They would have been left completely at the mercy of this new threat.

The Great Spirit was the power of the Earth made manifest. No man, woman, or child within the Warrior Nation could dispute that with the truth of it before their eyes every day. There was no denying the danger posed by Carpathian and his poison, or the Union and others who sought to use the same technology for their own ends. The relationship between the Great Spirit and the free people of the Warrior Nation was a flawless example of nature at its greatest, each helping and protecting the other.

He only hoped it would be enough, given the weight of foes arrayed against them.

*****

With the tall mountains stretching into the sky behind them, silhouetted by the sun rising far off in the east, Walks Looking stood, her breathing steady, and let her spirit vision take in the sweeping vista before them. The descent through the pass had been difficult, especially when one of the seasonal snowstorms had nearly swept them from the pass in one night of stark terror. But here they were, on the far side of the Bitterroot Range, farther than she had ever been from her father and her people.

She felt liberated.

Sky Spirit had spent more and more of their journey in his spirit form, flying among the sharp peaks, gathering the great eagles to him and pleading his case. Many had agreed, disappearing into the east. She knew, from watching the shivering of his aura, that each majestic bird departing for those distant battlefields was a sore charge on his heart. The Fire Eagles, like the Great Elks and the Energy Beast horses that willingly came to the Warrior Nation cause, would eventually die in the service of the Great Spirit, their bodies wracked with the pain and exhaustion of transformation.

Walks Looking shook her head. There had to be a better way. She knew there was a better way. Her own spirit guide had shown her the way, many years ago. Most warriors of her people felt sorry for her, seeing her lack of a spirit form as proof that she lacked a powerful connection with the Great Spirit. Her spirit sight was undeniably powerful, but as far as most knew, it merely compensated for the sight she had been born without. She was always careful to hide the full extent of her powers, and willingly suffered the silent pity of those who could never understand.

But the truth of her connection with the Great Spirit was far more awe-inspiring than any of them could ever know. As far as she had been able to gather, only a few of the greatest warriors and leaders of her people were granted the honor of the Great Spirit's direct communication, and even then only rarely. Her father had been so blessed on several occasions, guiding the tribes to unity, and then to war against the foreigners and their poison.

None of them spoke with the Great Spirit as often as she did. The Great Spirit visited her all the time, giving her advice, asking her questions, and offering her solace in the face of her cold isolation as the only warrior who truly understood what was happening. The Great Spirit came to her, its fiery eyes flashing, and revealed to her the secrets of the spirit world and of the waking world. It was through the power of the Great Spirit that she knew the true path to victory over Carpathian and his ilk was to turn their weapons against themselves, and then to destroy the weapons forever.

She knew that this would cause the Great Spirit much pain. He had told her so himself. But did not the beasts of the

Earth sacrifice themselves for their cause? Could the Great Spirit do no less?

But even if she managed to convince some of her people of this truth, they would need numbers to wield the weapons. And despite her distaste at following Sitting Bull's dictates, seeking the assistance of the far western clans was the best way to find those numbers.

"Will they come?" She asked Sky Spirit without turning around. He had been silent for nearly two days, since the last of the great eagles had vanished into the east. But before he had fallen into his deep malaise, he had told her that he had seen strange eagle warriors off in the distance to the west, and knew that they were being watched. There was no way they would arrive in the lands of these foreign tribes without the Thunder Wolf and the Raven Warrior knowing of their approach.

"They will come." His voice was soft, and she had to stop the rush of annoyance at his weakness from spilling out into her own response.

"Do you say they will come because their failure to do so would render all our efforts here useless? Or do you say they will come because you truly believe that they will come?" She tried to smile as she said it, but knew the words had emerged more biting than she had wished.

He did not seem to notice. "They will come because they must, and thus I truly believe it." His hooded eyes rose to stare into her face, and for the first time, she saw that her appearance had no impact upon his aura at all. It caused a strange mix of emotions within her, seeing that he was now beyond her reach.

"I hope you are right. If we can convince these westerners to join us, there is no way Carpathian and his rotting slaves can stand against us." She went back to scanning the land beneath them as they walked side by side, leading their horses to give them a well-deserved rest. She could sense that Sky Spirit had more he wanted to say, but with a sigh, he lapsed back into his dour silence. She could not summon the energy to coax him out of it.

It took them the rest of the day, even as she pushed their pace, to reach the flat lands beyond the Bitterroot Range. Forests rose up all around them, and soon their view of the land was swallowed in the deep greens of the enormous hardwoods. The long shadows of the afternoon were swallowed by the thick canopy overhead, and soon they were walking in a green twilight, the moist loam of the forest floor soft beneath their feet.

Walks Looking was lost in the wonder of the life around her, letting her spirit sight absorb the web of vitality that wove through the forest, when she felt Sky Spirit's hand fall upon her shoulder, drawingher to a halt. She shook her head, glancing at him in question. He was not looking at her, but straight ahead, into the forest. When she followed his gaze, she saw what her spirit sight alone would not have caught; the soft, shifting glow of firelight illuminating the forest far ahead.

"Is it—" He pulled her farther back, and then pushed on past her, hissing for her silence in a maddeningly-dismissive way that reminded her too much of her father. Who did he think he was?

"You can't—" He whirled around, his eyes narrow, and drew a hand slashing down between them. His aura darkened in anger, and she realized that there was nothing to be gained at the moment for fighting that old fight. She simply nodded, not trying to hide the frustrated snarl on her lips, and gestured with wide sarcasm for him to carry on ahead of her.

Together they moved through the forest, feet treading in utter silence on the wet earth. With a gesture, their horses had halted, uncomfortable at being left behind. As the two warriors skulked forward, drawing on every ounce of skill and instinct they possessed, she knew there was no way the people below could know they were there.

Except that they did.

"No need to lurk through the shadows, my friends." The voice was loud, shocking them both into stunned stillness. Someone chuckled in the darkness that hung between them and the light of the fires. "You are among friends, I assure you." Something moved, and before they could react, a large man rose out of the brush, a dark void in the soft glow of the firelight behind him.

Walks Looking felt her blind eyes narrow in suspicion. She had not even caught a hint of the man's aura as they approached. She had never encountered any of the free people who could disguise their deep connection with the Great Spirit from such short range. And from the man's appearance and attire, there was no doubting that he was one of the free people.

The tall man wore his black hair loose, draping over his shoulders. A sheet of woven reeds and bone hung on his chest over a deep red shirt. His legs were wrapped in rich, golden doeskin. His smile was wide, and matched by a twinkle in his eye that seemed almost to spark there like distant heat lightning.

"You are welcome, travelers from the east. It was truly a fortuitous calling of nature I answered this night, or else you would have clearly crept up on us all unawares, and conducted the Great Spirit alone knows what kind of mischief." His smile was open, taking any sting of accusation from the words, and he stepped back, gesturing with a sweep of one strong arm for them to join him.

Walks Looking and Sky Spirit shared a silent glance.

They went back for their mounts, and then followed, soon emerging into the center of a ring of large campfires. Many teepees were situated around the fires, disappearing into the shadows of the forest. People were emerging from the tents as they approached, their faces a mixture of curiosity and excitement. Walks Looking saw that there were no young in evidence, and no elders. In fact, all of the men and women she sensed echoed back to her the hard-edged auras of warriors.

It was a war party, prepared for a long journey.

"I am Qwoli, called the Thunder Wolf by my people. We have known for many days of your approach." The man turned at the center fire and gestured for them both to sit. "Plenty of time for those of us so inclined to prepare ourselves for the passage east."

Even in the full light of the flames, the man's eyes seemed dark, sky fire dancing in their depths. Walks Looking sat as the camp came alive, warriors taking up ranks all around to look at the newcomers and hear what news they might carry. Their horses were led away to join the mounts of the war party beneath the trees.

Another eminent looking warrior, a cloak of black feathers draped over his broad shoulders, pushed through the crowd. He lacked Qwoli's open warmth, looking at the two newcomers as if they did not quite live up to his expectations.

"You come from Sitting Bull, in the east?" His voice was clipped, as if he was in a hurry to be off.

Qwoli laughed, rising again to slap this new warrior on the back. "Bayaq, you do not even allow our guests a moment to rest before you seek to tear answers from their hearts?"

The feathered warrior, Bayaq, did not turn away, his eyes fixed upon Sky Spirit. As Walks Looking saw this, movement over the man's shoulder caught her attention. The echo-form of a great owl, its aura glittering crimson and gold, looked down upon her with inscrutable eyes. It cocked its head to one side as if passing judgment upon her silence. It was that, more than anything, that caused her to do something she almost never did. She stepped forward and assumed the mantle of leadership that her father's position granted her.

"I am Walks Looking, daughter of Sitting Bull and chosen emissary of the Great Council." She stood to her full height, her hands on her hips.

Both of the war leaders before her shifted their eyes from Sky Spirit to her own shrouded face, as her companion took a step back and bowed his head. Before they could speak, she continued.

"My father and the council request that you join your power with the rest of the Warrior Nation against the enemies of the Great Spirit, moving in the east. Your assistance could well mean the difference between—"

"Excellent." Bayaq's sour expression did not change as he broke into her speech with a gruff nod. "We leave in the morning."

Walks Looking watched the man disappear into the crowd

as Qwoli shook his head with a smile. "Many of us are eager to meet the devils from the east, but none so much as Bayaq. He feels the insult to the Great Spirit more personally than most."

She continued to concentrate on the direction Bayaq had taken, sensing him enter one of the larger tents, pulling the skin door down behind him. In the branches overhead, the great owl's majestic head dipped once in recognition. She turned back to the smiling stranger, granting a smile of her own.

"Excellent. That is exactly what I was hoping to hear."

Chapter 11

Ernest was not speaking at all as the Doomsday rolled beneath the dark pines of the Tonto Forest. The last few days had been more trying than even he had anticipated. There was definitely something off about J.P. Smith, and more and more often, he found himself hoping that the man was not a representative member of the other denizens of Payson. If their destination was entirely peopled with folks like Smith, or if F.R.'s childhood memories of his uncle and his father had hidden personalities more in line with the raving clockmaker, then he might have to think about finding a way back to New Zealand on his own.

"Now, there will be animations and other constructs guarding the road through the forest, so we have to be careful." Smith spoke in low tones, barely audible over the grumbling engine, as if the forest was having some sort of suppressive effect on his usually frenetic energy. "We will be fine, but you must trust me, if we are stopped."

Smith looked sideways at F.R., and Ernest thought he caught just a glimpse of concern there. "If you are still intending to surprise your uncle, we will want to keep a low profile."

Ernest found F.R.'s responding smile more unnerving than he would care to admit. "I have several surprises for my uncle and my father, J.P. Let's keep as low a profile as possible, by all means."

The dark forest around them grew thicker as the trees rolled past. Tension in the cabin seemed to rise with each passing hour, and Ernest was almost ready to scream just to hear a human voice, when Smith brought their wagon to a stuttering halt and cursed under his breath.

"Damn." The man seemed even more concerned than when the UR-30 had stopped them on their way out of Kansas City. "Damn the woman."

Through the narrow vision slit, Ernest could see a thin figure standing in the middle of the road, several hulking animations still as statues behind it. As he peered more closely through the slit, he saw that it was, indeed, a woman. She wore tight clothing that would have been a scandal anywhere in Europe, with a blaster on her right hip and a long, thin knife sheathed to her left thigh. She stood with one hip cocked out in a jaunty pose, her hand resting lightly on the weapon there.

There was something odd about the woman's face, but through the dappled sunlight, he could not tell what it might be.

"Damn the woman to Hell." Smith was clearly concerned. He looked at his two passengers, and there was no doubting the fear on his face. "I think you gentlemen should stay here in the cabin while I try to appease the infernal harlot." Without waiting for a response, the man turned, cranked open the door, and dropped from sight. The cool air of the forest flowed in through the opening, a relief from the heat they had suffered over the course of their journey.

Ernest watched Smith approach the woman, his arms gesturing with sharp, jerky motions. Looking sideways at his friend, the young New Zealander was surprised to see that F.R. was staring at the scene before them in rapt attention.

"F.R., are you alright?" In his experience, that expression seldom augured well for him.

Without a word, and quite against their guide's instructions, F.R. slid across the seat, behind the controls of the Doomsday, and dropped out of the open door after Smith.

"Damnit." Ernest's voice was bitter as he scrambled down himself.

"—just returning to Payson, Miss Mimms, as instructed." Smith's voice was heavy with exasperation, his body stiff with tension. "Doctor Carpathian knew I was out and about."

The woman's pose had not altered, but as Ernest landed with a grunt, he saw her hand slide from the butt of her blaster to curl around the pistol grip, as she stood a little taller.

Following F.R. toward the pair, Ernest could now see that the woman was wearing a mask. It covered her entire forehead, and then dropped down to conceal her right cheek and half of her nose, ending in a graceful curve at her jawline. A shiny cascade of golden-brown hair fell over one shoulder and down her back. Despite the mask, he could tell she was extraordinarily beautiful, and her frontier clothing certainly left very little to the imagination.

As the two young men came up even with Smith, the man looked first over one shoulder, then the other, in rising alarm. His speech stumbled to a halt as he shot F.R. an injured look. But the dark haired man paid him no attention, instead slipping past him to stand before the woman. Ernest felt the ominous gathering of bad karma, and wanted nothing more than to retreat back into the wagon.

Behind the woman, the animations swayed slightly, ready to defend her at a moment's need. Behind the standard-sized corpses was another enormous brute almost as large as 5. The thing's legs were metal constructs ending in wide, flat platforms offering greater stability than human feet. Instead of arms, two enormous drill assemblies poked out from its sleeves. Unlike most of the animations they had seen, this one was covered, its misshapen body hidden beneath a voluminous canvas long coat. The only visible element that identified it as an animated corpse was the pale, slack face. The lower jaw had been crudely removed, and a third drill poked out of the shreds of rotting flesh, nested in an assembly of pistons and tubes. As Ernest watched, the drill moved forward and then back slightly, and he realized it must be mounted on an elaborate hydraulic framework that could launch it out of the mouth during combat.
He shuddered at the thought.

Ernest shook himself out of his dark contemplation as he realized that an uncomfortable silence had settled upon the group standing in the middle of the road. Looking at the woman opposite them, he was not at all comforted to see that her lips had twitched into a sneering semblance of a smile, while her eyes had hardened as if reacting to a challenge.

"Please forgive J.P., miss." Ernest almost moaned aloud at F.R.'s tone. It was the low-pitched voice he used when he found a woman particularly intriguing, and it almost always had an effect on the opposite sex. Not always the desired effect, but there was always a reaction.

"He was only working on my behalf." F.R. shrugged with a boyish grin that kept its shine despite the woman's lack of response.

"Who are you?" Her eyes were hard, her mouth firm, and her pose a mixture of indifferent relaxation and readiness. Her voice was polished, with a strange, near-French flow that seemed to compliment her mask in some strange way.

At her words, F.R. hesitated. He looked to Ernest for a moment, then to J.P., then back to the woman with a shrug. "Well, it was meant to be a surprise. But I cannot fault the guardian of my family's domains for her vigilance." The dark-haired young man took a step back and bowed with more than formal grace. "May I please introduce myself as F.R. Caym, son of Vladimir Caym, and nephew of the great Doctor Burson Carpathian."

The woman's eyes widened at that. Her body, however, tightened further. She looked to Smith, and her expression was hardening before the echoes of F.R.'s declaration had faded from the trees around them.

"It's true!" Smith put his hands up as if afraid the woman was about to charge him.

"It is true, I promise you." F.R. had also raised a hand.

The woman's eyes flicked from Smith to F.R. and back again, only once gracing Ernest with a look that dismissed him so quickly he almost took offense. When she spoke, it was to Smith, and Ernest was alarmed to see that her blaster had risen an inch or so out of its holster.

"And how did you become the guardian of such precious cargo, Smith?" Her voice was dangerously soft, and Ernest felt a thrill down his spine despite the tension of the situation.

Smith started to stammer a response, but F.R. stepped in again, both arms raised, speaking calmly as if gentling a nervous horse. "Miss, J.P. has been a correspondent of mine for many years. In the heat and confusion of the moment, I imposed upon him for aid." He shrugged, and for the first time in weeks, Ernest saw again the young man who had lost his mother to a bloody, senseless attack. "I'm afraid something terrible has happened back in Paris, and I have outpaced the news." He paused for a moment, and the woman, her eyes now fixed firmly on his face, never wavered. "My mother has been killed, my home burned. My father knows nothing of this, and I had nowhere else to go."

It was a good story, even if the tale left out some key elements. Ernest watched the woman for her reaction, concerned that any lady who dressed the way this one dressed, and stood alone in the middle of a dark wood with only the company of decaying, animated, and surgically altered corpses to attend her, would not melt at a sad little orphan boy story.

He was not disappointed.

"I have a hard time believing that neither Doctor Carpathian nor Ursul would be aware of something that important." The blaster was all the way out of the holster now, although she kept the muzzle pointing into the road. "I think you'd better come with me. We'll straighten this out with them."

F.R. tilted his head as if conceding a point, but then raised a single finger, his tone shifting to playful bartering without missing a beat. "We can do that, but do you think either my father or my uncle will be pleased, if I am who I say I am, and you have brought me into my family's new demesnes in chains?"

The woman smiled at that, and Ernest allowed himself to feel a moment's relief. Then the edge of the smile struck him, and he knew this was not going to be easy. "I think Doctor Carpathian and his majordomo and chief of security would be pleased that I did my job, and followed their instructions." She gestured with her weapon with a casual wave, but the threat was not lost on any of them. "Especially given that we have had our own difficulties with mysterious strangers, of late."

"Miss Mimms," Smith moved forward again, his hands still raised. "I vouch for this man. He is who he says he is. You know I have the doctor's trust. If you still harbor doubts–"

Her smile widened, and her next words were floated on

a breathy chuckle that drained the color from Smith's face. "You have the doctor's trust, I know. I also know that you have singularly failed to gain Ursul's trust, or my own."

Seeing all of their plans and his grand reveal slipping away, F.R. could not stop a note of desperation from leaking into his voice. "Miss, please. We have traveled a long way to seek solace with my family in a very dark time. Allow me to meet my father and my uncle with dignity, and I will be forever in your debt." His voice smoothed out somewhat, and he gestured with one gloved hand. "You can accompany me all the way to meet them... you should accompany me! If, as we stand before them, they do not instantly recognize me, you can shoot me down where I stand!"

The woman stared at him for a moment that dragged on well into the realm of true discomfort, and then her eyes flitted to Ernest. "Who is he?"

F.R. looked back as Ernest, then to the woman. "A friend, companion, and fellow scientist of great renown. Ernest, come forward." He made a swift churning motion with one hand, and with a slight hesitation, Ernest stepped into their little circle.

"Miss... Mimms, is it?" She nodded, her face blank, and F.R. continued with a nod of his own. "Very good. This is Ernest Rutherford, of New Zealand. A Fellow at Cambridge, and a man of great intellect and academic accomplishment."

Ernest dipped his head in a slight bow. "How do you do." He muttered the words, lost in the surreal moment, speaking to a beautiful masked woman holding a very large gun in her seemingly very capable hand.

The absurdity of it all seemed to reach the woman as well, and her smile softened somewhat. "I do passingly well, thank you." She looked back to F.R., then to Smith, and then sighed, sliding the blaster home. "Smith, if this goes poorly," she tilted her head toward F.R., but her eyes stayed on the tall man in the armored bowler. "You will be the second to die."

*****

After sending her nightmare brigade back into the forest with a curt word of command, Misty Mimms had gestured for the men to remount the Doomsday, and they had continued on their journey. Ernest found himself grateful that she had demanded to drive, and so was clear across the cabin from him. Despite her alluring beauty and the strength of her personality, she terrified him.

The cabin was silent as the wagon bounced along the road, shadows from the tall trees streaking across the vision slits, causing the compartment to flicker with strobing sunlight. After about an hour of silence, F.R. had clearly had enough, and began to make conversational sallies, trying to draw Miss Mimms out of her professional shell. By the time the trees began to thin ahead of them, although her responses had not gotten any warmer, she was no longer trying to hide a slight smile touching the corner of her full lips.

But as they turned one last corner in the forest, even F.R.'s incessant talk trailed off, as the city of Payson opened out before them.

At first glance, Ernest could tell that the city owed a great deal of its design and layout to the more modern, industrial cities of America. Despite the wealth of timber all around, there was not a wooden building to be seen. Every structure was made of serviceable red brick, the buildings close together and the streets narrow enough to make negotiating them in the big wagon a challenge that demanded most of their fair driver's attention.

They moved through the narrow streets, occasionally seeing living denizens of the mysterious town moving about on their own business. They wore fairly standard fashions, considering how far into the frontier they lived. There were nearly as many bowler hats and stovepipes as there were Stetsons, and Ernest would have made a comment to his friend, if his mind had not been taken up with all they were seeing.

Most of the buildings were clearly manufactories, storehouses, or small businesses that catered to the inhabitants. At one point, he thought he could see a devastated swath of burned buildings slumping into a side street off in the distance. Given how clean and well-ordered the rest of the town was, he found himself wondering what might have happened, and if Miss Mimms was purposely avoiding other damaged areas.

Wherever he looked, he could see RJ power in prolific use. Signs glowed a dull red, smoke pouring from the tall stacks all around was tinged in crimson, and ruby light gleamed from many of the shuttered windows. Occasionally, he saw a large animation or construct, altered to carry heavy machinery or for other menial tasks. The street continued to slope downward for a while, then leveled out. The buildings around them were more widely spaced now;clearly residences of influential members of the community. Most of them featured high brick walls topped with glowing red wires for added security.

"I think F.R. would like to use a side entrance, Miss Mimms, to make an impact with his family?" Smith made the tentative suggestion, shooting a slanting look at their new driver, then at F.R. on the other side.

Miss Mimms sniffed, leaning forward to look at F.R. with an arched eyebrow, then shook her head. "It won't matter what door we use, if you're not who you say you are. We'll go in through the north side, then. The service entrance to the south is still in the process of..." She looked over at Ernest and F.R., and then shrugged. "Refurbishment," she finished with a sardonic twist. She took the next right hand turn, and the Doomsday continued to grind along the constricted streets, moving ever downward.

The wagon eventually pulled out into an open square, and Ernest whistled as he saw the enormous building stretching upwardinto the sky, built into a red cliff that towered above them. It was clearly modeled after some of the great fantastical castles being built across Europe as a last gasp of fairytale architecture. Turrets and sweeping buttresses stretched up into the sky, while countless narrow windows looked out over the town around them.

Two animations, fresher than the combat models they had seen and dressed in relatively well-preserved finery, shuffled out from a vaulted iron door and took possession of the Doomsday. The heavy doors boomed shut behind the vehicle as it disappeared down a tunnel, carrying 5 with it. Without fanfare, Misty Mimms led them into a small entrance, past a security checkpoint where two living guards looked them all over with suspicion, but retreated quickly from their guide's curt commands.

The halls were painted pristine white, and the architecture again reminded Ernest of European palaces. Fine furniture was scattered throughout in tasteful, distinct conversation groups where the halls swelled into rounded chambers, and paintings graced the walls that harkened back to countless classical schools in the Old World.

"There was a council meeting earlier today." Misty Mimms spoke over her shoulder as she led them through the baroque maze. "It should be finished now. Doctor Carpathian will be back in the tower room." She looked at F.R. with a grudging smile. "Your father might even be with him."

Ernest could see that her use of the word had struck a chord with his friend, who smiled broadly for the first time since they had reached Payson.

The four of them entered a large room with several sets of double doors along one wall. She turned curtly to Smith and gestured back the way they had come. "I think you can go, Smith. I will escort your friends the rest of the way."

"But—" He spluttered, his face aggrieved.

"You should go down and check on Five, should you not?" She turned away, unmistakably dismissing him.

Glaring at the woman's back, Smith snorted, but then looked apologetically at F.R. with a shrug. "Good luck, my friend. I am sorry I will not see the reunion with my own eyes."

F.R. reached out to take the tall man's hand. "As am I, J.P. It never would have happened without you, and I will be forever in your debt." He patted the man on the shoulder. "We will see each other again soon, however, I am sure."

Smith nodded, then gave Ernest a shallow bow, and turned to stalk back down the hall the way they had come.

One of the double doors before them slid open with a

ringing sound, and Ernest realized that they were lifts. He had seen several during his travels through Europe, and once in New York after disembarking from the Celtic. This variation, however, was much more spacious than any of the others, and moved more smoothly as they rose up through the palace for far longer than he would have thought possible.

Eventually, the doors opened again, and they moved out into a wide hall that looked much like the ones below. Misty directed them to move ahead of her, drawing her blaster with an apologetic tilt of her head. The hall grew lighter ahead, and soon they were walking through what had to be a bridge. Long, tall windows stretched out on either side, and the hall ended in a massive set of double doors with an elaborately carved 'C' decorating each.

"Both the doctor and Ursul are within." She did not bother to tell them how she could have known this, and Ernest was again reminded that they could well be playing with fire. They were now in the palace of one of the greatest men in the world, completely within his power, and moving forward with a gun literally pointed at their backs.

"Go in, slowly." The lady gestured with the weapon. "But remember our agreement. If there is a moment in which the doctor or Ursul do not recognize you, you won't even feel the shot that kills you."

F.R. nodded his understanding, staring fixedly at the door. Now, at the moment of truth, was he feeling the pressure of destiny? Ernest felt for his friend, but he wanted this moment safely in their past as soon as possible.

F.R. rapped on the door, standing awkwardly in the silence that followed.

"Enter." The single word, muffled as it was through the thick door, caused F.R. to jump nevertheless. He paused, took a deep breath, and then, with one sheepish grin at Ernest, pushed the door open.

The room on the other side was impressive in an understated sort of way. The walls were decorated with an eclectic mix of items ranging from war trophies from the past and present, to prototypes of various weapons and other inventions. Along one wall was a large map of the United States, silver pins twinkling in a swirling pattern of martial constellations, clearly indicating troop concentrations in an array of colors. Lighting in the room was provided by RJ lanterns in intricate wall sconces that cast a warm, flushed glow over the scene.

A number of elegant, wing-backed chairs were placed around the room in subtle groups, tables beside each holding small tokens and objects of idle interest. Windows dominated several walls in the rounded chamber, including a wide array of clear glass behind the largest object in the room, an enormous dark desk cluttered with papers and bits and pieces of technology.

Two men sat nearby, each holding a snifter, the liquid inside swirling as they turned to watch the newcomers enter.

Ernest had only ever seen photographs of the two men, but they looked exactly as he had expected. Doctor Carpathian was prim and proper in his evening coat, his cravat well-pressed, and his hair tussled. Only the gleaming red lens where his right eye should be marred the image of the fashionable country lord.

The other man had to be Vladimir Caym, called Ursul, or the Bear. He was clearly a soldier, his burly shape well-muscled beneath the smart tunic and trousers that he wore, more a uniform than any sort of stylish suit. A white fringe beard covered the top of his own cravat.

Both men bore similar expressions, their brows drawn down in curiosity mixed with annoyance. When the doctor saw Miss Mimms standing behind the two newcomers, he rose quickly to his feet, a smile replacing the emerging scowl in a flash.

"Miss Mimms! Welcome!" He moved toward them, only stopping when he saw her weapon drawn, pointed firmly toward the two young men. "Miss Mimms, is something amiss?"

"Hello, uncle." Ernest was surprised by the firmness in his friend's voice. Given all of the emotions that must be swirling through his heart at that moment, he sounded like a man casually greeting a relative on the street corner.

Only when he turned to his father, did F.R.'s voice waver. "Hello, father."

Both of the men stared at F.R. in shocked silence. The old soldier rose slowly to his feet, stiff disbelief drawing his face into a half-frown.

Ernest became keenly aware of Misty Mimms standing behind him with her gun drawn, and hoped one of the men would acknowledge F.R. soon, before her trigger finger got itchy.

"Son?" Vladimir took a step forward, and Ernest remembered that the man had left home so long ago, he would only have seen photographs of his grown son himself. "How..."

F.R. swallowed, looked down for a moment, and then dragged his eyes back up to meet his father's gaze. "Mother is dead."

Ernest watched the old man's face in fascination as the news hit him like a sledgehammer to the gut. His dark face paled, his mouth and eyes widened, and then his eyes sank inward as the meaning of the words finally dawned.

"Ce... cum..." He seemed to fold in on himself. Ernest did not speak Romanian, but he could imagine, after years and years of separation, how the moment must have struck Vladimir Caym.

F.R. rushed to his father, taking him by the elbow and guiding him back into his seat. "I know, father, I know. I have carried the knowledge with me for months now, and I can still hardly credit it myself."

Carpathian stood nearby, stunned as well. In his peripheral vision, Ernest saw Miss Mimms slip her blaster back into its holster: one less thing to worry about, anyway.

"Father, I did not know what else to do, or where else to go." F.R. shot a look at his uncle, an unspoken plea in his eyes. "Where else could we go? Surely, family... Hugo secured us funds, and we came—"

"Hugo." Vladimir seemed to cling to the name. "Hugo, the old tutor? How did he secure you funds?" As was often the case, in Ernest's experience, people cling to mundane details in the face of great tragedy.

F.R.'s look took on a slightly furtive cast, and he shifted his glance between his father and his uncle. "He... sold... several of my inventions and designs. We have the rest stored away in crates." He stood up suddenly realizing with an obvious chill that all of his cargo had been on the Doomsday wagon that had disappeared into the bowels of the palace. "At least... we did..."

"Your cargo will be fine." Miss Mimms said, with a hint of a smile. She seemed to have warmed a great deal since their story had been verified.

The doctor recovered himself and moved to stand beside his nephew. There was something deep in the old man's eyes, some tinge of suspicion or withheld warmth... and for a moment Ernest was concerned for his friend all over again. Could Carpathian know of their nighttime predations in Paris and beyond? Would he find fault with such practical experimentation if he did know?

"F.R., I can't tell you how glad I am that you did come." The words were right, and the tone was right, but for some reason, Ernest felt there was something else beneath the doctor's reaction that he could not fully comprehend. "Of course there is no other place you should have come. I have heard great things about your work, son; both from your father and from others in our field back in the Old Country."

Carpathian took F.R.'s shoulders and lifted him up, holding him close and then bestowing a formal kiss upon each cheek. As he pulled away, however, he looked down at his own hands, still gripping the younger man's arms. His fingers flexed, tightening so that the flesh across his knuckles paled, the metal framework creaking.

A look that could only be suspicion arose in the doctor's eyes. "Take off your coat, F.R."

Ernest felt his heart leap into his throat. He had completely forgotten that this moment must come, he had been so concerned with his friend's emotions and the pretty lady with the big gun.

But F.R. had not forgotten, and the grin that swept across

his face, with an anticipatory gleam flaring in his eyes, caused a dark chill to rush down Ernest's back.

"Of course, uncle." Slowly and deliberately, F.R. shrugged out of his coat, pulling his arms from the long, concealing sleeves.

The young man's arms were completely artificial: sleek, gleaming steel, detailed in dark, burnished iron and pins of shining gold. The glow emanating from them was not the angry crimson of RJ-1027, but a brighter, more vibrant vermillion. As he dropped his coat over a nearby chair, F.R.'s grin broadened, and he flexed his arms. He stripped off his leather gloves, revealing deft, supple fingers of shining metal, thousands of tiny, articulated plates shifting at each joint with every movement.

"They... they're beautiful!" Carpathian stepped back to get a more complete look, and his nephew held them out, turning them first palms upward, and then downward, so the doctor could get a good look.
Vladimir's stricken face paled even further as he saw the artificial arms. The limbs were far more elegant and refined than the replica they had seen on Virgil Earp, but there was no mistaking their artificial nature. F.R.'s arms had been entirely replaced. "Why..."

As all attention was riveted upon his friend and those gleaming, alien arms, only Ernest, who had been present during the surgery and integral in constructing the power supplies and the control runs for the limbs, had any attention to spare on the woman by the door.

As the metal arms had been revealed, a slight quiver struck through Misty Mimms' entire body. One hand had risen to the right side of her face as her eyes had widened in a look that could only have been described as shocked horror. She had taken two short steps backward, all of her grace and poise gone, and then without a word, silently turned and slipped through the enormous door, leaving the other three men in the room none the wiser.

"I could not very well expect to compete in the new world without marked advantages, Father." F.R.'s voice was the height of reason, but his father just continued to shake his head in denial.

"I knew something drastic would be needed to secure my place here. I had heard rumors of what uncle had done for the outlaw, Jesse James, and what he had been forced to do for himself, and I saw that this was the only road that would lead me to where I wanted to go."

As Vladimir continued to shake his head, Carpathian, a smile dawning on his drawn face, continued to study the arms. "They are magnificent, nephew. Who conducted the surgery? Did you design them yourself? What powers them?"

F.R. looked down at his own arms, admiring their lines and function. "I did design them myself, Uncle. And I directed several surgeon colleagues during the procedure." He looked at the silent Ernest for a moment, his grin turning sharper. "The power is entirely dependent upon a new science pioneered by my very good friend, here, Ernest. It is atomic in nature, using highly radical elements to supercharge a fuel cell in each arm."

Carpathian could not tear himself away from the constantly-moving arms, like a prey animal mesmerized by the eyes of a cobra. "Amazing." He muttered to himself.

Ernest could tell they had secured their position within Payson. But he could not shake the feeling that there was something more behind Carpathian's eyes than he could truly understand.

Chapter 12

The private dining room was small compared to most of the residential areas within the palace. Carpathian did not often take his meals here, usually eating in either his tower office or the council chamber on the floor below. When Vlad had received the invitation to dinner with the doctor had arrived that morning, he knew something strange was in the offing.

When he arrived at the heavy door with the ubiquitous 'C' engraved in the shining finish, he stopped, took a deep breath, and pulled his formal tunic down more snuggly over his broad shoulders.

F.R.'s appearance in Payson had set off an avalanche of change within Carpathian Industries that was still being felt days later. J.P. Smith, a man Vlad had distrusted since his shadowy arrival on the heels of some vague tales of Union persecution, was now viewed with at least some small amount of suspicion by the others as well. Had F.R.'s claim not proven true, if he had been an assassin working for the Union or for any of the factions that wanted the doctor dead, it could have been the end of everything they had all been working toward for so long. As most things in life, success was an excellent defense, after the fact. But the reality was that he had conspired with an unknown person to gain access to the secret stronghold of Payson, and that had to be eating, just a little, into the doctor's trust.

For Vlad, the impact of his son's arrival had been the most profound, and yet at the same time, the most subtle. News of his wife's death had rocked him, of course. He had been away from home for so long, had made so many promises that had been deferred, over and over again, that he could barely stand to think about the fact that she was gone. The woman he had loved all his life, the woman for whom he had worked all this time, would never see what he had helped to accomplish.

But his son would. In fact, his son saw more of it every day. Carpathian had kept F.R. and his foreign friend away from any of the major labs and most of the men and women who constituted the heart of the Enlightened Movement, but he had seen plenty already. Vlad had been excited to show his boy all over the town to prove to him, at least, that the separation had not been completely wasted. But the relationship between him and his son had been strained, understandably. F.R. had not been as warm and forthcoming as Vlad might have hoped. He now cursed every letter he had allowed himself to write, telling the boy to stay away. F.R. and his friend, Ernest, had kept to themselves for the past few days, waiting for the boy's uncle to formalize his position in the town and the organization. Vlad had tried to carry on with his duties, and had worn a polite mask throughout. But he had been nervous, and would not lie to himself about it. When Carpathian made his decision, it would be final. And Vlad was not entirely sure what that decision would be. If his son was to be sent away... he had no intention of letting that happen.

The summons to dine, unusual in itself, was almost definitely in regards to F.R.'s status. The moment Vlad had seen the detailed invitation on its crimson stationary, sealed with glittering golden wax, he had known.

And he did not wish to put off the discovery any longer.

Vlad knocked sharply on the door, and smiled grimly at the customary "Enter."

The room was not small by most standards. Roughly ten paces to a side; it was paneled in warm, rich wood. The floor was a black and white mosaic imported from Italy, and the furniture was all original work from the plundered palaces of France at the turn of the century. The table could comfortably serve ten without crowding, and Vlad's steps faltered as he saw that there were six places set. He had anticipated that it would only be him and the doctor for dinner, to give him some time to process whatever decision Carpathian had made. The fact that more places were set made him feel a little more hopeful. Carpathian would hardly have invited other people to witness his shame if the decision had gone against him, would he?

"Vladimir!" The doctor, in formal coat, vest, and silk cravat, rose from his place at the head of the table and approached for a formal embrace. The two men swung their heads for two perfunctory, traditional kisses, and Vlad did his best to keep his smile steady, allowing the doctor to speak in his own good time.

"I think I remember you enjoyed venison, yes?" Carpathian gestured for Vlad to sit beside him. As he did so, he scanned the table, thinking how bare most of it looked. He nodded when the doctor raised an eyebrow, waiting for a reply.

"Excellent! The hunting has been very good up north past Tolchico, or so they say." He sat back down, replacing the napkin in his lap. "Now, tell me. How is young F.R. settling in?"

Vlad eased back in his chair, eyeing the empty wine glass with some dismay. "He is vell, Burson. Sank you for asking." He swallowed, and then continued. "He is hoping to take a more active role in zevorkings of Payson, ven you have taken ze opportunity to vet his accomplishments."

Carpathian laughed at that, and then clapped his hands. "Oh, I have done that, don't you worry, Vladimir. Your son is quite remarkable, as I well knew long before his arrival. He was not unknown to the scientific community in Europe, even as a boy. I have no doubt that he will be an important, active member in our work here. As we strive to sever our ties from the mysterious past and forge ahead on our independent path, we need fresh young blood like your son's. All the better that the blood be of our family, no?"

"He vantsnossing so much as to serve, Burson." Vladimir would not beg for his son's position, but he knew that the doctor could sometimes act on impulse, and the looks exchanged between young F.R. and Misty Mimms had not gone unnoticed.

"I know, my friend, I know." A service door opened in the rear of the room, and a man in a ceremonial white duck uniform came stiffly in, standing by the doctor with an inquiring expression. The man's tunic was similar to Carpathian's in cut if not color or material. A red and gold crest had been emblazoned over the left side of the man's chest; yet another of the doctor's 'official' seals.

"Bring the wine, please, if you will." The doctor continued

to smile at Vlad, barely acknowledging the servant's presence. The man nodded, his face a formal mask, and turned to go. Carpathian brought him back with a sudden snap, and then turned to address him directly. "Please have my next two guests brought in. I think we're ready for more company."

Vlad was curious, but refused to show it, even for a moment. When Carpathian was in this mood, nothing could keep him from springing his little surprises. His only consolation was that the man could not be so far gone as to play with his emotions like this if the news regarding his son was bad.

Still, it never hurt to ask. "Have you given any sought as to vhat duties F.R. might be called upon to perform?" Carpathian answered with a sly smile, putting one finger alongside his nose. "No telling secrets out of turn, Vladimir." He tapped on the table with a finger. "All will be well, I assure you."

The rear door opened again and another servant in white came in bearing a large bottle wrapped in soft terrycloth. The man stopped at the doctor's side, but Carpathian waved away the offer of a taste. "Just pour us two glasses of wine, will you? I chose the bottle. I know what it tastes like."

Without reaction the man nodded, poured off a glass for the doctor, and then moved around to fill another for Vlad. He nodded his thanks, but the man was gone before he could say anything.

The wine was delicious, of course. Everything that Carpathian served was amazing, or what would be the point? A great deal of time and effort was being expended to manipulate the future of an entire continent. There would be little reason if the men and women who made that effort could not live in comfort through the fruits of their labor.

There was a knock at the main door, and Carpathian put his glass down with a sharp click. "Enter." Vlad was surprised to see a slight smile on the man's face as he said it. Was it possible he was being ironic whenever he gave his seemingly self-important response?

Vlad turned in his chair to look at the door, and was surprised to see two figures in flowing lab coats enter. The first was the broad Englishman, his florid face shining with sweat despite the cool of the room. Behind Thomas Huxley came the brush-haired German, Friese. The two of them, the newest additions to Carpathian's establishment, Smith notwithstanding, looked slightly out of their depth in the dining room, as well they might. To the best of his knowledge, neither of these men had really been accepted into the doctor's inner circle yet, and so dining with their lord and master was probably not something they had anticipated when they awoke that morning.

"Ah, gentlemen!" Carpathian arose from his great seat once again, gesturing at the two places to his left. "Come! Come! I trust you enjoy venison?"

The two young scientists mumbled their assent, nodding to Vlad as they approached the table. He nodded back, more curious than ever. Was F.R. going to be put in the care of these young men? He hardly thought that would be fitting, given his son's already impressive accomplishments. He could not even remember what these two men specialized in. Huxley studied genetics, if his memory was not failing him; something about the gradual or sudden change in the development of an entire species? As for the German, he worked with some sort of insect.

"Now, I know you are all wondering what brings us together like this, with so little warning." Carpathian smiled to each of the men at the table individually. Vlad had seen him do this before, playing a room like a fiddle. Even knowing to watch for it, he felt an answering grin on his own face. The two young men were completely lost.

"Vladimir and I were discussing my nephew, F.R. What do you boys think of him so far?"

Huxley and Friese looked at each other for a moment, both shrugging, at a lost as to what they should say. Huxley spoke up after another silent moment. "We have not spent a great deal of time with him, sir. But the boy's reputation precedes him, certainly."

Friese nodded, a smile shining out from his full beard and long mustaches. "A very respectable name indeed, sir. I have heard he has been doing great work with alternative power supplies and even exploring different aspects of flight." His excitement was getting the better of him, Vlad could see. Carpathian did not take kindly to people looking too closely into alternative power systems, considering almost all his influence was derived from his near-monopoly of RJ-1027. "I would be very interested, in particular, to see what he thought of my work with the bees, sir. I think—"

"Of course, of course!"Carpathian's smile was artful, but Vlad thought he saw some iron at its edges. Something in his stomach twisted slightly at the thought. "And how about you, Vladimir?Were you anticipating that the boy would join the ranks of my scientists, when he took his place here?"

The question sat there for a moment, and Vlad could not help but think of the opaque waters of the southern swamps and the dangerous monsters that lurked beneath the surface. "I did, Herr Doctor."

Carpathian seemed to mull that over for a moment, swirling a mouthful of wine around his tongue while the skin about his eyes tightened slightly in thought. "Indeed. He does have a fine, scientific mind. Of that there is no doubt."

With another sharp clap, Carpathian summoned a servant, and told the man to see that their final guests were brought in.

"I imagine, to keep everyone happy, the two young men come as a pair, yes?" This time there was no doubting the edge to the doctor's smile.

The three dinner guests looked at each other, not sure to whom the question had been addressed. Vlad shrugged. "F.R. seems fond of zelad, of course. I sink if given his choice, he vould-like to see a place found for him as vell."

Huxley nodded. "Never can have too many Cambridge men on the team, right?" He smiled, but his deep laugh fell flat in the big room. Watching his friend's failure, Friese merely nodded, his smile dimming.

For the third time that evening there was a knock at the heavy door, and for the third time Carpathian drew breath to issue his accustomed summons.

The door swung open before he could speak.

F.R. came into the room as if he owned it, a broad smile on his tanned face, his orange-tinted goggles drawn up over the brim of his Stetson. It was clear he had made no effort to dress for dinner, and looked like some fanciful image on a dime novel's cover. Tight denim trousers were tucked into heavy boots, while an elaborate leather jacket, collar turned up, was open to reveal a soft, dark shirt beneath. The jacket's sleeves had been artfully removed to show off the sleek metal arms to their best effect.

The vermillion light, orange highlights glittering within the ruby red, was a sharp contrast to the sullen RJ chandelier and the lamps hanging at intervals along the walls.

"Uncle, you wished to see us?" Behind F.R. stood his burly friend from New Zealand. The young man's pleasant face was pale behind his bushy mustache, and he seemed on the verge of apologizing for barging in.

Carpathian took the moment in stride, rising as he had done for his previous guests and gesturing for the new arrivals to take their seats beside Vlad. With a cocky grin, F.R. slouched to the farther chair, leaving the seat between himself and his father for the other boy.

Carpathian waited until both were seated, then settled down himself. He topped everyone's glasses off with his own hand, and then sat back in his chair, one arm dangling loosely over the armrest.

"We were just discussing your potential, nephew, and where we might all best profit from your most excellent set of skills." He took a sip of the wine. "Have you any thoughts on the matter?"

F.R. stared at his uncle for a moment without expression, and a vague, growing chill rose in Vlad's chest. "Well, uncle, I've had a few days to think about it, of course. I know you're working on daVinci's dilemma..."

Carpathian drew a single eyebrow up, gesturing with a finger for elaboration.

"Flight, of course." F.R.'s smile widened, but his eyes were cold. Clearly, he had not appreciated being made to wait, even for afew days. Vlad's chest tightened further. Did the boy not see what was at stake?

Carpathian looked first to Vlad, then to Huxley and Friese. It would have been difficult to completely hide the nature of their work, with tests being conducted regularly on the proving grounds across the dust-filled valley. But the work on the Hellions was not supposed to be something spoken of lightly. Someone had been telling tales.

"Interesting." Carpathian did not try to conceal the sour look on his face, and F.R.'s smile brightened another tick. "Tell, me, F.R., who have you been talking to?"

Vlad's son shrugged, sinking further into his chair. "Lots of people, Uncle.Anyone who would talk to me, really." His smile vanished for a moment. "It's not as if there was a lot else to do."

Carpathian pursed his lips. "Of course. I apologize for your lack of diversion." There was no apology in the man's eyes, though. Vlad's concerned tightened another notch.

The doctor's eyes twitched as he seemed to think of something new, and a different light smoldered in their tightening shadows. "Were you speaking with Miss Mimms, by any chance?"

That question seemed to catch F.R. as off-guard as it caught Vlad. The boy frowned, all artifice falling away for a moment. "No. I haven't been able to find her."

Vlad was afraid that the second statement did almost as much damage as the first avoided. A hungry gleam in Carpathian's eyetold him he was right to feel that way.

"A shame. Two young people such as yourselves, I'm sure you have a lot in common." He smiled slightly and his eyes flicked at F.R.'s brazenly displayed arms.

The doctor slapped both palms lightly on the table and

sat back, his face suddenly relaxed and friendly. "So, it looks like there is agreement here. Your past accomplishments, coupled with your clear aptitude and keen mind, would all seem to argue that your place here is with the men and women of science, pioneering the technologies that will see us pushed forward into the new century."

Everyone around the table but Vlad seemed to relax. Huxley and Friese leaned forward, grabbing their wine with relief, and even F.R. and Ernest sat back. Some strange, half-seen doom had apparently passed them by, and the released tension in the room was palpable, even to the newcomers.

Except that Vlad could tell that the moment had not passed, and watched the doctor with sharp eyes. When the change in the man's face happened it was subtle, but the old soldier saw it, and it made his blood run cold.

"I, however, am not so sure." Carpathian's words were casual, but they served to burn the calm from the room. Smiles slipped and backs straightened. "I have heard tell of other skills you possess; other duties you might perform." The doctor's smile grew predatory as he leaned over the table toward his nephew. "I've heard you might even like that kind of work more than you say you revere science."

The chill in Vlad's veins settled deep. All of the half-heard whispers, all of the dark rumors and accusations that had been made against his son over the years, charges that he had dismissed out of hand, came rushing back to his mind. And as he saw the look in his son's eyes, the understanding, the amusement, the total lack of denial, he felt like he was trapped in a nightmare.

"I have many interests." F.R. muttered the words, leaning forward in conscious mimicry of his uncle. "And I take joy in a great many things."

Carpathian's smile was that of a shark, slashing through the water at the scent of blood. "Excellent. So you would not shy away from more... direct, work?"

F.R. shook his head. "Speak plainly, Uncle. Tell me what you want me to do."

Carpathian's eyes were dark, hellish pits. "I want you to kill a man."

*****

F.R. clung to the steering handles of the Iron Horse. His uncle could not have known how eager he had been for just this sort of assignment. The time he had spent traveling through the desert, then cooling his heels in Payson, had driven him nearly mad with ennui. He needed to get out there and do something. He needed to get his hands dirty. And although his ultimate goal was to work beside his uncle and usher in this brave new world, it would not hurt for the old man to understand what other skills F.R. possessed as well. Besides, what were these outlaws to him?

All around him, a phalanx of the floating vehicles roared across the dry desert. Clumps of pale, spikey grass grew here or there, but for the most part, he was now in the midst of the desolation. He glimpsed sideways, squinting despite his thick goggles, and found himself wishing that Ernest had chosen to take this journey with him. But his friend took no joy in this kind of escapade.

The man riding beside him, however, looked like a prisoner escaped from the darkest jail in town. Thomas Huxley was clearly a man of action in the same mold as F.R. himself, and had been chomping at the bit to escape the laboratories beneath Payson, even if only for a short while. A heavy, wide-gauge shotgun was crammed into an undersized boot by his left thigh, and the young man from Romania found himself eager to see what the weapon could do.

All around the two young men, the rest of the metal machines were ridden by the most solid animations his uncle could assemble. There were no great Creations like 5 or the drill-beast he had seen in the Tonto Forest, but the firepower they carried in their desiccated hands should be more than enough to finish the job.

According to his uncle, the target was holed up in a run-down old ghost town on the very edge of the western desert called Tolchico. Aside from the outlaws, it was supposed to be completely uninhabited, abandoned decades ago. There were no clear roads out this way any longer, and F.R.'s posse flew over the dusty remains of the trail that had led to this border outpost in days long gone by.

Getting to ride the Iron Horse was an unsought bonus of the assignment. He had heard of them, of course; even seen several during his journey west. But he had not expected to be entrusted with one of the one-man transports so soon. The thing was like an iron rain barrel on its side, with a massive cowcatcher on the front, sled skis on the bottom, and a saddle on the top. An assembly of control handles, knobs, and levers sat nestled behind a grimy windscreen, and a nest of nozzles, tubes, and flared siphon-shapes stuck out the back end. When the things were turned on, they made a God-awful howl that would have put the now-dead Ironhide to shame.

F.R. knew they would have to leave the Iron Horses behind if they wanted to approach the outlaws unawares. Neither himself nor Huxley had ever been anywhere near Tolchico before, but the doctor had provided them with excellent maps, and he knew that they had only a few more minutes before they were going to have to stop and finish the trek on foot.

F.R. waved to get Huxley's attention, and they both throttled down their 'Horses, the constructs drifting to a stop settling into the dirt. They swung their legs over the saddles and dismounted, both stretching their aching muscles and shaking life back into their limbs. All around them the animations disembarked from their own vehicles, only to stand, stock still, waiting for their next instructions.

With a sidelong glance at several of the animations, F.R. turned back to Huxley. "What do you know about this William Bonney?"

The Englishman shrugged. "He's an outlaw, no better nor worse than any of 'em. I've only met him once, in passing. Not a very pleasant fellow."

F.R. looked out over the desert to the west. "How many men does he usually have with him?"

Huxley shook his head. "I don't know, mate. I don't know anything about the man." He pulled his enormous weapon from its sheath. "You're the expert at this type of thing, I hear. I'm only along to watch your back."

F.R. opened one of his saddlebags, pulling out two thick pistols, a bronze canister affixed to the back of each. "Why, by the way?" At a look from Huxley, he elaborated. "Why are you here to watch my back?"

Huxley's grin was barely contained within the margin of his muttonchops. He laughed. "You're a breath of fresh air you are! Do you have any idea how hard it is to get assigned to any sort of duty outside of the labs in Payson?" He rolled his eyes. "I've been trying to get out of that cell for months!"

That was something F.R. could appreciate, and he returned the smile with a nod. "Well, then, let's keep the excitement going, shall we?"

They gave the animations specific instructions and then headed out. They had a long walk ahead of them if they wanted to reach Tolchico at midnight. When hunting men, surprise was always paramount.

Chapter 13

From a shallow ridge overlooking the town, F.R. and Huxley watched through the red-tinged glow of monoculars. The contraptions took what little light there was and magnified it, bringing distant objects into sharp, clear focus illuminated with a ghostly crimson hue. The eerie lighting within the device made the blasted ruins look like a real ghost town.

They could just make out the sand-buried remnants of a fence that had once encircled the entire town. Twenty or thirty buildings had once defined tight, twisting streets within the wall, but none stood higher than six feet tall now. Much of the lumber thrusting up out of the ravenous sand was charred and shattered. Tolchico was a ghost town, and it had not died easily.

In the center of town was a large, slumped pile of a ruined building. Built from red desert stone, it looked to have once been over two stories tall, with a wide terrace all along the front and a grand staircase leading down to an open square before it. Now, the windows were smashed, dead eyes, any door that might have been there was long-since blown away, and the roof had caved in over more than half the structure. The walls were canted inward, and the whole thing looked like it was awaiting only a soft spring rain to blow it down.

F.R. was not used to the touch of fear that now settled down between his shoulder blades. He was the predator in the night, the haunter of the shadows. He was the thing other men had to fear. Except, as he looked down at that blasted old building, he seemed to sense an aura of unspeakable horror clinging to the very stones, rising into the night sky like an invisible column of thick, foul smoke. No man in his right mind should have gone in there.

But through the monoculars they could see a light glowing from within the irregular windows. It looked as if Carpathian's information had been correct. His uncle had not said what his interest in the outlaw Billy the Kid was, but he was at least involved enough to know where the man was hiding. F.R. thought for sure that was something he might want to think about when he had a little more leisure.

"There are at least three in the ruins behind the main gate." Huxley gestured with his own monocular to the gaping hole in the tumbled wall where the front gate had once been.

F.R. focused his own monocular on the area and soon saw the outlines of three men, each lurking in a different place, pacing around in the shadows. They appeared as red silhouettes in the monochrome image, living things showing much more brightly than the inanimate ruins around them. As he watched, one of them raised his own vision device to his face and scanned the desert. The Romanian almost ducked, before remembering what his uncle had told him about the devices. Living things, even grass and bushes, would make it difficult to discern men hiding within. So, hunkered down in the desert grass, they were probably safe.

"Anyone you can see out in the other direction?" F.R. moved his field of vision slowly over the far edge of the village, but at that distance there was nothing to see.

Huxley shook his head. "Not a nit, I'm afraid. But the foothills border that edge of town. We're right on the verge of savage territory. If they don't have sentries out that way, they're more ignorant than I've heard them given credit for."

F.R. stared down at the town, his monocular loose in one metal hand. Even without them, he could see the glow of RJ lanterns from the broken windows now. He looked back at the animations sitting on their haunches in random bunches, staring into the middle distance with their pale, milky-white eyes. Then he looked down at his monocular again.

"Thomas," his voice was soft as he thought. "Do these contraptions see animations as well as they see living men?"

*****

Billy sat at the crooked table and stared glumly into his empty glass. The bottle was on a small pile of boxes across the room, in easy reach of Smiley's grimy paw, but he didn't care to ask for more. He had been waiting in this burnt up, knocked down hellhole for over what seemed an eternity, and still Carpathian had not sent for him. He was giving the old man one more day, and then he was going to go out there and find Jesse James and rip those shiny arms right off his stinking body.

He shook his head, dizzy from the drink. They were running out of food, too. He was not eating nearly enough to counter the amount of rotgut he was pouring down his gullet. He had done too much for that crazy old man to be left out here to rot in the desert like this. No way was this fair. His eyes flicked up to take in the men lounging around the ruined old trading post. Men like these sensed weakness, they sensed when a chief was no longer able to hold his own. Much more of this, and they would leave him for another boss.

Or worse, one of them would take it into his head to off their current leader and take his place. As the current boss, that did not at all sound like a good idea to Billy.

"Smiley, y'gotta smoke?" Jake 'Smiley' Williamson looked up from where he was sharpening his gleaming stiletto and shook his head.

"No boss." The words did not seem entirely sincere, coming from that wide, empty grin.

"Well, then wha' the hell good'reya?" Billy lurched to his feet and began pacing. The men moved their legs to avoid getting stepped on, but he did not notice. Smiley had been with him longer than almost anyone. Only his old friend, Johnny Ringo, had ridden with him longer, and Ringo had been laying low ever since his run in with the Earps back around Tombstone. Without Ringo, Williamson was the only gun hand he could totally trust. Would they have to sleep in shifts, to avoid waking up with a slit throat?

Smiley was a butcher, without a moment's warmth in his heart for beast nor man. But when he gave his loyalty, he gave it completely. At least, he had when he had given it to Billy. The man might ride with other outlaw chiefs every now and then; hell, he had even ridden with Jesse a few times. But he always came a'runnin' when Billy called.

With the life they led, out here in the middle of nowhere, on the edge of nothing? That was worth more than its weight in gold.

The first gunshot caught them all by surprise. It was a distant, flat sound, coming through the front windows and the gaping doorway. There had been no outcry, no warning. A second blast sounded, and they all saw the brief crimson flash of an RJ weapon light up the night. Then there was a cry. It was an inarticulate scream, but Billy could tell straight away who it was. Doyle was not one of his brightest hired hands, but he was a good man, and one of the sentries watching the eastern walls and the main gate into shattered Tolchico.

Another scream echoed through the night, cut off abruptly in a gurgling, choking sound.

Doyle had been a good man.

"G'up! G'up!" Through the muzz of the drink, Billy scrambled back away from the windows, grabbing men by the shoulder and pushing them forward. "G'out there an' fight!" He grabbed one man by both shoulders and pulled him in close, screaming into his face, spit spraying into his eyes "W'am I payin' you fer?"

The man shook his boss off, wiping his face with a disgusted hand. Lyle: that was the man's name; another good man. What was he doing, shouting at his best hands? Had he really let the old man get that deep into his brain?

Billy drew one of his custom six shooters and moved toward the door. The haze from the whiskey was fading in the face of imminent violence, and the ways of a leader were coming back to him fast. You could not expect men to follow you when the bolts were flying if you were hiding, pushing them into danger.

"C'mon, boys! Must be Jesse, wantin' to prove who's the better man!" He drew the other six shooter and hit the ruined wall hard with his back, just left of one of the big windows. "Let's show him who the real big bug is, shall we? Get those lights!"

That did the trick, and his men were up and moving, scuttling to avoid possible fire from outside, grabbing weapons and power cells as they scrambled forward, dousing all of their RJ lanterns as they moved into position. Brooks and Grady, the two newest men, were not quite as fast as his old hands, Dale or the brothers, Rusty and Jake, but they all looked game enough. Smiley pushed himself up off the wall, pulling his shotgun from its scabbard over his back. He still held the evil-looking knife in the other hand. His grin never wavered.

Billy swung his head around to catch a quick glimpse of what was happening outside the old trading post. Without monoculars, he could barely see anything out there, but he thought he could make out some movement, coming down the rubble-filled streets toward him. After a quick breath he looked again, not quite believing what his brain had told him on first glance.

The creatures shambling toward the ruined building were animations: Carpathian's animations. The doctor had been lying to him all along.

"They're the doc's walkin' corpses! Get 'em!" Rage and fear burned the last hints of the whiskey from his blood. "Rusty, Jake, Dale, you guys take the left side." He waved them off to the gaping windows in that direction. "Brooks and Grady, get yer asses over here and help me hold off the shamblers on the right."

Billy held his six-shooters in hands that shook with anticipation, he looked over his shoulder, scowling. "Smiley, you get yerself to the front door and be ready to blast anythin' that makes it up the front steps." He looked back out over the ruined town, noting the animations still making their steady way toward the square in front of the trading post. "Stay in here, though. Don't go stickin' yer fool head out till we tell yayer gonna have a shot."

Smiley frowned slightly at that. Billy almost never put together a plan of attack that left him staying quietly in the back. Then he shrugged and settled back against the thick legs of an overturned table.

Billy looked out again and sent two quick bolts slamming down into the darkness. The ruins were momentarily lit up with the hellish hue of the RJ bullets, but the figures moving toward him did not cringe or pause. In fact, before the echoes of his shots had faded away, the figures had all raised their own blasters, opening up on the front of the building with haphazard fury.

Billy ducked back behind the brick wall as ruby bolts, dust, and bits of window frame erupted through the building. One of his greenlegs screeched like a banshee and fell over. Grady's heels kicked, his face mostly gone from the nose up, splinters sticking out of the wet meat that had once been his eyes and forehead.

The animations were holding their rifles like normal men, which explained how they had gotten all the way out here. The Doc's usual method was to take off the corpses' hands and replace them with weapons. Only the special carrion soldiers intended to ride Iron Horses were allowed to keep their own hands. He allowed himself a quick sigh of relief. At least there wasn't a Doomsday or Ironhide lurking out there, waiting to unleash its heavy weapons on his posse. They were probably only facing a group of animations and then one or two living and breathing mudsills from the doctor's team.

He liked those odds just fine.

With a guttural snarl, Billy rose from his crouch and shot down two animations with one shot from each of his custom pistols. The two animated corpses dropped like sacks of wet grain, their heads replaced with clouds of fine red mist and glittering machine parts that sailed off, still glowing, into the dark.

While he continued scanning for targets, Billy saw three more animations go down on his left, his old hands taking a heavy toll with careful, disciplined fire. There were only a few more figures picking their way out into the square below. The outlaw chief peered into the ruins further back, trying to find the breather that would be directing the attack. It would never be the doctor, of course, but maybe the day had come when he could prove himself against those damned German brothers, or maybe one of the brainy types from back in Payson that thought they were such great shakes with a shootin' iron.

But there was no movement out past the line of shambling carcasses. That made Billy a little nervous. There had to be someone out there somewhere, and they would not have started their attack if they were not going for the brass ring.

A grunt sounded off to the right, and Rusty went down, air wheezing through a glistening hole in his chest, splintered bone peeking out of the red. Jake cursed a blue streak as he spun around, seeing his brother fall. He moved toward Rusty, but even Billy, from across the dark room, could see the light fade from the gun hand's eyes. With a savage snarl, Jake turned back around punching bolt after bolt out the window as if he could impart additional force into the shots by snapping his fist after each one.

Billy regretted losing Rusty. They had ridden the river together for a couple years now. But there were only a few animations left moving toward the trading post, and if he could get out of this dry gulch only losing a couple of his hands, he would look at it like a gold bargain. He holstered the pistols and drew out his Gatling Shotgun, grinning like Smiley to think of the mess it was going to make of the last few dancing corpses when they got close enough.

The first bolt that flew from the back of the big room took them all as a complete surprise, no one more so than Brooks, who got thrown out of his window by the force of the bullet that struck him high in the back. The poor kid never even had time to scream as the ravening energy of the crimson bolt ate through his flesh, his spine, and into his lungs. In a flash and a tumble, the only thing left of him was a thin column of drifting black smoke rising from outside the window.

Billy spun around, his shotgun coming up to his hip, a snarl twisting his face into a terrible mask.

"Boss, no—" Smiley lunged for the door, his own shotgun barking a cloud of black smoke and thick red sparks. But Billy paid the grinning madman no mind. The black shadows at the rear of the long room hid an enemy out to kill him and his posse; a back shooter that had already cost him a man. He would be damned if he was going to turn his back on that kind of lowdown skunk.

More shots blasted out behind him. The animations must be making their final push. Several streaks of ruby light punched through the darkness into the shadows ahead as Carpathian's meat slaves fired their own last blasts. Ahead of him, the shadows remained impenetrable despite several small fires ignited by the blaster bolts. Nothing moved in the gloom, and his shotgun waved back and forth, tracking with his eyes as he sought the yellow dog who had thought to catch him unprepared.

Billy got tired of squinting into the black, and reached for the monocular on his belt as he continued to move deeper into the darkness. Behind him he heard another grunt, and then another scream. But he was in the midst of the wreckage-strewn rear section of the big room. If he turned now, he would be giving the coward a clear shot. With a steady hand, he lifted the monocular.

As his eyes pressed up to the lenses, the rubble around him sprang into clear focus, ruby gleams chasing each other around the edges of each object. He caught a glimpse of movement off to his left just as a massive explosion erupted behind him. He smiled beneath the heavy monoculars. That had to have been Smiley's shotgun, clearing the rest of the animations from his back field. That only left—

A moan from behind him sounded eerily familiar, and he jerked as it scratched at something in his mind. Again, something off to his left moved, and his mouth fell open as a tall figure rose from behind a pile of wreckage. He could not make out any detail, as even beneath the long sleeves of a great coat, the figure's arms blazed like the sun in the RJ-soaked vision of the monoculars.

His breath caught in his throat. "Jesse?"

The figure barked a laugh as it rushed toward him. "Not hardly." The voice was not Jesse's, although the arm arcing in from his left moved with the speed only the older outlaw could manage with his metal arms and their devil's blood.

The hand clapped down on his shotgun and pushed it out of true just as he pulled the trigger. Damn, but this Johnny Come Lately was fast! The Gatling Shotgun hissed into overdrive, and it spun through all three of its barrels, blasting an enormous swath of destruction through the room to his right, blasting the wrecked furniture into smoldering kindling and illuminating the room with a flickering light.

The man before him was definitely not Jesse James. He was much younger; younger than Billy himself, he looked. And the wild gleam in his eyes would have made Jesse look as sober as a judge. The man's smile was the worst thing of all, though. A wide grin equal to anything Smiley could muster on his darkest days.

"Sorry, Billy." The man spat through his grin even as his other hand came up and around, catching Billy on the chin with the force of a piston hammer and knocking him into the dust, and then deeper, into darkness.

*****

Billy gasped as the water flooded over his face and into his mouth and nose. He was drowning. He could not remember how he had managed to get into water, especially at this time of year, when the Little Colorado outside of Tolchico was barely a damp trail down the middle of the riverbed. But here he was, choking on a flood of water, without a doubt.

He sputtered and lunged forward, only to find himself tied to the arms of a chair. He was in a chair. The muzzy cotton in his head started to clear. He remembered animations, and his men being cut down around him. He remembered metal arms glowing a strange yellow red in his monoculars.

"Jesse?" He coughed. He knew there were things he could not remember, but there was only one set of arms like those in the entire world, as far as he knew.

"Sorry, mate. No one by that name here." The response was light-hearted and kindly. The accent was foreign, but not the harsh tones of Carpathian or that bastard of a slave of his, Ursul.

"What…Where…" He could not marshal his thoughts.

A sharp crack rocked his head back, and his cheek flared with agony. He had been slapped! Some four-flusher had dry gulched him, did for his boys, and then slapped him!

His eyes snapped open. He was in the trading post at

Tolchico. He was tied to one of the old chairs. His head whipped around. There was the man with the iron arms, standing in the open door, silhouetted by the rising sun shining behind him. He wore a broad-brimmed brown felt Stetson, orange-tinted goggles hoisted up over the hat brim. A thin beard sketched a line from his temples, down his jawline, and beneath his grinning mouth. He wore a vest-like leather coat designed to show off his sleek metal arms.

Beside the man in the door stood another man, stouter, in a light-colored duster. His face was open and friendly, his bushy eyebrows matched by thick muttonchops framing a pleasant smile. The man held an enormous shotgun by its cut off grip, the barrel resting on his shoulder. The floor was covered with the blood of his men, their bodies piled up in a corner. He began to panic as he counted. One... two... three, four, five...

He finally found Smiley, shaking his head in slow, groggy sways, tied to an exposed beam in the wall. He slumped there, hurt, his arms pinned behind him. But he moved. He was alive.

Billy looked back up at the galoot with the metal arms. "What do you want?"

The man laughed, his head thrown back in genuine amusement. He looked back down, shaking his head wryly. "Oh, that could fill a book, my friend: what I want. But as for the here and now of it? I'm here for my uncle."

Billy tried to make sense of that, but nothing came. "Your uncle?"

The man's smile widened. "Oh, yes. You know him. Dignified gentleman; rules over a little town to the southeast; metal from the waist down, I believe?"

"Carpathian." Billy spat the word into the blood-thick dust. "He's your uncle?"

The man nodded. "He is. And he sent me for you."

Billy nodded, straightening against his bonds, sitting as tall as he could, and looking off into the middle distance. His was amazingly calm, now that it had come to it. The trail of the outlaw did not have many endings. He had come to terms with that a long time ago.

"I won't beg." His voice was steady, and his chin raised another notch with pride.

"Good." The man with the metal arms sauntered toward him, settling down on his haunches in front of the outlaw chief. "Good. I'm glad. A man's got to have some pride, even when things have gone entirely pear-shaped on him."

The man stood, pacing back and forth with slow, deliberate steps. His smile never wavered. "My uncle had a message he wanted me to deliver, before I finished here."

The man spun, one glossy arm snapping down and then coming up with a strange pistol in his hand. If possible, the draw seemed to have been even faster than anything Jesse James could have managed. The strange, bell-shaped mouth of the weapon settled between Billy's brows, and he forced himself to meet the man's gaze, waiting for the end to come.

"No!" Smiley grunted from his place on the wall. "You get off'a him!" The enormous man was struggling against his bonds, and Billy looked at him in surprise. It was easy to think of Smiley as a soulless killer, completely lacking in human emotions. A swell of loyalty rose in his heart. He owed the big man whatever he could manage, before the end.

"You can kill me, but—"

The metal-armed man's smile deepened as he interrupted, "Oh, I'm not going to kill you."

Just as the words registered, the strange weapon seemed to float up on its own, gleaming at the end of that smooth metal arm, and settled on the center of Smiley's chest.

"Goodbye, Mister Williamson." The man's voice was low, a strange glitter in his eye, and he pulled the trigger.

It was over in an instant. One moment Jake 'Smiley' Williamson was struggling against his bonds on the wall, snarling beneath his thick mustache, larger than life itself. The next moment, with a soft thump, the enormous man was gone. The wall was saturated with gore, as was the floor around him out to a distance of at least ten feet. Gobbets and shreds of flesh, fabric, and leather were scattered around the room. Blood and guts dripped from the ceiling in a horrifying drizzle.

Billy heard someone screaming, but in his dazed confusion he could not tell where it was coming from. When the smiling man with the metal arms came back to stand before him, holstering his strange gun, he wanted to ask him who the hell was caterwauling, and to tell them to stop.

It did stop, just after the back of the man's metal hand connected with his jaw.

*****

F.R. stood with his glorious arms folded, enjoying the play of their orange-red light on the dull metal of the cell's bars. The man on the far side stirred, the shadows of the bars drawing stripes of darkness over his body. He lay in the clean straw, all of his possessions, except his weapons, in a neat pile on a bench at the back of the small chamber.

Payson did not seem to have a dungeon, or even a proper jail, since his uncle's purported allies seemed to have burnt down half the town. Most folks in the town were there because they really wanted to be, or they were too scared to leave. Neither group was terribly inclined to commit any serious crimes on the other members of the community. For those rare occasions when someone was feeling their oats, or was tempted onto the primrose path through any of the manifold temptations that even the most cerebral societies were heir to, Doctor Carpathian's punishment was generally swift, terrible, and did not call for an extended stay in a prison cell.

But this big cage, sunk into one of the cellars of the palace, had been constructed over a year ago, just in case the doctor decided he had need of holding someone against their will, and terror alone would not keep them still. The bars were crafted from stout iron, and it was said they were strong enough to defy even the fabled arms of Jesse James. F.R. smiled and looked down at his own arms. You just could not help but wonder about some things.

The man behind the bars stirred, and then moaned. Soon, he raised a bruised and battered face out of the shadows, and looked up at F.R. He started to shake his head, and then stopped, groaning at the pain it caused.

He squinted up at F.R. "Smiley?"

The young man could feel his grin stretch. "Oh, he's gone, I'm afraid, Mister Bonney. As gone as gone can be."

"Bastard." He spat into the straw, struggling into a sitting position against the bench.

A cloud briefly shadowed F.R.'s grin, but then it returned full force. "Oh, I assure you, Mister Bonney, my parents were properly wedded."

Billy the Kid spat again, looking up at F.R. through the fall of his disheveled hair. "What the hell you want with me? What the hell's your damned uncle want with me? I done ever'thing he ever asked o' me."

F.R. shrugged, going down to one knee beside the bars. "I'm not sure what my uncle wants with you, Mister Bonney. But for some reason, your actions and your words out in Tolchico have had a strange effect on me. I wanted you to know that I was only acting on my uncle's orders." He leaned in closer, making sure the man was looking him in the eye. "Everything that happened was at my uncle's express orders."

The man in the cell slumped farther down against the bench, shaking his head gently. "Don't matter no how."

F.R. frowned, shaking his own head. "Oh, but it does, Mister Bonney. I admire you. I admire you a great deal. And I wanted to share with you a little bit of history before I have to leave you for the time being."

Billy the Kid was not even looking at him now, but F.R. continued to talk. "I wanted you to reflect upon this: nothing lasts forever. Even this dark moment will pass, one way or another. And before it does, I wanted to make sure you did not do anything foolish."

Now the man looked up at him again, a feral light in his eyes. "Well, they do say foolish is as foolish does, friend. And I ain't no fool." The eyes tightened further. "I ain't no one's fool."

F.R. smiled as he stood. "Excellent, Mister Bonney. Then I hope we see each other again very soon. I'll be away for a little while, but when I return, I think we might have a great deal to discuss."

He turned on one heel and walked casually down the hall to the great wooden door. Behind him, Billy the Kid did not say a word, but F.R. could feel the weight of the man's gaze on his back all the way to the door.

He smiled even wider as he pushed it closed behind him.

Chapter 14

Vlad sat upright in the graceful wooden chair as if it were made of stone. His face remained a rigid, expressionless mask, as it had since Carpathian had sent F.R. after Billy the Kid more than a week ago. The man had sent William Bonney to Tolchico himself. Even though he had witnessed more than his share of double-dealings in his life, the cold, calculating heartlessness of this felt as if it had wrenched open his eyes.

The fact that his own son was the instrument of the betrayal may have made the sting all the harder to bear, but he hoped he was being honest with himself when he thought that he would feel the same way even if F.R. was not involved. But he knew it would be a lie if he imagined it did not have some impact on his reaction.

Carpathian had smiled after sending F.R. away, and they had sat down for an awkward, silent meal, the doctor, Vlad, Heinrich Friese, and his son's friend, Ernest Rutherford. Carpathian had acted as if nothing was amiss, bantering with his dinner guests, eliciting muttered, half-felt compliments on the meal, and generally pretending he had not sent his own nephew, the son of one of his closest advisors and friends, on a deadly mission on what seemed like a whim.

Later, Carpathian had taken Vlad aside and explained that the boy needed to establish himself with the rest of the Payson elite. Huxley, he said, was a devoted follower and a brutal fighter who would see F.R. safely returned to them if he, in fact, proved unequal to the task. The words had seemed sincere, Carpathian leaning in close for an intimate chat, his arm around Vlad's shoulder.

But those words had only touched upon a share of Vlad's fears. What if F.R. was equal to the task? What if even a portion of the tales he had dismissed as unkind rumor proved true? He knew, if his son returned with William Bonney, and the blood of Williamson on his hands, that there was far more to the boy than he had allowed himself to know.

And so he had nodded to the doctor's reassurances, setting aside his doubts and fears, and waited, like countless parents throughout history, for his son to return home from a battlefield not of his own choosing.

When F.R. had ridden into town only the day before, countless empty Iron Horses tethered to Huxley's mount, one with an unconscious William Bonney strapped across its saddle, he had felt his world shake.

F.R. had not come to him, but reported directly to the doctor upon his return. Bonney was below, in the cell they had constructed for Jesse James. Vlad had not been privy to the boy's debriefing, which had occurred while he was settling the still unconscious outlaw in his new abode. When he had once more been free to scale the tower, his son was gone, back to his rooms, and had asked not to be disturbed. He had felt the anger growing inside him every minute that ticked by, vowing that if something did not give soon, he would demand both the doctor and the boy tell him what was happening.

The summons to the council room in the tower had not come a moment too soon. The meeting, called for noon the day after the hunters of Billy the Kid had made their triumphant return, would not have raised the eyebrows of the most security-conscious advisor. But it raised the eyebrows of a father, and so Vlad sat brooding, rather than standing behind Carpathian's throne-like chair, when the others began to stream in.

Most of the assistants and technicians had not been invited this time around. This was not to be a grand unveiling, but rather a quick policy meeting regarding Billy the Kid's new condition, and an announcement Carpathian intended only for the ears of his inner circle. First to appear were Edison and Eiffel, conversing quietly together, their eyes dark. They each nodded to Vlad as they came in, their conversation dying, and slid along the far side of the long table, to their accustomed places. Friese came in with Huxley next, and Vlad tried to fathom within the Englishman's eyes what he might have seen out in Tolchico. But as usual, the bulldog face was blandly jovial, he smiled with a noncommittal gesture, and dropped himself into a chair opposite.

The Kaufmann twins were the only people in Payson who seemed to share any of Vlad's misgivings, but their own concerns probably dealt more with the fear of being supplanted in the doctor's good graces as his chosen gun hands. If even some of the rumors about what had befell Bonney and his posse were true, they had good reason to fear. They took their seats along the same side as Vlad after a moment's hesitation, and each of them glared at him as they moved past with barely-civil nods. Clearly, they blamed him as much as his son for their plight.

When a grinning Marcus Wayward made his grand entrance, sweeping into the room as if he owned it, followed by his ever-present watchdog, Jake Mattia, Vlad did not try to hide his sneer. These two, mercenaries of the last order and trash by any definition of the word, should by all honest accounts be sharing Bonney's cell at the very least, and if he were to be totally honest, he would rather they be strung up to die a slow, strangling death on a gallows out in the central square of Payson for what they had done to the town and the people in it. For what they had done to him.

Instead, Wayward moved through Payson as if he were a visiting dignitary, completely assured of his eventual ascension to the throne of the Confederate Rebellion. Jesse James' disappearance and eclipsing had happened without a mutter of regret or confusion, while Marcus Wayward, shiftless mercenary and honorless gun for hire, strutted through the streets he had attacked only a short while ago, a free man.

Wayward nodded regally to Vlad as he moved to sit directly to the right of the doctor's throne, Mattia standing behind him, thick arms folded over his chest. The old soldier blinked slowly, meeting the mercenary's gaze, and then looked away without acknowledging him. There would come a reckoning, but until that day, Vlad only had to tolerate the vicious pig, he did not have to be polite to him.

The door opened again, and Vlad almost rose as his son entered. F.R. looked healthy, happy, and completely at his ease. He had gotten some sun while he was on the trail to Tolchico, and the burnished color of his face agreed with him. His arms, polished as always to a deep shine, moved with a smooth silence that still filled Vlad with equal parts horror and admiration. His son nodded to him, grabbing his shoulder with a quick, reassuring grip and giving him a tight, honest smile before sitting down beside him. Ernest Rutherford came in behind his son, looking frustrated and annoyed, staring daggers at nearly everyone in the room.

The ten of them sat for several minutes in near silence. F.R. assured his father that he was well, the Kaufmanns shared a few muttered comments with each other, glaring at both father and son, and the scientists on the other side of the table were a study in contrasts; from Huxley in his relaxed, easy smile, to Friese's nervous grimace, to Edison and Eiffel talking to each other as if no one else in the room existed.

Vlad looked for a moment at the empty seats, wondering what each portended. The seat where Marie Laveau had sat was unsurprising in its vacancy. The woman had returned almost immediately to the free port of New Orleans to continue her research and production of her vicious animal minions for the coming war. But where was J.P. Smith? Sightings of the strange man had been scarce since F.R. had appeared, and he was one man Vlad liked to keep tabs on at all times. Something about the man struck him as wrong... more wrong than the usual run of villains and outcasts that had washed ashore in Payson.

When the silence had reached a sufficiently awkward level, the door opened one last time and Carpathian came in, Miss Mimms on his heels. She had been by his side practically nonstop since F.R. had left for Tolchico, and Vlad wondered if that had had something to do with his own feeling of unease. Maybe the Kaufmanns were not the only people worried about being supplanted?

"Welcome back, everyone. It truly is enchanting to see you in the light of day!" The doctor's smile was wide. "I trust you have all heard rumblings of young F.R.'s success in the west? Of our new guest, held in the palatial suite we have had installed downstairs?" The smile widened even more, and he chuckled at his own joke. Wayward grinned amiably, his eyes lingering on Misty Mimms with a mischievous glint. A couple of the scientists essayed a slight chuckle, but everyone else merely nodded in acknowledgement. F.R., of course, basked in the moment.

"So, yet another loose end has been dealt with, and our friend William Bonney will no longer be pestering us." He sat down, his fingers steepled before him. "I wish to keep Bonney alive, and relatively happy, in case we need him in the course of the next few months. And so, please, no unapproved experiments while he is in our care?" He tilted his head toward the scientists, who all began to protest, just a little too loudly.

Carpathian silenced them with a single finger and another smile. "In addition to the wonderful news regarding Mister Bonney, I have other information, perhaps of even greater value, to share with you today."

Vlad listened to the doctor, but he could not take his eyes off the young girl standing behind the throne. Was she truly poised to take his place? The old soldier knew the doctor's feelings for the beautiful, maimed girl in the enticing mask were confusing and entangled, but what were her feelings for him? He found himself staring at her eyes. He thought he could make out the hint of ridged scarring around her masked eye. As he watched, he saw something flicker there as Carpathian droned on. He could not be sure, but he was almost positive the expression was not favorable toward the doctor.

"You all know that I have, for some time now, been struggling to conquer the lofty heights of the world, for the betterment of all mankind and the consternation of our foes." He shook his head with wry chagrin, and shrugged. "You also know that these efforts have met with... mixed success, shall we say?" At this, the scientists all exchanged sharp,accusatory glances.

Carpathian raised his hands as if separating combatants. "Now, now, gentlemen, no need to get ornery, as they say.There

is plenty of responsibility for our lack of success to go around."
He lowered his hands to the tabletop, craning his neck to look at
each person individually. "You also know the greatest threat to our
mastery of the airy void is the unwashed savages of the Warrior
Nation."

The doctor seldom spoke of the native warriors with such
disdain unless he was getting ready to gear up for an assault, and
Vlad found himself tensing. He had heard nothing of such preparation. He looked quickly at Miss Mimms'eyes. He saw surprise
there, as well.

"I see, however, in all of this news, a very happy con-
fluence of events!" Carpathian clapped his hands together, then
gestured with a wide sweep toward F.R. "We have our new Achil-
les, returned home from battle, and by all accounts eager to once
again take the field." He gestured toward Huxley and Friese. "We
have our great Archimedes and Aristotle, minds of such force
and intricacy that the very laws of physics bow before them!" The
man's smile widened. "And today we have information on an entire column of savages headed this way from the west who, if
taken in ambush, could be defeated in detail, giving their entire
filthy Nation pause, and prove, once and for all, that our Hellions
are masters of the skies!"

The faces around the table ran the gamut of human emotions. The Kaufmanns were furious, probably at being left out of
the grand narrative being crafted. Likewise, Edison. Eiffel seemed
almost indifferent, while Friese looked as if he had just seen a
ghost. F.R. and Huxley, Vlad noticed, were still smiling as if all
was right with the world, while Rutherford's discontent had only
deepened.

Only Wayward and Mattia were unaffected, and Vlad was
not sure what to make of that. For a man whose entire future
was now inextricably intertwined with Payson, should he not have
shown some emotion at the thought of the best and brightest of
the city going after an entire war party in the wilderness?

And for that matter, what was Vlad's own reaction? He
was angry, certainly, that he had been left out of the planning

of the operation. Carpathian was a genius, and a man whose greatness could not be denied, even if his plans were sometimes so convoluted they made no sense to a man of direct action like Vlad. But he was no military or tactical mastermind. He had always counted on his brother-in-law in that regard. Now, having prepared an assault without Vlad's help, how would it fare?

Unless someone else had helped him with the planning. Mimms? No, she looked as confused and concerned as he was. Whothen? He turned to his son, saw the wide smile there, and knew the truth of the matter.

Carpathian must have been impressed by the boy's accomplishments in Tolchico, indeed. Maybe Vlad did have something to be concerned about after all.

*****

F.R. and Ernest rode on the fighting platform of the lead Doomsday. Behind them, ten more of the monstrous wagonsfollowed, each with a large metal box affixed to the top. Their transport bays were filled with squads of animations and hulkingCreations. A vanguard of 'Horse-mounted animations rode about a mile ahead, scouting the way, while more of the creatures rode along the flanks, coupled with the truly strange-looking monocav constructs. Desiccated torsos of human bodies had been affixed to towering metal platforms balanced on a single wheel that churned at the dry, dusty earth, hurtling the unlikely things forward at unnerving speeds.

"I just don't understand why we're out here, taking the field like two muscle-headed imbeciles!" Ernest shouted over the howling wind, holding onto an iron ring with a death grip as their wagon bounced over the rutted ruin of a road. "I thought you wanted to be a scientist, making great discoveries at your uncle's side! Not roam around the countryside killing at random!"

His friend's smile was infuriating. Ever since they had reached Payson, F.R. seemed like a different person. And the parts of him that Ernest was most fond of were being overshadowed by the elements of his personality that he most feared.

"We're in America now, Ern!" F.R. leaned in toward him, pitching his own voice to be heard over the wind. "This is how science is done here!"

"I won't be leaping around with a God-awful gun like that mad Englishman, F.R.!" Ernest knew it was mostly jealousy that had has spawned his growing antipathy toward Thomas Huxley, but he did not care. "I'm more than some grimy line soldier!"

Rather than being annoyed or angered, F.R. merely laughed. "Of course you are! And so is he! You'll like Thomas when you get to know him, Ern, don't worry!" He tapped the side of his orange-tinted goggles and gave a wink through the thick glass. "You're here to make sure my new invention works. Were you able to do what I asked?"

Ernest sniffed, and then almost choked on the dust he inhaled. "Of course. The units you produced before you left for your little hunting party are all attached to the Hellions, linked into their cerebral control nodes."

F.R. gave a close-mouthed smiledue to the flying grit. "Excellent!" He tapped two small buttons that had been newly affixed to the side of the goggles, and it seemed as if the orange tint deepened for a moment. Then he tapped them again, his eyes reappeared, and his smile turned impish. He hooked a thumb at the big, windowless boxes trundling along behind them. "Darkness, of course."

Ernest shook his head at his friend, and then turned his own goggle-protected gaze out over the desert streaming by. After a moment he turned to F.R. and leaned in again to ask another question. "How did your uncle know the natives were coming?"

That earned him a wide returning smile and a shake of F.R.'s head, his dark hair streaming behind them. "How does he know anything?"

It clearly did not bother F.R. in the slightest, and that bothered Ernest more than he wanted to admit.

*****

The long column of warriors swept down out of the mountain passes, shedding the lingering chills and the early snows, moving down toward the plains with anticipation flashing in their eyes. With the Thunder Wolf and the Raven Warrior leading the way, guided by Sky Spirit and Walks Looking, they had maintained an excellent pace throughout their journey, and were going to arrive in the east sooner than Sitting Bull had expected. They had seen none of the spirit people on their return, and Walks Looking wondered if there might not be some significance to that.

In addition to the massive column of warriors moving with them, several great eagles shadowed their progress, intending to fly east and join their brethren against the enemies of the Great Spirit. Sky Spirit was humbled and gratified, Walks Looking could tell. For her part, she was not sure how she felt about the giant birds constantly floating overhead. Something about them bothered her, and she found herself constantly gazing upward, trying to keep tabs on the monsters.

Traveling with the strange warriors from the west had been a revelation for Walks Looking. These men and women had only a passing knowledge of her father and the council that had brought the tribestogether. They owed no debts of fealty or honor to him, and did not feel the reverence for him that seemed to permeate the eastern people.

She had spent many nights talking with Qwoli and his warriors. Bayaq was a taciturn man, not easy to fathom. But the Thunder Wolf and his men and women were irreverent and kind, and they often laughed deep into the night. They knew little of the Union, or Carpathian and his poisons, and so did not have her own people's paranoia about such things. It had been an intriguing journey, indeed.

But they were on the plains at last, the Rockies rising up behind them, crowned in glittering silver. Riding at the front of the column, she opened herself up to the earth, her spirit vision showing her the infinite connections and flow of life through the view stretching out before her. Ahead she could see, in the faded ghost trails of past travelers, a fork in their path. The northern route would take them back to the main Warrior Nation encampment and her father. A return to the world she knew; the world that grew more and more tiresome. But the southern route would lead them down into the Contested Territories, toward Carpathian's hidden stronghold and the red poison.

To the south was a path free from her father and his influence.

As her mind wandered, she focused more on the southern fork. There was a blazing aura of life sitting directly across that trail. A long, sinuous line of vibrant spirit energy lay there as if waiting for her: a rattlesnake. The serpent reared up in the distance and regarded her with eyes that winked with ruby light reflecting the sun high overhead. Focusing on the creature, she watched it with a growing sense of wonder. Its aura was unique, glistening like oil, a thousand shades of crimson, ruby, and red winking along its length.

The Great Spirit, guiding her once again.

The serpent nodded once, and then lowered itself back to the parched grass, slithering off into the tangle of life within the ghost trail.

Walks Looking allowed her mount to continue for several steps, then raised a single hand, the horse rocking to a halt.

"Is something wrong?" Qwoli's smile was open and honest as he turned to her. His aura was easy to read, and a single hand on his shoulder was all it took to set it shimmering.

"I think we might want to think about heading south."

"What?" Sky Spirit urged his own horse toward them from where he had been riding in brooding silence, as usual. "We need to meet with your father. These warriors are a great boon, but only if we can coordinate—"

"We are no slaves to an eastern chieftain." Bayaq snapped. Walks Looking was gratified at the response. She would need all the doubt and confusion she could muster in the next few moments.

"If we head off across the plains, Carpathian's minions will learn of our arrival." She turned her blind gaze back to Qwoli, nodding to the Raven Warrior behind him. "If we move swiftly, striking now into the heart of his power, we will have the advantage of surprise. We can gut our enemy before he even knows we are near." She looked over her shoulder at Sky Spirit. "How much happier will father be, if we return to him with such a victory to hand, rather than mere allies, with battles still to fight?"

Sky Spirit shook his head with a scowl. "No. This is not what your father wishes." He turned to the western chiefs. "Even in your full power, you must see your strength is best employed in concert with our own."

Bayaq shook his head in dismissal. "I see no such thing. I see a finely-honed weapon poised over the heart of our enemy. At such a moment, you plunge the blade deep; you do not hesitate, waiting for permission."

Qwoli's usual smile was eclipsed with a grim, blank mask. "I agree." His eyes flicked to Walks Looking. "If we move toward him, will he come out?"

She looked back down the pathway. There was no sign of the snake, of course. There was no way for her to know what Carpathian would do. But she could trust the Great Spirit. There was a reason He wanted her on that path.

She nodded. "He will not be able to ignore such a challenge to his power. We may have to stage some raids on towns loyal to him, but when the cost is steep enough, he will emerge."

Sky Spirit's aura was like a churning storm cloud around him. He shook his head, not believing what he was seeing. "Sitting Bull must be made aware of our—"

"Go to Sitting Bull." Bayaq snapped. "Follow your heart. Your absence will not be felt."

That gave Walks Looking a moment's pause. The flying constructs Carpathian had been throwing into the sky were weak, but without Sky Spirit and his eagles, they could pose a serious problem. "You should stay—"

He cut her off with an abrupt gesture of one hand. "I know my duty, and my path." He looked toward the northern trail. "I trust I will see you all again, in time."

He left without another word, urging his horse northward. For the first time, Walks Looking was completely alone among the new warriors. As she watched Sky Spirit's aura fade and mingle with the ghost trail to the north, she felt liberated.

She turned back to the Thunder Wolf and the Raven Warrior. "Shall we continue?" Their auras glowed with anticipation, and she felt an answering rush in her own chest. As she saw the distant birds drift off to the north, she could not even summon a moment's care.

*****

Three days into the Contested Territory, the war party emerged from a small pine forest and looked out over the edge of the great desert. A small town lay before them, the tell-tale ruby gleam of RJ power prevalent throughout. Walks Looking knew that it would be no trouble at all for the western warriors to destroy the village. They would not even have to ask any of their mounts to sacrifice themselves to the Great Spirit's will. The town could not hold more than a hundred souls, and they would be farmers and shopkeepers, scratching a living from the dusty soil. There would be no warriors among them.

Qwoli stepped up beside her, his eyes taking on a yellow tinge, like those of a wolf. On the other side, Bayaq drew his cloak of ebony feathers more tightly about himself, his grim face nodding in satisfaction.

"We will make our first mark upon the east here." Bayaq gestured toward the tallest building. "When that building is engulfed in flames, it will be seen for hundreds of miles. There is no way your Carpathian will not see it, or be able to tolerate such actions against his people."

Qwoli nodded with a grin. "This day will be well-remembered by our people."

There was something not quite right about the town, but Walks Looking could not tease her doubt into the light of day, and so shrugged the inkling off as the typical chill before battle. All was quiet as the warriors approached. They made no effort to hide their presence, walking in the open, their weapons in their hand. A large herd of horses was left silent behind them, pawing the earth with nervous anticipation.

The leaders of the eastern warriors paced forward to either side of Walks Looking. They approached the nearest little house on the edge of town, and still there was no movement, no outcry. At this time of day there should be someone about. Someone should have seen the large war party advancing on them. Again, she felt that dark whisper of doubt.

"Perhaps we should send someone ahead." She nodded toward the house. "We should have seen someone by now."

"They are hiding in fear, or else sleeping through the heat of midday." Bayaq dismissed her concerns. "I will see that building burn before the sun travels another mile across the sky."

Something flashed in the corner of her spirit vision, and Walks Looking turned quickly, trying to catch it. There was nothing there but the line of warriors stretching off into the distance. Another movement caught her, and she looked in the other direction. Again, there was nothing.

She was looking directly at the house when it happened again, and she realized what she was looking at. A shadow had snapped over the house, vanishing as quickly as it appeared. A cold stone formed in her stomach, and she looked up into the air.

*****

In the stifling heat of the barn, Ernest wanted nothing more than a cool breeze. But he knew that his first chance at fresh air was going to come with his first taste of real battle, and so he forced himself to be satisfied with the heat.

In the center of the hay-strewn space, F.R. stood, his arms outstretched, and a maniacal grin stretched across his features. His eyes were hidden by a dark, shifting gleam that filled his goggles.

"It's amazing, Ern!" The other man's voice was louder than it should have been, hiding in a barn. It was as if he were shouting over the wind, or from a great distance. Either made sense, when Ernest thought about it. Still, though, it was not appropriate behavior while conducting an ambush, he was sure.

"I can see everything any of them can see!" F.R. tilted slightly to his right, his right arm dipping. "I can control one at a time." He frowned slightly. "The farther away they get, though, the more of a lag there is in their responses."

Ernest nodded, although he knew his friend could not see him. "Can you see the savages? Are they close?"

F.R. had been using the new Hellions to shadow the Warrior Nation party for more than a day now. When they had realized that there were no eagles or flying warriors protecting them, the Hellions had been given nearly free rein. The Romanian had been frustrated, time and time again, with the lack of control the Hellions suffered at higher altitudes, but the advantages far outweighed that limitation.

"They are approaching the northern-most house." Again Ernest had to force himself not to cringe from his friend's volume. "What do we have there?"

He took a moment to think. "Five animations, and Creation Seven, I think."

Creation 7 was a particular pride of Carpathians: the fusion of two brawny corpses, with two heads, their RJ units protected by iron helms. Two brawny arms each held a horrific close-work weapon, a wide buzz saw and a long, glittering drill, while two smaller metal armatures bore a frightening flame-spouting weapon and the dark metal bulk of a Heavy Gatling Gun, respectively. The titan was a testament to the durability of the doctor's Creations. Marcus Wayward had nearly destroyed 7, and yet with a few replacement weapons and some new flesh sewn on, it was as terrifying as it had ever been. They had thought that such a formidable foe so close to the probable point of first contact would be ideal.

"Excellent! They should react any moment now, then!" F.R. tilted slightly in the other direction, and Ernest could only imagine the view he was being treated to, seeing through the dead eyes of a distant, flying, animated corpse. "They are almost upon the first house."

Ernest rested his palm upon the pistol grip of the atomic ray gun he wore holstered by his side. He knew that he would be able to use it, if he must. He had no compunctions about taking the lives of the filthy savages approaching them, especially with a weapon of his own devising. Nevertheless, he was several steps farther removed from the lab than he really wanted to be.

In the distance, a sound like a ripping tear through the largest sail in the world echoed up into the sky.

*****

Walks Looking knew that her relationship with the Great Spirit rendered her nearly invisible to foes in battle. She did not know why this was so, but took it as another boon from her direct contact, without a spirit guide between them. When violence broke out around her, she was accustomed to seeing those near her felled by the weapons of the enemy while she herself remained safe. She knew this shield only protected her at a distance, but she was more than confident in her ability to look after herself in the swirling melee of close combat.

She slipped her two ritual blades from their sheathes, and in her spirit sight, they began to burn with a fierce sapphire glow. There was a reddish stain just visible within the flames, but she knew that it was merely from her contact with the Great Spirit, from which all energy flowed.

When a line of warriors off to her left were suddenly cut down by a spray of ruby bolts blasting from a narrow window in the house ahead of them, she felt relieved. She had known something was amiss. It was good to know she could trust her instincts.

With the eruption of crimson streams, and the accompanying grinding burr of a Gatling gun, the line of warriors scattered, many running wide around the house. Qwoli gave a low groan, his shoulders hunching, and his features began to shift beneath the flesh as bursts of blue lightning skittered over his body. Behind her, Bayaq cried out in pain as his own body was wracked with the agonizing, wrenching spasms that would see him emerge in a spirit-guided war form.

He shot over her head, taking off into the sky on shining black pinions as he screamed through the malformed beak of a great raven. His wings were huge, and tore at the air, carrying him up and over the house.

Qwoli, his own transformation now complete, was closer to a natural wolf in shape than her father was during battle. He lunged forward on all fours as blue energy continued to arc off his body and into the ground around him. He loped across the ground and leapt, crashing through the smashed window that had been spitting death since the ambush had first begun.

Walks Looking moved carefully toward the house, but kept her eyes on the sky. The flying carrion creatures were still circling overhead. They were not so high that arrows could not reach them, though, and several archers along the flanks of the Warrior Nation advance had stopped in their tracks and were launching glowing azure missiles up into the air. As she watched, one of the flaming arrow shafts pierced a creature whose wide, leathern wings were closing in preparation for a swooping attack. The missile caught the thing high in its chest, knocking it back into an uncontrolled tumble as its wings went limp and it burst into cobalt flames.

She was skirting along by the side of the house, watching for movement among any of the other buildings, when the wall in front of her shattered into countless flying splinters. She heard a familiar snarl as she watched the twisted wolf-form of Qwoli tumbling into the street, an enormous, reeking animation grasped to his broad chest. The thing was flailing with thick arms, a circular saw ending one and a growling, spinning metal drill the other. A web of lightning bound the two huge figures together as they rolled, and a strange howling filled the air. She reared back as she realized that the thing had two heads, both of which were screaming in frustration.

The massive Creations were horrible monstrosities, but this one seemed even more mangled and butchered than the others. There were angry red scars all around the bulging buzz-saw arm, as if it had been newly reattached. The flesh of the things' heads and chest were charred and ridged with burn scars, and a crude, fleshy patch had been sewn over the center of its chest. But Qwoli appeared to have the measure of the beast, and did not seem to need her help.

Walks Looking slipped through the blasted hole in the wall and scanned the room beyond. There were four animations standing loosely at the windows, firing blaster rifles out into the bright sunshine beyond. None of them were looking in her direction.

It was the quick work of a moment to spin through the room, her ritual blades taking each one in turn through the back of the neck, just below the glowing cylinders that gave them renewed life.

She took a last glance to make sure the building was empty, and then moved toward the front door, peeking out into the street beyond. It was a swirl of chaos as shambling corpses and proud warriors moved through the steps of a dance as old as man itself. She moved out into the light, counting on the touch of the Great Spirit to keep her hidden, and slid through the battle, corpses dropping lifeless behind her wherever she went.

There had to be a guiding force behind this ambush. The European's undead minions never attacked alone. While Qwoli and Bayaq kept the animations occupied, she would find where the leaders of the band lay hidden. She had some questions she wanted to ask them.

*****

F.R. soared over the burning town, glorying in the freedom of flight. He could feel his body tilting back and forth in sympathy with the Hellion whose dead mind he rode, and tried to ignore the distraction. The battle was going quite well, he could see from his high vantage. The savages had made it about half way toward the town hall in the center of the cluster of buildings, but the animations had boiled out of every building, stopping them cold.

A piercing agony flashed through his mind and he brought the Hellion he was riding back down to a manageable altitude. He was going to have to discover why they started to lose control when they went much higher than a hundred feet above the earth. He had already lost several to testing the boundaries, and was eager to test more. He was also frustrated by his inability to take a direct part in the battle. As far from the fighting as the barn that housed his body was, the lag in response time for the Hellion was too great for him to fight with any degree of skill. Perhaps if he was closer, he would feel differently, but for now, he directed the work of the other flying constructs, and observed from afar.

He had been glad to see there were none of the giant eagle-beasts he had heard so much about back in Payson present today. Nor did there seem to be any eagle-warriors. He winced and switched his consciousness to another undead mount as the Hellion he was currently inhabiting was knocked from the sky. The impact had struck from behind, with no warning at all.

The shadow of a flying warrior swept past, and he caught a glimpse as it fell upon another of his own minions. Not an eagle-warrior, but some darker bird, a carrion crow or something equally as distasteful. He sighed, wishing he could come to grips with the new enemy but knowing his control of the Hellions would not be sufficient to the task.

He could hear Ernest muttering darkly somewhere in the barn, but ignored him with an indulgent shake of his head. His friend was no coward, he knew that. But Ern needed to learn that the world was not changed in a laboratory buried deep beneath the ground, but out here, under the sun, where all the vagaries of the wide world could conspire against you, forcing you to adapt.

He had learned that he could guide several Hellions at once for brief periods of time, before his head started to ache. Again, not with fine-enough control to guide them in combat, not yet, at least. But it would come.

He had learned just about all he felt he needed to learn from this little skirmish. There was just one more thing he needed to do before he could declare the day a resounding success.

*****

Walks Looking had made it to the edge of the small square that marked the center of town. Overhead, Bayaq was making quick work of the flying corpses. Every few minutes one of them, torn and twitching, would fall limply to the dirt, often in several parts, and the shadow of the Raven Warrior would move on to its next victim. Qwoli was still matched in a fierce battle with the four-armed beast, while two more larger-than-normal creatures had come out into the open, blasting away with high-powered weapons or lashing out with blades and hooks.

Her first thought had been that the leaders of the ambush would be holed up in the large building across the square, probably in the bell tower that reached up into the sky. But an errant crimson bolt had struck the tower while she made her way closer, and the entire structure was now engulfed in flames.

Bayaq's wish had been fulfilled, but probably not in the way he would have wished. From her own experiences, that was the only way wishes were ever addressed.

A pained howl echoed off the buildings all around. Somewhere behind her, the battle must have turned against Qwoli. She shook her head, again scanning the area around her. A barn on the far side of the square caught her eye, and she saw a hint of movement in the shadows within an open side door.

Again, the howl wavered up into the sky, and she cursed. Spitting into the dust, she pivoted and ran back toward the sound.

Qwoli's wolf-form was torn and bleeding, one leg stretched out painfully behind him as he tried to move away from the towering form of the two-headed construct. Blood flew from the circular blade, and crimson fire licked from the snout of the flame-throwing weapon. The metal arm holding the large, multi-barreled cannon rose to point at the downed war leader even as he struggled to stand.

With an ululating cry, Walks Looking broke into a sprint, her arms held wide, blades glittering with spirit energy. The towering thing started, turning at the waist to watch her approach. With a shiver of revulsion she realized that the two heads appeared to be talking to each other behind their elaborate metal helmets.

She leapt into the air just as the thing unleashed a torrent of flame in her direction. Her leap took her over the wash of fire. One doeskin boot tapped lightly on its massive forearm, launching her up and over its heads. She spun as she flew, coming down facing the construct's back, her glittering ritual blades flaring with spirit energy and streaming black and red ichor.

For a moment it appeared as if Walks Looking's attack had failed. The gigantic thing stood, its dead muscles flexing with the power coursing through its veins. Then a wash of foul fluid burst from its two necks, each one sliced deep on the outside, arteries opened to the light. The construct seemed to shrink, deflating, as the black and red flood continued to sap it of strength and power. With a soft, gurgling moan, it toppled onto its faces in the street and was still.Where the brute strength of Qwoli's wolf-attacks had been insufficient to best the creature's defenses, her own weaponry, guided by the Great Spirit, had made short work of them.

She moved towardQwoli, his body resolving its shape back to that of a strong human man. His wounds were bad, but not life-threatening.

"Well done." He looked at the towering giant still leaking dark fluid into the dust of the street. His aura was colored with admiration and thanks, and just a shade of jealousy.

"You had distracted it." She smiled. "Now, let us find further diversion."

He started to smile in response, but then the expression froze on his handsome face.

"No need, my dear." The voice had a trace of an accent, not unlike the European, or his thick henchman. "We're right here."

She turned to see a tall man standing near the fallen construct, his arms folded over his chest. Behind him stood another man, his eyes shadowed, fixed upon the wounded chief behind her. Both men looked young, but under the foul influence of the devil's blood, she knew that meant very little.

Walks Looking started as she realized that the noise around the town had died down.

All around her, animations were emerging from the surrounding buildings, their weapons held at the ready. Another living man, this one with wild hair down the sides of his face and a massive gun in his hands, grinned at her from behind a small group of corpses that held their weapons in their original hands.

"I must say, that is an intriguing trick, to fight as you do, and blindfolded? There must be a great mystery there, I am sure. Sadly, there's really just one more thing I want from you all, and then I think we'll be done here!" The man unfolded his arms, and she saw with a start that they were metal. Jesse James? But no, she had seen the outlaw many times during skirmishes between his shiftless band and the Warrior Nation. These arms were sleeker, more finished, and their aura was different. They lacked the pure ruby glow she had come to associate with the European's devil's blood.

"Who are you?" She stood, knives at her side, her head tilted. She had never seen an aura like his before.

"Well, that is a sad tale, my lady." He drew a long, flashing blade of his own. "I'm afraid, fate has conspired to cast me as the man that will regretfully end your life, today."

She looked from the knife back to the man's grinning face. All around her, the animations and their larger cousins were closing in.

The man with the metal arms took a step toward her, and she crouched down, her own knives coming up into a ready position.

A hurtling mass of black feathers and screeching muscle struck the stranger in the stomach and they both went rolling down the street. Knives flashed within the tangled ball of limbs and dust, as all living eyes in the town watched the two battling forms come to rest in the town square.

Walks Looking saw that Bayaq was bleeding from several shallow cuts as he stood, his wings flaring out behind him. The man with the strange arms had managed to cut him three or four times as they tumbled, despite the confusion of the moment.

No one was looking at her or Qwoli, and she realized with a burning snarl that there were no surviving native fighters. The bodies of her new allies were strewn across the ground, and in the distance she could hear the screams of their horses as even they fled back into the distant mountains. Their entire force had been reduced to the two chieftains and her. She knew that if she slipped away now she would be able to catch up with one of the horses and ride hard back to the council.

Her vision flicked from the prone form of Qwoli, to where Bayaq fought a titanic battle with the poison-armed European, and the fleeing horses. She should leave now, while she had the chance. She looked down at Qwoli again, on the verge of abandoning the wounded chieftain to his fate. But, if her vision for the future was to be victorious, she would need allies in the battles to come. She knelt down beside Qwoli's shivering form.

The man's body was rigid with tension, wanting nothing more than to rush to his friend's aid. But he was torn up. He could not even stand unaided. She bent to him again and whispered in his ear.

"He is trading his life for yours. Do not render that bargain meaningless." Tears of frustrated anger streamed down the big man's cheeks as he stared at the swirling combat that now dominated the town. Then he nodded, allowing her to help him stand, and she began to move him toward the edge of town, giving a silent prayer that her special relationship with the Great Spirit might protect him as well.

The thought of the Great Spirit gave her pause, and she stopped. Why had the Spirit led her to this? Why had the guiding energy of the earth wanted all of these warriors sworn to its cause to die in such a way? She shook her head. Thoughts of that nature were for another time and another place. For now, it would be enough that she survived, and dragged one man with her, if she could.

As they made their way around the last building, and the furious duel and its audience of apathetic walking corpses slid from view, she would have sworn she saw the other young man staring at her, his face still, his eyes dark and fathomless.

Chapter 15

Sound was deadened by the moist brick of the distant walls and the looming weight of the low ceilings overhead. The light, provided by gleaming RJ lanterns all around, did nothing to dispel the impression of claustrophobic containment in the deep lab. None of this, however, registered in Ernest's mind. He was standing at a gleaming metal table with F.R. and the two Payson scientists, Friese and Huxley, staring down at a collection of mechanical parts that represented the accumulated work of years for all of them.

The object before them appeared to be the breast plate from a suit of ancient armor lying on its chest. From its back grew a lumpy, irregular shape like a metal tinker's pack, with gleaming metal wings emerging from either side. Small nozzles and metallic balls were scattered across the surface holding the wings in place, and thin tendrils of almost clear smoke drifted up from the nozzles to swirl across the low ceiling.

The men stood in one of the deepest laboratories of Payson, putting the finishing touches on what each knew would be a masterpiece. They had addressed each of the challenges that had arisen during the ambush of the savage war column weeks ago, and were almost ready to unveil the pack to the doctor and his team.

When F.R., Ernest, and Huxley had made their triumphant return, presenting Doctor Carpathian with the twisted head of the bird warrior, the entire city had greeted them as conquering heroes. All four of them, eager to put what they had observed to use, had spent most of the time since working in the lab. The armored vest and the package on its back was the final result of years of work that first F.R., then Ernest, had been working on in Paris. Not only would it protect a man in combat, it would allow him to become what they had taken to calling an Air Walker.

But their time in Payson had opened their eyes to a world of new opportunities, and they had made many modifications to the design during their sojourn in the scientific enclave. In addition to fine-tuning their work with the help of the doctor's new assistants, many more advanced elements had been added since the flight pack had been made a part of the Hellion Project.

Friese, in particular, was excited to be working with them now. As a biologist specializing in insects, and bees in particular, he had spent nearly all his time in Payson trying to show Carpathian the possible connection between the various control and flight problems the Hellions had suffered and an array of evolved patterns and processes of the various species of bee that could be incorporated into a new generation of control runs for the flying creations. Huxley, the local proponent of the more radical theories of evolution, had championed the cause as well, but to no avail until F.R. had arrived on the scene.

A small but powerful generator placed on the back of the suit incorporated much of Friese's latest work. The mechanisms within would interact with similar generators placed within the control assemblies of the Hellions, powered by their RJ-1027 cylinders. The theory being, of course, that the Air Walker would be able to lead the Hellions more directly in battle, where range and degraded communication would be less of an issue, given the swarm-mentality with which the creations would now be imbued.

"I still don't understand why we are toying with the power supply." Friese's German accent always got thicker when he was being challenged. It was obvious to Ernest, at least, that Friese saw the addition of their smaller atomic power source as an unnecessary burden to the design.

Bending over the flight pack, F.R. was sliding a vermillion cylinder into place behind one of the short wings. As it clicked home, several tell-tale lights winked on along the flank of the pack. "I'm concerned with interference, Heinrich. The atomic power is less likely to interact with other power sources on the battlefield. Anything that reduces the vulnerabilities of the Hellions can only be a good thing, no?"

Friese was unconvinced. "We have never had an issue with RJ-1027 interacting on the battlefield." He put his fists on his hips. "If this new power interferes with the balance of chemicals and the apian mechanical elements within the construct, I will not be held responsible for the failure." The latest iteration of their design was the first to include his own work, and he had fought, tooth and nail, the inclusion of other new technologies in the design, afraid they might impact the effectiveness of his own components.

That was another thing Ernest had had to get used to. The scientists of Payson were so concerned about failure in general, and regarding the Hellion project in particular, that they were nearly paralyzed in their efforts, each trying to ascertain how much credit or blame would be assigned, depending upon the outcome of a given experiment. He shook his head. Things here were not living up to the dreams he had developed during those long discussions back in Paris.

Ernest had found Payson to be more trying than he could have imagined. More and more as the days crawled by, he found himself fondly remembering his small, unprepossessing labs beneath the Gibbs Building back at Cambridge. He looked over at F.R. His friend was fitting another fuel rod into the flight pack. He experienced a twinge of guilt, thinking of the letter he had recently snuck off to the headmaster, asking if his old position might be available, should he return.

He did not want to abandon F.R. now, nor did he want to lose out on the advances that were being made every day here in America. But he found the atmosphere stifling to his creativity, the casual lack of respect for life in general was a heavy weight on his mind, and he knew that he would never be his best self while trapped here in this benighted little city.

"It's just a fallback system, Heinrich." The soothing tones of Huxley's suave accent, delivered with the familiar open, friendly smile, barely held the German in check. Huxley looked across the table at F.R., one bushy eyebrow raised in question. "Correct, F.R.? Your combined RJ-1027 and atomic fuel will be a boon on the battlefield, in case the Union discovers the doctor's ion technology."

Ernest gave a jerk at that. The ion technology that Carpathian and Edison had discovered during their first years together was one of the most carefully kept secrets in a city filled to the brim with mysteries. The fact that ion energy interfered with RJ-powered machinery, in some cases even managing to deaden it completely, was a secret capable of undoing the work of decades. Every denizen of Payson knew that handing such information over to the Union would be tantamount to destroying them all.

But many whispers were making the rounds of Payson these days concerning the melodramatically named 'Wayward Eight' and their attack on the city, as well as all the unpleasantness that followed. There was a great deal of speculation concerning what might have transpired in the little tower room between the mercenary captain and Doctor Carpathian at the culmination of their attack. Ion technology often figured prominently within those rumors, despite the doctor's most stringent denials.

And yet, all along, F.R. had been insistent upon them using a combined fuel cell rather than the pure RJ. In Paris that had made sense. Ernest's connections made acquiring the atomic fuel much easier than pure RJ-1027 on the continent. But even in their work in Payson, where RJ was nearly as easy to get their hands on as air, F.R. had insisted they work with the combined cells. It made no sense unless you gave credence to the stories. It was just another of the mysteries that made his life here among these strange men and women so trying.

F.R. nodded, his head still down. "We have plentiful access to both types of fuel. There is no reason not to use the combined system."

Friese continued to mutter in German, and then said, "I don't trust this atomic material. God alone knows where the material goes as it boils off."

"God alone may know, but we've all got a pretty good idea." Huxley's smile was still firmly in place. "If it works, leave it alone, right, chap?"

Ernest could feel the sour look on his face, but made no effort to hide it. "I can't believe you're worried about God, while here we are, bringing back the dead on a daily basis."

Huxley's smile widened again, while F.R. shot Ernest a glance that told him such statements were not welcome. That was another thing: in Paris, the two of them had worked as a team. There had been other scientists, of course. F.R. had a reputation that reached across Europe and even into the Sultan's court. But here, in America, with his uncle to impress and Carpathian's cronies to coddle, God forbid Ernest say the wrong thing, or get on someone's bad side.

Meanwhile, they all seemed determined to get on each other's bad sides until the bloody sheep came home.

Friese waved away the statement, and Ernest knew he was going to get yet another lecture from the pedantic German. "Of course, we are only using the bodies of the dead as a framework upon which to place our material. Each animation retains no more autonomous thought than the metal frames used by the Union, once their mechanical brains have been removed. It is simply easier, less-expensive, and quicker to use the bodies of the dead."

"And there is nothing ghoulish about that to you?" Ernest felt his frustration converting to anger, and tried to bring himself under control as Friese, eyes wide, stared at him as if he had just slapped the man.

"Ernest, would you mind finishing up with the flight pack?" F.R. stood, wiping his hands off with a clean rag. "I have an appointment I would rather not miss, and you know this system better than anyone."

He recognized it for the blatant attempt to change the subject that it was, but he was thankful all the same. However, the atmosphere of enigmas within mysteries still rankled. "An appointment with your uncle?" It would not be with his father. F.R. had been avoiding Vladimir Caym since they had returned from the battle with the Warrior Nation. Ernest did not know why, and had detected no animosity in his friend toward the man, but the effort was clear nonetheless.

"No." F.R.'s smile widened. "A far more pleasant appointment than that, I hope." He moved through the lab gracefully, grabbing his wide-brimmed hat from a stand by the door. "Gentlemen, if I'm not back by morning, feel free to take the Air Walker out for a test flight without me."

As the door closed behind him, the three remaining men exchanged blank looks of confusion and annoyance. The others' eyes betrayed a level of frustration at F.R.'s mystery that bothered Ernest.

The New Zealander cursed himself as he realized that. He was becoming more and more a creature of Payson each day he remained.

* * * * *

Misty Mimms walked through the streets of Payson with her shoulders back and her head held high. She was someone here, not some anonymous dance hall entertainer; a dime a dozen in the dusty towns of the western territories. Here she was the educated, mysterious killer standing beside the doctor nearly every day. It was an elevation in status she could never have dreamed of, especially before that terrifying moment in the small garret room over the Arcadia back in Kansas City.

A lot had happened to her since she had suffered the blow that shattered her jaw, permanently scarring the right side of her face. Carpathian had provided her with preliminary training, and then sent her off to New Orleans to Marie Laveau, to study everything from combat and field medicine to poise and diction. She owed a great deal to the Voodoo Queen.

She had thought back to her time down south often since her return. Marie Laveau was a deep woman, with plans within plans stretching out from her in all directions. But she had always made Misty feel like she mattered, like her opinion was being heard. Since her return to Payson, she knew that Carpathian valued her, and had watched with delighted awe as she demonstrated the many techniques and tactics she had learned in New Orleans. She had spent a large part of every day with him ever since.

But as time passed, she could feel his regard for her shifting, and something in his eyes and his voice told her that there was more than pride and appreciation for a clever pupil and gifted professional behind his smile. As she walked, she shook her head. That gleam in his natural eye and that soft burr in his voice had probably been there all along. She had been a frightened, wounded child when she was first found by the doctor's people and brought to Payson. He had healed her, provided her with a place of safety and comfort in which to recover, and, most important of all, he had promised her a chance for vengeance.

That chance had been the driving force behind her every living breath since she had recovered. Somewhere out there, Jesse James walked the earth, his conscience clear as a baby's despite the death toll the man had piled up behind him and the pile of broken and bleeding bodies he had left in his wake. A pile that included her own, she remembered, whenever she caught sight of the half mask staring back at her from a mirror.

The doctor had plans for Jesse James; she knew that. But he had promised her that, when he was done with the outlaw, she would have her chance. She was beginning to doubt the truth of that promise. She was not foolish enough to believe everything the doctor told her. But she was sure that being in Payson would afford her the best chance when her moment came. The strange adoption of Marcus Wayward into the doctor's schemes, a man very similar to Jesse James in so many ways, seemed to bode well for her chances.

As she walked, she reflected on the empty streets. So many had died when the mercenaries and Union agents had attacked. The scars ran deep, she knew, along their line of assault, and the destruction wrought by Wayward and his band, many wielding the stolen technologies of Payson itself, would be a long time in healing. But for some reason, despite all that, Carpathian had forgiven Marcus Wayward, had taken the survivors of his band into the employ of Carpathian Industries, and even brought the captain into the inner circle of the Enlightened Movement itself. It was one of the more confusing mysteries of life in Payson.

Her feet, working on their own, had found the establishment the people of Payson called simply the 'southern saloon', as it was situated on the southern edge of town.

The place did not have a proper name. There were too few saloons in Payson for them to require anything so mundane as a name. In fact, Doctor Carpathian had encouraged the few independent businesses in the city not to display signs or names, as part of his plan to defend the city should it ever be invaded. There were no street signs or identifying markings in the twisting lanes of Payson, either. The idea was that if an invader managed to infiltrate the Tonto Forest and find Payson, they would have to navigate blind as they fought through the layered defenses of the city.

Of course, that was exactly what Marcus Wayward's little team had done. That event, and the subsequent escape of the other mercenaries, had cost the town the sense of security it had once derived from such ruses.

Misty took the small flight of wooden steps two at a time, moving under the cool shade of the saloon's covered porch. She pushed the heavy door open, and then turned to close it behind her; no batwing doors in security-conscious Payson. Inside, the room was dim by design rather than for want of RJ to power the lanterns. One of the many benefits of life in Payson was the plentiful energy. But people generally came to the southern saloon for a chance to get away from the sound, noise, and heat of the manufactories, laboratories, and mines.

Misty had made a new habit of coming to the southern saloon in the late afternoons for weeks, now. The more her unease around the doctor grew, the more she needed these brief chances to get out from underneath his gaze. Slipping off to the saloon for a single whiskey had become her favorite part of almost every day.

That had to be her unconscious mind trying to warn her about her current situation, but she did not want to look at it too closely. Her entire identity was now entangled with the doctor and his hidden little city. If she was forced to leave, she had nowhere else to go.

And then, there was her quest for vengeance. It was far more probable she could realize it with the power of Payson behind her than if she was wondering the territories on her own.

The man behind the bar nodded to her and met her at the corner table she had claimed as her own, drink in hand. He placed it before her, waved away her offered payment, as he often did, and left her with a pleasant nod.

Her table was lit by a small lantern hanging from the ceiling. Deep within the shifting crimson glow, she watched trails of deeper reds and vibrant yellows chase each other through the ruby sea. Much of her time here was spent contemplating that lantern and the strange movement within. RJ provided so much to Payson and the rest of the country. And yet, most people knew so little about it. How did it give forth light, heat, and power, but at the same time bring animated corpses back to some semblance of shambling life? And what of its restorative properties?

Her idle thoughts were disturbed as a man sat down opposite her. That had never happened here before, where the other patrons all knew her, and respected, or feared, her enough to leave her alone.

She looked up, several sharp retorts rising in her mind. They all vanished, and she sat up straighter, as the man's identity registered. His hat was in one metal hand, and his tousled dark hair was in utter disarray, but F.R. Caym looked as boyishly handsome as he had the first time she had seen him, out in the shadows of the Tonto.

She had been avoiding him since that first day. Her eyes flicked down to the alien metal arms folded before him on the table, and then back up to his youthful grin.

"You've been avoiding me." There was no heat behind the accusation, and the smile widened to take any possible sting from the words. But she still reared back a little; the words were too close to her own thoughts.

"I'm sorry." Her pride responded before her mind could process the statement. "I'm afraid I don't know what you're talking about." She certainly did not consider him important enough to avoid. Did she?

"You've been avoiding me since my first day here." He shrugged, settling back in the chair, one metal arm whirring as he threw it up over the back. "It's alright. I enjoy a good chase."

Stung again, her pride reared up inside her. "Is that what you're doing? Chasing? You might want to watch it, before you catch more than you've bargained for."

The smile was maddeningly wide now, and she cursed herself as she realized she was playing his game.

"Well, that's a chance I'm more than willing to take, Miss Mimms." He waved one metal hand at the bartender and then waited, pleased smile stubbornly unmoved, until the man brought him a drink of his own.

"This is a quaint establishment you've found." He made a show of looking around at the unprepossessing saloon. "Your own little semi-private retreat, eh?"

"What do you want?" She forced herself to take a sip of whiskey, trying to use several techniques Mademoiselle Laveau had taught her to bring her breathing and temper under control.

F.R. took a sip of his drink, made a face, and shook his head. "I came to see you, of course." He held up his glass. "Certainly not for the quality of the drink."

"What do you want from me, then?" Her anger was rising, despite her best efforts.

"To talk, is all." He put one hand out as if calming a skittish horse. "You left before I could thank you on that first day. And you've been devilishly difficult to find since then."

His words seemed so normal. And his speech was refined, his accent softer than his father's; even than his uncle's. But her eyes flicked down to his hands again. She could not think about those arms without the rage and pain rushing back. She knew they were shaping her thoughts and responses, but she did not really care. What was he to her?

"You needed to be alone with me to thank me?" Her cold, even stare usually turned men aside at a single glance, but instead, he was looking right back at her and she felt more conscious of her damned mask than she had been in a very long time.

"Well, I know you had gone against your instructions, letting Ernest and me into the tower like that. It didn't seem like something I should be thanking you for in front of my uncle or my father, to be honest." His smile mellowed, becoming more genuine as he pulled back with a slight shrug. Then he stroked his chin with one sleek metal hand, and she blinked at the darkness that rose again behind her eyes.

"I had my gun on you the whole time. You didn't pose any danger."

He raised both hands, as if sensing that he had been making a little ground with her, and it had slid out from beneath him again. "I know! Believe me, I know. Thank you, nevertheless."

It was her turn to shrug. "I followed my instincts."

"You had good instincts." He leaned forward over his arms, the smile firmly back in place. "What are your instincts telling you now?"

She sighed, putting her drink down with a firm clink. "That I need to get back to the palace. Doctor Carpathian will be wondering where I've gotten off to."

"He won't need you for a while. My father is with him this afternoon."

She did not try to hide the suspicion that rose up at his words. "He is? How would you know that?"

Again, the smile, this time accompanied by an infuriating shrug. "I've developed friendships around town. People tell me things."

"People tell me things too." She leaned forward now. "Like you have been avoiding your father since you came back from the plains."

He nodded, the smile fading. "I've got some things to think

about, and I don't want to bother my father with my idle musings."

That day in the tower room of the palace came back to her. She had been thinking about him more than she wanted to admit, and something that had been in the back of her mind came rushing out while she looked down at the last sip of whiskey, swirling around in her glass. "I'm sorry about your mother." That slipped out before she knew she was going to say it. She continued, however, coming to her question. "Do you blame your father? For not being there?"

It seemed to catch him off-guard, and he sat back, his face thoughtful. Then he shook his head. "No, I don't. I blame him for leaving us, and for being gone so long. I blame him for not sending for us sooner. But at the same time, I understand his reasoning." A strange shadow came into his eyes as he continued. "Besides, the final say was always my uncle's."

She knew that was true. She had witnessed more than one argument on the subject herself. "Do you blame him, then?"

This time F.R. took a lot longer to think about his response. "I don't know, to be honest. He has suffered his own losses, and I think that might have colored his perceptions of America, and how unsafe it might have been for us." He shrugged. "That might have affected my father, as well, of course."

Carpathian did not often speak of his wife or her murder at the hands of the Union, but she knew it figured prominently in his drive to destroy the nation and replace it with something more malleable. "And yet here you are, having traveled half way around the world to be with them both."

He nodded, his eyes thoughtful. "I love my father, and my uncle is a great, great man." He drummed on the table with his damned fingers, and she had to stop herself from shivering with the chill it sent sweeping down her back.

"So you came here to study, to learn?" Her voice was not nearly as cold as she had intended.

A completely different light ignited in his eyes, and his voice became far more animated. "The world is changing, Miss Mimms. The boundaries of science are being pushed back every day." He waved his hands around him with a low whir, and it took a moment for her to realize the chill it caused had lessened. "And the greatest work is being done here, by my uncle."

She surprised herself as she felt a smile on her lips. "I've been told. So you have come to take your place beside him?"

F.R. shook his head, and her smile faded at the seriousness in his eyes. "No. My uncle does not realize the power of his own creations. His vision of a Confederate America is nothing compared to the potential of what he has created. By filling the world with these thoughts and machines, he has caused it to go mad."

She sat up straighter at the anger in the young man's words. As he continued, the energy and the anger intermingled. "The entire world is in chaos and disarray. Only here, in Payson, is there the power and the ability to bring peace to the Earth and usher in the new age of Enlightenment that threatens even now to slip from our fingers. My uncle, my father, and the others lack only the will to reach out and seize that new world and make it our own."

"And you are here to provide that will." She already knew the answer, and was shocked to realize that not only did he truly believe it, but that she was coming to see it as well. The power and energy behind F.R.'s words had touched off an excitement in her as well. If the world was taught to bow down in thanks and praise to Payson, then there would be nowhere that was safe from her rulers. No one would be safe from those who directed the power of the secret stronghold, especially two-bit road agents like Jesse James.

She did not restrain the smile that rose to her lips at his nod of agreement.

"I am, Miss Mimms. I am." He settled back in his chair. "And I will."

His confidence reminded her of something Carpathian had mentioned. "Was the grand summit your idea, then?"

His frown was immediate and genuine. He knew nothing about his uncle's newest plan, then. "He has given me a list, a very extensive list, of men and women he wants to bring to Payson in about a month."

F.R.'s frown deepened. "Who? What kind of men and women?"

"You honestly don't know?" His growing concern made no sense. "He said it was all to do with your latest work. I assumed you knew."

The frown did not fade, and his eyes seemed to grow distant with thought. When his eyes cleared, his face had settled into neutral, impenetrable lines. "What kind of men and women?"

She shrugged. "All kinds, really; scientists, industrialists, military and political leaders. It's quite an extensive list."

The blank expression thawed slightly, and one corner of his mouth rose in a small grin. "Well, the old man must be more impressed than he's let on."

"But you knew nothing about this?" Carpathian's plans were rather extensive, including the building of a great wooden stage in the square before the palace, and seating for hundreds of visiting dignitaries. The security concerns alone had been keeping her up at night for weeks.

"I did not, but there is only one thing it really could be about." He relaxed and tossed his whiskey off with a wide smile. "You know? This isn't half bad after all."

She shook her head. "But, if whatever you're working on is so important, can you tell me what it is?"

He placed his empty glass on the table and gestured for another, then leaned forward. "No. I'm done talking about myself and my work. That's not what I came here for."

She felt herself stiffen, the old defensive walls rising up again. "What did you come here for?"

There was no predatory edge to his smile now, and his eyes glowed only with a kind, gentle mischief. "To talk about you."

She was shocked to feel the smile return to her own face, and when he took a new glass from the bartender in his agile metal hand, there was hardly a chill at all.

Chapter 16

The map had not changed in months. Vlad stared at the old parchment in its fancy frame, glittering pins summing up bloody death and tragedy in nice, clean little clusters. Most of the Union pins had not moved in over a year. Most of the Warrior Nation pins had not moved in months. Even the Confederate pins, so energetic only a few months ago, were still.

Despite years of effort, the battle lines had been drawn, and they did not seem to be moving anytime soon.

He shook his head, looking down at his strong but wrinkled fingers. He had fought in many wars, across three continents. He had seen so many ways men could die, and he had killed more than his fair share of enemies. He recognized a bloody stalemate when he saw it. The forces of Payson were poised to break the careful balance and usher in a new tomorrow. Joined with the forces of the Confederacy, there would be no way the Union could stop them.

He eased himself back into the cushions of the chair. His son's victory against the western Warrior Nation band had been eye-opening, on several levels. He had gone over the events of the battle with the Englishman, Huxley, several times. The tactics employed had been sound, and the casualties more than justifiable. Even that two headed brute had been easily repaired in the field, and shambled its own way back into its Doomsday transport. His son had won a great victory, and proven the weakness, and importance, of the Hellions in the process.

Thoughts of his son brought a sour frown to his face. The boy had been avoiding him since his return. He had sensed no animosity, but there was no denying F.R. seemed to be hiding something, and avoiding him. Was it fear of discovery that kept him away? Or shame? What was the boy up to?

The grand doors to Carpathian's tower office swung opened and the man himself strode in. Vlad quickly rose, nodding a greeting, and the doctor reached out to embrace him with a wide smile. "Vlad, I am truly glad to see you."

"I came as soon as I got vord." He stepped back, trying to gauge the doctor's mood. "Vhat is it?"

Carpathian waved the question away as his heavy metal legs thumped around the big desk, dropping him unceremoniously into the heavy chair behind it. "We can talk about that in a moment. How are you, old friend? You spend so much time with the repair and salvage crews, we hardly see each other anymore!"

Vlad lowered himself back into his chair and shrugged, feeling his lip curl dismissively. "I don't much care for ze air around here lately."

Carpathian's fingers were steepled beneath his chin, and he nodded sagely. "Wayward? You object to his presence?"

Vlad's head snapped down. "I object to ze man breazing, Burson. After eversing he did to us, after eversing he did to your people, you embrace him and threaten to raise him up to be a king." He shook his head. "Your methods are your own, Burson. I trust you. But zat man, and his mongrel pack, are a foul breed. I vould razer the stink of a souzand animations in my nostrils, zan a moment more vis zem zan necessary."

Carpathian looked like he was on the verge of laughing, and Vlad sat up straighter. After everything he had sacrificed for Payson, he would not sit idly by and be mocked for his concerns now.

Carpathian's hand rose and he shook his head. "No, no." The laugh was replaced with a more serious expression. "You are right to doubt him. But the world is as we find it, Vladimir, not as we would have it. With Jesse gone, we needed to fill his dusty boots anyway, and Wayward will be far more malleable, I think, than our half-tamed outlaw. Whether we like it or not, Wayward will be the next ruler of the Confederate States, and we will be better for it than if we had not had that position to offer in the first place."

A bitter taste flooded Vlad's mouth at the reminder. "As you say." He looked back up at the map. How many more would die across the continent before Carpathian's vision was made a reality?

The door burst open and F.R. rushed in, his face a boiling cloud of fury. Barely giving his father a second glance, the boy stormed past and rocked to a stop in front of the desk, metal hands balled into fists, crashing down onto the cluttered wooden surface. His chest was heaving with angry, gasping breaths, and his eyes burned with a fire that put the RJ lanterns to shame.

"What is the meaning of this newest interference in my work, Uncle?" He spat the words, and the familial title came out like a mortal insult.

Carpathian did not react with so much as a raised eyebrow, settling back in his chair, his smile undimmed. "Ah, welcome, young Master Caym. I don't believe I issued you an invitation to this meeting?"

"Several of your mindless automata just broke into my laboratory and confiscated my Air Walker without so much as a by-your-leave!" He took a deep breath, obviously reining in his anger with great effort. "I ask you again, Uncle, what is the meaning of this?"

Carpathian grew thoughtful for a moment, and then settled back, looking up at the ceiling with a gentle nod. "Ah, yes. I had forgotten. My apologies." The smile he gave the boy had all the sincerity of a crocodile's.

Vlad looked to his son, concerned for his reaction. The boy had proven to be extremely level-headed since his arrival in Payson, but he had shown himself to have a temper as well. Carpathian knew this as well as Vlad himself, and the old soldier found himself wondering what the doctor's game was.

But F.R. was still in command of himself, and although he spoke through gritted teeth, his voice was cold and calm. "To what end did your animations seize my work?"

The doctor's smile widened. "You have been spending a great deal of time away from us, Nephew. I thought it was time you showed your work to the rest of the community."

The fires of anger guttered, doubt fighting for its place on his son's face. "But... we're not finished. There are elements..."

Carpathian nodded amiably, playing the role of gracious

uncle to the hilt. "There are always elements that get away from us, F.R. We are scientists, and the first thing about science is that we must admit we will never know everything. There is always a new mystery peeking around the next corner." The doctor's gaze had a predatory gleam that gave Vlad pause.

He could not have said why he felt the sudden urge to rise to his son's defense. "F.R., I'm sure zere vill be more zan enough advancement—"

"Are you going to use it?" The question was cold, like a lash snapping out into the quiet room, and the challenge in F.R.'s eyes was undeniable. It bought Carpathian up short, his smile fading.

"I beg your pardon?" The older man straightened, his hands falling to grip the arms of his chair.

F.R.'s scowl gave way to a tight smile as if he had just seen his shot strike a distant target. His chin rose challengingly, and an answering fire lit in his own eyes. "Are you going to use the Air Walker, and the new capabilities it will grant the Hellions?"

Carpathian's voice was dangerously low as he responded. "I don't know—"

"Or will you let my work rot just as you have let your own rot down through the years, as the world rushes into the future without you?" The boy's smile was fierce now, and Vlad turned to look at Carpathian as the momentum of the confrontation shifted. He did not understand what was happening, and a sickening feeling rose in his stomach as watched his son and his brother-in-law squaring off.

"Excuse me?" Carpathian whispered the words, and they were filled with potential tragedy.

"You have hidden away here in Payson for years, Uncle." Vlad's son paced as he spoke, tracing a short track, only three of four steps at a time, before swinging around, his metal hands clasped behind his back. "You have done great things. You have brought many wonders into the world." He stopped, and pivoted to stare at his uncle. "But you refuse to accept your true position in that world. You allow inferior enemies to mock your strength, to stand tall when they should be bowed down! You tie yourself to foolish alliances when within your mind you have the strength to prevail over all who stand against you!"

The abrupt change in tone and tactic had caught Carpathian and Vlad equally by surprise. Drive the doctor to the very edge of rage, and then shower him with back-handed compliments? Both older men watched F.R. with a mix of fascination, confusion, and concern.

Carpathian shook his head as if to clear it, and replied. "With the help of the Confederacy, when the time is right we will—"

"No!" The tension flooded back into the room. Carpathian's own eye flared at the single, abrupt syllable. "The Confederacy is nothing but a nest of old women more terrified of the future than you are! They sit upon literally tons of material, and even their strongest fighters are tied to the weak-willed vermin they call their leaders. They are not worthy of your consideration, Uncle!"

"You try my patience, boy." Carpathian's tone had hardened. "I assure you, I am the master of the situation, and everything is unfolding according to my will. When the Confederacy rises up to replace the Union, we will be in a position to usher in exactly the future of which you speak, without lining the bodies from sea to sea and watering the fields of America with the blood of her people."

F.R. was nodding at this, although his expression had not wavered. Vlad found himself hoping that the boy was hearing the doctor's words, and sensing in them the wisdom of a slower, surer path.

And then that hope was shattered.

"How, Uncle, did a mind capable of mastering the powers of God himself, settle upon a vision so infinitesimally small?"

Vlad and Carpathian both stared at F.R. in dumbstruck awe.

Without waiting for a reply, the boy continued. "You have forgotten the wider world, Uncle. You set your sights upon one backward, adolescent society, when nations both ancient and great stand ready to succumb to your every desire!"

An uncomfortable silence stretched out across the room. Carpathian seemed balanced on a knife's blade, tottering between violent expulsion and tolerant amusement. Vlad held his breath, waiting to see in what direction it would fall. When the doctor smiled a tight, forbearing smile, shaking his head as if to a wayward child, Vlad relaxed. Color eased back into his knuckles as he released the arms of his chair.

"You have grand vision, Nephew, and that will serve you well, coupled with the tempering of experience. But you misunderstand my motives and my goals, if you believe I wish to rule the world. My technologies will allow mankind to realize his full potential, under the guidance of the wisest of men. We will first bring America into the new age, and then, through our influence and example, the rest of the world will follow. We will, all of us, live as kings, without the burden or price of monarchy. I—"

"You will fall into obscurity, a victim of your lack of ambition and vision." There was nothing but contempt in F.R.'s eyes, and Vlad could sense the moment when all hope of reconciliation slipped away.

F.R. stood in the center of the room, glaring defiantly at his uncle. "The world is yours for the taking, Doctor. If you do not take it, someone else will." His meaning was clear, as was the insult in his words and tone.

Carpathian sat silent for a moment, and when a rigid smile slowly sketched itself across his features, Vlad saw no warmth or kind regard behind it. "You may go now, Nephew. Please see that you are in attendance at the proving grounds, on the far side of the valley, at noon today."

F.R.'s entire body was rigid, poised as if he believed he would have to fight his way out of the room. When his uncle's reasonable tone registered, he blinked, tension rising at the note of dismissal.

"Uncle, you need to—"

"That is all, Nephew." The iron in the words was unmistakable. "You have been dismissed."

F.R. stared in disbelief, and then looked to his father for

the first time. Vlad saw the thwarted rage guttering in his son's eyes, having risen to a fever pitch and now offered no release. He knew he had to get his son out of the room before the boy did something that would destroy his future completely. He nodded, his eyes kind, and nodded to the door.

A flash of pain warred with the anger in the boy's eyes, and then with a snarl and a curt nod, he turned without a word and stormed from the room.

As the crash of the door's closing faded away, Vlad looked back to Carpathian, eager to begin mending the tatters of the doctor's regard for his son.

"Ze boy is so young, Burson. You remember ze fires of your own youth, yes? After ze Montage von Medizin und Wissenschaft refused to see ze genius behind your vork? If only—"

"So," Carpathian looked thoughtful, his eyes on the ceiling. "You would cast me in the role of the benighted old men of the Assembly of Medicine?" He shook his head. "I understand your concern, my old friend, but your analogy does no credit to your cause."

He felt a tightness around his chest. "Burson, I only meant—"

Carpathian held up a hand, and looked back down at Vlad. The ghostly red lamp of the doctor's right eye seemed to bore a hole into his own mind. "I know, Vladimir, I know. Have no fear. The boy will settle down, I have no doubt." He moved forward, his hands resting back on the desk. "You will see that he remembers his place in the future, yes?"

"Of course, Burson." He could hear the eager relief in his own voice, and he hated it.

"Of course. And of course the boy will be a great asset to us, in time." He smiled, the red lens winking. "He will need to learn his place, but he will be a great asset. It is not as if these are sentiments I have not heard before, correct?"

Vlad nodded, his relief giving way to a wary concern. "Correct."

And it was correct. Because in the silence of his own heart, Vlad knew that he agreed with nearly everything his son had said.

* * * * *

The proving grounds beyond the blighted valley was a vast scar of sand and rock that cut through the dark pine forests of the Tonto just north of Payson, visible from Carpathian's tower office. A tent had been raised near one edge of the desolation. A small group of men were seated there, talking quietly among themselves, when F.R. came up over the rise.

A field table sat before the tent. His flight pack lay on it, along with an assortment of tools, and several pairs of goggles that looked exactly like the pair he had worn since his arrival. As he walked up to the tent, he scanned the group, hoping to find Misty, but she was absent. His father was there, sitting next to Carpathian, and his heart lurched in his chest to see them talking together, given how badly the morning had gone.

F.R. had almost decided not to attend this farce of a gathering. Who was going to be operating the pack, anyway? No one knew the system as well as he did, and he had had nothing whatsoever to do with the planning of the day's demonstration. The heat of anger and frustration had not settled from his veins. The thought of his genius being held for ransom by a coward incapable of grasping the golden moment haunted him. It burned with such a raging combination of frustration and disappointment, just thinking of it threatened to cost him his calm demeanor again.

He took a deep breath and forced himself to stroll into the shade of the tent. In the front row sat his most recent collaborators. Heinrich Freise was there, sweating and uncomfortable in a heavy, formal suit. Beside him sat Thomas Huxley, his sardonic smile firmly in place as he nodded to F.R. Beside Huxley, closest to the glaring sunlight, sat Ernest. Ernest, who had been his friend and confidant for years, who had crossed an ocean and half a continent with him. Ernest, who had become more and more distant as their time in Payson had stretched on.

F.R. nodded grimly to Ernest, but his friend would not meet his eyes. In fact, the young New Zealander showed no recognition at all. F.R. frowned, and for the first time, he wondered exactly what was supposed to happen beneath that pounding sun.

Off to the side, sitting with Carpathian and his father, three other men made brave attempts to seem at ease. Marcus Wayward was the most successful, sitting in amiably silence and taking in the scene with a slight, enigmatic smile. Beside him, his man Jake Mattia took the prize for least successful, gripping his massive heat rifle in white knuckles and glaring at anyone who ventured too close. Next, but set apart by enough space that F.R. could tell the distance was deliberate, sat Gustave Eiffel: one of Carpathian's very first disciples. He looked as sour as F.R. had ever seen him, and the most out of his depth, sitting in his dark suit in the blazing heat of the proving grounds, his face red behind the full dark beard.

Along with Misty, Thomas Edison, the supposed first among equals within Carpathian's inner circle, was absent as well. And rounding out those who were absent was his strange ally, J.P. Smith. The man had apparently been persona non grata since facilitating F.R.'s breach of Payson security. He hoped the man's punishment was not permanent. He had honestly looked forward to working with him when his own situation had stabilized.

Standing at the back of the tent were the Kaufmann brothers, cool and aloof in their long gray coats, their goggles down and entirely opaque. They stared at him with unseen eyes, and he felt the skin between his shoulder blades crawl with the strength of their animosity.

He suddenly realized how hostile this group was to him. These people were not his friends, and the people who should have been the most supportive; his father, his uncle, and his best friend, had barely acknowledged his existence.

Well, if this was the game they wanted to play, he would be damned if he went down without playing the best hand he had.

"Are we waiting for anything in particular, or can we see what there is to see?" He kept his tone light, his smile firmly in place. "I don't think it's a surprise to anyone that we all have pressing business elsewhere?"

The whispered conversations beneath the pavilion subsided, and F.R. gave them all a wide smile, sweeping his hat off in a grand gesture he had seen in a dance hall show back in Paris. "Do not let me interrupt your conversations, by any means. But I was led to believe we were all here for a reason?"

He gestured eloquently to the flight pack with one graceful, metal arm. He was inordinately proud of his arms, which he knew were masterpieces in every sense of the word. They were far more elegant and efficient, and far less vulnerable, than the work his uncle had done for others here in America; far better, even, than the metal replacements Carpathian himself now wore throughout his body. A reminder of that would not go amiss, he thought, as he dropped into one of the vacant wooden chairs in the first row.

Carpathian nodded, a tolerant smile combining with the snowy white of his mustache and side whiskers to make the man look like anyone's favorite grandfather. The act was nearly perfect, but F.R. could see the iron in the man's eye, and knew that his punishment for that morning's audacity had not yet begun.

"Well, I suppose there's no reason to put things off any further." The doctor stood, muttering to F.R.'s father and Wayward. Vladimir Caym nodded brusquely, looking away, while the mercenary smiled and gave a quick snort of laughter.

Carpathian stepped out into the blazing sun, the brim of his top hat throwing a dark, almost impenetrable shadow across his eyes. His teeth flashed in his good-natured smile, though, and he moved to stand behind the table.

"Gentlemen, we are at a crossroads in our effort to show the people of America the true path to liberty and happiness." He patted the pack before him, and as he touched it, F.R. had to stop himself from lurching to his feet. This would all be over soon, and he could return to his lab and his work. There would be plenty of time to find a consensus within the Payson community for his grander vision. And when that day came, his uncle would have to see the light or step aside for the younger generation.

"This lovely piece of machinery here is the result of the tireless work of my own beloved nephew, F.R., as you all know." Everyone under the awning nodded, some even smiled at him. But a growing sense of dread had begun to churn in his own chest, and he watched his uncle, hoping that he was wrong.

"With this flight pack, and the other technologies you all have created to augment it, our Hellion Project will soon be a bright reality." As he spoke, the old man's energy picked up. He became more and more animated, and F.R. caught a glimpse of the man his father had followed to America all those years ago. "Soon, the savages will have no choice but to flee before us. The Union will be helpless below us as we dominate the skies." He took the pack by the wings and grunted as he hoisted it over his head. "With this, all of our dreams will be made real!"

The doctor's sense of excitement was contagious, and soon F.R. realized that almost everyone in the shade of the overhang was smiling, leaning forward in their seats, hanging on Carpathian's every word.

"Contrary to what you probably believe, however," he lowered the pack back onto the table with a hollow thud. "We are not here to see a man take flight this day."

F.R.'s eyes tightened in suspicion as the disappointment of the group around him swelled.

"It has come to my attention that things are not progressing as quickly as I might wish." The doctor shook his head with dramatic disappointment, looking at all of them like a school teacher with a particularly unruly class.

"The men working on the flight pack have been distracted by myriad diversions, while the temperament of some on the project has proven more of a hindrance than an advantage." He looked at the group, his face blank, his hands folded peaceably over his belt buckle. "Young Ernest, for his part, has asked to be returned to Europe to pursue his studies, and perhaps further our own business, there."

F.R. felt a cold rise up in his face as he turned to his friend. Ernest would not meet his gaze, only nodding briefly to Carpathian.

"We will miss him, of course. But we hope that he will continue to be a friend to Payson in the future, and we look forward to the great accomplishments we know are ahead of him." Carpathian looked down at his entwined fingers. "Sadly, there is a more serious cancer within the project that needs to be addressed." His focus snapped in on F.R., the red lens of his RJ prosthetic flaring in the sun. "Nephew, thank you for your work on this and so much more. But I believe it is time you step away from this project." The hard gleam of satisfaction in the man's one human eye felt like a dagger.

F.R. was standing without any memory of coming to his feet. He had some vague awareness of his father rising also, but it was as if the world had resolved itself into his uncle's face, and nothing else existed but himself, the grinning old mask with its glaring red eye, and the tunnel of solidifying air between them. From within that tunnel, Carpathian's next words echoed with almost Biblical strength.

"Your lack of discipline and respect cannot be tolerated, F.R. You are no longer associated with the Hellion Project, or any of the hardware it has created. You will return to your rooms in the palace and consider yourself removed from all research until further notice."

The burning sense of shame and anger washed all thought from F.R.'s mind. For this he had abandoned his position in Europe? For this he had crossed the world? For this humiliation and shame he had run to this man, his own uncle, in this strange, twisted world he had created?

F.R. was stalking toward Carpathian without realizing it. He felt hands on him, pushing him back, but in the swirling chaos of his mind he did not even know who had risen to confront him.

He could hear the droning voice of his uncle, however, as the man continued to speak as if a raging madman had not erupted in the midst of his little audience.

"I am pleased to announce that Heinrich Friese will now be providing unified oversight of the Hellions." F.R. knew that his arms would make him the equal of any man who tried to keep him from his uncle, but even as the rage threatened to boil over inside him, a cold voice in his mind spoke in a frigid, chattering tone. He shook off the arms that had seized him, and saw Jake Mattia and the Kaufmanns step away, all of them watching his face for signs that he would make another lunge.

"I am sorry, F.R., but we must all think of the good of Payson and the Enlightened Movement." There was no regret in the man's eye, however. F.R. could see nothing there but vindication and triumph. "Now, Schultz and Dieter will accompany you back to the palace, and we will talk in a few days, yes?"

The twins were careful not to touch him as they moved up on either side, but it was clear that they were offering him no choices in the matter. Their hands were not far from the elegant daggers they wore at their waists. F.R. scanned the faces one last time, committing each reaction to his disgrace to memory.

His father's face was drawn; surprise, anger, and concern warring across its craggy surface in equal measure. It was clear that his father had known nothing about this. Eiffel looked bemused and slightly affronted, but in an impersonal way, seeing this as no fit way to treat any scientist, probably, rather than any personal feelings for F.R. himself. Neither Ernest nor Friese would meet his gaze, again, and of course Huxley's smile was still firm as he shrugged; as close to an apology as the man ever gave. Mattia scowled at him with an expression unchanged since the first moment he had met the man, and the Kaufmanns were blank-faced, their vindication and enjoyment carefully hidden from their master's view.

But the two faces that pulled the corner of his lip up into a spasmodic snarl were Carpathian's and Wayward's. The doctor's smile was small, but vindictive and full of poison. While Marcus

Wayward looked at him as if the man had just taken him at poker, bluffing off a pair of deuces.

In a flash, F.R. realized that his uncle had told Wayward of his own contempt for their plan for the Confederacy. The man had been offered a throne, and no upstart kid from the Old Country was going to take that away from him.

F.R. stood watching them all for a moment longer, a thousand words struggling to spew from his mouth and seal his fate. But in the end discipline prevailed, and he merely nodded to his father, gave Ernest a last look, and turned away.

He could play the long game. After all, he had more time than anyone else under that tent.

Chapter 17

His metal fingers flexed against the cold marble of the work table, and he reveled in the sensation brought to him through the subtle lines of pseudo-nerve woven through the hard carapace of the artificial limbs. He smiled despite the anger burning through him. The pseudo-nerves were just one of the many advances his own arms' design had over his uncle's crude efforts. He tapped his fingers against the stone, creating a rapid tattoo that echoed off the far walls. With a tight grin of self-satisfaction, he forced the fingers to move faster and faster, harder and harder, until it sounded as if a Gatling gun were being fired within the confines of the old laboratory.

The fingers were a barely-discernible blur in the dim light. With a grunt he brought them all up and then down sharply. There was a crack, and the table before him fell to pieces, chunks of marble and cascades of powdered dust showering to the floor. With the stone and sand fell the various components of experiments and half-finished mechanisms that had been left behind when Friese and his crew of animations had stripped the lab of any sign of the Hellion Project or the flight pack.

With a savage snort, F.R. gave one of the tumbled stones at his feet a kick that sent it skittering across the bare floor. The room served as little more than a reminder, now, of his fall from grace, and of those few glorious days when he had thought he had realized the full potential of his foolish, youthful dreams. He spat into the dust, his arms shaking with the nearly uncontrollable urge to destroy something else.

F.R. shook his head sharply. He refused to give in to these base impulses! It had been days since they had taken his work from him. He had not seen his uncle or his father since his humiliation on the proving grounds. Ernest had left for England soon after the ordeal. He had come around to say his goodbyes, but their moments together had been tense and awkward. All of the material had been removed from the lab already, and his friend had found him, desolate and alone, in the midst of the empty room.

Ernest had begged F.R. to return to Europe with him. Payson was no fit place for either of them anymore, where their research could be taken from them at the whim of a single man. By the end of the conversation, his friend's tone had turned positively pleading. They could do so much back in Europe, out from under Carpathian's thumb. They would not return to Paris, for fear of questions from the Sûreté concerning his mother's death and the destruction of the family home. But they could go to Cambridge, where Ernest's reputation and relationships with the faculty would assure them the space and material they would need. Hiding from Reid and the other Detective Inspectors would not be that difficult a task, and might even prove entertaining.

The metal fingers tightened, creaking at the leavened joints, as he remembered those last moments. He had been sorely tempted. After the way his uncle had treated him, stealing his work and relegating him to little more than prisoner in his own rooms, his emotions had been a raging torrent of white fury, overturning any rational thought that tried to take hold. But even within the buffeting winds of his own inner storm, he knew that he could not run now. To leave Payson with his own dreams lying in ruins would be to admit defeat to the very man he had spent his entire life admiring.

And that was the core of his wrenching inner conflict. He had grown up hearing tales of Uncle Burson and how similar the two of them were. His entire education was predicated upon his following in Carpathian's footsteps, earning a place at his side. Even in the darkest moments of his childhood, his father gone and his sad mother mourning the life they had lost, F.R. had been comforted by the knowledge that somewhere out there was a man, beholden to him through blood and family ties, that would understand and appreciate the drives and desires that moved him. He felt a deep kinship to the young man who had been moved to flee Romania so many years before.

All of that had come to a crashing halt in the sun-scorched dirt and stone field of the proving grounds. As his father looked on and did nothing, the man who had been his spiritual father for as long as he could remember had insulted him and humiliated him in front of his friends and colleagues. He had been stripped bare before the people whose opinion mattered most to him, and not a one had stood up in his defense.

On the long walk back to Payson, flanked by two men he knew despised him, he had been sustained by his anger. His rage had kept him upright, his face pale, his gaze steady, and his lips silent. But after they had deposited him in his rooms, he had collapsed on his bed, staring at the wall, his world in disarray. It was the night of his mother's murder all over again.

F.R. had carried the grief and horror of his mother's death with him into the new world. He had lost the foundation of his world that night. Everything had turned to shifting sand beneath his feet. But as he pushed those feelings of despair and misery into the shadows, as he had struggled to reach his father and his uncle in America, his soul had latched onto the new possibilities, the new life he could make for himself in this new world. It had not only given him a goal to strive for, but it had made the loss of his mother more bearable, somehow.

He kicked another chunk of stone, sending it careening into the darkness. Even the RJ lamps had been dimmed. The laboratory was useless now as a work space. It only stood as a reminder of what he had lost. When Carpathian had disgraced him out there in the hot western sun, he had taken everything away. He had not just lost his uncle's affection, and everything the man stood for, it had torn open the wound of his mother's loss as well.

But deep within the swirling rage, tangled up in his anger with his uncle, was a much larger pain; a nearly unbearable pain that overshadowed everything else. All that his family had suffered through the years would be rendered bearable, would be at least mitigated, if they were allowed to reap the benefits of their sacrifices. Everything they had been forced to give up along the paths down which fate had forced them, could be made good, if only the ends could be achieved. The road to vengeance for his aunt's death, for his mother's death, for the humiliation of his uncle at the hands of the world's scientific community, all of it could be made

good at last, if they were allowed to rise as high as those sacrifices should allow.

But his uncle would never permit that. There, in the dark of
the basement lab, he finally understood. Burson Carpathian had
been blessed with a brilliant mind and a spirit whose indomitable
energy made it possible to reshape the world. But somewhere
along the way he had lost his strength of will. He was settling for
being a petty king in a dusty, worn-down little realm, an island in a
rushing river of time that threatened to leave them all behind.

In the great brick palace, the twisting streets of Payson,
and even in the mindless obedience of the stinking animations,
F.R. now saw pale imitations of the faded glory of their ancestral
homeland. Carpathian had done nothing more than recreate his
only little shadow of Romania in the Wild West of America, and
he was perfectly happy to play make-believe, strutting around followed by his ghost army, fighting in these trivial skirmishes for the
phantoms of exaltation he had been denied in his youth.

They had reached a world historical moment, when the
right man at the right place could apply the lever of science and
change the course of history forever. And his uncle refused to
push on that lever, rendering everything they had lost completely,
tragically senseless.

F.R. collapsed into a hard wooden chair. His head fell
heavily into his upraised hands, and he stared at the gritty wreckage between his booted feet. How could he have been so wrong
about so many things? Even in the midst of his rage, he still believed in the greatness his uncle had once achieved. Payson
could be a perfect launching point for the future he envisioned,
and in that, Burson Carpathian had been entirely correct. But now
it was nothing more than a trap, an illusion that allowed his father
and his uncle to revel in past victories and put off the final efforts
that would carve their family name into the heavens for all time.

He sat up. There was a sound behind him. Someone had
pushed open the door to the lab, and stood there, looking in. He
was in plain sight of anyone standing there, and yet whoever it
was had not said a word.

His first thought was of Misty. She was still gone, and even in the midst of his own torment, he had been concerned. Edison had not returned either, as far as he was aware, and others had been sent away in the past weeks as well. Whatever Carpathian had planned for his grand summit, he must be using his highest-ranking people to usher the guests to Payson.

He didn't know why he felt this way, but he was certain that speaking with Misty would calm the turmoil churning through him. She might be able to see a way through this; perhaps even a means of making his uncle see reason. If some sort of reconciliation was possible, he could try his best to move past his anger. There was still so much they could accomplish together, if his uncle would only meet him half way.

There was a grinding crunch behind him as the person took a first step into the rubble-strewn lab. F.R.'s anger had not been kind to the room, and he felt a slight twinge of guilt as he realized what it must look like to a person coming upon him in the dark like this.

He stood and turned, hoping to see Misty's tall form silhouetted in the doorway. He felt his shoulder slump as he saw a lab assistant standing there in a long white coat, one hand on the door frame.

He could make out no details on the man's face, a dark silhouette in the hall light. Many of the assistants and technicians had been kind to him during his time here, however, and he reined in his anger, knowing that this man most likely did not deserve the weight of it, no matter what his mission might be.

"Can I help you?" His voice was rusty. He had not spoken to another person in days, his vocal chords only ravaged by the occasional primal scream in the dark of his ruined lab.

"Mister Caym, sir?" The man took a hesitant step into the lab, his head turning from side to side at the destruction. "I thought I would stop by to see if you were alright."

The man's voice was low and diffident, but there was no denying the concern there, and it gave F.R. a small jolt of shame. He still had friends in Payson after all, it seemed.

He walked toward the man, marshaling as realistic a smile as he could. If he could not be with Misty, he wanted nothing so much as to be alone with his anger. But he forced himself to mind his manners, intending to send the man on his way with a reassuring smile and his thanks, before he could go back to his brooding.

"I'm quite alright, thank you... mister...?" F.R. had not made much of an effort to learn the names and faces of the men and women who worked in the background of the labs of Payson, and he cursed that offhand callousness now.

"Dalton, Mister Caym. Kyle Dalton. I work primarily with Mister Huxley." The man moved into the shadows, and F.R. could finally make out his face. It was still no one he recognized, but that was no great surprise.

"Well, this is kind of you, Mister Dalton; and kind of Mister Huxley as well. I trust he is well?"

Dalton shrugged. "Please, call me Kyle, sir. Mister Huxley is Mister Huxley, of course: smiling widely as ever." The man's own smile was wan, and he cocked his head as he looked at F.R., as if trying to gauge his state of mind. "You're sure you're okay, sir?"

F.R. waved away the concern, turning back into the lab. He really wanted the man to leave. "I'm fine, Kyle. Nothing that a few more days of languishing in my own misery won't cure, eh?" He pushed a light tone into his voice and gave his own shrug. "Honestly, I'm sure I'll be back in the sunlight in a few days' time."

The man took a few more uncertain steps into the lab. "I wanted you to know, sir, that most of us think you've been very poorly treated, considering what you've done for Payson and the cause."

F.R. turned at that. "Thank you."

"It's just the truth. There's a lot of resentment toward your uncle and your father right now. A lot of people feel there's been a terrible miscarriage of justice." He gestured around the dank room. "A lot of folks are wondering if Payson is a safe place for anyone anymore, if the men in charge will do this to their own kin."

F.R. found himself shaking his head in a reflexive response, but then stopped himself. "Well, I'm sure everything is going to be fine, Kyle. My father and uncle will calm down when they feel I've learned my lesson."

The man shook his head, stepping even closer, into the beam of one of the remaining RJ lanterns. A strange, luminous red glow cast back from the man's eyes. "No, sir. Many of us feel that you have nothing to learn; that it's Doctor Carpathian that has to learn something." He moved even closer, now back-lit in the crimson glow. "A lot of us think you're the person to teach him."

That stopped F.R. as he reached up to steer the man gently back toward the door. "I'm sorry?"

The man hesitated, ducking his head. "I didn't mean to speak out of turn, sir. It's just that, a lot of us here in Payson agree with you. It's torn us up, seeing how you've been treated. It's not right."

F.R. straightened, looking around the ruins of his once-proud laboratory. It was not right, and he knew it. But he had been completely stripped of his machinery and material. He was one man in his uncle's center of power. He felt his lips twist in a bitter half-smile and he turned back to the lab technician.

"Well, you may be right, Kyle, but there is precious little to be done about it now."

"You must make him see sense, Mister Caym." The man's gaze was suddenly intense, gleaming in the shadows with a power that had not been there before. "You must show him what you are capable of, and prove to him you are the man to carry his banner into the next generation and beyond."

F.R. blinked. Hearing those words in another voice, from another mouth, lent them weight and solidity that the same thoughts, in his own head, had lacked.

The man looked back to the door as if nervous of discovery. "I should really leave now, Mister Caym. I've got to get back to the laboratory before I'm missed." He backed toward the door, hands open apologetically.

"Wait," F.R. followed the man. "I want to thank you—"

"No need to thank me, sir." The man's grin was strange and thin. "You owe me nothing, Mister Caym." He stopped, retreated for a moment, again beneath the crimson light, which flared in his eyes. "But what do you owe yourself?"

And then the man was gone.

F.R. stood alone in the ruined lab for several moments. Kyle Dalton was gone, but his words lingered in the air like an echo trapped in cloudy amber.

He felt his body loosen as he chewed on those words in his mind.

What did he owe himself?

* * * * *

F.R. stalked through the streets of Payson, tall brick buildings passing along on either side, a whirlwind of confusion roaring behind his eyes. All around him, the city was a study in contrasts that echoed the conflict in his own mind. RJ power was everywhere, and every building overflowed with the latest innovations and discoveries coming from the countless laboratories and manufactories. And yet, the buildings around him were dingy and tired-looking. The city had been churning out clouds of dark smoke for decades now, and that had taken its toll on the brick and the stone and the painted wood.

As he walked, his mind wandering even darker paths, he realized that his uncle's position was even more untenable than he had first thought. Not only did Carpathian lack the strength of his convictions to take the world firmly in hand and wring from it the future of his dreams, he was not even living in a glorious past. No one took care of the buildings and streets of Payson. As far as he had been able to tell, only his father had even tried to organize the rebuilding after Wayward's invasion and the explosive escape of the other mercenaries. Everyone else in the town seemed content to build around the wreckage, take alternate streets, ignore the scars.

His mind continued to spiral downward. Why would a man like Wayward, who had led a mercenary attack on the city at the behest of the Union itself, be allowed to thrive here now? Why would his uncle be promising a confirmed enemy control of a continent? He knew there was still great resentment toward Wayward among the survivors of Payson. The man went nowhere without that mongrel guard dog of his. He surrounded himself with the surviving vagrants of his little band whenever they were in town. Without that protection, he would have been dead months ago. And yet, Carpathian was apparently willing to grant him one of the most powerful positions in the world. The position the doctor himself should be taking.

It made no sense to F.R., and he could feel the muscles of his face bunch in distaste even as his mind continued to wander in the shadows. Wayward was some kind of war hero to the south, apparently, and that was all well and good for the manipulation of the Confederate remnant. But there was only so much use to be wrung out of that defeated bunch of fatalists. Certainly not enough benefit to justify the rulers of Payson giving up the power for themselves.

But that was the crux of the issue. His uncle, apparently, did not want power. Or rather, as he constantly maintained, he did not want political power. But as F.R. wandered the streets of Payson, having been stripped of everything that mattered to him in the world, he found himself wondering if there might not be quite so many gradations of power as his uncle believed. If they did not control the government directly, and one day those that did turned against them... would their situation be any better than the one they found themselves in right now?

F.R. sensed the shadow of someone turning a sharp corner in front of him, and made to step out of the way to continue on his brooding trail uninterrupted. When the person moved smoothly with him, stepping into his new path, he was barely able to pull up in time to avoid crashing into them.

F.R.'s metal arms snapped up to the person's shoulders to steadied them. His eyes came back into focus from his dark reverie, and he was staring into the deep green eyes of Misty Mimms, her red and gold mask glittering in the sun.

"Misty!" The flood of emotion he felt at seeing her would have been embarrassing, if he cared what others thought. He pulled her into a tight embrace without another word.

Her eyes had widened as she realized who she had crashed into. She murmured "F.R." as he reeled her in, her own arms coming up around him.

They stood like that for longer than seemed appropriate, but not as long as he would have liked. When they pulled apart, he kept his hands on her shoulders. "Where have you been? What are you doing here?"

F.R. had wandered into a dark, rundown section of Payson while he brooded. There was almost no reason for Misty to have been there alone in the normal course of her duties.

She shook her head, her long honey-brown hair billowing out behind her in a way that was almost enough to take his mind off his worrying thoughts. "He sent me to Washington. I'm sorry, but no one was to know."

"Washington?" That gave him pause. "The Union? What were you doing there?"

She looked around, seeming to realize where they were for the first time. "Your uncle has friends everywhere, F.R. I was sent to bring some of them back to Payson for the summit."

F.R. shook his head, gesturing with a lift of his chin toward a side street that would bring them back up and around to the more pleasant parts of the city. She nodded, and the two of them separated, moving at a slow pace toward the alleyway.

"Things have been... difficult, since you left." He would not meet her eyes as they walked. He had wanted nothing more than to be with her and tell her everything, but now that she was here, he found himself loath to recount his embarrassment at the hands of his own blood.

She nodded, glancing aside at him every few steps. "I know. I never finished my business in Washington... I came back when I heard…"

That made very little sense, and he finally looked at her. "You know? How?" The thought of someone else telling her about his humiliation on the proving grounds caused his stomach to churn.

She shook her head, looking away. "There was a man... a stranger. I don't know." She shrugged, smiling to dismiss her own thoughts. "He just said some things that made me think of you... that made me think you might need me. I couldn't shake the feeling, so..." She raised both of her hands in a graceful gesture of surrender. "Here I am."

He shook his head, stopping her and turning her to face him in the narrow alley. "What do you mean, you talked to a man? Who? What did he say?"

She shook off his hand and stepped back. "I told you, I don't know. And he didn't say anything specific at all. It just made me think of you." She shrugged again, sheepish, and looked like she now regretted telling him. "I couldn't get it out of my mind, so I made arrangements and came back as quickly as I could."

"Does my uncle know you've returned?" His mind churned into motion once again. If Carpathian knew she was back, he could summon her, separating them before they got a chance to really talk. "What have you heard?"

She shook her head, again looking up and down the alley. He looked as trapped and confused as he felt, and he pulled her closer to the wall, seeking what little shelter he could from the mouths at either end. "I haven't spoken to anyone, I just started looking for you. I found your lab..."

He bowed his head, remembering the damage he had inflicted on the room. "Not my lab anymore. He's taken my work away from me."

She looked shocked at that. "Why? He was so impressed with all your work! He said it would be essential in moving for-ward!"

F.R. laughed. "Moving forward is not something I think my uncle has in mind."

"What about your father?" She looked into his eyes, and

he could tell she saw the pain there, no matter how deeply he tried to bury it. "What about Ernest?"

F.R. looked up, fighting down the rage that rose again in his throat. "There's nothing my father can do. Nothing that he did, anyway. Ernest left for Europe. He didn't want to stay in Payson." He looked back down into her eyes. "I should have gone with him. There's no place for me here."

Her own face twisted in anger behind the half-mask, and she shook her head. "Nonsense! There is nowhere you belong more than here!"

He smiled slightly at that. "Why Miss Mimms, I didn't know you cared."

She did not smile. "F.R., you can't let them freeze you out of Payson. This place needs you. Your uncle needs you, whether he realizes it or not." She pulled further away. "Without you, I don't know if he can succeed."

"And you won't be able to get what you want, either." She had told him a little about her past, and he had guessed more. There was something she thought Payson could do for her, although he had no clear idea what it might be.

She nodded, her chin raised boldly. "And what of that? We all want something out of life, and we owe it to ourselves to grab as much of it as we can."

Her words echoed the lab technician Dalton, and he stepped back. He wanted to stay. He still wanted everything that had driven him across the ocean to this strange, dry place. He shook his head. "Even if I stay, there's nothing I can do here. He's burned down the trust between us." He looked into her eyes, trying to make her understand how trapped he felt. "I honestly don't see that there is any way for me to reach the man. I've fought his battles, worked on the projects he told me to work on, and toed the line for as long as I could. I did everything a dutiful nephew might owe his own blood." He looked away, his shoulders slumping, his eyes still tight with anger. "He's as blind as the ignorant men and women he despises."

She nodded, biting her full lower lip between glittering teeth. "You need to prove to him that you are capable of standing on your own. Meet him on equal terms and show him that you're no slave or wage worker, but a partner."

He barked a laugh that echoed off the close brick walls. "How? I have nothing, Misty. Nothing! The man has taken everything from me!" He could feel the fury burning behind his eyes, and did not even try to control his voice. "He has left me with nothing." He spit this last into the dirt at their feet.

Again, she nodded, but there was an edge to her eyes now that reached him through his desperate, angry fog. "Do you know anything about Jesse James?"

That seeming non sequitur brought him up short despite his growing anger. "I know what everyone knows. My uncle seems to have built a relationship with the man in the past."

She nodded, her own bitterness clear in her eyes. He could see she was edging closer to her own inner demons. "Carpathian had been grooming Jesse James to take the Confederacy and help him destroy the Union."

That made some sense. "That's why he gave him the arms?" Such mechanical marvels were not cheap, nor were they easy to emplace. He flexed his hand; he should know. He had often wondered, in idle moments, what a dusty frontier outlaw might have done to earn that much interest from his uncle.

"That is why Doctor Carpathian gave him the arms." Her eyes flicked toward his own metal limbs before she continued. "And a great deal more."

"But... Wayward?" He felt the more she was telling him, the less sense the situation in Payson made.

Misty shook her head. "I don't know. There's something between Carpathian and Wayward that he hasn't told anyone. It might have something to do with why Wayward and his mercenaries halted their attack on the city. Jesse James disappeared from the doctor's care a couple months before Wayward arrived. None of us know where he went, or what he intends to do." She smiled at him. "Despite working together, he is not the greatest admirer your uncle has ever had."

F.R. tried to summon a smile for her, but he could not. "I can imagine."

"But I think the most important strand of this knot, to you, is not going to be Jesse James, but William Bonney."

Again he found himself nonplussed. "Billy the Kid?"

Her head jerked up and down once, sharply. "Haven't you wondered why your uncle wanted Bonney in the cell beneath the palace, instead of dead like the rest of his posse?"

F.R. shook his head. "I don't know any more about Billy the Kid than I know about Jesse James, and all I know about either of them is from the penny dreadfuls."

Her own bark of laughter was softer than his had been. "Those silly books don't get a lot right... but if you've read them, you know that Billy and Jesse don't get along."

He felt his sluggish brain start to move. "I do."

"Bonney has always felt that your uncle was unfair with the distribution of his favors. He has always been jealous of Jesse James, and despite jumping whenever Doctor Carpathian snapped his fingers, the man never felt he had gotten his due." She pushed a single finger into his chest. "Which is why he sent you to go and fetch him. Now, he's in a prison cell where he can't team up with Jesse James now that that outlaw has gone rogue, where he can't cause any further mayhem, especially given the big summit your uncle is planning, and where he cannot make a further nuisance of himself."

"Why not just have me kill him?" F.R. hooked his metal thumbs behind his blasters. "Why go through the trouble of capturing him and keeping him in a bell jar?"

"William Bonney is not the sharpest spoon in the drawer, F.R. Your uncle believed that, after things quieted down again here, he could convince the man that everything had been in his best interests, and then probably use him to track down Jesse James, if that still proved necessary."

"But he had me kill the man's best friend before his very eyes." Pieces were clicking into place, and he realized that his uncle's mind was a constantly shifting puzzle, sliding along on more levels than most people could even conceive.

"Exactly. Maybe so, when the time came, his anger could be redirected away from the good doctor, and toward someone else."

F.R. scowled. "Are you telling me that my uncle was planning on betraying me from the very beginning?"

She shook her head. "Who knows? Probably not, but he's a deep thinker, and he likes to keep all of his options open. One thing I've learned, watching Doctor Carpathian: if you think you know what direction he is about to turn, walk the other way."

"So what are you trying to say?" His was soft. If his uncle was familiar with manipulation on so grand a scale, he might not hold a grudge if he was administered some bruises in the course of his own lesson, if the curriculum was important enough. He thought he saw where Misty was heading.

"You feel alone and without resources. But you need to prove to your uncle that you are a true member of the family, and a worthy heir, when the time comes." She shrugged, reaching out and resting one hand on his shoulder. "Maybe you're not as alone as you think you are."

His eyes lost their focus as he weighed her words. What did he owe himself, after all? And maybe this was exactly what his uncle wanted him to do. Maybe he was only waiting for F.R. to prove himself worthy of the family legacy. What did the concept of family mean, after all, if he let the current situation stand?

Chapter 18

The room was cool and quiet. Filtered sunlight streamed through wide windows overlooking the grand square far below. The massive space was filling up rapidly, hundreds upon hundreds of seats placed in neat rows almost entirely occupied by guests that had been pouring into Payson for the past week, led to the mysterious hidden city by Doctor Carpathian's most trusted agents and assistants. Around the edges of the square, the occupants of the city itself were gathering shoulder to shoulder, every one of them eager to know what was going to unfold in front of the palace.

Carpathian could feel the smile stretching the taught old skin of his face. He refused to allow the pull of the dark iron augmentation within his right eye socket to detract him from the glory of the moment. Below, as the tide of people swelled, the culmination of a lifetime's dreams sat just beyond the horizon, waiting only for the right moment to rise up into the sky and blaze forth, heralding a new age for Payson, himself, and the whole world.

He had come to this continent decades ago with the sole purpose of restoring a war-torn nation, using his advanced technology to heal the wounded of both the north and the south. He had intended to usher in a new age of reason and Enlightenment in the New World. Instead, the moment his foot had touched American soil, everything had been taken from him. He had been stripped of even the most basic materials, every one of his trained servants, even the crew that had brought him. And his beloved wife, Veronica, had been murdered before his very eyes.

His old hand, wrapped in its supporting iron frame, clenched with remembered sorrow and anger. General Grant and his butchers had slaughtered everyone, then savaged his body and left him for dead. If it had not been for his strange, fiery-eyed benefactors, he would surely have died on that beach.

Benefactors. He almost choked on the bitter laugh that rose in his throat at the thought. It had taken him many years, and many painful lessons, to learn the brutal cost those benefactors exacted from each transaction. Over the years he had watched the best laid plans of soldiers, outlaws, and statesmen collapse in the most horrific ways. His scientific mind told him there was a pattern behind the bloodshed and the failure even as it refused to believe the evidence. There was no way he could embrace the concept of an all-powerful, supernatural force abroad in the world, stalking the best intentions of men and reveling in their fall.

In the window before him, he saw his reflection sneer. How wrong he had been. The ancient relics had taught him that, among many other things. This Dark Council which haunted the shadowy corridors of history were real, and they were alive and well. Only a unified power would be able to stand against them. And only he was in a position to forge such an alliance here and now.

No one, not even Vladimir, really understood the threat posed by these shadowy, crimson-eyed creatures. Even his oldest friend and confidant, the brother of the woman who had meant everything to him, looked at him with an infuriating mixture of pity and condescension whenever he mentioned the Dark Council. He knew, now, that he needed to first bring the continent under his control, and then gather the best minds in the world together and force them to understand. The reflection's sneer twisted with even more bitterness as he remembered the Assembly of Medicine and Science...

But all of that would soon be over. Below, gathered together for the first time, were some of the greatest minds from two continents. There were scientists, politicians, military leaders, and philosophers. Each would see the power of Payson on full display, and would have no choice but to agree that, in the face of what he would soon be able to bring to the field, there had to be a better way than war. The Union would be destroyed, of course. There was no way that could be avoided, nor would he avoid it if he could. But afterward, his real goals could begin.

The door behind him opened, and Vladimir came in. The old soldier was dressed in a suit of severe design that called to mind military uniforms of an earlier age. His face was pale, as always, its expression grave. Since F.R.'s disciplining, Vladimir had been quiet and distant. He knew his friend found watching the rough handling of his son difficult, but he also knew that Vladimir was a strong man who could do what must be done.

"It is nearly time, Burson." His tones were flat beneath his accent, and Carpathian found himself missing the bantering tone that had so often colored that voice in the past. He hoped that closeness would heal, in time.

Carpathian nodded, pulling his vest down tight over his stomach and straightening the lapels of his formal coat. "Of course, Vladimir. Thank you." He moved toward the door, Vlad stepping out of the way, and paused to ask, "How is F.R.?"

A flash of uncertain annoyance passed over Vladimir's face before he schooled it back to immobility. He responded with a shrug. "You told me he needed to be left alone."

Carpathian smiled, patting his friend on the shoulder. "And he did. But have no fear, Vladimir. I have no doubt these weeks have taught him a valuable lesson. He will come back to us stronger and more valuable than ever."

Vladimir straightened within his tunic. "He may, Burson. But vill he forgive us ven he does? Vill he forgive me?"

The doctor clapped Vlad on the shoulder once more and moved on past into the hallway. Vladimir moved to follow. "You remember being young, Vladimir, do you not? Emotions are strongly felt, deeply felt, but also quick to pass when a new set of circumstances dawns. Once this great unveiling is complete, and all of these people have returned to their homes, we will bring the young man back into the fold. He will be eager for a chance to prove himself, his soul set ablaze by what he will witness today."

They moved along the hall in silence for several minutes. Here, security was provided by the freshest, most advanced animations, and the smell was almost negligible. A particularly surly-looking animated corpse recalled something to his mind, and he craned his neck to speak over his shoulder. "Has there been any further sightings of James?"

Vladimir shook his head. "No. Nossing ve can confirm, at any rate. Ze man is a ghost, moving through ze territories vith impunity. Not even ze full power of ze Marshal's Service has been able to detect anysing."

"Hmmmph." He wanted to spit. He had spent a great deal of his political capital cementing that alliance, and it had proven far less efficacious than he had hoped. "Well, perhaps Bonney might be persuaded to hunt him down for us, after all of the excitement dies down."

"Zhat explains certain sings."

The man's tone was so noncommittal, Carpathian had to laugh. "You think too highly of people in general, old friend, and of the outlaw variety in particular. William Bonney will be back on the trail in no time, and he will fall into his same old patterns of behavior."

They stopped at the bank of lifts, and Carpathian saw Vlad eyeing the row of double doors with discomfort; remembering Wayward's assault, no doubt. He turned to his oldest friend, his face serious. "Vladimir, this really will be a day to remember. By the end of today, the world will know our true worth, they will know what we can achieve. After today, there will be no way we can be stopped."

Vladimir tucked his chin into the collar of his tunic. "I pray to God you are correct, Burson. If you are wrong, ve may never recover."

Carpathian clapped Vladimir on the shoulder with as much force as his powered exoskeleton could summon. Sometimes, he admitted to himself, the augmentations had their uses. He grinned as the other man winced. "Nothing will go wrong, Vladimir. We will have allies around the world, your son will be with us once again, the savages and the Union will have no recourse, and we will finally have the time to hunt down Jesse James, remove him, and move forward with our plan for the continent; and the world."

Vladimir's blank face bobbed in a half-bow, but he remained silent as the heavy doors slid closed before them.

Far below, the most prestigious group of men and women ever gathered in one place in the New World awaited Carpathian's arrival with baited breath.

The thought made him smile.

* * * * *

Far beneath the palace, down abandoned halls far from the common paths, security was provided by far less fresh and more odiferous cadavers. They stood at their assigned stations, their small, RJ-powered cells pushing the crimson substance through soft, decaying veins, surveying their allocated stretches of empty hallway.

Rance Bollivar had been a farmer for most of his life. He had made a decent living working for old man Loder, married well, raised a family, and always had enough left over at the end of a given week that he could toss a few back with his friends down at the local tavern. But then he had heard about the western territories, how a man could head out west, stake a claim to a beautiful piece of land, and be his own boss, master of all he surveyed. There would be land to leave his children. He would be able to live a life of relative leisure, keeping what he made for himself.

That's not how it had panned out, though. Rance had forced his wife to drop everything and dragged her out into the desert. They had lost their first boy to a fever, with no doctor around to tend him. That winter they had near starved, and his wife had taken their second boy and gone back east, leaving him along to scrabble at his dusty little plot of land alone. When the same fever had struck him not long after, there had been no one to help him, and he had died screaming at the injustice of it all until his throat was raw, and all he could summon was a weak, pathetic croak.

There was little left of Rance Bolliver in the animation watching the stretch of hallway but the meat and bones. The soul was long gone, fled, hopefully, to some better place. Only faint echoes and shadows of the man he had been remained, wandering the halls of his mind dull, and listless. A contraption had been rammed into the back of Rance's head, reanimating his body, and a vestigial machine intelligence looked out through his cloudy eyes at a world composed entirely of swirling, glittering reds. Within that sight, the hallway before the animation was empty. It had been empty since a servant had left a tray of food for the prisoner four hours and fifteen minutes ago.

The animation that had been Rance never saw the blow that took it down. It had no way of knowing that a back door had been left open that night, nor that every animation between that door and its own station had been eliminated in turn. It had not died when the heavy axe slashed through its back and knocked it to the ground, but it found it had been paralyzed. Its field of vision was far more limited from its current vantage point; it could only make out heavy, dusty boots trooping past toward the cell.

When the boots returned, a single voice was speaking, its sound moving with the group as they stepped over the body and continued down the hall, heading toward the upper levels of the palace.

"—gotta remember, we wait fer the boss's signal. An' we don't do nothin' he don't tell us to do."

Another voice responded, and although Rance might have recognized the bitter anger in the voice, the animation had no such frame of reference to go by, only hearing and recording the words themselves.

"We'll see, pal. He might be yer boss all o'sudden-like, but he sure as hell ain't mine. We'll see what's what."

"But, he got us to you, Billy! We follow his lead, we're gonna be gettin' the copper ring outta this one!"

"We'll see."

The boots and voice faded away, and the sentry could only lay, its eyes recording an empty hall, and wait for reanimation.

* * * * *

The sheer presence of so many people pressed in upon him even through the heavy doors of the palace. He had walked through this portal thousands of times over the years, and never had it felt more portentous than it did at this moment. Even the first time he pushed the heavy doors open and took possession of his new seat of power, he had not felt this thrill of excitement and destiny. As soon as he pushed through these doors today, he would be stepping into a whole new world.

Not all of his invitations had been well-received, of course. But the crowd beyond was larger than he had dared to hope. There were more than enough opinion-shapers and policy makers sitting in the hot sun to ensure that his words were going to reach all the right ears. What they were going to see would spark a revolution that would change the world, elevate him to a position of greater power than any man had ever known before him, and free him to prepare humanity for the true battle that lay ahead.

He felt a momentary skip in his heartbeat as he remembered the only person who had seemed to understand his plans at all, no matter how hard that was to credit. Jesse James had been more than a pawn in his intricate machinations. The man would have been a leader for the war to come, and he could have been a great one. Marcus Wayward was no leader of men. He would follow instructions, he would do what he had to in order to secure his own power and position, but the spark of fate was not in the man. He was too much his own creature to play the role of true ally.

His mouth lifted in a tight, distasteful grimace. Damn Jesse James anyway.

Outside, the surf-like mutter of a thousand voices surged for a moment, and then died away. He had ordered his animations and some of his more fantastical Creations to take up station around the crowd before he made his own appearance. They would set the tone for the rest of his presentation, as well as serving as proof of his power to some of the less-informed guests. There were hundreds of people from around the world sitting out in the hot sun, few of whom would credit the stories of his work as anything more than exaggerations, or even outright fabrications dreamed up by the sensationalist press and dime novel writers.

Vladimir had spent nearly a week constructing the vast stage, with its voice-amplification contraptions and an elaborate system of pulleys, curtains, and counterweights that would make the Paris Opera House proud. His smile lost its sour edge as he thought of the coming drama. What was theater without a grand reveal, after all?

He turned behind him, to where his brother-in-law stood at stiff attention: ever the military man. "Everything is in order?"

Vladimir gave the merest jerk of his head. "I believe young Huxley vill be demonstrating ze flight pack at ze height of your grand pantomime."

Huxley... Carpathian nodded. He would do nicely. The young British biologist was perhaps the most pragmatic of all the scientists currently working in Payson. He was also physically intimidating, with his stocky, athlete's build. It should make quite the scene, watching him rise into the air under a clear sky in broad daylight.

"The rest of them are in position?" He straightened his lapels, adjusted his cravat, and shrugged his shoulders within the heavy coat.

"Thomas and Gustave are on ze stage avaiting your arrival. Vayvard and his dog vill be in ze front row, vith Miss Mimms, ze Kaufmanns, and ze ozers." He reached out to wipe away a stray bit of lint on the doctor's shoulder. "Ze rest of ze front row is given over to ze special guests."

Ah, yes. The smile widened: his special guests. Two princes, five dukes, several foreign ministers, and even one ambassador plenipotentiary. He felt a thrill run up his spine as the boy who had once confronted the assembled geniuses of Europe in Vienna rubbed his hands at the thought of what was about to happen.

"Well, I believe it is time we began, is it not, old friend?" He gave Vladimir's arm a warm squeeze, took a deep breath, and pushed open the grand doors.

* * * * *

The sea of faces stretched as far as he could see. Closing his natural eye with a squint, he focused the RJ-enhanced lens on the far edges of the crowd and smiled to see the towering Creations patrolling the boundaries of the square. He even nodded to J.P. Smith, who had suffered his exile long enough, and was now watching the perimeter with his beloved Creation 5. The man responded with a thankful, ingratiating smile, and Carpathian knew the punishment had been effective.

As the people in the front of the crowd saw him within the doorway, they stopped speaking, hushing those around them. A wave of soft hisses rushed backward through the mass, leaving quiet expectation in its wake. Soon, the entire square was completely, eerily silent.

Carpathian stepped off the high veranda of the palace and onto the wooden ramp leading to a wide stage. A podium had been placed front and center on the platform, echoing the placement of a similar lectern that had once stood on the dais of the Assembly of Medicine and Science decades ago.

Doctor Burson Carpathian forced his spine to formal stiffness, and walked across the ramp with careful, measured strides. Leaving the cool shadows of the sheltered gallery, he felt the weight of the sun beating down upon his tall hat and broad back. There was almost no movement in the crowd, save for the turning of heads following his progress and the occasional flutter of a fan or hat under the brutal heat. The creaking of the wood beneath his heavy tread was the only sound, echoing off the distant buildings, the grand sub-palaces, and administrative complexes from which Payson controlled its growing empire of influence and advancement.

The doctor stepped behind the podium and grasped it with both hands. It was old, polished wood, and he found himself wondering where it might have come from. He knew his mind was wandering, wanting to forestall this moment for as long as possible. His entire life had been focused on this day, and the rest of his life would be a glorious counterpoint in its honor.

A large ball-topped wand stuck up in the air from the center of the podium. Modeled after the vocal reiterators used by the Union, it would send his voice out to the crowd through an array of amplifiers that Edison had created for just this purpose. Every person in that vast crowd was silent, watching him, waiting to hear what he had to say and see what he had to show them.

Carpathian took a moment to look up at the clear blue of the sky, high white clouds scudding by, casting phantom shadows that drifted across the crowd. Tall buildings rose up all around, their intricate designs and gothic architecture a reminder of the best Europe had to offer. It had all had been built through his efforts, and for his purposes. He had risen from that humiliating day in Vienna all those years ago, to this stage, poised to shift the course of history forever, and take the first steps toward defending mankind, and Earth itself, from the enemies that had unknowingly plagued them since the dawn of time.

With a smile, the doctor reached up and tapped the soft ball at the end of the wand. The sharp report of the contact echoed across the square, and a ripple of surprise swept through the crowd as the amplifiers threw the sound out into the warm air. People all around began to crane their necks, looking for the source of the sound, while others smiled appreciatively, seeing this as what it was: the opening of the doctor's grand presentation.

"Please, ladies and gentlemen, do not be alarmed by the sound of my voice." His smile broadened as the deep, echoing tones washed out from the stage. "This technology is the least of the wonders I have to show you today. If we cannot get past the amplification of mere sound, we shall be here suffering under the heat all day!"

A low rush of soft, nervous laughter washed across the square, and he saw many of the men and women in the front row smile tentatively. These were the truly important people, the ones would go back to their homes and begin to implement the changes in attitude and preparation needed to turn the world around. Sitting in the very center of the front row was Marcus Wayward, his smile glittering in the sun and more than compensating for his companion's dour expression. Wayward was being introduced to some of the most important, powerful people in Europe this day, and the legend of his rise to power over the entire continent of America would begin here.

Carpathian found himself sparing a wistful thought for his old contentious partner-in-crime, Jesse James. Now that man had a sense of drama and style. He forced himself to smile warmly at Wayward, and then let his gaze fall upon Misty Mimms, sitting demurely beside him. She had followed his advice and left her frontier leathers in her rooms, wearing a beautiful gown of red and gold that complimented her mask. She looked truly beautiful, regal even, among that collection of lords and princes.

Beside Misty, uncomfortable in their formalwear, sat his two oldest assistants, Thomas Edison and Gustave Eiffel. Thomas had travelled all the way to Washington and then on to England for him, and had brought back all of his proposed targets. The man was one of his best servants, and would be central to the expansion of the Enlightened agenda in the days and years to come.

In the second row, face shadowed by a large Stetson, was a big man with shoulder-length gray hair. Although there was no sign of a shiny metal star upon the chest of his duster, Carpathian was glad all the same that Virgil Earp had come to his senses and attended. Despite their failure to find Jesse James, the Marshal's Service had a large part to play in the future of the territories, he knew. It was nice to know that some servants stayed bought.

He looked back up at the crowd, and drew in a breath of the clear forest air. He had had the manufactories closed for the better part of a week, to ensure that their stink would not pollute the great day. For the same reason, only the freshest animations had been assigned to guard the crowd, and the Creations had been washed and treated the night before, and told to patrol upwind of the vast group. Payson was on display to the world for the first time, and he would be damned if it did not put its very best reanimated foot forward.

He exhaled the breath slowly, enjoying the pure, animal sensation of the clean air in his often-raw throat.

He tapped the sphere again, just for the fun of it, and shrugged. "I never tire of that." He smiled at the responding polite chuckle, and then cleared his throat. "Ladies and gentlemen, first and foremost, I wish to thank you for making the journey here to Payson. I know many of you have travelled for thousands of miles, braving all sorts of hardships and dangers, and I will never be able to convey to you how important it is to me that you have come." He raised a hand. "And I know that means very little to most of you, as you do not know, truly, who I am."

He tapped his chest with one metal-shrouded finger. "I am Doctor Burson Carpathian. I am a man of science and rational thought, like many of you. And I am a man who has spent years fighting for peace and justice not only for the high and the mighty among us, but for all people, wherever they might be." He gestured to the beautiful buildings that formed the borders of the square, feeling the majesty of the palace rising up behind him. "I created this place to be a center of learning, design, and advancement for my adopted homeland. I took the squalid little burg of Green Valley, and through my own work, I grew it into the metropolis you see before you."

The guests had all been brought into Payson through very carefully prepared routes. His minions had avoided the damaged and rundown sections of the city, sticking to the more impressive thoroughfares and tree-lined promenades that had been designed and built, nearly two decades ago, with this very day in mind.

"I know many of you are asking yourselves why I invited you here. Why I have spent every ounce of political capital and good will I had amassed through a lifetime of collaborative work and tireless effort on behalf of the human race, to assemble such an august company in one place, at one time, so far from civilization." He smiled and nodded, and many of the people in the first several rows nodded in response, their own smiles not quite as wide.

"We are on the cusp of a great new world, my friends. Science, philosophy, manufacturing and technology are all advancing at a breath-taking pace, and we are now poised to enter a new epoch in human evolution, if we, the Enlightened, can only see the time for what it is, and seize the moment, and make it our own!"

That got a quick, muttered conversation moving through the crowd, and Carpathian raised a hand to quiet them before continuing. "The technologies that we here in Payson, and many of you around the world, are creating today can be used to raise the common press of Mankind above the mud and the squalor of previous centuries, and point him toward the very stars themselves! This Industrial Revolution is only the beginning, my friends. When every man, woman, and child may feel the benefits and the succor of our burgeoning advancements, then we will have truly made this world our own, and placed our seal upon it!"

The faces in the crowd nearest him were wavering. He could see confusion and doubt building there, as he knew he would. There were many reasons to shape the future of the world, but for most petty-minded cretins, no matter how highly-placed they might be in the world, having their names writ large in history for a selfless gesture in the name of humanity did not factor highly in their personal calculus. Most of these men and women would require a more mercenary reason to make the right decision; just as he had planned.

He raised one hand, tilting his head as if forestalling an argument. "I know, often in the past such rhetoric has led to great conflict and unrest, with the ever-present battle between the wealthy and the poor clouding the issue. But I am here to prove to you, my friends, that the power of technology is not to level the playing field by dragging the highest of us down, but to raise the lowest of us up." He unleashed his brightest smile. "And for those few of us here at the beginning, there will be great rewards to reap, as well." He needed to be careful here, he knew. No one wanted to be accused of greed or meanness of spirit. Like the average run of humanity, and possibly more than most, these wanted to be given their due while being told what good souls they had. He wrestled the sneer that thought threatened to conjure under control beneath the wide smile.

"As mankind rises from the ashes and the mud of centuries of warfare and conflict, it will crave leadership and guidance." He nodded, pointing out over the crowd. "If we are able to band together here today, a new generation of leaders will be needed. And who do you think that will be?" He nodded again. "I think you know who it will be."

The crowd was made up entirely of men and women in positions of authority and privilege. They would make the connections he intended and come to the proper conclusions. In a world dependent upon his new technologies and powers, there would be a great deal of wealth to be made. They would see that surrounding them in the city he had made in the middle of the desert, and they would know that from a lifetime spent at the top of the ladder. He needed them to make these connections, but could not explicitly state such vulgar realities for fear of being branded a profiteer. He smiled wider at the thought. He was a profiteer; as was almost everyone sitting before him. And there was nothing wrong with that. Yet he could not speak the words aloud. He almost laughed. Truly, what fools humans were.

He saw the speculation igniting behind many of the eyes before him as they began to see the potential. And yet, the profit they saw would be to the advancement of mankind, as well. Profit and purity in equal measure; it would be a heady mixture for most of them.

But there were still those who doubted, who would deny the sanctity of what he had to offer, or find the profit to be insufficient to the work ahead. For those, there were two more roads he had prepared, and he brought his hands down to grasp the edges of the podium as he leaned into the growing rush of whispers as advisors and counselors bent to murmur in their patrons' ears. Conversation stopped again as they realized he was looking out at them with an expectant eye.

"Of course, such advancement will not come without a price. There will always be those who wish to keep all the power and the profit for themselves." Many of those in the audience were perfect examples of the type. "There will always be evil men who seek to chain science and advancement for their own benefit, denying it to others."

He reared back, still gripping the podium, and this time there was no need for a dramatic flair to add fire to his words, and he unleashed the anger and resentment that was never far from his heart. "We, on this very continent, have suffered long and grievously beneath the yoke of just such a regime. Many of you know of what I speak. Those of you who have traveled here from abroad know of the iron-hard embargo the United States government has placed upon the technologies that have emerged here in recent times. You have seen for yourselves the advancements readily available to many here that have been denied to your people at home. We of Payson have waged a constant war against these tyrants for many, many years. For the plight of the little people who cannot stand for themselves, we have met the forces of the despotic Union time and time again."

But he was not appealing to their sense of righteousness, no. This next step would be to shake those in doubt with fear. To show them what Payson was capable of bringing to bear against those who did not share its vision. He ignored the looks of concern Virgil Earp shot him from beneath his wide-brimmed hat. The man had known was he was signing up for long before he had gotten that shiny new arm.

"You have by now seen the automatons that guard Payson with tireless devotion." He waved a hand out over the crowd and toward the buildings beyond. "You have seen the awe-inspiring Creations that even now watch over us all." At the words, the Creations moved forward into plain sight. The two headed 7, refurbished and as good as new, dominated the forward part of the audience as it stepped out onto the veranda. Creation 9, moving out of an alley on the other side, stood before the assembly, its enormous drill arms extended, a discreet veil covering the bottom of its face where its lower jaw had been removed to make way for a long proboscis borer. J.P.'s Creation 5, with its massive battering-ram forearms and the huge Rail Gun affixed to its back, was a particularly impressive specimen.

Nearer at hand a massive Creation scuttled out of the shadows to his left, wide-spread metallic spider legs moving in a blur of coordination as the upper body of a strong, albeit dead, man pivoted back and forth, tracking the movement of the crowd with its blank crimson stare.

All through the crowd he could hear gasps and sharp curses.

"To those of you who might doubt our ability to combat the evil Union, that blight upon the land that would hold all men not of the Union down in the mud, I have decided to reveal to you a secret or two that I think you will find both illustrative and intriguing." He turned away from the audience, presenting them with a view of his noble profile, and gestured behind him to the right of the stage, where a massive curtain hung suspended on a beautifully-crafted wooden frame. Servants in the livery of Payson stood at attention on either side, loosely holding ropes that disappeared up into the bunched fabric.

"First, I would like you to see something I've been working on with several of my best people." He gave a nod to Eiffel, who was beaming with pride. "We find it difficult to confront the Union's heavy armor on occasion, or to deal with the savages' warped and twisted animal allies, and so we created this—" He made a grand gesture with one hand, and the servants pulled on their ropes, dropping the curtain that shrouded the right side of the stage.

The Skorpius was truly a beautiful work of art. It was enormous, standing proudly on its four thick metal legs, each bowed slightly to give the monstrous machine a threatening pose, as if it were preparing to leap. It was entirely metal, the child of Eiffel's affinity for working with automatons rather than the malleable flesh of the dead, and he was very glad he had allowed the Frenchman to follow his muse this time around. An enormous drill protruded from the main chassis, a feature that had dug deep furrows through the proving grounds north of the city. The maw of a powerful blaster cannon protruded from between its forward shoulders, capable of destroying even a Union Rolling Thunder wagon with a single shot. Curving up over the machine's arching back was an articulated assembly of joints and armored plating that held aloft a pair of smaller, rapid fire blaster cannons that would make short work of any soldiers intent upon doing the vehicle harm.

Carpathian watched as a large portion of the audience recoiled from the sight of the Skorpius. Nothing like it existed outside of Payson, he was sure, despite some whispered rumors of walking artillery that the Union was said to be working on. He would put his glorious creation against anything that hack Tesla and his brood could come up with in a New York minute, as the saying went. The man had done nothing but latch upon every innovation to come out of Payson for more years than he cared to count.

"Ladies and gentlemen, faced with the overwhelming firepower of the Union, we of Payson give you the Skorpius. A mobile weapons platform capable of destroying the most armored enemy, repositioning at a moment's notice, and decimating intervening infantry at the same time." He smiled widely. He believed there was nothing in the Union arsenal that could stand against it. He knew that nothing fielded by any of the nations represented in the crowed below could challenge the beast. And each and every one of them knew it as well.

The Skorpius crouched lower, coming to life, and the vents and tell-tales along its flanks and down its legs flared to crimson life. Again, the audience gave a start, and Carpathian could not help but smile. "Powered by my proprietary energy source, the inestimable RJ-1027, the Skorpius will be the unstoppable vanguard of our cause." And there was the true sticking point. Decades ago back in Vienna, as a very young man he had offered the world all of the healing properties of his RJ-1027, and he had been laughed off the stage. He noted with a smile that no one in the crowd was laughing now.

He moved back to the podium, leaning into the speaking wand, and cleared his throat. He had their full attention now, even though many eyes flitted back and forth between his face and the hulking iron menace behind him.

"There is one frontier that mankind has yearned to conquer for millennia, but that has forever been beyond our grasp." He spoke in low tones, and the murmuring stopped as people were forced to quiet down to hear him. "One desire that we have never been able to fulfill." He looked up into the clear sky with a perfect sense of drama that had every head in the square tilted upward, wanting to know what might come next.

He looked back down at them, one side of his face curled into a half-smile. "I speak, of course, of powered flight." He put up a hand even though no one had spoken. He had them now. "I do not mean the quaint balloons of the Montgolfiers, or even the fantastical powered wings of Leonardo da Vinci. I speak of a man being able to soar, on his own, through the clouds. The image alone is enough to bring tears to the eye!"

He frowned, and then smiled again. "I have worked, on and off, upon this conundrum for years upon years, as have many of you, I have no doubt." He shrugged. "Of course, where the greatest genius of the Renaissance failed, many of us have had very little hope of success." Many heads turned toward each other in the crowd now. They were debating, he knew, if he could truly do what it seemed he was on the verge of claiming. The thought brought another genuine smile to his lips. "I did meet with failure after failure, of course." He waved one hand up into the air. "It appeared, at times, that this would remain the one, inviolate frontier." He brought his hands back down to grab the podium, leaning forward once again, and gave them a conspiratorial smile. "But no barrier can stand forever, when the greatest minds of the world are applied against it. And I assure you, ladies and gentlemen, we of Payson have now conquered the very sky herself!"

There was a rush of talk and movement. Many of the people in the crowd looked up again, expecting to see something above their heads. They were fools, if they thought he was so poor a showman as to reveal his prize so soon.

"Of course," he continued in an almost casual tone. "The military men among you can easily see the benefits, once one admits of the possibility of flight, of weaponizing such potential." With another grand sweep of his arm he waved at the left-hand curtain, and it, too, fell, leaving only a small space behind the stage shrouded. Standing behind the curtain was a line of six Hellions. The raw materials were as fresh as could be obtained, although the inhuman attachments across their upper faces and heads would have hidden many of the signs had they not been. Their metal talons rested heavily upon the wood of the stage, and their massive wings, a framework of metal and tubing, were shrouded in fine leather. Each bore a heavy blaster rifle at port arms, thanks to Vladimir's suggestion. They made quite the martial display, he was happy to see.

"Now," Carpathian turned back to the crowd. "There were some difficulties, of course. I don't have to tell you all that the road of progress can be a bumpy one." He smiled, and scattered throughout the crowd, some smiled in response. "But we have finally defeated the last barriers to our mastering the skies. Lead by a living, breathing man, these creations, my Hellions, will be the most powerful force for good on or above any battlefield on Earth!"

A figure stepped out from behind the last curtain. Tall and straight, he could see at once that it was not Thomas Huxley. With the wide-brimmed Stetson, the cut-away leather jacket, and the gleaming metal arms, he realized he should have known all along.

F.R. Caym stood on the stage, his iron arms crossed, grinning widely into a crowd of the most influential people in the world. Upon his back was strapped the flight pack he had worked on for so long. The vestigial control surfaces swept over his shoulders like the wings of Nike herself, and the flare in his eyes was a combination of challenge and unalloyed pride as he basked in the awe and amazement of the crowd.

Carpathian looked blankly at his nephew for a moment. Behind F.R. he could see Huxley, resting easily against one of the curtain frames. The Englishman gave an infuriatingly casual shrug, his usual smile unaffected by the situation. The doctor looked back at his nephew.

F.R. met his gaze with bland eyes. He was wearing his goggles, but now there was a smaller pair of lenses fixed above the standard set, and flashes of light and movement skittered across those smaller circles as he watched.

Carpathian's straight mouth slowly curved into a broad, proud smile.

He turned back to the audience and snapped one hand toward the new arrival. "And now, my own nephew, and one of the heirs to the legacy of Payson, F.R. Caym, will demonstrate my newest addition to the canon of human knowledge!"

With his head turned toward the crowd, Carpathian could not see the narrowing of the young man's eyes as credit for his greatest accomplishment was stolen. And blinded as he was in his moment of victory, he did not see the looks of horror that flashed across many of the faces before him as he said the boy's name.

Chapter 19

Vlad's eyes were locked on his son's as Carpathian made his sudden, unscripted introduction. It took a moment for the doctor's words to sink in. 'My newest addition to the canon of human knowledge!'...

F.R. wore his heavily tinted goggles, the strange second set of frames set above the first making it even harder to see the eyes behind the glass. But a sudden ripple of tension ran through the young man's entire body as the words registered, and Vlad's heart turned to frigid stone in his chest. He pushed through the servants by the door, not knowing what he should do. He could not interrupt the doctor's grand reveal, but with a dread, nightmarish certainty, he knew that he was trapped in a moment in time that would haunt him forever.

Was it his brother-in-law's betrayal of his son that would haunt him? The knowledge that he had stood silently by while Carpathian had robbed F.R. of the greatest accomplishments of his life? He thought not. He knew that the doctor was overreacting, but he also truly believed that Carpathian had the boy's best interests at heart. There would be a reconciliation, if only they were all given enough time.

Was it fear of what his own son might be capable of? He had heard the horrible rumors out of Paris, of course. The scientific community might be a parade of effete, girlish old men who enjoyed nothing so much as belittling each other across continents and centuries. But they were also a close-knit community. He had heard the rumors that had circulated throughout Europe about his son's... unorthodox experiments and field trials. But he had dismissed the vast majority of those tales as nothing more than the petty jealousies to which these men of learning where so often prone.

His dark eyes flashed out over the audience, a sea of still, silent faces, their eyes fixed upon his son. Many of those faces belonged to the men and women who had taken an inordinate glee in retelling those tales about F.R., he knew. And many of them were shocked, some even terrified, at the sound of the young man's name. It was the look of honest terror in those eyes, more than anything else, that finally began to wear away his blind, paternal trust. What if F.R. was capable of those terrible things? The frozen stone in his chest doubled in weight.

"And now," Carpathian spoke out over the crowd. "My nephew will demonstrate this great new step in human evolution and advancement for you all!" The looks of horror gave way to awe and excitement. Vlad turned and saw plumes of white mist boiling out from the bottom of the pack on F.R.'s back. The small wings jutting over his back extended, and with a smile, his son rose gracefully into the air.

* * * * *

The rush of success was so intense, F.R. almost lost himself in the moment. He felt his feet rise off the stage as he concentrated on rising up, and he was suddenly as weightless as a cloud. He could feel the lift of the control vanes on his back, and could not resist the temptation that swept over him. He stretched his arms out to either side and bowed his head in humility. The effect was partially ruined, he knew, because nothing could have wiped the wide smile off his face at that moment.

It had taken some of the most strenuous debating he had ever conducted to convince Friese and Huxley to agree to this route to reconciliation with his uncle, but it had been worth every moment of stress and strain. Both of them had sworn that the pack had worked flawlessly in trials, and once they had come around to his way of thinking, they had managed a few short, late night test flights inside the spacious laboratories to which Carpathian had moved the Hellion Project.

That flash of memory brought him back to the present as he floated there above the stage, thousands of people watching him with wonder and amazement.

And every one of them thinking that his uncle, the great

Doctor Burson Carpathian, was responsible for the miracle they were seeing.

Deep within F.R.'s mind, something dark strained against the glory of the moment.

* * * * *

As F.R. continued to hover above them, as if he were standing upon a column of solid mist, the hushed stillness of the crowd shattered; a roaring wave of amazement and approval crashed against the stage.

Vlad watched in disbelief as the most important men and women of science, politics, and a score of other disciplines lost all sense of decorum as they watched the last great barrier of man shattered before their eyes.

He saw people in the surging crowd weeping in ecstatic disbelief, others were laughing, tears streaming down their faces, slapping their companions on the back. There was not a hint of the horror or fear of a moment ago.

Vlad felt himself begin to relax. It would appear that the doctor's scheme had succeeded beyond their wildest expectations. Judging from the faces he could see, there was not a single hoped-for alliance that would not come to fruition now. Carpathian's dream future stretched out before them in glorious, concrete splendor. A small smile formed on the old soldier's face. Perhaps there had been nothing to his fears after all.

The loud, raucous cacophony of the audience defied reality and redoubled itself again as the six Hellions behind F.R. all shot into the sky in sharp, military precision. The line of animated corpses, their pale, slack flesh obscured behind the shining metal contraptions attached all over their bodies, looked glorious as their large wings extended out behind them, casting a dark shadow across the facade of the palace.

Carpathian raised both of his arms out in imitation of the Hellions behind him. "Behold, the fall of the last great barrier to human advancement!" The crowd went insane, surging toward the stage. Vlad watched as Marcus Wayward staggered with a sour look on his face as the people around him tried to push forward for a better view. Misty Mimms had lost her smile as well, and was looking around as if something she had expected had not happened. The cold stone returned in Vlad's chest as he watched her searching.

"I have conquered the sky!" Carpathian's voice echoed out over the square, its amplification ensuring that it would drown out even the draconian roar of the adoring crowd. "Behold, my friends, the day that man became greater than God Himself! The day that I became greater than God!"

Something in Vlad's chest shifted at the words, and he knew that the moment he had sensed had arrived. He whirled around, one hand reaching out toward his son's floating form. He could not see F.R.'s eyes behind the flickering goggles, but something about the set of the boy's face told his father that they had all entered a moment from which there would be no returning.

F.R.'s face was cold and still, his flaring, inscrutable gaze falling upon his uncle's back from on high.

At first the audience did not notice the change in tenor on the stage. It could easily have been part of the overall presentation, for F.R. to draw both of his shining custom blasters. It might have been part of the show when he flourished them up into the air, sparkling in the high sunlight. But when they began to drift downward, momentum in the crowd began to shift, their movement toward the stage to slow. When the weapons continued to move down, more and more of the spectators noticed, and started to push back at the rest of the surging mob, growing unease on their faces. Pockets of realization erupted throughout the square as the muzzles of the two weapons tracked down past the horizon and began to slide across the audience itself. A growing horror began to mix with the excitement and adulation, but the spectators farther back continued to press onward, pushing the enclaves of reluctance forward against their will.

F.R.'s pistols came to rest pointing firmly at Carpathian's back.

Time had frozen for Vlad; one hand reaching out to his son, a cry dying on his lips for lack of breath. He could only watch, helpless, as his world died before his very eyes.

The first bolt hit the doctor square between the shoulder blades, punching him with an audible grunt into the podium and throwing a shower of steaming blood and meat into the audience. Tracking his victim's movements, F.R. placed the next bolt lower. It blasted through Carpathian's abdomen and continued through to shatter the lower half of the lectern, sending the wreckage and the doctor tumbling off the stage and into the front row. The dignitaries there tried desperately to leap away, but met the continued resistance of the crowd surge behind.

F.R. floated forward, his teeth fixed in a skull-like grin, and fired two more shots into his uncle's struggling form. Vlad could see, from his vantage point to the side of the stage, each terrible, searing crimson bolt strike home. One took Carpathian in the left shoulder, blowing his arm to ragged shreds of flesh, the other struck him high in back on the right, spinning him around and sending another shower of gore across the screaming, churning audience.

Vlad stumbled to the edge of the stage, looking down at his brother-in-law's still form. As he watched, a wash of blood spread out beneath the body. Enormous craters of blacked flesh marked the exit wounds of the RJ bolts, glistening wetly, forming a network of cracks and fissures. As he stared down, numb with shock and horror, he saw the ruby glow of Carpathian's artificial eye flicker, dim, and die, as the doctor's remaining natural eye drifted toward him, widened in surprise, and then lost focus, fixing on a point high in the air overhead.

The doctor's brother-in-law and majordomo staggered to one knee as he watched the man to whom he had devoted decades of his life die on the dusty cobbles of the grand square.

Behind him, he heard the continued rush of the flight pack, and a splintering crash from the great doors of the palace.

Feet thundered across the stage, setting it shaking. Barbaric, ul-ulating cries echoed off the surrounding buildings and bolts of crimson force flew in all directions at the unmistakable sounds of a Rebel yell.

Vlad's body would not respond to his urgent commands. He could not tear his eyes away from Carpathian's steaming corpse. He was vaguely aware of fighting around the outskirts of the crowd as someone began to target the Creations towering there. He saw a bright ruby line stretch out from his left and pierce Creation 7's chest just below where its two necks merged, in the middle of an old scar. The towering construct jerked once and then tumbled over like a felled tree.

There was only one kind of weapon that left a heat trail like that hanging in the air... a Rail Gun. And there was only one Rail Gun in the square...

The growing sense of betrayal and tragedy began to thaw his frozen joints, and Vlad turned his head to see Creation 5 stumping forward, walking on all fours like a giant ape. J.P. Smith danced gleefully beside the beast, pointing his flashing staff at another target, and another line of red death traced out and took the veiled Creation 9 in the head. The cranium evaporated, a mist of red spraying out as metal components scattered widely across the onlookers standing nearby.

An ear-shattering detonation erupted behind him and his head, finally freed from its paralysis, swung around to stare in dis-belief at a band of ragged men and women brandishing an array of weapons out over the crowd. At their head was a familiar, fresh-faced young man whose skin bore an unmistakable prison-pallor, cradling an enormous Gatling shotgun in both hands, a wild grin stretched across his face.

The Gatling shotgun whined for a moment as its barrels spun up to speed, then with the sound of a colossal sail tearing in a gale-force wind, a tongue of blinding crimson flame lashed out and blasted a row of animations off the stage, spraying metal, cold flesh, and tattered cloth out over the audience.

Billy the Kid let out with another raucous Rebel yell as he slammed a quick-loader of three massive shells into his weapon's breach.

"Let's get this party started!" The Kid's face was twisted with gleeful rage.

A cold, empty resolve filled Vlad's chest, and he stepped toward the outlaw chief, his small hold-out blade, Vendetta, slipping into his huge fist.

A thunderous blast from behind him brought him up short, and Vlad whipped around to see an outlaw standing just behind him, gun extended toward his back, a huge smoking hole where the man's chest should be. With a perplexed look on his scruffy face, the man's knees gave way and he fell to the gore-spattered boards of the stage, revealing F.R. floating behind him, one blaster held high, barrel smoking.

His son did not acknowledge him as he brought the weapon back down to bear upon the outlaws, and confusion reigned in Vlad's mind as his son barked at the renegades, now pausing in their sweep across the stage.

"Not him!" Vlad watched as his son gestured in his direction with the smoking blaster.

"You got it, boss!" Billy seemed perfectly content to turn his posse against the remaining animations. In the crowd, even the soldiers were still, knowing their mundane service pistols and ceremonial swords would be no hope in the titanic struggle that had erupted around them.

Vlad turned back to his son, and saw the wide muzzle of the blaster on him. His son's smile was nowhere to be seen, and he dipped the barrel toward the stage floor. "Drop the blade, Father. Your work is done here."

The clatter of the heavy knife on the boards surprised him, as he had no recollection of having dropped it. He could not tear his eyes from his son's face as the young man turned away to survey the crowd. Behind him, the line of Hellions still hovered, their weapons held ready in their corpse-arms.

"No, no, no... damnit, no!" The muttered words emerged from the chaos around him, and he found himself turning back to look down at his brother-in-law's body.

Marcus Wayward had staggered to the corpse, collapsing onto his knees in the spreading pool of blood and black ichor. In the depths of his own confusion and pain, Vlad frowned down at the wretched mercenary. The old soldier might have lost his entire life's work in this explosion of violence, but Wayward had just gone from heir apparent to a shiftless, unemployed gun-for-hire.

It was clear, as Wayward shook his head violently back and forth, that he saw the situation in exactly the same terms. The man's hopes and dreams had been snuffed out, his very real, human reaction raw and unfeigned. And in that moment, his own grief etched deeply into his heart, Vlad's hatred for Marcus Wayward guttered and went cold.

Behind Wayward, Jake Mattia stood over his boss, his enormous heat rifle stabbing out threateningly in all directions. Around them, the seats of the great and the mighty were vacant as those powerful men and women pushed at the edges of the widening circle of space expanding around the doctor's body. Only Misty Mimms, Thomas Edison, and Gustave Eiffel remained in their seats. The two scientists stared in numb shock at the doctor's still form, while Mimms' expression was unclear behind her glittering mask.

"No, no, no!" Wayward repeated again, his voice growing more guttural with each word.

F.R. floated toward the edge of the stage, looking down at the ring of pale faces staring up at him in paralyzed terror. He holstered both of his blasters with a smooth, practiced flourish, his smile flashing for just a moment as the weapons slid home, and raised his gleaming metal hands up in a placating gesture. His grin returned, disturbingly wide beneath his strange goggles. "Ladies and gentlemen, please accept my humble apologies for the slight change in our program today." He flipped one hand toward the ground where Wayward sat collapsed over the doctor's body. "But the substance of the situation remains unchanged. I—"

"No!" Wayward lurched to his feet, his Rebel hand cannon leaping into his fist. "You little squirrelly bastard, NO!" The gun rose, and Vlad's battered psyche lurched back into life as he staggered toward his son, one impotent hand rising again to ward off what he saw approaching.

The bark of a single shot echoed out over the square, and Wayward staggered to a halt. His face looked mildly perplexed as his head tilted questioningly to one side. His arms fell as if the gun in his grip had turned to lead, dangling loosely by his side. He took one clumsy step, trying to turn around, and Vlad saw that a perfect hole had appeared in his forehead, just above his right eye. A fine stream of blood welled up from the hole, his eyes rolled up in his head, and his body collapsed backward on top of Carpathian's still form. The blood continued to pump out of the dark hole, mingling with the fluids already soaking the ground.

Still seated behind the dead mercenary, Misty Mimms blew the delicate trace of smoke rising from the small barrel of her hold-out derringer. There was no mistaking the smile that stretched across the woman's lips.

"You bitch!" Mattia was bringing his ludicrously large weapon around to bear on Misty, his face twisted in rage, when the hovering Hellions all froze in place, their weapons snapping up, and unleashed a tidal wave of flickering ruby light. A fusillade of RJ bolts took Jake Mattia in the back.

For a moment, the mercenary stood, outlined in the terrible fury of the attack, then his body disintegrated as bolt after bolt slammed into him. A shower of gore sprayed out over the empty seats all around, leaving nothing behind but tattered fabric and chips of bone.

As F.R. shouted out over the crowd, trying again to calm them after this latest gruesome display, Vlad's arm fell to his side. His body felt numb, the sounds of the square growing distant, echoing within his ears, slowly overwhelmed by a rushing sound he could not identify. Occasional barks of blaster fire welled up out of the leaden wash of noise, but they faded quickly. He felt a strange jolt, and dully realized that he had collapse to his knees.

He stared down, dazed, at Carpathian's body, metal eye socket dark in his pale, blanched face, natural eye wide and still in one last expression of pained surprise, dully reflecting the crystal blue sky high overhead.

The End

Zmok Books – Action, Adventure and Imagination

Zmok Books offers science fiction and fantasy books in the classic tradition as well as the new and different takes on the genre.

Winged Hussar Publishing, LLC is the parent company of Zmok Publishing, focused on military history from ancient times to the modern day.

Follow all the latest news on Winged Hussar and Zmok Books at

www.wingedhussarpublishing.com

Look for the other books in this series